The

# TELEVISIONARY
# ORACLE

To commune further with the Televisionary Oracle, go to
www.televisionaryoracle.com
or send e-mail to
zenpride@televisionaryoracle.com.

# The
# TELEVISIONARY
# ORACLE

# ROB BREZSNY

Frog, Ltd.
Berkeley, California

The Televisionary Oracle

Frog, Ltd. books are distributed by
North Atlantic Books
P.O. Box 12327
Berkeley, California 94712

Cover art and design by Stevee Postman
Book design by Paula Morrison

Printed in the United States of America

ISBN 1-58394-000-6

1  2  3  4  5  6  7  8  9  /  04  03  02  01  00

Welcome to the Televisionary Oracle

Coming to you on location from your repressed memory of paradise

Reminding you
that you can have anything you want
if you'll just ask for it in an unselfish tone of voice

Programmed to prevent the global genocide of the imagination

Hi, beauty and truth fans, and welcome to The Most Secret Spectacle on Earth, brought to you by the Menstrual Temple of the Funky Grail, Beauty and Truth, Inc., and Twenty-Two Minutes of World Orgasm.

We're your hosts with the Holy Ghost grins, and we're proud to announce that this is a perfect moment. This is a perfect moment because you, my beloved friends and teachers, have taken the first step in a ritual which could lead to the end of your amnesia.

At this perfect moment you have somehow managed, by fabulous accident or blind luck or ingenious tricks, to tune in to the Televisionary Oracle—proving that you're ready to recover your repressed memories of your sublime origins, and know again the Thirteen Perfect Secrets from Before the Beginning of Time.

Welcome to the end of your nightmares! The world is young, your soul is free, and a naked celebrity is dying to talk to you about your most intimate secrets right now!

Just kidding. In actuality, the world is young, your soul is free, and at any moment you'll begin to feel horny for salamanders, clouds, toasters, oak trees—and even the ocean itself!

Whoever you think you are, whatever friendly monsters you've tried to make into your gods and goddesses, whatever media viruses you might have invited into your most private sanctuaries—you can decide right now that your turning point has arrived. You can decide that you're ready to change your lives ... and change your signs ... and change your changing. Because when you tuned in the Televisionary Oracle, you tuned into your own purified, glorified, unified, and mystifying self.

We're your hosts for it all, beauty and truth fans. Your MCs for the Televisionary Oracle. Your listeners and your protectors and the sacred janitors we hope you've always wanted.

Does it matter what we call ourselves? You can refer to us any way you want. Your Sweet Fairy Godparents. Your Spirit Guides or Extraterrestrial Midwives or Personal Diplomatic Representatives to the Queen of Heaven.

Do you remember your dream of the saintly anarchists burning heaven to the ground? That was real. That was us. We can't in good conscience tolerate institutions that kill people with love.

Do you remember your dream, from the night before your seventh birthday, of the janitors with the pet vultures taking the garbage out from under your bed? That was real. That was us. We own all trash everywhere, after all. We were just ministering to what's ours.

We're inside your shadow, beauty and truth fans, helping you use your terror to become rich and famous—if that's what you want.

We're percolating up from the ground beneath you, bringing you the Gnostic African Buddhist music of the ever-growing roots—if that's what you want.

Like a tick in the navel of the seven-headed, ten-horned beast of the apocalypse, we're even riding on the underbelly of tonight's satellite transmission from CNN, MTV, UFO, and CIA, broadcasting to you on location from wherever we happen to be at the moment—if that's what you want.

We're all around you—if that's what you want—or nowhere to be seen—a secret keeping itself, like nature—if that's what you want.

So. What *do* you want, anyway?

The Televisionary Oracle
is brought to you by the ten-thousand-year-old lupine seed
that Yukon miners found in frozen silt and turned over to scientists
who planted it and grew a perfectly healthy bush.

I'm at the Catalyst, the biggest nightclub in Santa Cruz, California, looking for trouble on a Friday afternoon in April. Later tonight, my band World Entertainment War will be playing here, and I'm working myself into a righteous frenzy so I'll hit the stage in just the right mood.

For twenty minutes I sit alone at the bar swigging a lemonade under a sunny skylight. Meanwhile, I monitor the traffic in and out of the women's bathroom, glad to see only one visitor in all that time. Finally I'm ready to move. Acting as if I'm headed for the men's room, I instead slip into enemy territory, primed to perform my benevolent terrorism.

The yellowish white walls are an unruly pastiche of smooth and rough surfaces. The mirror over the sink is blistered with cracked orange stains, and the faint stench of bleach adds just the right touch to the ambiance. Pulling out my fine-point felt-tip marker, I print neatly on the wall:

> Macho feminist seeks cunning Goddess-worshiper with high IQ for experiments in raw friendship.
>
> Do you want to be listened to with a luxurious concentration that no one—let alone a mere man—has ever given you before? Are you looking for a savvy servant and sidekick in your holy quest to cultivate your own flaming genius?
>
> Try me. All my patriarchal imprints are incinerated, all my locker room jokes obliterated. Even better: I know how to play.

Let's dress up as teenage hoodlums and go hunting for pet grasshoppers in a dandelion meadow next to a trailer park while chanting passages from the *Bhagavad Gita.* Let's put on dorky floral shower caps and climb a hill at dusk in the rain to stage a water balloon fight while we sing songs from *West Side Story.*

Check my credentials: a roomful of books about the Goddess revival; a talent for channeling the spirit of Gertrude Stein; and ownership of a pair of red shoes once worn by Anaïs Nin. I'll write songs about you, memorize the story of your life, massage your booboos. I have a ten-inch tongue, short fingernails, guaranteed no beard stubble. Foreplay isn't a means to an end—it's a way of life.

Call Rockstar at

As I'm writing my phone number, the lavatory door slams open. In strides a tall, athletic voluptuary with a waist-length auburn mane and a bemused expression. I'm in love instantly. Her emerald eyes are kind but skeptical. Her crooked grin is a work of art that announces that she's uttered a lot of smart-ass benedictions in her time. My fantasies are already going full bore. I'm inventing her from scratch. She's a Qabalistic witch with dancer's instincts, steeped in the magical lore of herbs and the art of turning men into salamanders. She's a beauty queen who renounced her crown in solidarity with her ugly sisters everywhere. She's a stand-up comedienne with a slapstick streak, and she cackles when she comes.

Probably none of this is true, but I can't help myself. Her thick auburn eyebrows and flared nostrils and top-front-teeth-gap and freckled cleavage are the exact features my dreamwoman would have. Her high forehead and total lack of make-up are clear evidence that she's an earthy idealist with a massive IQ. Gorgeous sphinx with a prankster heart; part-Italian, part-Ethiopian, part-Irish, part-Czech, and part-extraterrestrial. Definitely not raised as a Catholic. Her loose-limbed body language says she loves sex and treats herself with joyous respect.

True, the purple baseball hat and purple windbreaker are a little strange—they're accessories favored by redneck babes—but on the other hand the logo on the front of the hat is a double-headed ax, which is a notorious code, at least in bohemian Santa Cruz, for feisty feminism (having been an important symbol in ancient Crete, among the world's last-known matriarchal cultures). Maybe she's the star shortstop of an all-woman team sponsored by a pagan coven. Hell, maybe she's the high priestess of the coven herself. I picture her sky-clad in an oak grove, holding a carved willow-wood thyrsus as she leads a circle of worshipers in a bacchanalian dance under a full moon.

Sorry. I'll stop now. I silently apologize for sculpting her out of my private raw materials. In real life, she's probably a single mother scratching out a living through a combination of welfare payments and a typical Santa Cruz under-the-table job like scraping barnacles off boats down at the yacht harbor. Of course this is also weirdly attractive to the part of me that yearns to save the world by erotically nurturing all the world's most psychically wounded (yet physically beautiful) women. In the interests of objectively reporting on the current state of my lust, though, that's not the specific version of the divine feminine I'm in the mood to lose myself in today.

I command myself to take a tantric breath of fire. It's amazing how profoundly my imagination can blind me. As the first flush of my testosterone-fueled fantasy subsides, I realize I've encountered this siren on at least three previous occasions, each time in circumstances where my receptivity to her charms did not fully combust due to my preoccupation with making a spectacle of myself. The first meeting was the night she jumped on stage during one of my band's shows here at the Catalyst. I was histrionically imitating a homeless person and screaming out the paranoid lyrics to "Get Out of My Head."

> Get outta my head
> Leave me alone
> I wanna think my own thoughts now
> Get outta my head
> I'm never alone
> My brain feels like a radio

But as I yanked on a long shank of my hair, which was secured in a topknot by a white sweat sock, this wacko babe wearing a baseball uniform—the same voluptuary who now stands before me in the women's bathroom—grabbed the guitar player's microphone and tried to outshout me, chanting, "Brainwash yourself before somebody nasty beats you to it" until one of the bouncers ushered her off.

I also remember seeing her at a performance art ritual, "A Happy Birthday for Death," which a friend of mine staged for about sixty pagan hipsters in a cemetery at dawn a couple months ago. As the sun rose, I caught a glimpse of Gorgeous Sphinx doing a dance on top of a sepulcher to the accompaniment of harp, tabla, and didgeridoo. Even if I'd wanted to, I couldn't stop and stare because I had a major role in the proceedings. I was playing the goat god Pan, complete with furry leggings and horns strapped on my head. My job was to dance obscenely and blow my panpipes and offer everyone sips of wine from my goatskin and in general stir up an orgiastic mood.

The third time I saw her was a month ago, at a party thrown by a local newspaper that carries the stories I write now and then. I was entertaining a gaggle of yuppie drunks with a rap about how I was a dream doctor; that if they prayed to me before they went to sleep, I would make a house call to their dreams and surgically remove the demons from their nightmares. Absolutely free! No further obligation!

Suddenly a green-eyed woman with stunning auburn hair elbowed her way through the champagne-swillers. Though I had never talked with her before in my life, she announced, "You said in my dream last night that I should not under any circumstances play soccer in bunny slippers at dawn in a supermarket parking lot with a gang of sado-masochistic stockbrokers who've promised to teach me the Balinese monkey chant. I'm extremely grateful for that advice, and I wanted to do something for you in return. Please accept this talisman. I made it myself."

Whereupon she handed me a purple origami in the shape of a bull's skull and disappeared.

"Are you lost?" she says now, here in the ladies' restroom, her tone a perky blend of sarcasm and affection.

"Doing some undercover political work," I say, trying to sound enigmatic but self-effacing, cocky but harmless. "Slipping some benevolent propaganda to the feminist masses."

She scans my graffiti, then turns to the mirror and stares my reflection

7

in the eye with mock gravity. "Stick out your tongue," she commands.
"Huh?"

"Stick out your tongue. I want to examine your tongue."

I'm in no mood to be rational. Besides, I've just announced in my
personal ad that I want to be of service to strong, mysterious women.
I thrust out my tongue.

"You don't have anywhere near a ten-incher," she laughs. "It's
maybe five at most."

Am I dreaming? Is it possible this person is one of the rare grown-
ups who likes to play as much as I do? My heart feels a warm, tickling
rush as I dare to imagine that my initial fantasies about her might be
accurate.

"My tongue always becomes exactly as long as the woman I'm with
needs it to be," I reply, pretending to be defensive. Her next statement
will be crucial. It'll tell me if she's prepared to join me here in a spontaneous act of performance art, or else retreat into a boring old literal
conversation.

"But if it's true that you're a macho feminist, I would think that
you might want to demonstrate the strength of your convictions by
wearing women's clothing."

Eureka. Please O Goddess in heaven, let this woman be the kindred spirit she seems to be.

"My therapist has strictly specified which fetishes and addictions
are good for me," I jive. "She says for now the only feminine garments
I should wear are lesbian pumps." And in fact I do have on what are
called in Santa Cruz "lesbian pumps"—lavender hightop Converse
sneakers.

"Uh-huh. OK. That is an acceptable answer. By the way, I should
tell you that I have been sent by the Feminist Bureau of Standards to
determine whether you meet the certification requirements. Do you
mind if I ask you a few more questions?"

"I'm eager to prove my worthiness."

"First question. You say you've got a roomful of books on the Goddess revival. Then give me a capsule summary of the importance of
Marija Gimbutas' work.

"Question two. You say you've incinerated all your patriarchal
imprints. Then give me a very practical example of a way it's changed

one of your relationships with an actual woman.

"Third question. Let me feel your face. Hey, I thought you said you're stubble-free. I'd never let you slide that sandpaper across *my* cheek."

There are few exchanges with *any* beautiful woman that I don't find at least mildly erotic. (Whether this is a sick compulsion or a gift from the Goddess is still in question.) But when the beautiful woman is also skilled in the art of improvising irreverent psychodramas, mere titillation evolves into atavistic hunger.

Before responding to her test questions, I decide to make a pre-emptory strike. I will alert her to the possibility that my testosterone could at any moment boil over and sully my standing vow never to objectify any woman, ever, for any reason—even women who're begging to be objectified. My egregiously selfish, gloriously empowering, accursedly sickening, ecstatically inspiring TESTOSTERONE might, at any moment, assume its priestly shamanic disguise and attempt to transubstantiate Gorgeous Sphinx into archetypal Goddess food—that is to say, sneakily objectify her in a *spiritual* manner.

By the way, I am in awe of everything I just said. I inwardly genuflect in rapt admiration of my ability to confess my male sins in such a way as to make myself more attractive to women. Somehow I have been chosen by the Goddess—I alone of all the men I've ever known—to have discovered this brilliant technique of transcending the assholeness which is my legacy as a male—by *capitalizing* on it.

I take my felt-tip marker to the bathroom mirror and carefully print at the top, "Official Document Ensuring That All Further Interactions between the Male and Female Will Be Fully Consensual."

Gorgeous Sphinx grows a mocking grin of horror on her face and stage-whispers, "My hero! Thank you so so very, very much for your oh-so-courtly courtesy and romantic old-fashioned respect. You're worried, aren't you? You're afraid you're going to commit an act of sexual harassment against my poor, defenseless female person. How flattering. I appreciate your sensitive concern for my delicate feelings ... *Now quit waffling, bitch, and say what you fucking mean!*"

She slaps her thigh histrionically and doubles over with guffaws.

With her head still inverted and down near her knees, she edges her way towards me and begins to tie my shoelaces together. Blissfully stunned by this brazen act of prankful intimacy, I don't resist.

Trying to recover my composure, I shuffle back to the mirror to write some more. "Whereas, the male and female parties to this agreement earnestly desire to speak freely, but also recognize that the male, despite his most earnest efforts, has yet to fully debug himself of crude patriarchal metaviruses which could cause him to unintentionally hurl lust-bombs at the aura of the female."

Then I draw two lines for our signatures, and sign my name on one.

Gorgeous Sphinx takes the marker from me and signs her name with her left hand. "Rapunzel Blavatsky."

"I'm afraid I'm going to have to subtract points for your residual patriarchal metaviruses," she says solemnly, "but your admission of guilt has awakened in me a possibly idiotic compassion which may well aid your cause in the long run. On the other hand, however, I'm getting impatient for your erudite discourse in reply to my three questions ... *you goofy slut!*"

A new attack of chuckles convulses her, and she slaps me on the back like a drunken ex-classmate at a high school reunion.

I take my Swiss army knife out of my jeans and open the biggest blade. I turn on the water faucet and squirt some of the yellow soap from the dispenser onto my hands. Soon I'm engaged in a primitive scraping of the stubble from my face. To show off my reckless poise even more, I don't even look in the mirror to guide my hand.

"Let's see," I begin. "Marija Gimbutas. Maverick archaeologist who for forty years doggedly tracked down ancient goddess figurines from under the soil of Eastern Europe and Asia Minor, singlehandedly digging up the concrete proof that up until four thousand years ago, God was a woman—and a woman with a big fat ass at that."

"Good, good. Though at the Bureau of Standards we prefer 'plump buttocks' to 'big fat ass.'"

Rapunzel is now facing away from me, hard at work drawing and scribbling on the wall with my felt-tip pen. I'm freshly invaded by the musky coyote scent of her grandiose hair as she squats down. That and her bouncy, muscular body language beam a wave of rubbery heat directly at my knees, which in reply threaten to crumple.

"Now as to your second question, Rapunzel. About giving an example of how I've incinerated my patriarchal imprints. Let me tell you about the laws of making love I learned from my lesbian girlfriend, Lourdes."

"You're a brave fool."

"Here's the first law: Whatever you, as a man, might think is the proper length of time to keep up a particular stroke or maneuver, take that and at least double it. Don't just rub your cheek against her belly for a couple minutes and then move on to swabbing your hair against her thighs. Continue doing that cheek and belly thing forever, like you're playing the childhood game 'Slow Motion.'"

As I speak, Rapunzel's creation is taking shape. It appears to be a cartoon strip.

"The second law is this: Figure out a way, using your imagination and magic, to get your thrills as much from giving your companion pleasure as you do from receiving pleasure from her. Remake your body, do whatever it takes, so that you have the sensation, when you're stroking your lover's erogenous zones, that you're literally touching yourself."

"And have you actually mastered these two laws yet?" Rapunzel interrupts.

"Well, I'm still working on the second. But the first is thoroughly ingrained."

"Uh-oh. Sounds like I'm going to have to take a few points off for not putting your money where your mouth is, my friend."

"I understand. But maybe you'll reinstate them when I tell you the other three laws. All of which I have perfected."

"I'm open to an appeal."

"The third law is that the top of the tongue and the underside of the tongue have very different textures. You should use them to create different effects.

"Fourth law: It's a wise soul who sings songs into his lover's flesh; who literally places his lips against various parts of her body and croons away."

Rapunzel shuffles over while still squatting and presses her mouth onto my left hand. To my delight, she sings a few lines from one of my songs, "Television":

Don't kill your television yet
Have another cigarette
in your imagination
Tiger tiger burning bright
Take back the airwaves of the night
in your imagination

Finished with her guerrilla action, Rapunzel sidles back to work on her artistic masterpiece.

I continue my presentation as if I'm unfazed.

"The fifth law is most important. That's this. There are hundreds of erogenous zones to choose from, all created equal. A fully democratic allotment of sensitive nerve-endings. The back of the knee needs as much attention as the tender spot where the underside of the breast joins the chest. The lobe of the ear and the crook of the shoulder demand equal time. And don't neglect the place where the top of the thigh makes the transition into the butt; it deserves as many kisses as the nape of the neck.

"I should also mention a crucial corollary to the fifth law: *Every* part of your body should eventually caress, soothe, fondle, rub, and vibrate against *every* part of her body. No exceptions!"

"Elegant," Rapunzel says. "I think the Bureau of Standards will be impressed."

I've finished, as well as can be expected, ripping the whiskers off my face. The whole time I've delivered my monologue, my companion here in the restroom has been working. She steps away now, apparently satisfied, and I examine the piece in detail. It is indeed a comic strip. It features a male character with long hair and a wiry build, sort of like me.

In the first panel, the dude is shown bowing down as if in prayer or homage to a creature that has the body of a vulture and the head and breasts of a woman. A dialogue balloon coming out of the supplicant's mouth says, "I'm your humble serpent."

In the next panel, the vulture woman is aloft, carrying him away through the air. The mode of transport is unusual. Her buzzard beak is grasping the most sensitive part of his anatomy. The balloon emerging from his mouth says, "I always wanted to be stolen."

In the third panel his abductor has dropped him from a great height head-first down into a giant goblet on the ground. She's saying, "Into the Grail with you." The fourth panel shows the same scene, only now it's encapsulated within a TV around which a group of women is sitting and applauding. "Our very first volunteer!" one woman's balloon exults.

What gives me the chills more than anything else about this artwork is that it has an eerie similarity to a certain set of events in my own past.

When I was a kid I loved six subjects: girls, astronomy, music, baseball, dreams, and vultures. At age nine, I was the founding father of the Vulture Culture Club, which included among its products a series of homemade comic books not unlike the work Rapunzel has splayed on the bathroom wall.

To this day, no one but me has ever seen those carefully drawn creations. Everyone, especially my parents, hated my fascination with the lowly buzzard, so I learned to be covert. My entire oeuvre, collectively titled "Raptor Rapture," was kept in a locked metal box which took me three weeks' worth of allowance to buy. Each installment in the series had a complex storyline, but of equal importance in the overall message was my benevolent propaganda. I often reiterated the fact that though from one point of view the vulture is the ugliest of birds, with its bald head and scraggly neck, it also happens to be the most graceful of all the soaring raptors. If you didn't know that their appearance in the sky is an announcement of death, you'd marvel at the long gliding dance of their flight.

Another fact about vultures which intrigued me was that they're misunderstood helpers. They don't, after all, kill the things they devour. In fact, most are peaceful creatures that never hurt a living thing. Their job is to assist nature in processing carrion; to clean up the messes that others have made.

But of all my reasons for becoming obsessed with vultures, my recurring dreams about them were the strongest. Though I shiver whenever I think of them now.

"Well, old boy," Rapunzel sighs, interrupting my reverie, "I'm quite impressed with your testimony about Lourdes. So impressed—and I assure you this is highly irregular—that I've decided to qualify you for admission right here and now, without submitting a full report to the usual committees."

Suddenly she sinks to her knees in front of me.

"Qualify me for what?" I gulp, trying to prevent my body from convulsing with lust.

"By the authority vested in me as Supreme Arbiter of the Feminist Bureau of Standards, I hereby declare you a candidate for admission into the Menstrual Temple of the Funky Grail."

Pulling my shirt out of my pants, she undoes its lower buttons and writes on my abdomen with the marker: WANNABE. Above it she also draws the profile of a vulture woman similar to the one on the wall.

As she finishes and stands up, she gives me one of the strangest looks I've ever seen. It's simultaneously conspiratorial, full of compassion, amused, didactic, and, if I'm not mistaken, a bit lustful. "Next question. Would you be interested in taking on the power of those who bleed but do not die?" she asks.

"And what the holy eucharist is that supposed to mean?"

She pulls a smooth, grey, oval rock out of her pants pocket and hands it to me. It's about six inches high and three inches wide, with two flat surfaces on which a text is printed in small red letters.

Men! Are you jealous of the emotional potency experienced by menstruating women?

Do you yearn to walk between two worlds with the same ease, grace, and mournful flair that they do?

Are you sick and tired of living by the unforgiving rhythms of phallocratic clock time?

Do you ache for regular dips in the stream of eternal consciousness?

Are you exhausted by the absurd pressure to act as if you're in control all the time?

Would you enjoy getting way way away from it all at least four days of every month so as to refresh your *duende*— thereby making it unnecessary for the Dark Goddess Persephone to sneak up from behind and knock you on your ass when you least expect it?

If you answered yes to even one of those questions, the hour of your liberation is at hand.

Now, for the first time since 4323 B.C., the Menstrual Temple of the Funky Grail will begin initiating men into the mysteries of menstruation—and you could be one of the first.

Hallelujah and praise Persephone! The ancient phallocratic curse on menstruation is withering. As the fearful lies of the Scared Old Boy Network lose their stinky magic, eons of disinformation about the peach flower flow are giving way to the New Menstrual Millennium.

And the payoff? Now even a few selected men will be able to undo the alienation bequeathed them by the Big Dickheads Who Turned the Tender, Poignant Penis into the Berserk Cosmodemonic Doomsday Machine.

Now even a few selected men can find out how to correlate their cycles with the tonic rhythms of the Dark Goddess.

Will you be one of the chosen? Stay tuned!

MENARCHE FOR MEN! COMING SOON TO A SACRED GROVE NEAR YOU!

Guaranteed to be at least ten times less painful than circumcision.

"Where do I sign up?" I say when I've finished reading the rock for the second time.

"If you truly think you're up for it, there'd be some preparatory work you'd have to master."

Up till this moment, I've been nurturing the fantasy that Rapunzel is a bullshit artist of the first magnitude—a play-acting lunatic as devoted to creating hyper-real performance art on the spur of the moment as I am. My confidence in this interpretation has been shaken somewhat by the speed and ease with which she materialized the mature vulture masterpiece on the wall. It seemed rehearsed. Now, with the appearance of the "menarche for men" announcement, I'm forced to consider the possibility that Rapunzel's behavior is at least partially premeditated.

Whether it is or not, I can't let that issue dampen my own contribution to the entertainment.

"Supreme Arbiter," I say, "I'd kiss your buttocks and wear a cardboard crown from Burger King and write a whole album's worth of songs just for you if that's what it took to earn the right to a female-mediated experience that no man has had since 4323 B.C."

She points to her ankle-high army boots. "You are indeed precocious, my boy, but not so much that you get to kiss the buttocks of the Supreme Arbiter on the first date. I will, however, let you take a stab at another part of the holy vehicle. See if you can transmit your tantric awe into my feet—but without taking off my shoes, thank you."

I lean over to unlink the shoelaces that Rapunzel tied together earlier. Then I drop down to the floor and do ten push-ups, grunting like an army recruit. With my arms as props, I lift my upper body to her derrière-level and feign a quick strike at my preferred target, barking fake karate yells. But this is just psychodrama, a strategy to heighten the foreplay and impress Rapunzel with my erotically attractive unpredictability. In fact, I'm determined not to blaze in on a fast, direct course and bang my lips ineffectually against the unyielding black leather guarding her toes. Instead, I plan to spiral in from the side of the left boot and descend on that sensitive borderland where the smooth hood of the boot meets the latticework where the laces begin.

Like a cobra I dart and feint with my head, approaching the target with a teasing caginess. Rapunzel seems patient, standing calmly with her legs apart about shoulder width, her eyes gazing down to catch my show. To add to the drama, I hiss almost subliminally.

My final descent is in slow motion. With reverent tenderness, I rest my lips gently against the targeted area and begin to chant a mantra evoked specially for the occasion: SMOOOOOOCH. Now and then my tongue slips out to seal the prayer, tasting the leather that separates me from Rapunzel's sacred skin.

"I'm pleased," she says blithely when I'm done. "That was one of the most lion-hearted boot kisses I've ever been worshiped with. I can see you're willing to take blasphemous liberties with your tantra. You don't do it by rote. Shows your great promise."

16

"Thank you thank you thank you."

"Now what's that hype you spouted about writing a whole album's worth of songs for me? Are you really prepared to follow through on that offer, or was that just your sex making promises the rest of you can't keep?"

"It'll be like a rock opera," I riff without hesitation, "based on a story of a macho feminist rock singer who before a show at a big nightclub sneaks into the women's bathroom because he's heard there's a lot of horny graffiti written about him in one of the stalls. Only while he's in there he has a fortuitous encounter with a mysterious woman with a fairy tale name who he quickly realizes is smarter than he is and who also isn't totally gaga about his fame and charisma like all the other girls, which turns him on so much that he cooks up a plan to get to know her better. And the plan is that he offers to write a whole cycle of songs about her based on the story of her life, which he has no intention of actually doing because it's just his sex making promises the rest of him can't keep. She falls for it. She agrees to let him interview her and follow her around and plagiarize her life. To his own amazement, the rockstar gradually realizes she is the most fascinating and powerful woman—no, the most fascinating and powerful *person*—that he's ever met. He becomes so infatuated with the epic sweep of her fate that he sets to work composing a great song cycle about her after all."

"Doesn't exactly fit into the World Entertainment War esthetic though, does it?" Rapunzel replies in a compassionately skeptical tone. "I love what you and your band do, but you're not especially renowned for your poignant storytelling, are you? I admit that you've got the formula down for funky rock anthems and comic shticks. You do the pagan chant thingee pretty well, and the anarchist politics. I truly enjoy your whatchamacallit, your bombastic ritual therapy. But I've got to say that all that hypermasculine flash leaves me a little hungry in the emotion department. Aside from the shock and laughter and rebellious dissidence, you don't seem to know squat about how to arouse the whole rest of the spectrum. You know what I mean? I'm talking about *creature* states. Sadness, restlessness, astonishment, the longing to belong, gratitude, mourning—you know, *real life*. You're always so goddamned mental. So relentlessly masculine."

"I can explain—"

"Now on the other hand, I *have* seen signs of a budding tenderness in those stories you write for the local paper. Most of the time they've been as relentlessly arch and clever as your rockstar shtick. But lately there's been just a hint of a softening. It's like you're tiptoeing up to getting ready to invoke your readers' soft deep achy feelings. Now and then you condescend to telling an intimate tale about the way the love and pain get all mixed together out here among us common folk.

"You keep going in that direction, and *then* I might let you write a song cycle about me. But not now. Not yet."

I feel deflated. Her critique is truly insightful—a pithy articulation of thoughts that have only recently appeared on the frontiers of my self-awareness. But I can't believe she's suddenly abandoned the bubbly spirit of our theatrical improvisation and regressed into serious conversation. She's broken the rules of our fun game.

Before I can summon a rejoinder, she slips into one of the stalls and closes the door. She starts singing one of my songs, "Apathy and Ignorance."

> In the land where nothing's sacred
> Where the doctors make people sick
> If you stand on your head
> you might see things more clearly
> But then again you might become
> addicted to conflict
>
> I ... I have a problem
> I know that lawyers cause all the crime
> And the banks make the drugs flow
> The priests make the porno
> And you might be responsible
> for poisoning the sunshine
>
> What is the difference between apathy and ignorance
> I don't know and I don't care
> What is the difference between apathy and ignorance
> I don't know and I don't care

As she croons, she's rustling around inside the stall. I see she's taken off her windbreaker and draped it over the top of the stall. Finally she finishes the song and yells out, "Take off your shirt and throw it over to me."

I obey. A moment later a shirt flies out. I guess she was wearing it under the windbreaker. "Let's trade," she says.

I don my new costume, a short-sleeved baseball jersey. It's dark plum with black pinstripes. The number thirteen is on the back. A big, buttoned pocket graces each side. On the front of the right pocket are the words "Menstrual Temple of the Funky Grail," along with a picture of a rather queenly gold and red vulture, who has a woman's face and crown on a body which is thoroughly buzzardly except for two exuberant breasts. This is a more majestic version of the creature in Rapunzel's comic strip.

I soak in the new scent that now clings to me. *Silken saltiness* are the words that come to mind to describe it. Ancient freshness. I flash on an immaculate spider web after a summer rain, and the leathery sweetness of the Dead Sea Scrolls, whose fragments I once sniffed in a museum. Weirdly, I'm also reminded of a vivid smell from childhood: my mother's sweetly musty old khaki cloth bag full of marbles from her own childhood. She kept it in her closet, and when she wasn't home I would sneak it out to examine the beautiful antique marbles. Strange that this specific old aroma would emanate now from the shirt of a stranger. It's indescribably unique. There are no words for it besides the pictures and feelings they stir: chilly autumn Saturdays playing alone in the basement of the family home in Michigan while football games drone on the TV.

All these fragrances together evoke in me a delirious happiness, a kind of dreamy unselfconscious joy from my childhood. It's very different from the alert, calculating excitement that Rapunzel's presence has provoked in me up till now, though also oddly synergistic. Adding to the celebration is my instinctive sense that all of her delicious smells are utterly natural. Nothing artificial in the mix, thank Goddess. No pheromone-destroying perfumes or deodorants.

As I meditate on these glories, another item of clothing sails over the top of the stall and alights on my shoulder.

"Sorry to say I don't have a cardboard Burger King crown with me," Rapunzel says. "Would you accept these instead?"

I drink in the lovely sight of the dark plum-colored, silk bikini underpants. They sport the picture of a regal buzzard much like the one that graces the shirt pocket. The only difference is that this one has long, Rapunzel-like hair.

I pull the panties over my head, dipping them down to nose-level before raising them back up and arranging them like a crown. Immediately I'm spinning in a hurricane of synesthesia. A collage of half-remembered, half-imagined tastes and visions from my childhood billows out of a mutating whirl of aromas. I'm slurping raspberry sorbet in a rowboat with my mother as we float on Otsego Lake in northern Michigan shortly after catching my first fish, a scared rainbow trout flipping around and pooping in a red bucket next to me. Or I'm lolling in a plastic swimming pool beneath a tree full of ripe pears in Marty Maxwell's backyard while eating his mother's delectable peanut butter and banana and maple syrup sandwiches as his younger sister Debbie lowers her bathing suit and shows us what girls look like down there. Or I'm lying at night in my bed dreaming of listening to the static-y radio broadcast of the Detroit Tiger baseball game when a ball of mist puffs in through my open window, smelling of lavender and vinegar and new-mown grass.

Fermenting dreamily in this ripe vortex, I'm startled when Rapunzel bolts out of the stall and slips by me. "Catch you later," she says and glides out the lavatory door.

"Can I call you?" I yell after her, but the door smacks shut. I do a series of five tantric breaths of fire to refocus my awareness, fasten a couple buttons on my new shirt, and burst out of the bathroom myself. Rapunzel, wearing my favorite Indonesian-print shirt, is already trotting out the front door of the club. I lope after her, but by the time I reach the street, she's disappeared. Gambling that she's turned down Cathcart Street, I bolt that way. But when I arrive at the corner she's nowhere in sight.

Why is it so important
to the future
of daffodils and sea urchins and the jet stream
that childbirth be shown regularly in prime time?

What is the best way
for you to undo
the black magic
you've performed on yourself?

What exactly do we mean
when we predict that
hedonistic midwives will one day rule the world?

Why are we so sure that sooner or later
each of us
will be a well-rounded
incredibly kind
extremely wealthy
genius
with lots of leisure time
and an orgiastic feminist conscience?

As you bask here in the sanctuary
of the Televisionary Oracle
all will become puzzlingly clear.

Congratulations, beauty and truth fans, for the courage you've shown by throwing yourself into our sacred chaos. The celebration you've joined is scheduled to last for twenty-two years, or until you undo the black magic you've practiced against yourself—whichever comes first.

Whether you've chosen to approach your ecstatic falling apart through dream incubation, accessing your inner child's pet dragon, or talking about your problems until you've talked them to death, we're sure you'll find your time here at the Televisionary Oracle to be the most rewarding vacation you've ever had.

We trust that you've all done the recommended preparations before launching into your initiation. For best results, you should be in the third day of your fast. You should have used a chainsaw to destroy any belonging that has made you feel you're better than other people. And you should have done a meditation to implant simulated memories of great happiness right around your second birthday, the moment our research has determined is the critical turning point in developing trust forever.

Later, after the opening festivities, you'll be invited to find a comfortable place in your personal dream incubation temple. There a vision will come to you during sleep, perhaps in the form of a visit by a god or goddess, perhaps in the form of a dream of some deed or mission which you must accomplish in order for your healing to take place. Whatever divine prod you receive, we urge you to translate it expeditiously into some action that will change your waking life forever.

One thing before we start. As the Televisionary Oracle begins to pour into you, fight it off—just a little. Flex your willpower to see if you can resist its delicious onslaught. Not to the point of keeping it out, of course, but enough so that you feel confidence in your ability to take only what you need from us. Why? Because as much as we believe you will benefit from becoming one with our lyrical and restorative propaganda, it's just not healthy for you to surrender blindly to *anyone's* infomania.

Now we're ready to go to work on the solution to your spiritual emergency. To begin, release yourself into the emotions of the following affirmation:

*I will interpret every experience in my life*
*as a dealing of the Goddess with my soul.*

4

Once upon a time, right at the beginning of the end of that tragic success known as the phallocracy, that sad miracle, a girl child named Rapunzel Blavatsky—whom I also call me myself and I—was born to quirky parents in a place which many have come to call "Goddess' Country": Santa Cruz, California. The child's mother, Magda Zembrowski, was a dollmaker who had taken up her art as a form of permanent mourning about her four abortions. The abortions had all been invoked in the name of poverty, not fear of children. Magda had in fact long yearned to nurture a helpless little being fresh from the spirit world, and each time the abortionist's vacuum had sucked the budding clump of cells out of her womb, she'd suffered a Hiroshima.

"Not enough money" had always been the mantra. Magda, though her hands and wit sporadically conspired to create masterpieces in clay and feathers and wood and found objects, depended on dumpster-diving and house-cleaning jobs to stay alive. Her partner, Jerome Blavatsky, had always been too ... well ... *insane* to support a child, let alone Magda or himself. When Jerome wasn't reading books about occultism or writing fairy tales or playing "chaotic piano," he enjoyed slipping into marathon trances (sometimes lasting as long as three days) during which he would experience himself—he wouldn't say *imagine* himself, he would definitely say *experience* himself—living, in exquisite detail, in any one of seventeen "other incarnations" he believed himself to be connected to via "astral tunnels." In one life he was a follower of and helper to Joan of Arc. In another incarnation he was a follower of and helper to the early American religious dissident Anne

Hutchinson. In yet another life he was James, the younger brother of Jesus Christ, enmeshed in a mix of awe and jealousy and the desire to serve Jesus' mission. All of his trips and sojourns in these other worlds were faithfully reported to Magda, or in his journals, with lush detail and an encyclopedic knowledge of local conditions that seemed impossible to accrue merely from reading history books.

His journeys might have had a greater measure of credibility, however, if among them there had never been lifetimes spent in lands that existed only in fairy tales. Living in Florence as a sixteenth-century painter was one thing. Living the life of Jack in a cottage next to a giant beanstalk that reached to the clouds was another.

A year before the first abortion, when both were twenty-five years old, Jerome and Magda were married by a Universal Life Church minister on the bumper cars at the Santa Cruz Boardwalk. And though they'd stayed married and loyally monogamous, they lived apart more often than they lived together for the next six years. This was due not so much to bouts of mutual irritation, which their equally dreamy natures rarely indulged in, as to the fact that Jerome had a deep and abiding need to sleep in caves on beds of leaves (and not simply as a way to save money), whereas Magda found it hard to spend a night without a roof and a few thick layers of foam padding that she'd once pulled from a dumpster behind a warehouse on Coral Street.

Maybe it was this curious non-domestic arrangement that fueled the mystically romantic approach they took towards each other. There was not enough familiarity to breed contempt. For many years, even after their girl child was born, Jerome and Magda kept a notebook in an old leather bag stored high in the crook of a climbable oak tree in the backyard of a mutual friend. The notebook was a kind of diary for their relationship. In it they wrote each other poetry, scrawled dreams and fantasies, made up stories about each other and spoke the unspeakable thoughts that were too private to communicate in person.

It was this perverse insistence on staying in love, as opposed to accumulating furniture together, that provides a clue about how they could have been so careless as to have conceived a fetus they didn't intend to keep on four occasions. Romance had precedence over pragmatism.

Jerome had a notion based on an ancient Greek word *idoni*. He'd learned this term, he said, during his lifetime as a student of Pythagoras, which was not a *past* incarnation, mind you, but an incarnation that was simultaneous with all his other incarnations, including this one in twentieth-century Santa Cruz. (I once consulted a scholar of ancient Greek to find out if such a word as "idoni" exists, and she told me that "i" never ends ancient Greek words.)

But Jerome nonetheless believed that *idoni* was a term describing a magically potent electromagnetic substance that's exchanged between lingam and yoni during sexual intercourse. Most people waste it, he thought. They don't sublimate it and direct it to any worthwhile task, like, say, saving the world or healing their own pain (as Magda and Jerome did, in the grand tantric tradition). Most lovers didn't appreciate the occult power of the idoni, but let it stop cold in the neurons that register pleasure. For Jerome, that idoni was rocket fuel for the psyche. It was, he believed, what allowed him to squeeze through the wormholes that led to all his other lifetimes, and what allowed him to make extended stays there. A three-hour erotic dance with Magda might translate into a three-day vacation with Jesus in ancient Palestine.

Here's the kicker: Jerome believed there was just one form of birth control that didn't do terrible damage to the exchange of idoni: the heroic withholding of the semen. He had cultivated a talent for controlling his ejaculatory muscles, and wielded it like a master. While he knew that wasn't a foolproof hedge against pregnancy, he didn't acknowledge until the third conception that he and Magda were too fertile a combination to allow even a few spermatozoa from his pre-seminal fluid to leak out.

The very worst violation of the idoni, Jerome thought, was the condom. Rubber was a fascistic insulator, a crime against idoni. Birth control pills were catastrophic in a different way. They inhibited the flow of Magda's copulins, a key ingredient in the generation of the idoni (not to mention the source of her yoni's sex scent). The diaphragm and IUD: dissonance, disruption, interference. Abortion, in the prodigal mind of Jerome, was the only acceptable way to stave off children.

Only trouble was that it was a rather expensive form of birth control for poor folks like Magda and Jerome. Perhaps they would have rethought their position if the initial abortion hadn't been given to them at a steep discount by Dr. Ooster, a Dutch-American doctor who felt an odd sympathy for the two lovable weirdos. The first easy surgery invited the second and third and fourth, all courtesy of Dr. Discount. Without naming the womb-scraping as a ritual, Magda and Jerome turned it into a kind of sacrificial act to propitiate their love.

A complication: For a long time Magda was unaware that there was, for Jerome, another reason for the abortions. Though his obsessive fantasy life—or certifiable schizophrenia, whatever you want to call it—meant that he wasn't much good at hiding anything from Magda, he somehow managed to conceal this one secret. He believed that in his incarnation as Jesus' brother, James, Jesus had communicated to him a mystical truth about how to preserve his ability to live in seventeen lifetimes at once. "You must become your own child," Jesus told him. "You must not let your reproductive power be diverted into the creation of offspring. *Reproduce yourself.* With the first cry of your first child, the astral paths would close with a violent gulp and you would be trapped in just one body." Those were, Jerome believed, Jesus' exact words.

Nothing, not even death, scared Jerome more than the threat of losing his connection to his other lives, and so he had risen up with each of Magda's pregnancies and smote it down. Magda had her own fears—of trying to nurse a baby on a diet bought exclusively with food stamps, of the child becoming sick and her not having the money to care for it, of devoting her attentions to a child Jerome didn't want, thereby chasing him away so far that he would disappear forever. And Jerome preyed on all those poverty-induced fantasies, manipulated Magda for the good of his magic.

For more than five years, as abortion followed abortion, Jerome nurtured in private his unique conflict. On the one hand, he could never use birth control for fear of extinguishing the idoni that powered his journeys. On the other hand, if he permitted any of the resulting pregnancies to come to term, his journeys would end.

But as I said in the beginning, there was a girl child born to Jerome and Magda. Me, Rapunzel Blavatsky. How did that come about? Why, upon Magda's and Jerome's fifth conception, did he withdraw his demands to terminate the pregnancy?

Liberation Day—at least that's what I call it—arrived during a cool, cloudy spell in the middle of August. Magda had been up since

4 A.M. cleaning a laundromat, which she did five days a week. Jerome was deep in the woods behind the university campus, coming down from three days of healing the sick with Jesus and company in Galilee. As was often the case when he returned from one of his time travels, he was in a voracious and horny mood. Fantasies of making love to Magda competed in his feathery, aerated organism with an intense longing for French onion soup and grilled salmon and artichokes dipped in mayonnaise. Before he rode his bike to the cafeteria in town where he would scam the food people left behind on their trays, he visited the oak tree where his and Magda's joint diary resided.

Magda was used to Jerome's extended absences, and to keep things equal she pulled off her own disappearing acts from time to time. But on this particular day she was horny and voracious herself. Maybe it was the dream that had awoken her minutes before the alarm clock: swinging joyfully on the erect, bouncing phallus of an enormous satyr. Or maybe it was the little twinge she'd felt to the southwest of her navel last night, sure sign that she was ovulating. Riding her one-speed bike to work in the predawn mist, she felt like the Slut of the World; fantasized like a happy lunatic about copulating with rock stars and construction workers and tigers. By the time she was unlocking the double glass doors of the laundromat, the raw sexual craving had softened into a yearning for the kind of empathic listening that Jerome, of all the people she'd ever known, did best. Though there were many days when her husband was as narcissistic as a child, he would regularly slip into a state of grace during which he became the most tender reflector—wildly curious about her life, and full of interesting questions that, when she answered them, made her real to herself.

After work she pedaled straight to the oak tree where the diary lay nestled in a fork of branches some twenty feet up. While perched up there, she read his most recent entry, dated just hours before. It said something like this:

"Ascetic Dionysian with idiot-savant tendencies seeks flexible doll-maker with crafty riffs for experiments in organized chaos. Guzzle my poetry, baby, and I'll be your disciplined wacko. Trick me with your cunning stunts and I will taste you all over with my forked tongue. Scavenging tonight? Meet me here at 9:03 P.M. and we'll go raid the witch's garden. Wear your costume from 39 in Grimms'."

What made Jerome's insanity even more insane was that he was so precise, so punctual, so perfectionist, and not at all in the compulsive way that schizophrenics sometimes have. His exactness was very relaxed. You could be sure that the peculiar time for their date, 9:03, had a baroque numerological import for him, and you also knew that he'd be there not a minute later. Yet he didn't mind if you were late, and he never harangued you with the cosmology of it all.

Magda was there early, having enjoyed an afternoon nap to compensate for the sleep she'd probably be missing later that night. Thanks to a visit to the Bargain Barn, a used clothing warehouse where clothes sold for twenty cents a pound, she'd assembled "a costume from 39 in Grimms'." That seemingly cryptic reference in Jerome's note was no mystery to Magda. She'd known to turn to page 39 in her edition of *Grimms' Fairy Tales*, where she found the story of Rapunzel. What it all meant, she knew, was that Jerome was enlisting her, as he had on numerous occasions, in another one of his "mythic reconnaissance missions" in preparation for an attempt at "mutating the old imprints."

Jerome was a writer of fairy tales. He was convinced, in fact, that his stories were to be his greatest gift to humanity. He wasn't so intent, though, on creating new myths from scratch as he was of messing with the old standards. Long before the word "deconstructionism" became a shibboleth for academic elites, Jerome used it to describe his modus operandi. If traditional stories and myths were records of the outdated patterns that characterized the collective unconscious long ago, Jerome wanted to be the one who disrupted those moldy patterns and rearranged them into fresh imprints more conducive to creating the utopia that he staunchly believed was humanity's destiny.

At 9:03 Magda was under the oak tree dressed as a German peasant woman might have dressed in the thirteenth century—if, that is, she'd had access only to the Bargain Barn: long muslin dress over grey leggings, brown suede vest and faux leather work boots. Jerome's outfit was more authentic: the materials of his shirt and tights were made of extremely rough tan fibers, and his primitively sewn leather boots were a throwback. Where'd he get them? Chances are he'd try to make you believe he'd somehow managed to smuggle them back over the dimensional threshold from fifteenth-century France.

"What if in the new, updated version of Rapunzel," Jerome said conspiratorially as he hugged Magda in welcome, "the witch never catches the husband in the act of stealing the lettuce?"

"Then you wouldn't have much of a story left," Magda retorted sensibly. "In fact, you might as well say, 'They all lived happily ever after, the end' after that."

"Ah, but wait. Let's theorize that the witch's garden represents the mystical knowledge of herbs, the old wise woman lore passed down from mother to daughter since before the beginning of history. And what if in the new version of 'Rapunzel,' the husband scales the walls of the witch's sanctum and brings its delicious secrets back to his wife—again and again. Let's say the witch, the guardian of the old womanly ways, never stops him. Maybe she never even notices. Or maybe she notices and still decides to let him do it. Maybe she says to herself, if this man is so devoutly in service to his wife's needs, then I will allow him access to the old wisdom. I will permit him to become mediator between crone and maiden."

Jerome was a man out of time. The cultural trends of his historical era brushed up against him, but his dearest passions were fed by the madnesses and fetishes of other eras and places. He was also, in a curious sense, a man of action. It was true that when he was in his learning mode he could close his eyes in broad daylight and remain virtually motionless for hours while he traveled hundreds of years and thousands of miles away. But when he was in his creative mode, working on one of his mutated fairy tales, he needed to create rituals in *this* time and this place. Maybe it was the Aeschylus in him—he believed that in another incarnation he was the ancient Greek playwright—that compelled him to dramatize his ideas in order to explore them. There was something about physically recreating the conditions of the story he was deconstructing that aroused buried reserves of inspiration.

A half hour later, after pedaling their beat-up bikes a couple miles to the spot Jerome had selected for his "mythic reconnaissance mission," the two crouched at the foot of a stone wall that surrounded a garden and a cottage with one light on. Jerome motioned for Magda to hop on his back and peer over the wall. After she did, he eased her down.

"You know what to say, wife," Jerome whispered.

"Oh husband," Magda said without hesitation, "In that garden is a bed of ripe rapunzel greens. They look so fresh and delicious that my mouth is watering. I simply must have some to eat. I think I shall die if I don't."

"I cannot let my wife die of longing," Jerome said. "I will bring you some of that rapunzel, no matter what the cost."

He clambered up over the wall. In a few minutes he returned with a wad of freshly picked spinach. Magda wolfed it down and lay her head in Jerome's lap. After a few minutes of silence, she spoke.

"Oh husband, I cannot stop thinking of that rapunzel. It was so good, so very good, that my craving for it has grown. Please, I beg you, fetch me some more."

Jerome paid a second visit to the garden and brought back another handful of spinach. Again, Magda gorged herself. But minutes later, her yearning returned yet again. "I am famished for rapunzel, my love. It seems the more I eat, the more I want. Don't make me wait."

Jerome leaped over the wall again, and this time, instead of slinking and skulking, he stood up, faced the cottage, and waved his arms. Did a jig. Sang an excerpt of the Hallelujah Chorus. And then snitched some spinach and returned to Magda. This time she only pretended to eat. The fairy tale wife might still be fascinated with the taste of rapunzel, but the actress needed a break from the spinach. The green leaves got stuffed in the waistband of her leggings.

"Husband," she said as she massaged his shoulders and neck, "My hunger for rapunzel has become so wild that I can no longer contain it. I beg you now to become hungry for rapunzel yourself. For only if you eat the rapunzel until it is gone can my own hunger ever be satisfied."

Jerome pulled his wife's long dress up above her waist and kissed her just below her navel. Then he heaved himself over the garden wall. Taking a small notepad and pen out of his pocket, he wrote the following: "Dear Witch: Thank you for helping us to change history. With your gracious permission, I have fetched my wife so much of your rapunzel that I, too, have become hungry for it. Now there is no longer any need to protect my daughter from me, for I have renounced the ignorance of my gender and the sins of the fathers. With deep reverence, Rapunzel's Daddy."

Jerome strode up to the cottage and slid the note under the back door. Returning to the garden, he plucked the remaining spinach and carried it back to where Magda lay. Slowly and methodically, he chewed and swallowed it all.

"Shall we consecrate the mutation, wife?" he said. Licking her forehead once, he removed her vest, pulled her dress over her head, undid her boots, and shimmied off her leggings. Then he lay back passively while she performed the same ritual on him. As she finished and lay down next to him, he said, "Nope. Got to give our love to the promised land. Come on."

He urged her over the garden wall. Once there, she took his hand and led him to the pumpkin patch. Under the scarecrow, he sat on the soft, damp night earth and she settled down on his lap. There for the next how many minutes—the time it took for the two-days-past-full moon to slither from behind the hill yonder to the top branch of the apple tree in the garden—they did the eye-fucking game. Tip of lingam lightly poised against tip of clitoris, no penetration except their amused and hallucinating eyes, slinging dusky amber light back and forth, fantasizing daimons and elemental spirits flowing from each other's nerves, wishing nothing else but that this moment be what it was.

By the time the moon reached the lowest leafy cloud, lingam and yoni had begun to blend, no official moment of entry but only a slow misty merger of yoni electrons and lingam electrons. In this happy-birthday-for-all-sentient-beings, the mask of Jerome's face glowed transparent for Magda, overflowing with a fountain of momentary portraits—of Aeschylus, perhaps, and Jesus' brother James, and Jack of Beanstalk fame; but also every man that had ever motivated Magda—that brush-cut warlock with the broken nose who taught her yoga, the fourth-grade teacher who told her she was a good artist, the smart boy she loved in second grade, the face of Jesus in the painting on her *Child's Book of the Bible*, the doctor who caught her as she pulsed free of her mother's yoni, her brother, her father.

Never any pressure to "fuck" or "screw" with Magda and Jerome. The mingling, not the friction, was the Grail. If alchemy meant anything, it meant this cooking, this slow, simmering mesh of *why* and *how*. As Magda steamed and marinated his prima materia, Jerome found leopards in her face, quetzalcoatls, the Queen of the Faeries, his mother and grandmothers, his old girlfriend, Billie Holiday, the woman who had served him ice cream every day of the summer of his ninth year.

And then ... who was that last face? He lifted his trance eyes away to find the moon, then looked back. It was still there, shimmering like all the others, but more solid.

Mary Magdalen. The wife of his brother Jesus. A face—unlike the others that were coruscating through his wife-goddess' eyes—that he felt himself retreat from. Not from lack of love, but from absence of gnosis—as if he weren't old enough, or smart enough. He wanted to love her, but didn't know how. As James, he had always felt shy and strongly drawn to her. Taboo.

He felt an infinitesimal gush in his lingam: a small, partial ejaculation—a safety-valve release which he, as a conscientious tantric lover, had trained himself to have so as to avoid a shoot-the-whole-wad explosion.

Feeling the need to anchor himself, to come down a little, he lifted his hands from where they'd been resting on Magda's hips and brought them to her face.

"Magda," he croaked, his voice rusty.

"Magdalen," she replied.

"Magdalen?" he whispered.

"Jesus has changed his mind," she spoke softly but firmly. It wasn't exactly Magda's voice. Huskier even than her usual sex voice.

"Jesus wants me to tell you. That what he said before. No longer applies."

"No longer applies," Jerome repeated. He knew what she was talking about but wasn't sure he was ready to know.

"Jesus says that he wants you to have a child—a real, physical child."

"But I haven't become my own child yet. I haven't reproduced myself."

"There's not enough time for that luxury any more. Jesus needs you—and I need you—to help us."

"I want to help you," Jerome said bravely. Magda's yoni muscles had begun a series of rippling squeezes, and though the temptation to ejaculate had been partially relieved by his mini-orgasm, he could feel his pleasurably diffused sexual charge starting to contract again towards his lingam. He resisted, concentrating on spiraling the energy back out to the top of his head and the ends of his fingers and toes. He exerted his will, trying to draw his attention away from the tingling confusion he'd felt since Mary Magdalen had begun to speak through Magda.

"I want to be alive in your time," she said. "I NEED to be alive in your time."

Suddenly he felt a burst of sweetness, the promise of an exotic species of orgasm he'd never negotiated before, at the center of his brain.

"I want you to reincarnate me as your child."

A loop of honeyed lightning swooped from that whirlagig spot in his brain, traveling down his spine to his lingam and back. Maybe ten times the loop circulated, building a charge as it sluiced. It was like the feeling of soaring higher and higher on a swing, and he couldn't see who was pushing him higher and higher but he liked it but he was dangerously high and couldn't control himself and then he was flying off the swing and swirling down the longest slickest slide on the biggest playground he'd ever seen. Magda was clutching webs of skin on either side of his abdomen and she was somehow with him slithering down this long silver slick tunnel. Firecrackers were singing inside violet waterfalls. Strawberry cream was splashing down his throat forever but thank you he wasn't drowning, only breathing a pink river. He could see his grandfathers and his great-grandfathers barreling towards him with arms outstretched as if to welcome him or grab him, but then they were shooting by him, shouting some joyful greeting he couldn't understand. As Jerome and Magda fell—now, somehow, they were falling up—Jerome could feel himself soften at the edges, unravel, dismantle. It was a sweet sensation, like falling asleep as a child. The night peeled away, exposing a strange sky teeming with winking, teasing stars. There was almost no space between the stars. They were nestling up against each other as far as he could see, like the jam-packed nest of throbbing frog eggs he'd once seen at the edge of the creek. He imagined that each of these billions of pulsing lights was an intelligent creature, and that they all loved him and were happy to see him and wanted to show him something very funny and very interesting.

Gradually he became aware of the wet dirt of the garden chilling his butt and of his swollen but soft lingam drooping out of Magda's yoni.

The moon had reached zenith. Magda's eyes were fluttering gently as if in REM sleep, though she was still upright on his lap and drumming her fingers playfully against his sides.

"You came inside me?" she laughed quizzically. "I'm shocked."

"Not half as shocked as I."

"Should I go hurry run home and douche this load out of me?" she offered.

"No, let's go to Golden West and eat some buckwheat pancakes. Did you get paid today? I'm suddenly starving."

Nine months from the night in the rapunzel patch, in the dead of a full moon night in mid-May—a time celebrated by some as the Buddha's birthday—my wet, feathery Rapunzel head bobbed twice at the threshold where Magda was cracking open, and then I splashed out in a flood of blood and amniotic juice, falling into the weathered hands of an old bird-woman. My father, his shoulder snug against the bird-woman's, laughed for a long time.

I am not describing a scene recounted to me by the three who attended my birth. I am not speculating that this is how it happened. Through my training in the occult art of *anamnesia*, I have lifted the veil of forgetfulness which, for most people, remains closed until death. I remember—not in words, of course, but in fuzzy images, in vivid smells, in telepathic textures—I remember that my father kissed me on the forehead as I took my first breath. I remember I was an inside-out star drinking in the smells of sweat and alcohol and camphor and shit and jasmine candles.

And I remember my father holding me, my umbilicus just cut, as I nodded expectantly towards the moist, shivering gate out of which I had just emerged. More to come, I knew. Still inside was the creature I had swum with for my first nine moons, my twin brother. Our separation hurt, blotted out the other separation from my mother. Why was I here and he was still there?

When finally the gate opened again, it was not with his head, but with the sac of nourishment I'd fed from, my placenta. The bird-woman stiffened at this, squawked an alarm, and grabbed two long silver scalpels. Cutting through my mother's skin and muscles and membranes, she plumbed for my companion.

Years after this event, when I'd learned enough words, I could describe what technically happened: abruptio placenta, the premature separation of my brother's placenta from the uterus. We were both supposed to be born before either placenta popped out. The appearance of mine while he was still inside meant that his placenta was peeling away from its source, depriving him of oxygen before he was ready to breathe.

That's what I know now. Then I knew only that my companion hurt. I felt him shrinking, fighting, stiffening—and then withdrawing. Even as my father put me down on a soft, white place to help the bird-woman, I sensed my Other leaving. I smelled or tasted or felt his growing absence. And with an unmistakable act of will—any expert will tell you a newborn infant has no will, but I'm telling you I made a clear decision—I swallowed my brother. I ate him up so he couldn't disappear. On his way out of this world, some diamond mist that was him—a sweet-tasting cloud with a pomegranate red heart pulsing at its center—slid down my throat and joined me in secret marriage. Since then I have always had two hearts.

The earth body of my brother, which I never saw again after that day, was, I have always imagined, perfect—as mine was not. The loss of him was of course not the cause of my three shining flaws, but I thought otherwise for many years.

My three shining flaws. My loves. My wounds. My treasures.

One flaw was visible to all, a beacon and magnet for anyone excited and repulsed by an otherwise beautiful girl with a grotesque disfigurement. In the middle of my forehead, exactly in that spot where Hindu women draw the dot to mark the mythical third eye, was a large, dramatic birthmark. It was—no other way to name it—a bull skull, a more squat version of those shapes Georgia O'Keefe always painted. It was a big, ugly, radiant brown oval with horns, the left horn slightly longer than the right.

My second flaw was on the inside of me, visible to no one at first. It was only after I entered my second year of life that outer signs of the flaw began to alert Magda and Jerome to it. Increasingly, the top of my head was warm to the touch and my eyes bugged out of my head and my skin broke into curious sweats. That was when the bird-woman, who had hovered around the three of us since the birth, took me away to live with her. It was she who paid for the doctors who discovered that my tiny heart was working overtime to compensate for a missing part.

When I was eighteen months old, surgeons stretched my twenty-eight-inch body out on the table and sliced open two vertical and two horizontal inches of my chest in a good approximation of a cross. They reached inside to clip and sew my most important muscle, repairing the flawed circuit.

So my head cooled down. My eyes bugged back into my head. The strange sweats stopped. And that two-inch by two-inch scar on my chest began to grow. With each passing year, it expanded, just like the rest of me. By the time I was nine years old, the horizontal line of the cross had stretched to four and three-sixteenths inches, and the vertical to three and five-eighths. I know, because I measured it regularly with my red plastic ruler. Meanwhile, my bull skull tattoo had grown too. It was one and one-sixteenth inches in diameter, with a left horn three-eighths of an inch long and the right a quarter-inch.

As I know now, both of my flaws—my signatures—were responsible for me leaving Magda and Jerome and moving in permanently with the bird-woman. Just as they had been before I arrived, my birth parents were so poor they could barely take care of themselves properly, let alone a third member of their family. When my heart's growing malfunction expanded beyond the scope of their financial resources, they turned to the person who had offered to care for me all along, and took her up on her offer. From a tiny, dingy apartment, I moved to a plush, luxurious mansion. From stained, secondhand baby clothes, I changed into vividly colored silks and satins and velvets.

My heart's flaw was the trick of fate the bird-woman used to claim me. My head's flaw was the reason she wanted to claim me. It was the bull skull on my forehead—along with similar but less grotesque birthmarks behind my right knee and inside my labia majora—that convinced the bird-woman I was the long-prophesied reincarnation of Mary Magdalen, and future high priestess of her ancient mystery school.

The third shining flaw? I'll save that story for another time. Suffice to say that it was a secret to everyone, even me, until I reached the age of sexual maturity.

While you commune with the Televisionary Oracle

Your lucky number is 3.14159265

Your secret name is Squeeze

The colors of your soul are diamond-hatched and marbled blue

Your special emotion is skeptical faith

The garage sale item you most resemble
is an old but beautiful and sonorous accordion with a broken key

Your magic smell is candy skulls
being crushed on graves by dancing feet

Your holiest pain comes from your ability
to sense other people's cracked notions about you

Your sacred fungus is yeast

Your special time of day is the moment just before the mist evaporates

The shape of your life is oval with soft dark sparks

Your lucky phobia is epienopopopontonphobia,
or fear of crossing the wine-dark sea

Your power spot is here and there

The flavor which identifies you most is grapefruit smeared with honey


The following exercise is designed to upgrade and refine your screaming skills. It is not meant to be a decadent indulgence, but *a means to an end*—a technique for flushing away any resentments, terrors, and rages that might be threatening your ability to feel horny for spiders, museums, lightning, crayons, mountains—and even the Internet itself!

To begin, curl yourself up into a fetal position, make your breathing shallow, and tense all the muscles in your body as tight as they'll go. Try to include even your obscure, little-used muscles, as well as those you might not even be aware you have. The hundreds of muscles in the face are especially important.

Tense every muscle in your body.

Hold.

Hold.

Keep holding. Keep holding.

And release.


Now even as you withdraw your concentration from this full-bore constriction, try to keep a great deal of residual tension active in the background. Give the command to your subconscious mind to remain on high alert, with maximum stress. Begin to envision what it would be like to tense up your organs themselves.


To assist in this process, you may want to visualize your worst fears.

Imagine a person who hates you, and picture all the terrible qualities this person attributes to you.

Summon the memory of the worst betrayal in your life, the most traumatic violation.

Envision yourself dying alone in a horrible way.

While holding those scenes in the forefront of your awareness, work yourself up into the most galling discomfort you're capable of.

Tense every muscle in your body, every nerve, every organ. Turn yourself into a taught bundle of astringent fear and hatred.

Hold.

Hold.

Keep holding. Keep holding.

And release.


Now allow yourself to squeal a low whine in the shape of the sound "no."

Take a breath and again emit a pitiful, desperate moan that circles around the curse "no."

Draw another breath, and spurt another "no."

Begin to uncoil yourself from the fetal position, all the while spilling the holy "no" from the abyss inside.


Now stand up.

Straight and tall.

Bend and stretch and reach for the sky.

Stick out your tongue and cross your eyes and put on your ugliest face.

Take five fast breaths and then unfurl a yowling "no" against all of the wounds life has forced you to endure.

Wave your arms and leap off the ground and punch the air.

Spin around in erratic circles while slobbering and mussing your hair.

Shriek "no."

Wail "nooooooooo."

Faster.

Harder.

Wilder.

Feel nothing but your own juicy, red, oozing, unscratchable pain from the beginning of time.

Lurch, gnash, writhe, and twist until you realize there's no longer any need for you to pretend to be in control.

And now unleash the sound of a hurricane lashing an erupting volcano.

Ululate the cacophony of an earthquake in a forest fire.
And keep screaming until the alphabet is gone.


Everyone in the world
secretly died of disinfotainment
while watching a holocaust
of boring love
on TV
during a nuclear war
back in 1999,
and therefore
WE ARE ALL LIVING IN PARADISE
AT THIS VERY MOMENT!

**6**

I'm crushed. Crashed. Thoroughly crunched. Rapunzel abandoned me right in the middle of our love feast in the Catalyst bathroom.

Sulking, I contemplate my next move. I sit down on the sidewalk in front of the nightclub, leaning against a wall. My attention is drawn to objects weighing down the pockets of my new shirt.

In the right pocket is a small hardback book. In the left is a sealed envelope which contains a soft, puffy object. Both items are plum-colored.

The book cover shows a familiar image: the statuesque vulture with the lovely face and alluring breasts. The only difference here is that the strange creature is not naked, but scantily clad with a lacy red bustiere and red panties. The book's title: *Menstrual Lingerie Fashion Show*. It lists no author or editor. Inside are fifty-five pages of glossy, full-color photographs of female models posed on a runway. But most of these are not ordinary models, and this is no ordinary fashion show. I spy only a couple of women who come close to matching the pouty, anorexic specifications of the icons who populate the runways of Milan and Paris. Buck-teethed, pear-shaped, midlife women are the norm here. Saggy-titted, cellulite-proud, pigeon-toed women. Crone-faced, hairy-legged, big-nosed women.

"Demeter," for instance, a wild-eyed Caucasian woman in her fifties, has unkempt sandy grey hair—including quite a bush under each arm—and breasts that must have nursed several kids. I could easily picture her pushing a shopping cart full of all her wordly belongings down a city street. But here, instead of being garbed in a ripped 1950s-style house dress over baggy khaki work pants and moldy sneakers, she's in a sheer mauve lace bodystocking with embroidered butterflies and a tall, conical, violet witch's hat. Unlike the sleek, steely body language of all the models I've ever seen, Demeter has one leg bent and raised, and her arms are akimbo like a praying mantis doing tai chi.

"Hecate" is a pregnant woman in her twenties with dyed purple hair and countless body piercings, as well as a metal brace on her right leg. She's sporting a lovely emerald silk charmeuse camisole beneath a cape of white eagle feathers. Around her surging waistline is what appears to be a live snake, grasping its own tail in its mouth.

Holding a broom between her legs, "Tiamat" models a tapestry merrywidow with a gold bull skull talisman woven into the crook of the bra. A tall woman with glasses, a large forehead, and heavy legs, she looks remarkably like my third-grade teacher, Mrs. Byrd. It couldn't possibly be she, though, could it? I always had an inexplicable crush on her, which of course I never admitted to anyone, especially because all my friends thought she looked weird.

My favorite model in the *Menstrual Lingerie Fashion Show* is "Vimala." A vigorous-looking old crone sporting shoulder-length dreadlocks, she's one of the few models with an anatomy approaching the red-blooded American male's 36-23-36 ideal. In addition to purple cowgirl boots, a lacy red bra, and a red leather mini-skirt, she's wearing a tall crown of inflated pink and purple balloons tied together in the shape of a vulture. Further accessorizing the look is a necklace of tiny skulls, the candy kind that you get in Mexico during the Day of the Dead ceremonies.

Yow. I mean hallelujah. I mean what the fuck. Feminist pornography. Goddess-sanctioned lust-arousers. I'm dizzy. Itchy. Alienated but fascinated. Repulsed yet totally turned on. I've got to explore this further.

After studying each photo intently, I close the book and my eyes. My thoughts drift, in an inevitable comparison, to my customary experience of viewing the naked bodies of women I don't know. I must confess that when I'm at the liquor store buying cherry cider and olives for a post-midnight snack, I now and then fail to avert my eyes from the porn magazine section. I especially fail to avert my eyes from *Swank* magazine, which I've adjudged to be the least demeaning towards women and the most titillating to me. Yes, it's true that a suspiciously huge majority of the models are well within the criteria by which my conditioned reflexes evaluate beauty. But at least they're not depicted in degrading poses. They're not portrayed as being abused or dominated. They actually appear to be enjoying themselves. All that's got to count for something.

What vexes me even about the women in *Swank*, though, is their universally scoured, waxen, alabaster look. Profuse make-up has been applied to camouflage their "flaws." Photographic touch-up techniques do the rest. There's never a hint of leg hair or, for that matter, a cut from shaving. All underarm fur is scraped away. If it's there at all, the pubic hair is manicured like an English garden. Far too often the bodies reveal the grotesque blend of anorexia and silicon. Unlike real women, whose breasts differ in size and shape, many of the *Swank* siliconites have a perfectly matched pair.

There's a part of me—and not just the moralist and feminist in me, either—that hates this approach to beauty. Lately I've taken to boycotting any porn rag unless it features at least a few women whose breasts have never communed with silicon. And I truly prefer the presence rather than the absence of underarm hair.

But I'd be a slimy patriarchal dissembler if I tried to pretend that *Swank* and its ilk don't provoke in me an instant hard-on. I'm proud to say, however, that it's a sterile, dessicated hard-on. A like-eating-highly-processed-junk-food hard-on. A temperature-controlled, artificially-scented, recycled-airplane-air, muzak-in-the-elevator hard-on. In short, an impotent hard-on.

I may get lathered up for the wrong reasons, in other words, but at least I feel guilty about it. And to my further credit, I'm aware of the fact that there are right reasons—which ideally I'm on the verge of mastering.

So how am I doing with this project, anyway? To what degree have I purged all non-feminist hormones from my lust? Maybe I should take advantage of the opportunity afforded me by Rapunzel's little picture book to take an inventory. Can I truly say I'm sincerely turned on in the most spiritually correct way by the women of the Menstrual Lingerie Fashion Show? Women who in their deviation from the freakish standards established by professional models are the very embodiment of normal? I would like to say yes. I would love nothing more than to be able to testify without any qualification—passing a lie detector test if necessary—that these pear-shaped, pigeon-toed, big-nosed women do indeed prime my kundalini for all the right reasons.

A judgment in my favor would serve many noble purposes, besides opening up a vast new repository of candidates for seduction. Most importantly, it would launch a healthy new chapter in the sordid history of my relationship with my conscience. The fact is that whereas the bulk of the population has installed in their superego a variation on the pissed-off, misogynist God of the Old Testament, mine is occupied by a very different archetype. Though sometimes she takes the form of a cagey, tender goddess like, say, Sophia of esoteric Christianity, more often she's a frowning fanatical harpy who has much in common with Medusa-clones like anti-porn crusaders Andrea Dworkin and Catherine MacKinnon. The endless streams of bile that spew from this aspect of my nasty inner critic may be the closest a patriarchal stooge like myself can ever come to knowing what it means to be battered. But I can imagine in thrilling detail the freedom that would burst out in my heart if I could convince the Dour Matriarchal Judge I was fully aligned with her agendas.

"No, Judge, I am not a looksist," I could appeal to her with a totally straight face. "I am not a bigot who evaluates women first of all on their appearance. My attraction depends more on their inner than outer qualities. I may be a slobbering lecher, but at least my slobbering lechery is fueled by only the most righteous motivations."

Before I could in good conscience approach the bench with this plea, however, I'd have to convince myself of its verity. The Judge deals harshly with self-deception.

So what about it? Do I believe my own wishful assertions?

There is a certain amount of evidence in favor of this interpretation. Exhibit A: Ever since I explored the "feminist porn" in Rapunzel's book, I have been luxuriating in a most sumptuous blooming of what the tantric poets refer to as the jade stalk. What further data could possibly refute that ringing empirical documentation?

I bask now in the fantasy that I could actually feel happy and festive and self-respectful about being a testosterone-possessed fucknut.

Emerging from my meditation, I leaf through the last few pages of the *Menstrual Lingerie Fashion Show*. Tucked between the last page and the back cover is a loose, rumpled piece of lavender paper folded into quarters. I open it up and find a text printed by hand. "Dear Rockstar," it begins. I feel a flush of excitement as I contemplate the possibility that Rapunzel didn't abandon me after all. She's just playing an interesting game with me. This is her next gambit. I eagerly devour the message.

Dear Rockstar,

Memorize every word of the text you're holding in your hands. You <u>will</u> be tested.

There are two doors between this world and the other world. Womb and tomb. Coming and going. Imagine a menstruating woman as one who opens both doors at the same time and peers both ways. When the uterine nest begins to disintegrate, the unfertilized ovum dies. Yet in the same instant, a hormonal message zooms to the ovaries, triggering the bloom of a new candidate.

So yes, women flirt with a little death every month. But it's a good death, a friendly death. When the magical "wound" between our legs bleeds, it purifies and renews us. No such luck for men. They can go on for months without any physical crisis that forces them to purge accumulated toxins. Or at least they <u>think</u> they can go on for months. In fact, many phallus-bearers walk around half-poisoned most of the time, unaware of how frenetically their rational minds are working to concoct logical explanations for their nasty, unacknowledged feelings.

The upshot is that women have a more convivial relationship with blood. For them, its flow symbolizes regeneration. For most men, the loss of blood portends plain old literal death; the ultimate humiliation; the ghastly annihilation of their one and only body.

There <u>have</u> been a few exceptional men who've courted the power of those who bleed but do not die. Maybe you'll be one?

Ancient tantric texts advise male initiates to make love with menstruating women if they want to grow wiser and stronger. Many shamanic cultures from Siberia to America were more likely to choose a man to be chief boohoo if he acted like a woman.

And we can't overlook good old Jesus. After he died, a soldier pierced his side with a spear, unleashing a stream of blood and water. In that lucky moment, he acquired a symbolic vulva; he mutated into an honorary menstruator. The bleeding slit was the seal of his immortality, the sign that his death was merely prelude to resurrection.

The Fisher King in the Grail legends wooed the same potency. The wound in his thigh gave him the chance to imitate a menstruator. He wasn't just an average dickhead, but a magical androgyne who'd taken on the power of a woman to regenerate herself.

What do you think?

Beauty and Truth,

Rapunzel

The letter is a little deflating, even if it does present an intriguing challenge that appeals to the poet in me. I have a hard time imagining what concrete actions I could take to become an honorary menstruator like Jesus or the Fisher King. Though I'm not a big fan of Aleister Crowley, I recall an experiment he once did to train his will. It involved the shedding of blood. He resolved not to use the pronoun "I" in his speech for a period of two weeks. Every time he violated his intention he slashed his arm with a razor blade. Quickly enough, his subconscious mind got the message, and added its considerable resources to the project.

As eager as I am to learn from Rapunzel's teachings, I don't know if I'm ready for a commitment as extreme as Crowley's. Outrageous meditations are more my style. There are certain Buddhist visualizations, for instance, that might help me, a mere man, cultivate a less literal relationship with death. One of the practices is called the corpse pose. The meditator lies utterly still for many hours, imagining himself mouldering deep underground as if he were a dead body. In another exercise, the practitioner imagines his body being ripped apart by carnivorous animals.

There's one other treat left for me to explore from the pocket of the shirt Rapunzel bequeathed me. An envelope with a soft puffy something inside. Opening it, I find a rectangle of cotton inside a cover of waxy sheer violet paper. The corners are rounded, and it measures maybe six inches long and two inches wide. The edges of the object are decorated with glyphs and pictograms, which I recognize from Marija Gimbutas' research as more of the hoary symbols of the ancient Goddess religion: lozenges, double-headed axes, snakes, and butterflies.

One side of the object has a strip of sticky substance that extends from end to end. The other side is tinctured with what appear to be reddish brown blotches. They feel moist and sticky. I imagine or maybe actually experience a pleasant shock in my fingertips.

I bravely but gingerly bring the object to my nose to sniff. The fragrance is sweet patchouli with a hint of butterscotch and eucalyptus.

Making sure no passers-by are spying on me, I linger in this olfactory investigation. The longer I sniff, the more penetrating the odor. There seems to be no saturation point. Usually, if I sniff a strong smell over and over, its potency gradually fades. But if anything, the aroma emitted from the cotton pad is growing stronger.

Another strange thing: New sub-scents continually rush in. Raw unsweetened chocolate. Fermented apples on the edge between wine and vinegar. Roasting coffee. And then, impossibly, there's an unmistakable aroma from childhood: my pink night-night, the blanket I carried around with me for most of the fourth year of my life. I'm transported to the heart of a moment in which my four-year-old girlfriend Dulce Weil and I wrapped ourselves up tight in my pink night-night and rolled down a grassy hill covered with clover.

Other smells invade. Baking cinnamon buns. Moist carrots freshly plucked out of rainy dirt. Musky skin of Kerry Kastle, the first girl I ever touched on the inside. The honeysuckle blooming outside the window next to our bed that night.

I feel dizzy but entranced. I love how the scents explode at the root of my nose and radiate out into my brain and body. My fingertips drink in the redolence; my heart; my lust. It's almost as if the circulation of blood centered in my heart is running parallel with the circulation of aromas centered in the cotton pad. My dizziness becomes a whirlpool. But I can't bring myself to pull my nose away from the magical artifact.

I open my eyes, trying to anchor myself. The reddish-brown Rorschach blotches on the pad begin to undulate and weave. I feel my pupils jiggling in my sockets, stimulating further animation.

And then I'm hallucinating deep into the history of the blotches. Their ancient origins. A giant, naked, blue-skinned Goddess with snake-like auburn hair and eight arms erupts out of a salty tidal pool in an autumnal estuary. She seems as inhuman as the wind or the ocean. I fantasize or hallucinate myself lying naked below her on marshy ground under a twilight sky. Her right foot is on my chest and her left on my thighs. She's over me like a holy mountain. She's inside me like a slit in my heart. I hear my voice inside me growling, "I *know* you! I *know* you!" As if in response, she breaks off a branch of wormwood from amidst her prodigious hair and shoves it in my mouth. As she squats, her smells fan out. Absinthe, marijuana, ammonia, eucalyptus, seaweed, rose. They're all over me, saturating me like a soft electrical shock. My eyes fibrillate, seeing her thousands of times per second. Bending her sweaty blue face down, she shoots a steaming river of words into my ear: "I'll make you famous with no one but me." Her necklace of severed human heads drapes across my chest, and I'm flooded with still-pulsing blood. She licks my face with her enormous tongue, inundating me with the tastes of the gall bladders and nasturtiums and comets she has devoured. She does not eat my face but rises again like a yew tree growing impossibly fast. Now she's swarming. Fireflies and maggots glisten in her gnarled hair, and her pendulous blue breasts ooze yellowish milk. One of her eight hands wears a baseball glove filled with a pomegranate and another cradles a toilet plunger topped with a diamond. Still others carry fresh figs, colored Easter eggs, and a silver Grail cup sloshing with reddish-brown liquid. In one of her hands swings my own bleeding, decapitated head. Even though I can plainly see it there, my face frozen with surprise, I still, somehow, have my head on my shoulders too.

I feel like vomiting but can't because I'm paralyzed. The only part of me that's able to move is my jade stalk, which is pronged straight up towards her and far bigger than usual. She leaps off me, grabs this handle with a free hand, and pulls me to my feet. My body is stiff and straight, like a hypnotized volunteer in a stage magician's levitation display. Still clutching, she drags me through a jungle of brown cattails to the inside of a purple canvas dome. She arranges me on the dirt floor, then squats down on me, engorging my sex with hers. Bright-eyed women in plum lingerie are arrayed around us, watching and murmuring prayer songs that sound like running water. I feel vulnerable, fascinated, humiliated, afraid, curious, and totally turned on. Waves of erotic pleasure rip through me, but they're so unlike anything I've felt before that they push me to the verge of panic. It's like *she* is penetrating *me*. As if she's ejaculating some ocean of electricity into the end of my lingam and gushing it down into and through my whole body. Time and time again her body is consumed by a rising spiral of shudders, then stiffens and climaxes. Each time she yowls triumphantly, "You're changing! You're really changing!"

Only when I feel sure that she has squeezed all the bliss she can from me do I give myself permission to release into an orgasm. But before I can surrender, one of the women from the circle hands her an antlered animal's skull. Grasping it by the horns, she presses it down against my belly. Miraculously, as if my skin were suddenly porous, the skull penetrates me. I feel my insides gurgling and rearranging to accommodate it. The agony is so novel, so interesting, that I hear myself screaming "Thank you!" as my eyes roll back into indigo sky. The anguish is not an event or a feeling. It's my whole world. I'm disappearing into the Land of Pain. With each heartbeat, an icy hot burst of shattered diamonds explodes at the base of my spine, shooting out a web of acid rivers which sluice through my legs, to the ends of my fingers, ripping out the tip of my tongue with a memory of the last nanosecond before the Big Bang. It's like I swallowed a bomb. Vultures and moles and hyenas and praying mantises are cannibalizing me. I'm being spanked with knives from the inside.

I'm aware of a perverse and yet poised longing to keep a record of the pain. I want to preserve every nuance of my relationship with it, as if this were the first flush of falling in love: the moment of imprinting.

But the stress of the revelation is too great. I cover my face with my hands and pass out.

Next thing I know I'm floating down a dark red river on a raft. On one end of the vehicle is a television made of bushes and clay and glass and jewel-like beetles. Standing at the other end is Rapunzel. Wearing a rainbow batik mini-dress and unlaced black army boots, she propels us along with a pole. I'm reminded of Charon, from Greek myth, who guided dead souls across the River Styx. "Did you steal Charon's job?" I joke weakly to Rapunzel. "The archetypes are mutating, Rockstar," she replies.

I gaze at the TV. It has no images, but keeps scrolling the same printed message.

> During your time of the month, meditate on the following questions:
>
> 1. What feelings and intuitions have you been trying to ignore since the moon was last in the phase it is now?
>
> 2. Which parts of your life are overdue for death?
>
> 3. What messages has life been trying to convey to you but you've chosen to ignore?
>
> 4. What red herrings, straw men, and scapegoats have you chased after obsessively in order to avoid dissolving your most well-rationalized delusions?

7

What if
Arthur C. Clarke was correct
when he said
that any sufficiently advanced technology
is indistinguishable from magic?

What if such "supernatural machines"
exist on this earth,
and are not commandeered
by military or government elites?

What if
there really are,
as have always been rumored,
mystery schools
that harbor
enlightened masters and shamanic geniuses and witchy saints
who ceaselessly conspire to
foment beauty, truth, love, and justice?

And what if
these magi have conjured
a supernatural machine
which can,
with your permission,

beam carrier waves
directly into your brain tissue,
using your skull as a transceiver?

And what if
the sole purpose
of these transmissions
is to link
your conscious ego
to the inaccessible part of your brain
called
your higher self
or guardian angel
or inner teacher?

Relax. Breathe sweetly and deeply. As you inhale, become aware that every one of your heart's beats originates in a gift of love directly from the Goddess Herself. As you exhale, allow every cell in your perfect animal body to purr with luminous gratitude for the enormity of the blessings you endlessly receive. Become aware that any residue of hatred still tainting your libido is draining out of you into the good earth.

Continue to breathe sweetly and deeply. Now gently explode yourself into an even more serene shimmer of reverence. Feel the lustful compassion flowing from your mitochondria in spiral hallelujahs. Sense the flocks of blood-red angels floating across the grey-green pupils of your eyes, dropping bunches of fresh beets to celebrate your homecoming.

You are now more at peace than you have ever been in your life. Your body feels the way it does after you've floated for an hour in warm seawater. The calcium in your bones and the iron in your blood are swarming with memories of how they were originally forged at the core of a red giant star that died billions of years ago.

Now imagine that you're dreaming, but you're also wide awake. You're both and neither. It's not exactly like an out-of-body experience and it's not exactly like virtual reality, yet it feels like both. You're in the Drivetime, the wormhole that connects the Dreamtime and the Waketime. You have become one with the Televisionary Oracle.


What if
by merely imagining these possibilities
you have cast a brainy love spell
on yourself,
linking
your conscious ego
to the inaccessible part of your brain
called
your higher self
or guardian angel
or inner teacher?

I'm back. It's me, Rapunzel. The chick with the crazy parents and the heart problem and the blotch on my forehead and the twin brother who died in childbirth. I'm getting geared up to tell you another story about myself.

But first I need to say a prayer.

Dear Goddess, You Wealthy Anarchist Burning Heaven to the Ground:
    Charge me up with Your Death Medicine, that I may die every single day of my life.
    Trick me into figuring out how to kill my own death.

O Goddess, You Sly Universal Virus with No Fucking Opinion:
    Teach me to incinerate my own hype. Not just other people's sorry-ass self-promotion and megalomania, which are so infinitely easy to scourge—but my own, no matter how elegant and subtle I might imagine it is.
    Guide me to drop my act again and again, even the part of my act that is covertly proud of being the kind of wise-guy who drops her act again and again.

Hey Goddess, Who Gives Us So Much Love and Grief Mixed Together That Our Morality is Always on the Verge of Collapsing:
    Brainwash me with your freedom
    so that I never love my own pain more than anyone else's pain

Amen. A-women. Ommmmmmm. And Hallelujah.

I can already feel Vimala cringing. She's my adoptive mom—not to mention the midwife who delivered me into the world—and she doesn't like me to die so much.

Especially when my dying requires me to lovingly rebel against the gorgeous system of secret gnosis preserved and nurtured for thousands of years by the mystery school now known as the Menstrual Temple of the Funky Grail. A task, by the way, which Vimala knows I was born to do, and which she poured all her love and care into me so that I could do.

Vimala, sweet Mommy, you know you want me to say this: As much as I am devoted to every last menstrual meme, as much as I believe the Menstrual Temple of the Funky Grail and all of its creations are the best antidote to the phallocratic celebration of soul death, I can't bring myself to dramatize our precious treasures with unironic literalism, as if they were the the Sole Truth and the Ultimate Way.

For instance, it's my dharmic duty to announce that when I speak of the phallocratic mentality, I'm not just referring to white men and Republicans. Women and leftwingers and poor people and sexual outlaws, with whom I'm more likely to feel sympatico, are just as likely to be phallocrats.

An example: A certain socialist feminist soul sister whom I'll call Juneau, a fellow shamanatrix with whom I've shared bellylaughs and trance-dancing, would turn off her love light towards me the moment she discovered that not only am I staunchly and passionately pro-abortion, but that I also understand and sympathize with all those people who hate and fight abortion. My socialist feminist soul sister couldn't comprehend or accept my belief that *both* sides are right—any more than a Catholic priest could.

How does my friend Lamorte put it? "I'm totally opposed to duality."

Everyone who believes in the devil, in other words, IS the devil. There is no enemy. There can be no enemy. I will fight to the death for the right not to believe in or have enemies. IF there could be such a thing as an enemy—which there can't—the enemy would be literalism. Fundamentalism. That appalling certainty and arrogant simplicity—whether found in Islamic zealots or the priesthood of the Cult of Science—that fosters the belief that MY story is truer than YOUR story. That the truth of MY story sucks all the truth out of YOUR story. That YOUR story cannot possibly have even an ounce of truth. OK, maybe an ounce, but I'll halfheartedly admit that as a debating strategy only so I can disguise the fact that I have utterly dismissed you and renounced forever the possibility of seeing your humanity.

I guess I've just implied that as much as I want to hate literalism, I can't even do that. Which of course leads me to make my next shocking admission about the champion of literalism, phallocracy. Though my passionate commitment to the Drivetime and all it stands for sometimes requires me to act AS IF phallocracy is nothing but an evil poison and AS IF the Menstrual Temple of the Funky Grail is the safest and most effective antidote, and though my personal temperament resonates intimately with the subtle themes of the Menstrual Temple of the Funky Grail, I also know with all my heart that the six thousand-year-old experiment known as phallocracy was an inevitable and necessary phase of the evolution of the human race.

Yes, I'm ready for it to be gone now; I want its ugliest creations to die off; I detest its violence and oppression and sickening abuse of the feminine. But I recognize too the beauty of its individuating force, its striving to explore and transcend and expand, its celebration of the rational, analytical mind, and its mysterious struggle to master nature.

I die daily. And saying what I just said about the redemptive features of phallocracy is a decent death for the first part of the day. But it's just for starters. It comes all too naturally. It's easy destruction. Hardly mourned. Good riddance. How about if I dare myself to kill even more lethal treasures; force myself even further into the threshold where dear life rots away and smuggles a message of resurrection back through time?

Do you dare me to tell you more of the story of my life, beauty and truth fans, thereby killing my cherished privacy and self-protectiveness? Thereby incinerating the superstitious fear I have that in telling you my story I will diminish its magic and potency?

Do you double-dare me to burn down my childlike cocoon, to slaughter the perfect fantasy about my life story that I and everyone who loves me have been all too eager to nurture?

I do. Dare me. Even if you won't, I double-dare myself to tell you profound secrets about my life that you might criticize or disbelieve or satirize, or worst of all, that you might not be particularly interested in. I triple-dare myself to expose to you everything that's true and holy about my experience, knowing that whether you treat it like treasure or garbage, I will have annihilated forever the sweet protective seal I have built around my life, the bubble of protection that has always preserved my innocent infantile belief that my life is important and righteous and good.

I want to direct your attention now, beauty and truth fans, to the archaeological evidence remaining from a death I created some years ago. It's one of my favorite deaths, one of the bravest.

Look at the center of my forehead. Do you see the beauty mark I was born with—the icon-like bull skull with one horn slightly smaller than the other? Of course you don't. Because it's not there. Or is it? Better make sure. Deaths can be faked, after all. Zoom in and examine the area in question very closely. Maybe my treasure is simply buried beneath a slab of special-effects make-up. I'm rubbing. I'm scraping. Any pancake coming off? No. Because there isn't any.

The grotesque yet beautiful glyph, the signature the Goddess imprinted on me in the womb, is gone. The birthmark that the ancient prophecies of our mystical order said would be the single most irrefutable sign of the female messiah. Disappeared. Erased. All that remains is what for all you know is a couple of worry lines.

My body has been re-engineered. I'm not the organism I was born to be. How? Why? Divine intervention? Miracle hands-on healing?

No. My gift is gone because I had it scoured away. At the tender age of sixteen-going-on-seventeen. Without parental consent. In a distant city, where I'd run away. With the help of a mere dermatologist who had never heard and will never hear of the Menstrual Temple of the Funky Grail.

But wait. Not so fast. My personal story makes no sense unless I embed it in a bigger, older story. And the victorious death I want to pull off for your entertainment pleasure won't have the finality it deserves unless I prove to you the profundity of its ignominy.

Let me then show you how my sublimated suicide depends for its authority on evolutionary trends that are thousands of years old. They feature an organization whose money and wisdom are making it possible for me to be talking to you right now. This organization, the Menstrual Temple of the Funky Grail, is so old and vast—yet so precise and slippery—that only a fool would try to describe it. It's a hundred organizations in one. A mystery school that's more ancient than the sphinx. A think tank that's so young most of its research is in the future. A media coven. A dream hospital. A gymnasium where mystical athletes hone their physical skills.

Picture a dating service for single mothers, or a secret society of occult astronomers that knew of the planets Uranus and Neptune and Pluto thousands of years before modern astronomers "discovered" them. Imagine a lobbyist for the rights of menstruators, or a ritual theater group that fed ideas to French playwright Antonin Artaud in his dreams. Visualize a gang of sacred janitors, or the world's oldest manufacturer of sacred dolls.

Most of all, beauty and truth fans, picture a hidden sacred city of the imagination—temples, dream sanctuaries, gymnasiums, theaters, healing spas, love chambers—kept so secret that it's invisible to all but a very few in every generation. Call this place a thousand names. Call it the College-Whose-Name-Keeps Changing-and-Whose-Location-Keeps-Expanding, or call it the Sanctuary-Where-the-Thirteen-Perfect-Secrets-from-Before-the-Beginning-of-Time-Are-Kept. Its official name as of today is "Menstrual Temple of the Funky Grail," and it has headquarters on all seven continents. Five thousand years ago, it was housed solely on two continents as "Inanna Nannaru," derived from Akkadian words, translated roughly as "Inanna's Nuptial Couch in Heaven." Six thousand years ago: "Tu-ia Gurus," from the Sumerian, loosely meaning "Creation-Juice, Bringer of Good Tidings to the Womb."

Two thousand years ago—so this story goes—our mystery school that is always both outside of time and yet entering time at every moment was called Pistis Sophia—in English "Faithful Wisdom." Its most famous member—its *only* famous member—was Mary Magdalen, visionary consort of Jesus Christ. Not a penitent prostitute, as the Christian church later distorted her in an attempt to undermine the radical implications of their divine marriage. Not an obeisant groupie who mindlessly surrendered her will to the man-god.

On the contrary, beauty and truth fans. Magdalen was Christ's partner, his equal. More than that, she was his joker, his wild card: his secret weapon. They worshiped the divine in each other. So say the ancient texts of our mystery school.

But you need not believe the secret texts to guess the truth. Even the manual of the Christian church itself, as scoured of the truth as it is, strongly hints at Magdalen's majesty. While all the male disciples disappeared during the crucifixion, she was there with Christ. While the twelve male disciples were cowering in defeated chaos, she was the first to find the empty tomb. Jesus appeared to her first after his resurrection; she was the first to be called by him to the mission of apostle.

The Gnostic texts from Nag Hammadi, discovered in 1947, reveal even more of their relationship, which violated all the social norms of their time. She was a confidante, a lover, an Apostle above all the other Apostles. Jesus called her the "Woman Who Knew the All," and said she would rule in the coming Kingdom of Light. Even an early Christian father, Origen, helped propagate these truths, calling her immortal, and maintaining that she had lived since the beginning of time.

The traditions of our ancient order say all this and more: that Mary Magdalen's performance on history's stage was an experiment—Pistis Sophia's gamble that the phallocracy was ripe for mutation.

That the risk failed is testimony not to Magdalen's inadequacies, but to the virulence of out-of-control masculinity. Magdalen, alas, was too far ahead of her time to succeed in being seen for who she really was. Her archetype was not permitted to imprint itself deeply enough on the collective unconscious. Sadly, the divine feminine barely managed to survive in the dreams of the race through the defanged, depotentized image of the Virgin Mary—Christ's harmless mommy, not his savvy consort.

From her cave in Provence, twenty years after the death of Christ, Magdalen foresaw that the future Church would suppress her role in the joint revelation. She predicted the Council of Nicaea, which in the year 325 excised from the Bible all texts that told of her complete role. She even prophesied that the spiritual descendants of Peter, the Apostle who had hated and feared her most, would trump up the absurd story of her whoredom, conflating her with Mary of Bethany and three other unnamed women described as sinners and adulterers in various books of the freshly canonical New Testament.

In the last years of her life, Magdalen, knowing that her work with Christ would be foiled and distorted, prepared for a renewal of the experiment at a later time. The records of Pistis Sophia tell us that she wrote of the signs by which future members of our order would know she had reincarnated. These signs were as follows.

1. Her return would come in the last half-century of the second millennium, and she would be born in the astrological sign of the Bull.

2. She would be born "in the place called Holy Cross, in a land blessed by Persephone."

3. She would endure "a living crucifixion that would save her life."

4. She would "be conceived double but be born single." In recording this prophecy, Magdalen added the following words, which are attributed to Jesus in the Gnostic *Second Gospel of Mary Magdalen*:

   When you make the two one, and when you make
   the inside like the outside and the outside
   like the inside, and the above like the below
   and the below like the above, and when you make
   the male like the female and the female like the
   male, then you will enter the Kingdom.

5. She would have a signature of the bucrania (or bull skull) in three places on her body: behind the left knee, in the right fold of the labia majora, and in the middle of the forehead.

In 1948, the Pomegranate Grail, which is what the Menstrual Temple of the Funky Grail was called at that time, began its preparations for the return of the avatar. Members all over the world were put on alert. Much attention was focused on all those places that were literally called "Holy Cross"—or in Spanish, "Santa Cruz." Pomegranate Grail members congregated around Holy Cross College in Maryland, as well as in Santa Cruz, Bolivia, Santa Cruz de Tenerife in the Canary Islands, and Santa Cruz, California. Of these three, the Californian city aroused greatest excitement because according to one interpretation California was "Kali's land." Kali, in the canon of the Pomegranate Grail, was the Hindu equivalent of Persephone.

In anticipation of her search for the reincarnation of Mary Magdalen, Vimala Nostradamus, one of the thirteen chiefs of the Pomegranate Grail, settled north of Santa Cruz, California, in October of 1949, where she began to build the community that was to serve as the nest for the coming again of Mary Magdalen. Vimala had spent the previous ten years in Pondicherry, India, which at the time was the world headquarters for our order.

I faithfully report these facts to you, beauty and truth fans, because I can say without much exaggeration that my body is made of them. They were fed to me with my childhood meals, sung to me as I fell asleep, repeated to me as I was bathed, by the people who've loved me most and treated me best in life: Vimala and my six other mothers, Artemisia, Dagmar, Cecily, Sibyl, Burgundy, and Indigo. How could I doubt the veracity of these stories, when they come from the same nurturers who've helped make me so strong and healthy and confident?

And yet I have to say that it has always been easier for me to love those big, ancient tales than the implication they have for my personal life. The glory and the mission of Mary Magdalen are myths I have been able to appreciate best when I've tried to pretend that she wasn't me.

But the people who've treated me best and loved me most say that Magdalen *is* me. I am, according to them, the fulfillment of the prophecy. Their avatar. The reincarnation of the divinity that last inhabited the earthly body of Mary Magdalen—come again to formulate and disseminate the new covenant of the ancient feminine mysteries, the dispensation for the next cycle of evolution.

And oh by the way, there *won't be* any next cycle of evolution if I fail to do my job. The prophecies of Magdalen, supplemented by those of her most esteemed interpreters down through the ages, are unambiguous about this. Unless I successfully lead the charge to restore the long-lost balance of male and female, patriarchy will literally exterminate the human species. By what means is irrelevant—nuclear holocaust, germ warfare or genetic engineering gone astray, global warming or ozone-layer destruction or rain forest depletion. There is only one logical outcome to misogynist culture's evolution, and that is to commit collective suicide.

According to the prophecies, it would almost be too late by the time Magdalen was born again. The patriarchy would be in the final stages of the self-annihilation it mistakes for aggrandizement.

Maybe you can begin to guess why I began to impose, at an early age, a buffer of skepticism between me and the role I was supposed to embrace. How many children are told that they have come to Earth to prevent the apocalypse?

At moments like these, I hallucinate the smell of a cedar wood bonfire. Visions of magenta silk flags flash across my inner eye, and tables heaped with gifts for me. These are psychic artifacts from midsummer's eve six weeks after my sixth birthday—the day of my "crowning" as the avatar. For a long time my recollections of that day were a garbled mass of other people's memories, which I had empathized with so strongly I'd made them my own. With the help of a meditation technique I call *anamnesis,* I have in recent years recovered what I believe to be my own pure experience.

I awoke crying that morning from a terrible nightmare, which of course I wasn't allowed to forget, since Vimala was there, pouncing from her bed in the next room with her cat-smother love, asking me what I dreamed and scribbling it down in the golden notebook she kept to record every hint of an omen that ever trickled out of me.

I dreamed I was doing somersaults down a long runway, dressed in a flouncy red-and-white polka dot clown suit and big red flipper shoes. Thousands of people were in the audience, but they were totally silent even though I thought I was being wildly funny and entertaining. Then I picked up a violin and began playing the most beautiful but silly music, and the crowd started to boo, and some people walked out. Vimala jumped up on stage from below and stripped off my clown suit and flippers. Underneath I was wearing a long magenta silk dress. From somewhere Vimala produced a ridiculously big and heavy crown that seemed made of lead or iron. It was taller than my entire body, and when she put it on my head I reeled and weaved all over the runway, trying both to prevent it from tumbling off and to keep myself from falling. The audience cheered and whistled and clapped. I broke into huge sobs, which woke me up.

"Did your dream make you sad?" Vimala soothed me, as she kissed my birthmark.

I said nothing, but slumped and wiggled my front tooth, which was hanging loose by a thread of flesh. Although I'd been crying in the dream, I stopped soon after I awoke.

"There's no need to feel sad," Vimala said. "How can you feel sad for even a moment when you are such a very powerful queen of life with so many blessings to give?"

I wanted to cry but I couldn't bring myself to. Instead, I yanked at my tooth.

And then suddenly it was free. Blood geysered down onto my red silk comforter and I started to shake. Vimala instantly removed the sash from her kimono and pressed it against my wound.

"Lie back down, wonderful one," she comforted me. "Rest a while. Here, give me that tooth and we will wrap it up for the fairies to come and take tonight."

She climbed under the covers with me and held my head in the crook of her arm. I fell back asleep.

When I awoke Vimala was gone. I decided I would lie in bed until she came to summon me. As I wandered back to the memory of my dream, I wanted to cry again and even felt the beginning of a sob erupting in my chest. But by the time it reached my throat, it was forced, a fake. I let it bellow out anyway, and the pathos of it almost ignited a real sob. But that too aborted itself.

As I looked around my giant, pie-piece-shaped bedroom, trying to penetrate the numbness I felt about the signs of luxury I beheld there, I allowed myself to experience, for the millionth time, my oldest, most familiar emotion: a blend of gratitude and guilt for all my blessings.

There in the corner where the curved outer wall of my tower met one wall of this, my "Moon Room," Sibyl had built me an astoundingly authentic play castle, complete with drawbridge, crenellated battlements, and three pint-sized rooms. Inside were all the accessories a child queen could ever hope for, including a treasure chest of jewels, conical hats topped with banners of silk, and a magic mirror.

Beside the castle was my art station, with every kind of clay, paint, and crayons I would ever need to create my masterpieces, along with feathers, leaves, crystals, glue, a small hammer and other tools, pieces of wood and nails—everything. Beside that was Sibyl's handmade, three-story oak dollhouse, filled with perfectly crafted miniature wood furniture. The entire room was a riot of toys, dolls, books, music, and countless other objects designed to nourish my imagination and overwhelm me with the knowledge that I was the most beloved child who had ever lived.

The emerald green walls—what could be seen of them through the swarm of toys and props—had been handpainted by Artemisia with scenes depicting the thirteen stations of Mary Magdalen (as opposed to the fourteen stations of Jesus). The figure of Magdalen was portrayed by the most successful female characters from fairy tales, including, of course, Rapunzel herself.

And this was just one of my huge rooms on just one floor of the four-story enchanted tower where I lived with Vimala. And in each of six other homes which formed just a part of our larger community— which seemed for all I could tell to be centered entirely around my happiness—there was a special room just for me where I could go to stay with my other six adoptive mothers. I had—and still have—seven mothers! And each has always doted on me as if I were her only child, even though Sibyl, Cecily, Artemisia, and Burgundy have natural-born children of their own.

My blessings were prodigal, supernal, monstrous. My meals were without exception masterpieces; the recipes came from cuisines as varied as my mothers' ethnic backgrounds. I had a thousand different outfits to wear, a hundred different shoes. My mothers conducted intricate, mysterious rituals at least once every new moon and full moon— mostly, it seemed, for my benefit—and streams of interesting women who seemed equally in love with me were constantly visiting on these and other occasions. I was read to, played with, massaged, hugged, and taught by a tag-team of seven smart, psychologically healthy women who never grew bored or impatient with me, because the moment they might be on the verge of submitting to those feelings they handed me over to a fresh substitute.

Not one of my mothers, not even once, ever gave me the slightest suggestion that I should be overawed by my abundance. No one ever manipulated me into behaving the way they wanted by threatening to withhold their love. And yet neither did they spoil me. I was expected to work in the garden, and clean up my toys, and be responsible for my emotions.

The guilt I swam in was apparently my own invention, devised under my own inspiration. Without any direction, as if drawing telepathically on the frustrations of underprivileged people I had never met, I somehow managed to conjure a chronic reflex that combined the feelings of "How can I possibly deserve such wonderful treatment?" and "Thank you so much, beloved Goddess."

Not infrequently, I daydreamed about what it would be like to experience real pain. Having my hands cut off was a good fantasy, fueled by the Grimms' fairy tale about the girl with no hands. I tried, ineffectually, to imagine what it would be like to have my mother die, as Sibyl said hers had when she was a child. At times I felt something like envy for the sorrow and agonies of characters in books.

Maybe this wouldn't have been a problem if my seven mothers had decided to tell me about the experiences in my early life that qualified as tragic. Those traumas—the loss of my twin brother, my heart surgery, and my biological parents giving me away to Vimala—had all happened before I could talk, at an age when memory was shaping its records out of materials that could not easily be retrieved later.

By the time I was informed, at age nine, of just how difficult my early life had been, it was too late to erase the imprint. That weird blend of compulsive gratitude and guilt was always there, preventing direct communion with the divine favors forever flowing my way. As a result, I half-wasted my blessings for years. I was caught up in my self-conscious dialogue with them, forever missing the point.

The point being: Don't get all bound up in worrying about the implications of the blessings; just get out there and use them, spread them, multiply them. Respond to them with the same spirit with which they have been given to you.

In light of this failing of mine, beauty and truth fans, the disaster I am about to describe to you may seem forgivable.

I lay in bed that morning for as long as it took to realize that I wasn't going to be able to cry right then. Finally I rose and wandered out of my Moon Room.

From the window that runs the entire length of the Sun Room's outer wall, I watched my seven mothers and other women at work out-side, preparing the grounds for the ritual ahead. Each of the other three towers was already festooned with long trains of silk magenta flags. On the circular green at the heart of our community, there were a harp and drums and the tall effigy of Persephone and a cauldron stacked on top of cedar logs and five huge round black marble tables with a silver cup and piles of gifts on every one. More prayer flags had been strung between the myrtle trees, whose branches held feathered ser-pents and corn dollies and colored eggs and bull skulls and balloons. Around the periphery of the green was a boundary of giant pump-kins, miraculously full-grown here on the first day of summer, as well as ripe tomatoes and pears and fat white candles.

It all looked very festive—and dismal. As I watched the arrival of women I had never seen—pilgrims, I had been told, from chapters of the Pomegranate Grail based all over the world, visiting especially for this joyous occasion—I could feel my entire body tightening into a rigid coil. It was one thing to be queen in the spontaneous play and fairy tales I had always enjoyed with my mothers and the three other children who lived in our community. I could slip in and out of these roles according to my whims, and just as naturally try on the person-ality of the witch or the king or the dragon or the wise old man. But today that slippery, delicious freedom was to be stolen from me. My face was to be forever locked inside the visage of the remote heroine I had heard so much about.

For as long as I could remember, I had felt everyone—my moth-ers and the forty or so other members of the Pomegranate Grail who hung around from time to time—sneaking looks at me that oozed long-ing, expectancy, adoration and, the most bizarre of all, worship. It rarely failed to unnerve me, or cause me to flinch (at least inwardly: I learned to hide the outward signs). At times my mind would rational-ize that they were mistaken to feel this way, that I was not who they thought I was. At other times, I fantasized that I was not just myself as I experienced myself, but also a stranger who was sort of like an unsprouted seed in me. That last image was the hardest to bear. I often felt as if I were standing beside myself, that there was another version of me, invisible and mute.

Maybe all my loved ones thought they were hiding these "attacks" on me. After all, the blatantly innocent look of wonder that would sometimes possess their faces would usually only emerge when they thought they were out of my direct field of vision. But though the looks themselves always came from sideways and behind, the other signs were laughably obvious. Every gesture that I made, every skill I learned, every goddamn bowel movement I emitted, seemed like a revelation to them, to be noted, named, registered, studied, and celebrated.

At least I had my childhood to escape into. I could always break into a hoppity jig or nonsense song when one of my caretakers-cum-devotees would ask me some absurdly portentous question like "What is the quality in me you would most like to see changed?" or an occult riddle like "Where can Persephone find the stone that the Builders rejected?"

As I gazed down from my Sun Room at all the remarkable women preparing for my special day, I began to mourn. I sensed a growing wordless fear that by tomorrow my childhood would be killed; that I would no longer be able to escape into it.

A few hours later, as the sun neared its highest ascension into the northern hemisphere, I was stripped naked by Vimala and the twelve other chiefs of the Pomegranate Grail—lovingly and with reverence, of course—and ritually bathed in the giant cauldron there in front of more than two hundred women and children. As Vimala dunked my head beneath the tepid holy water, I kept my eyes open, trying to stay focused on the two dead bugs I'd spied floating on the surface.

After that, all in attendance lay face down in the grass, ritually turning themselves into stepping stones for me. I did what I had been instructed to do: walked, still naked, across the backs of every adult woman with my full weight, and lightly tapped the backs of the children and babies with my left foot. I enjoyed this. I relished being able to look at everyone without them staring at me. I loved the utter, humid silence being punctuated by the series of grunts from the women I pressed into the grass. I felt like I was a musician playing a new kind of instrument: a field of living bodies, each of which emitted a different tone. A crazy idea occurred to me. If I was now the Queen of Heaven and the Underworld, maybe I had more power than I realized. I decided to see if I could get the grunts to play one of my favorite songs, "Row, Row, Row Your Boat." Amazingly, as soon as I set my mind to it, it seemed to happen. It made me happy for a while.

When this pleasure ended, I was finally allowed to be dressed. Vimala and the twelve other chiefs covered me with a silk magenta robe and slippers. But in trade I had to submit to a greater indignity. Vimala drew my bangs off my forehead and bobby-pinned them to the top of my head, destroying the function I cultivated them for. Now my birthmark was glaringly revealed.

In the best of times, I bought the Pomegranate Grail's party line that this was a beauty mark of messianic distinction. But right now, feeling exposed and humiliated even as I basked in the strange triumph of playing the music of grunting backs, I hated the blotch more than I ever had before. In fact, it was at that moment I decided I would get rid of it, somehow, someday, I didn't know how.

I was guided to sit upon a rose-bedecked throne on a litter that was picked up and held three feet off the ground by four strong women. My valets then circumambulated me very slowly, throne and all, thirteen times counterclockwise and thirteen times clockwise around the entire assemblage. While this excruciating part of the ritual dragged on for what must have been an hour, Vimala and the twelve other chiefs intoned from the holy texts of the Pomegranate Grail, from the most ancient to the most recent. The last section had a particularly spooky part.

> Will the patriarchs kill the world? Until today we feared the worst. Until today we staved off their murderous mandates with stealth and sidelong snipes. But no more! No more! Our Queen is among us! Our answer to the destroyers! Preserver of the ancient matrix! Singer of our strength and resurrector of eternity! Praise Her who outwits the global death blow of the cruel fathers!

Finally the reading and the circumambulations stopped. My four valets set me down beneath the myrtle tree where the effigy of Persephone leaned. A group of five singers then droned on with sacred hymns to Persephone for a long time. Their voices were pretty but the melodies were quite boring. As they sang, the thirteen chiefs came up to me one by one and kissed my blotch. When they were done, Vimala crowned me with a half-gold, half-silver headdress.

Darshan followed, a creepy event in which my job was simply to sit and radiate my direct connection to the Goddess while everyone else squatted and stared, soaking up my channeled beneficence.

The awkwardness didn't end but changed form as I oversaw the ritual of the divine feast. After placing my now-magical hands over the bread and salt and wine and flame, I distributed the blessed food to the assembled. Following this mirthless adventure, I opened my gifts interminably, the polite performance of which distracted me from the heavenly music of harp and drum and three singers.

Finally the mood lightened. The real feasting began, with unconsecrated salads and broiled fish and home-baked breads. The bonfire was lit, I let my bangs down, and the dancing began. For a time I was a mere sprout again, not a stiff old queen. I skipped and squealed and tumbled. I grass-stained my ceremonial gown and used my crown to play catch with Parvati, a friend my age, until Vimala stopped me.

But my temporary happiness hatched the miserable panic that had been pregnant in me all day. Without words, yet with unmistakable consciousness, I registered the fact that I had become a living symbol. I no longer belonged to myself; didn't even belong to my seven mothers. I was a possession and creation of the scores of loving, nurturing women who had all day gazed towards me with infinite expectation. I was too young to have this realization, but that's the story of my life.

As the first star burst out over the hill behind Isis Tower, I heard myself thinking a prayer. I didn't understand it for many years, yet the words were unmistakable: "I will never be the queen you want. I will never be the queen you want unless you give me back myself."

9

The Televisionary Oracle
is broadcast
LIVE FROM THE DRIVETIME:
the eternally inbetween mood,
the ambiance or tunnel or threshold you inhabit
as you flow back and forth
between the yes and the no,
between the lost and the found,
between the me and the you.

The Drivetime is
the sweet sanctuary where you
always pretend you mean the opposite of what you're saying
and vice versa.

Always vice versa.

In the Drivetime
everything you know is wrong
and yet you still have as much confidence and authority
as people who love to kill with their opinions.

Brainwash yourself before someone nasty beats you to it. Study
the difference between wise suffering and dumb suffering until

you get it right. Commit crimes that don't break any laws. Visualize Mother Teresa at the moment of orgasm. Build illusions that make people feel so beautiful they can't stand to be near you. Pretend to be crazy so you can get away with doing what's right. Sing anarchist lullabyes to homosexual children. Love your enemies in case your friends turn out to be jerks. Review in detail the history of your life, honoring every moment as if you were conducting a benevolent Judgment Day. Eat money. Fuck gravity. Drink the sun. Dream like a stone. Sing in the acid rain.

The Televisionary Oracle
is brought to you by
the white plumeria flowers
that fall at your feet
as you stroll towards the cove
where the sea turtles swim.

10

As I open my eyes, I find I'm not in a marsh being ravaged by a blue, eight-armed goddess. I'm not floating down a red river on a raft piloted by Rapunzel. Instead I'm sprawled awkwardly on the sidewalk in front of the Catalyst in Santa Cruz. There's a rip in my pants near the right pocket, and blood stains the hole. It seems that while I was zonked—was it a dream or some hypnogogic hallucination generated by that strange cotton pad?—my flesh intersected with a broken bottle lying nearby.

Ruefully, I fully register the fact that I've returned to the state of mind that hundreds of millions of people all over the world ingest drugs and alcohol daily to escape. How long have I been away? Too long. The sun is going down. Twilight isn't far away.

I try to slide back into the vision. The last thing I recall is the message scrolling on the weird, "organic" TV.

During your time of the month, meditate on the following questions:

1. What feelings and intuitions have you been trying to ignore since the moon was last in the phase it is now?

2. Which parts of your life are overdue for death?

3. What messages has life been trying to convey to you but you've chosen to ignore?

4. What red herrings, straw men, and scapegoats have

you chased after obsessively in order to avoid dissolving your most well-rationalized delusions?

An unwelcome image weasels its way into my mind's eye in response
to the first question. I see myself quitting the music business cold turkey,
abandoning the work to which I've devoted so many years of my life.
It's a painful thought that has become increasingly hard to suppress
these last six months. I've truly grown to hate playing unventilated
nightclubs where my lungs fill up with a year's worth of secondhand
cigarette smoke in one night. And I despise those odd nights when I'm
totally uninspired and have to rely on professional tricks and techniques in order to fake boisterous abandon and improvisational fun.
And I abhor it when my band members aren't satisfied with a mere
one hundred ten decibels, but feel compelled to crank their volumes
up to eardrum-curdling levels that make it impossible for me or the
audience to hear a word I'm singing. Worst of all, I can't even bear to
think about how much I despise dealing with slimy record company
executives.

I force my imagination to slip over into more pleasurable meditations. I remember how utterly relaxed I was sailing along with Rapunzel in my vision. As I sneaked peeks up her rainbow batik mini-dress,
I was flooded with memories from other times in my life I've felt perfectly at home. I can almost taste the white paste I licked from my fingers as I made a Valentine for Karol Darnell, the girl I had a desperate
crush on in kindergarten. I can smell the cherry candies my grandma
used to keep in a cedarwood bowl in her kitchen. I'm back at the Christmas pageant in church when I was eight years old, awash in smoldering myrrh and entertaining obsessive visions of growing as strong as
Superman by drinking the hot blood of Jesus.

Two resolutions grip me. First, I've got to find out how to get in touch
with Rapunzel. Second, I've got to summon every shred of wisdom
I've accumulated about the arts of seduction and devote them to invoking that moment when I will gaze into Rapunzel's adoring, lustful
eyes—not in a dream but in concrete reality—as we weave our actual
physical bodies together.

Censor that.

74

The previous fantasy belongs to an obsolete version of myself which I've earnestly sought to outgrow. Only in the old days would I have said, "I vow to do whatever it takes to win Rapunzel's love." Since then I've become wiser about the ethics of imposing my will on others. Witchy hexes definitely work—temporarily. As do manipulative stratagems copped from self-help books about love and relationship. But in the end there's always sick-hearted, soul-withering karma to pay.

I recall an event from years ago, when Arlene, in a demonic show of strength, ripped out a half-broken piece of a curb across the street from the Dragon Moon dance club and hurled it through the windshield of my blue VW van. That was the night she fully registered how much I hated domestic routine and how unlikely it was, therefore, that I would satisfy her need to nurture me with regular doses of her fantastic cooking. The love spell I'd used to snag her infatuation three weeks previously had failed to take that detail (and many others) into consideration.

The shattered glass was easy to tolerate, I should add, compared to the revenge Arlene sought in the ensuing weeks. With lunatic clarity, she launched a letter-writing campaign to my friends, the local newspapers, and anyone else who'd listen, accusing me of all manner of crimes, from refusing to wear condoms to kicking a cat to using the term "cunt" in violation of my feminist principles.

No. The safer and wiser approach to seduction is to never never never seek to bend anyone's will but my own.

"If it's meant to be, it will be," is how the New Agers phrase it.

Therefore I will now beseech the Goddess to reveal Her divine will for Rapunzel and me. Is it best for all concerned if Gorgeous Sphinx Prankster and I become temporary consorts? Best friends? Sisterly-brotherly comrades collaborating on some as-yet unimaginable project? Till-death-do-us-part soul twins?

"Dear Goddess," I pray, "In the coming days please reveal your intention concerning the relationship between me and Rapunzel which will serve the greatest good for all concerned."

Having said all that spiritually polite crap, of course, gives me at least half a license to lust and plot and scheme with all my heart and soul and mind to make Rapunzel my lover. After all, my job as a human being is to master the art of being both a generous idealist and selfish narcissist at the same time. The two impulses should balance and complement each other. One should not overwhelm and cancel out the other.

Besides, the Goddess sometimes takes a while to reveal Her intentions. While I wait, I sure as hell am not going to be courteously passive. Instead I'll proceed on the hypothesis that Rapunzel is my Queen and Chosen One, my soul twin and splitapart. Yes, I'll be alert for signals from the Goddess telling me to cease and desist. But till those clues filter in, I'm full speed ahead.

So how will I track down my future muse? I think back to the performance ritual "A Happy Birthday for Death," where I glimpsed her dancing atop the sepulcher. Were there any friends of mine there who might be able to slip me some intelligence concerning my heroine? Yes. Stim and Katrina. They were among the instrumentalists playing music to accompany her wriggle.

I hop to my feet as if I'm totally in control—nodding to the confab of skateboarders ten yards away as I gather my menstrual gifts from Rapunzel and pluck her underpants off my head—and bolt to the pay phone in front of the Catalyst.

Stim's not home and his answering machine's not on. I can't remember Katrina's number, and it's not listed in the directory. She lives just a few minutes away, though. I decide to make the trek to her house immediately. Whether or not she's home will constitute the first omen from the Goddess about whether She approves of the union of Rapunzel and me.

Oops. Another pang of conscience intrudes. A big, inconvenient pang. My love nausea recedes just enough to remind me that I and my band World Entertainment War will be taking the stage at exactly 11 o'clock tonight, which means that a few hours from now I'll be called upon to generate fountains of virile energy. The singing and dancing and performing I'll do during the show will be the equivalent of playing three consecutive full-court basketball games. If I expect to endure till the end I've got to approach the delivery of fuel to my body with a scientific discipline similar to that of a long-distance runner. By rights

I should have loaded in one high-carbohydrate meal within the last hour, and should plan another between 8:30 and 9:00.

Then there are all the other pre-gig rituals I haven't done yet: yoga, meditation, vocal warm-ups, pep-talking the band, method acting exercises with my assistant Marijka, and coordinating with my stage manager Erica on the organization of costume changes and props. These are very serious matters. My many years as a professional performer have pointedly taught me that there's nothing worse than arriving on stage unprepared, my voice not ready to hit the high notes, my body unlimber, my improv instincts unlubricated.

This gig is our maiden voyage since we divorced both our giant record company, CBS, and our giant management team, Will Boehm Management (WBM). After struggling for years to link our fortunes to powerhouse institutions with the clout to make World Entertainment War a household name, it turned out that we could not bear the ignominious compromises imposed on us by their corporate hackdom. Our relationship with WBM lasted fifteen months, with CBS eighteen. For the foreseeable future, we've opted to uphold our creative integrity at the expense of disseminating our music to as many people as possible. So begins our headlong plunge into the hype-less, fund-less void.

Do I know what the hell I'm doing? The entire mess scares and depresses me.

When I stumbled onto my career in music way back when, I had two main ambitions. First, I wanted to be a sacred entertainer: a shamanic clown conducting poetic rituals of catharsis for my tribe. The second motive, composing maybe thirty percent of the total, was to be worshiped as a rockstar. This sub-personality of mine, which I call the wannabe sexgod, was not and has never been in it for the joy of being of service. He's greedy for all the fame and adoration he can suck up.

To my credit, the sacred entertainer has held the upper hand in the relationship for most of my career. It has only been recently that the rockstar persona began, like a smarmy parasite, to gobble up more than its rightful share of psychic energy. I've found myself performing more and more acts of self-violation which I'd once sworn off as taboo.

Capitulating to WBM's wishes for us to do absurdly inappropriate shows was just one example. Nothing made me more embarrassed in front of myself than opening for the sweetly polished Neville Brothers at a sit-down concert in a Sacramento auditorium filled with yuppie baby-boomers. World Entertainment War is a radical chaotic tantric pagan dance band, for Goddess' sake. In contrast to the Nevilles, as well as ninety-nine percent of all other famous rock bands, we don't do no stinking love songs.

And then there was the bit about working with the CBS-assigned stylist, she whose aesthetic must have been imprinted by the anorexic pouting robots that populate the Neiman Marcus catalogues. Her attempts at sleek, chic makeovers made the rowdy faces of me and my fellow band members resemble evil but goofy harlequins.

And those humiliations are mild compared to the worst stuff, which I will not allow myself to obsess on for the thousandth time.

But that's exactly why my music career, after many years of slow, steady ascent, has in the past year begun to degenerate. I've discovered, to my amusement and horror, that I'm one of those rare and unfortunate men whose success—maybe even my very survival—depends on maintaining my integrity.

Which is the reason I had no choice but to bail out of my contracts with one of the world's biggest recording companies and a management group founded by a legendary name in the rock biz.

If this were any other day, even any other gig day, I would immerse myself in the delirium of the encounter with Rapunzel and its aftermath. I would cultivate and savor this mood for as long as it would last; would spend the next ten hours or three weeks in a dreamy haze of erotic nausea, revving up a master plan of seduction, composing love letters and creating gifts and staging surprises for my new-found goddess.

Tonight I'd compose an invitation, handsomely printed on a pumpkin I've saved since last fall, for her to meet me on Mt. Shasta, where, with the power of our combined voices uttering thunderous prayers in the language of the angels, we would precipitate avalanches that would lay bare the secret entrance to the fabled pleasure dome of the Atlanteans which they built eons ago inside the mountain.

Tomorrow I'd buy a Barbie doll and, with the help of modeling clay, surgically alter it to resemble the figurines of the obese mamas found all over old Europe by the archaeologist Marija Gimbutas. Taking my inspiration from "Venus of Willendorf," the most famous of those ancient big-assed goddess statues, I'd call my creation "Barbie of Willendorf" and impale her on a homemade crucifix. Rapunzel would find the gift on her doorstep wrapped in an Easter basket together with colored eggs emblazoned with bull skulls, alongside of which would be a real double-headed ax fresh from the hardware store, inscribed with the faux autograph of famous feminist sexpert Susie Bright.

But I won't launch any of that fun stuff tonight. The show at the Catalyst is too important to shortchange. In my personal mythos, I've already built it up into a landmark. I intend it to symbolize a turning away from my ego's cheap agendas; to be an exacting and final cure for the rockstar virus.

Redemption and resurrection are words too pretentious for me to breathe in the presence of anyone else, but alone with myself they're my mantras.

I decide on a compromise. I'll give myself the next hour to be utterly irresponsible in service to my infatuation. Who knows? Maybe I'll actually be able to get in touch with the Menstrual Temple's most tantalizing witch and offer to put her on the guest list for tonight's show.

With guilty triumph, I head towards Katrina's house. I pray she'll be able to tell me where the Grail resides.

As I leave the Catalyst parking lot and head into the residential neighborhood behind the downtown area, a wry voice from my higher self's funny bone adds a corollary to my recent musings. There is, of course, another impetus that has propelled my musical ambitions since they were first spawned, I mean aside from the urges to be a sacred entertainer and a famous rockstar. It's the desire to pick up chicks. Or to be more candid and specific: In lieu of being independently wealthy, I imagined that a job as a sacred entertainer-cum-rockstar was the best possible position from which to execute my yearning to make love with every decent-looking, halfway-smart woman I met.

I hasten to add that I'm painfully aware of how common and tawdry this aspiration is. Often I've wished it could be easier to sustain the delusion that my omnidirectional lust is more noble and unique than the dumb lust of the other two billion males on the planet past the age of puberty. But I was almost thoroughly deprived of that luxury long ago.

The earliest I recall admitting the ugly truth was one warm October afternoon in a college anthropology class taught by the witty and acerbic Dr. Tacker. My testosterone was burbling and gnashing in response to the vistas of flesh visible on three different nubile coeds seated within pheromone-sniffing distance. The sight of Joanie Rivalson's freckled back screamed at me from the plunging scoop of her purple tank top. The shimmering vision of Hilary Clark's slightly spread thighs hovered at the edges of her denim miniskirt, which I could steal glimpses of if I turned sideways in my chair and pretended to gaze out the window thoughtfully. The bulge of Tara Worthington's breast where it overflowed from her pink bra was begging me to stare at it through the gap between her upper arm and her sleeveless white blouse.

Together, the three muses had launched me deep into a ritual fantasy I'd been regularly invoking since kindergarten. For maybe the five-thousandth time in my life, I found myself on a gorgeous green and blue planet much like Earth, with one exception: There were no other human males in all the world except me. As I stood atop a verdant hill wearing nothing but a red silk robe, I surveyed hordes of females streaming towards me from all directions. They were all ages, all races, all shapes and sizes. I turned slowly in circles to drink in the abundance. They gazed at me with tender longing or fierce lust, spilling out of their clothes as they converged.

As it had each of the four thousand nine hundred ninety-nine previous times I'd invoked it, the fantasy's prologue gave way to an utterly unique scenario. In other episodes, for example, my English teacher from junior year in high school smeared her entire body in virgin olive oil and gave me the ultimate full-body massage, or the German female double agent from the TV show "Hogan's Heroes" brought forth six of her cohorts to conduct a ritual that combined the Episcopalian eucharist with a psychedelic orgy.

But in this particular version of the fantasy, Hilary Clark, Joanie Rivalson, and Tara Worthington pushed to the front of the horde riding on a sweaty black bull. They were yodeling and ululating like mad-women, their faces painted like nineteenth-century Native Americans going to war. The three of them slipped off the beast and ran around to face it. Joanie grabbed its horns and launched herself in an airborne somersault lengthwise over the bull, in the style of the daredevil maidens portrayed in frescoes in the Temple of Gnossos in ancient Crete. The other two women followed suit. As soon as they landed, they raced in my direction. Joanie rammed her shoulder into my midsection and tackled me. Hilary scurried over and threw her mouth over mine. Tara untied my sash and threw open my kimono. But as Joanie sat on my shins and began to swoop down devouringly, the voice of my anthropology teacher, to which I'd previously been oblivious, somehow injected its way into the scene.

"The human male," Dr. Tacker was saying, "is driven by a biological imperative to disseminate his genetic material to as many members of the female gene pool as possible. He really is an automaton, a hostage in blind service to the All-Powerful DNA."

In response to this awful magic, my lyrical fantasy collapsed. I was propelled into a humiliating line of thought about how much I resembled a robot. Tara and Joanie and Hilary and I explored no further intimacy that day.

Or for many days. For a few months following Dr. Tacker's rude hex, I grew so self-conscious about my "Planet of Women" fantasy that I half-heartedly abstained from it. Eventually it raged back stronger than ever, though, and served me again as a talismanic meditation and beloved recurring dream.

Still, in my darker, less self-forgiving meditations, I fixate on Dr. Tacker's assertion. My virtually indiscriminate lust could easily be seen as the damning proof that I'm little more than a slave exploited by my DNA—that resourceful matrix of amino acids—to disseminate its signature to as many different collaborators as possible. In this theory, DNA tricks me into believing I'm acting out my own designs so that I won't notice it's working to maneuver me into endless situations where I might conceive children, thereby making possible its infinite proliferation.

In my nobler moods, though, I envision an alternative. In this model, the human species is a single unimaginably complex intelligence. Call it the Goddess or the Christ or the Oversoul. Individual people are in a sense the body parts of this Gorgeous Supercreature, each with a unique assignment to carry out. I may be more like a lung cell and you may be more like a white blood cell. Because each of us gets so carried away with our specialized tasks, though, we lose sight of the larger purpose we're in service to. I forget that I can't be a good lung cell unless I coordinate my efforts with all of you white blood cells.

The good news is that just as every part of a hologram contains a tiny image of the entire hologram, each of us carries the master plan of the God that we collectively compose. The bad news is that the master plan is buried so deep beneath more immediate agendas that it might as well be a repressed memory. If we could only access it, it would detonate our passion to collaborate purposefully not just with a mate or a lover or a few special people but with every single one of the other cells in our shared body.

This is, in fact, the Root Desire masked by every one of our mundane desires. It's the engine that secretly drives evolution and that will one day become fully conscious in all of us. It's the original, divine agenda that we incessantly shortcircuit by chasing after inferior and incomplete unifications. Most of us can manage no more than a narrow little obsession with a particular human who we mistakenly imagine can satisfy our gargantuan yearning for the real, primordial thing.

According to this scenario, the reason I'm such a fucknut is that I've begun to tap into the Root Desire. I've awakened the drive to achieve conscious unity with all my fellow cells. I'm increasingly at one with the master plan of evolution, which intends for us to collaborate with all, not just a few. How, therefore, could I not help but lust for liaisons with as many different aspects of the Gorgeous Supercreature as possible?

According to the model implied by Dr. Tacker's formulation, on the other hand, I'm just a pawn of my measly little DNA's drive to reproduce itself everywhere.

Whichever is more true, the end result is that the wellspring of my life can be reduced to one pithy formula: cruising for babes. And if that's the case, then those other obsessions feeding my music career—

to be a shamanic high priest and rockstar—are really only in service to the ultimate obsession.

Wait. Wait. Wait. Here comes another voice demanding to be heard. From out of the subconscious depths it erupts, begging to offer a further nuance to the master theory.

It's true that on the face of it I may seem to be just another sleazy patriarchal drone possessed by my own testosterone (even if I rationalize it with spiritually savvy abracadabra). But in my defense, there is a considerable body of evidence suggesting that my testosterone's imperatives might be developing a distinctly *womanly* bent. I could even go so far as to say that for some mysterious reason—either through my own craftsmanship or some divine favor—I am in the process of re-engineering my generic male lust so that it serves feminist agendas.

Theorem 1: I never seek out women who honor and obey obsolete gender roles, or who willingly participate in their own objectification, or who rely so utterly on their fabulously beautiful appearance that all brain cells not contributing to that project have ceased to grow. While my libido may reflexively and atavistically flow in the direction of such throwbacks, I'm never moved to act on it.

Theorem 2: More and more I find myself doing unto women as women have traditionally done unto men. I try to read the moods of any female companion I'm with, for instance, and use this information to play to her needs. I'm an enthusiastic listener; I ask catalytic questions; I'm acutely attuned not just to what *I* want to do, but to the ways she and I can blend and collaborate. Most importantly, I don't do any of this merely out of duty. I enjoy it. It fulfills me.

Theorem 3: I love to give women gifts; I *need* to give women gifts. Not in the typical style of a generosity-addict, though: My goodies are not a means to control and manipulate the recipients. I confess I'm not perfect; if I were I'd bestow my blessings anonymously so that no one could ever puff up my ego with her gratitude. But I've worked hard to eliminate the compulsion to attach any strings.

Theorem 4: Nothing excites me more than a woman who's able to express a balance of "masculine" and "feminine" qualities. I demonstrate my commitment to this ideal in the way I treat her. For instance: I encourage her independence with tenderness, not aloofness. I reward her objectivity without punishing her subjectivity. I jack up her ambitions by being supportive, not competitive.

Theorem 5: I get off almost as much from invoking my companion's pleasure as I do from my own.

Theorem 6: Unlike the majority of the male population, I know the identity and location of the only human organ whose sole purpose is to experience pleasure, the clitoris. Unlike the majority of the male population, I know a woman's sexual engine can't go from zero to eighty miles an hour in ten seconds. Unlike the majority of the male population, my hard and fast rule about orgasms is, "After you, dear."

Theorem 7: I feel sheepish about the kind of bragging I'm doing, since I know that doctrinaire radical feminists who think all men are rapists would regard me as a self-deluded poseur. And it's *good* that I feel sheepish. It keeps me humble; it drives me to continue checking in with my true motivations; and it encourages me to cast that big frowning dyke in the role of my superego, which is far better for my moral growth than a big frowning patriarch.

11

Think globally,
but act locally.

Plan for the future,
but act in the present.

Dream of all the masterpieces you'd be thrilled to create,
but work on just one at a time.

Lust for every enticing soul you see,
but only make love to the imperfect beauty you're actually with.

Allow yourself to be flooded
with every last feeling that bubbles up from your subconscious,
but understand that only a very few of these feelings
need to be forcefully expressed.

Be passionately attuned
to all the injustices and hypocrisies you see around you,
but be selective when choosing which of those you will actually fight.

Live forever,
but die a little each day.

Watch the Televisionary Oracle,
but be the Televisionary Oracle.

**D**ear beauty and truth fans, please remember that you are always in control. While communing with the Televisionary Oracle, *you* are the chief programmer. *You* decide which songline to tiptoe along. *You* decide which wormhole to shimmy through.

Now take a look at our selection of Drivetime spectaculars, and choose the one that tickles your kundalini best.

- *Menarche for Men.* For the first time in more than six thousand years, members of the male gender get to plunge into the shamanic fun that comes from being dead and alive at the same time.

- *Mary Magdalen's Monster Truck Rally and Tantric Cryfest.* Saintly voluptuaries get doped up on poignant eros and whirl their souped-up pick-ups around hundred-foot-tall scarecrows of Persephone, Queen of the Underworld.

- *Do What You Fear Orgy.* First, you make a list of the one hundred things you're most afraid of. Next, you rate them from one to one hundred in order of how badly they scare you. Then you agree to stop worrying about the bottom ninety-five fears because they just distract you from the five really interesting ones. Finally, you conquer those top five fears—by doing them.

- *Destroy the News.* Sacred newzak, weather, and sports channeled live from menstruating shamans who're dedicated to annihilating the pathological obsessions of the mass media in the kindest way possible.

- *A Feminist Man's Guide to Picking Up Women.* Self-help book from one of the Drivetime's most macho feminists.

- *Get Out the Guilt Binge.* Write a list of each source of your remorse. Then compose an atonement and give a gift to each person on that list whom you've wronged. Next, write a love letter and give a gift to yourself, forgiving all your sins. Finally, eat the list.

- *Sex Riots.* Travel with our roving band of Sex Rioters to Tadzhikistan, Albania, Malaysia, and many other hotbeds of phallocratic repression. Simply sit back and enjoy the uproar, or join right in in stirring up some erotic agitation.

- *The Archetypes Are Mutating: The Heroine with a Thousand Ruses.* The autohagiography of a close personal friend of the Sly Universal

Virus with No Fucking Opinion.

• *Brag Therapy Marathon.* Brag about yourself willfully and wildly, stopping only to provoke nods of agreement, either in front of a mirror or in the company of companions who won't hold it against you.

• *The Kundalini Pledge Drive.* A telethon designed to mobilize the *SHAKTI* that has been groggy for more than six thousand years. (Also known as *witchy dragon gumbo, pearly crone thunder,* or *riot grrrl orgone.*) The goal: to pave the way for the celebration of Twenty-Two Hours of World Orgasm.

*Homework*

Write an essay on at least two of the following topics:

"How I Used My Nightmares to Become Rich and Famous"

"How I Exploited My Problems to Become Sassy and Savvy"

"How I Fed and Fed and Fed My Monsters
Until They Ate Themselves to Death"

"How I Turned Envy, Resentment, and Smoldering Anger
into Generosity, Compassion, and Fiery Success"

"Why Perfection Sux"

12

Hi. It's me again. The reluctant queen. The apologetic spoiled brat. This time I want to invite you into the story of how I learned to kill the apocalypse in spite of the efforts of dear Vimala, my beloved mother and teacher. To begin, I need to describe my menarche. But there's a problem. I had so many menarches. Which one shall I tell you about? The false alarms? The dress rehearsals? The harrowing rituals in which my well-meaning moms did just about everything but punch me in the groin to induce my tardy first flow?

Maybe I should tell you about the first time Vimala tenderly manipulated me into guzzling two large cups of noxious tea brewed from pennyroyal and false unicorn root. Didn't cure the problem as advertised, but stirred up a riotous night-dream straight out of the medieval tapestry starring a unicorn with its paws in the lap of the sensuous virgin. And that was mildly consoling to Vimala, who has always been a sucker for any of my portentous sleeptime artifacts from which she can wrangle prophetic interpretations.

In case you have not yet sniffed out what the bloody hell I'm talking about, I'll spell it out. My menarche was late. Not just a little. It was so late that some feared it might never start at all. And this was most disturbing to the members of the ancient order which prided itself on preserving the sacred menstrual mysteries through the dark ages of the phallocracy. How could their girl messiah embody and illustrate those mysteries if she herself didn't menstruate?

It's what I've always referred to as my Third Shining Flaw. A worthy companion for the ugly birthmark and heart trouble I was born with.

From an early age, of course, I had been thoroughly saturated with the logistics as well as the mythology of the menstrual cycle. Beginning with my first crayon drawings of the magical rainbow womb, no teaching imprinted me more deeply than the meaning of the moment that the ovum and its nest die. As they slough themselves free of the womb, I'd learned, they give a signal to the pituitary gland to secrete the hormone that begins the ripening of a new follicle in the ovary. This was the primal mystery of our order, a core symbol of how thoroughly the forces of life and death are interwoven.

"She's a late bloomer," the Pomegranate Grail's muckamucks clucked to themselves when their storied princess reached her fourteenth birthday without so much as a clot of the moon-flow. This despite the inconvenient fact that my breasts were growing exuberantly; my pubic and underarm hair were already thick thatches.

There was a thing like a wave of cramps in the month before my fifteenth birthday. Something that might be construed as an announcement of being on the verge of tiptoeing up to my menarche. And preparations were duly made. My seven mommies wove garlands of roses and peonies. They consecrated (for—what?—the fifth time?) my all-natural linen menstrual pads—made out of flax, don't you know, as in matriarchal days of yore. And then there was the unbelievably corny poetry, which I couldn't help but swoon over despite myself, it having been so thoughtfully chosen by my preternaturally loving mommies: "You're about to take a trip to the moon in a boat powered by fireworks and wild swans. . . ."

I'm sure my guardians had often whispered the word *amenorrhea* in worried discussions before I ever heard it, but the first time it hit my ears was a cold December day when I was closer to my sixteenth birthday than my fifteenth. In retrospect I know how awful a curse word that was; how rudely it threatened to refute the visions on which my mission hinged. That there might be something amiss with the menstrual potential of a messiah whose mission it was to restore the menstrual mysteries?! Impossible! Unthinkable! Downright heretical! To even ruminate on the possibility veered dangerously close to an admission that either, one, they'd fingered the wrong person for the job of serving as their holy one, or two, restoring the menstrual mysteries would not proceed in the way they'd always imagined.

At least amenorrhea was a concrete, physical problem, though. It might possibly be due to causes that didn't have to do with divine disfavor. In that sense my moms were rooting for it.

Unfortunately, the facts were not in their favor. Primary amenorrhea—failure to ever begin menstruating—occurs most often in young ballet dancers or gymnasts who're used to torturing their bodies with strenuous physical exercise. And while I was in good shape—danced a lot, walked all over creation, played softball—I was no Olympic-bound superfreak.

There's another cross-section of teenage girls whose ovaries don't produce estrogen in the proper way to goad the uterine lining to thicken and shed: the anorexics. But I was no ninety-pound weakling patterning myself after the concentration camp imitators stalking the fashion runways of Paris. I never bought into that skinny-is-prettier bunk. And the food my moms made was too tasty to avoid, anyway.

Vimala took me to three different gynecologists. Were my ovaries producing normal amounts of estrogen? Not exactly. Did I have polycystic ovaries? No. Was there any disorder that might be suppressing ovulation? Well, ovulation *did* seem to be absent, but not because of any discernible cause.

At least not any cause that mere doctors could discover.

Just goes to show you how supernaturally strong my own willpower is when I give it an assignment.

Did I just say what you thought I said?

Yup.

The reason I didn't menstruate when I was supposed to, even though it placed in jeopardy all the credibility I commanded as the prophesied messiah of the Pomegranate Grail, was because I *didn't want* to menstruate. I *didn't want* to give my beloveds what they desired from me—just as I had promised myself shortly after my sixth birthday on the occasion of my coronation. "I will never be the queen you want," I'd silently vowed. "I will never be the queen you want unless you give me back myself."

And they had not given me back myself. As the years went by, they'd stolen more and more of me for use in constructing their perfect little idol. I was not a person, but a projection screen onto which they cast bigger-than-life prophecies and breathtaking visions, many of which had been dreamed up long before I was born.

I forgive them, by the way. How could they have done anything different? They are and have always been passionate and idealistic women who live their lives in service to the good, the true, the beautiful, and the just. In their eyes, I was the magical agent by which they would supercharge their struggle to restore the divine feminine to its proper glory—and literally save the world from the doomsday machine of the berserk cosmodemonic phallus.

My mothers' cause was a sublime one. How could I not love and admire and forgive them for giving me a central role in carrying it out?

More than that. I also loved my mothers because they were so good to me. They gave me all of themselves, with alacrity and grace, as if being my mother was the service through which they honed their devotion to Goddess. They were expansively indulgent when the moment required, or compassionately stern, or cleverly motivational. I swear I understood the profundity of their gift to me. I knew that few children in the history of the world had been privileged to bask in the artful concentration of seven intelligent adults.

But back then I also hated my beautiful mothers at least ten percent of the time. Sometimes it was my lessons in ancient Greek and Sumerian that provoked my enmity. Other times it was when I had to not just study and analyze, but for Goddess' sake *memorize* endless top-secret ultra-sacred texts written in stuffy, obscure prose. And then there was the huge task of learning the difference between the *true* science and *true* philosophy and *true* herstory that Big Bad Daddy Culture had suppressed and the twisted patriarchal versions of all those subjects.

And that was the easy part. Far more oppressive was having to think and behave in a manner my mothers deemed proper for an avatar who was born to embody and teach the new matriarchal covenant. It wasn't that I disliked being molded into a strong, decisive, articulate, prayerful, athletic supergirl. I actually became quite proud of that, especially after I turned eight and my mothers began to let me meet girls from outside our community. I couldn't believe what fuzzy-wuzzy sissies they all were.

What I hated, though, was this. My loving mommies were shaping me into a strong, decisive, articulate, prayerful, athletic supergirl not primarily because it would make me happy and free. The real reason, the only reason that mattered, was to ensure that I would be of maximum use to the Cause. In other words, I wasn't here to live my own life. I was a cog. A mechanism. An object. I had come to Earth to serve as a living symbol in some grand design I didn't have any hand in formulating. And I didn't have any choice in the matter.

It seemed like such a drastic sentence. And so unloving, so inhumane. What was I supposed to do with the part of me that just wanted to *look* at things, not *think* about them; the part of me that liked to run and jump and climb and dance not because it was good for me but because it was fun; the part of me that couldn't bear to see my friends gazing at me with a mix of awe and envy and fear, but only wanted to be their fallible equal?

But there was another unspeakable torture I was forced to endure. Excuse me if I raise my voice as I name it. EVERYONE WAS ALWAYS SO GODDAMN SACRED AND SERIOUS AND POLITE! SO TERMINALLY LITERAL AND SINCERE AND REASONABLE! SO FILLED TO OVERFLOWING WITH SMARMY INTEGRITY AND PORTENTOUS PURPOSEFULNESS AND HIGH-MINDED NICENESS! It's a miracle to me that I even discovered what playful irony was, let alone disputatious spunk or wild-spirited edginess or the messy but fertile chaos that renews the heart. Thank Goddess my imagination was sufficiently robust to glean the existence of these states through the books I read.

And at least those states weren't forbidden. They may not have officially existed in the Pomegranate Grail pantheon of permissible states of mind, but I managed to covertly carve out a space in my psyche for them to thrive.

On the other hand, there was a host of darker, more unruly emotions that were almost completely proscribed. Rage and frustration and grief and fear had only one justifiable target: the crimes of the patriarchy. If I fell victim to them at any other time, say in reaction to Cecily's silly overprotectiveness or Vimala's elusiveness about my early life, I was expected to transmute them on the spot. "You have felt that way, at least, until now," was the ritualistic response my mothers made to me whenever I was less than my shining avatarish self—implying that from that moment on I must concentrate on overcoming the conditions that had led me to near-defeat.

"I just can't stop thinking about how Isis died," I remember saying to Vimala one October night, referring to my cat that had been ripped apart by a raccoon. And my mother said, "You have felt that way, at least, until now, my dear. Beginning at this moment, you know beyond any doubt that Isis' time in this world was done and she has gone to a better place."

How else could I respond to this oppression? My life of rebellious humor-crime began one April Fool's Day when I put salt in the sugar bowl in the homes of every one of my mothers. On Beltane, a month later, I slipped into the temple to offer a smelly incense made from burning an old shoe. Next I began a tradition of gleefully celebrating Vimala's *unbirthday*, bestowing on her several *no-gifts*, beautifully wrapped packages with nothing inside.

Soon my pranks grew more subtle. I remember studying an ancient Sumerian poem with Vimala one summer afternoon. (The School for One that I attended didn't have summer vacations.)

"I, Inanna, will preserve for you," I read, dramatically declaiming my English translation of the words the goddess Inanna speaks to her husband Dumuzi. "I will watch over your scrotum."

"Now that's an interesting translation," Vimala said neutrally, as if I had just made a thoughtful if creative attempt at scholarly accuracy. "But I think the better translation is 'I will watch over your *house of life.*' Not scrotum."

As so often happened, my dear mother and teacher had simply missed, or possibly ignored, my wry point. Which was LET'S TURN THIS SUCKER UPSIDE-DOWN AND INSIDE-OUT LOOKING FOR SOME MISCHIEF TO SATISFY THE LAUGHING SOUL.

But at least I'd entertained *myself.* At least I'd fed the strong, decisive, articulate, prayerful, athletic part of me that never ever wanted to take anything, no matter how dear, at face value.

I do have to say that there was one of my seven mothers who was receptive to my jokes. Dear Sibyl always winked or wrinkled her nose affectionately or gave me some tiny sign that yes praise Goddess she had duly noted my slash at dignity and propriety. And that's what I wanted most. Not necessarily even to be praised for my pranks, or to be pranked back. But simply to be duly noted. To be seen and understood as something besides a little automaton of the Goddess.

Kiss, kiss, Sibyl my love. You *saw* me.

It wasn't enough, though, I'm afraid.

Most of the real, raw me—the me that wasn't a sacred living symbol—more and more sought refuge in a place I called Melted Popsicle Land. To get there, I had to ditch my omnipresent mothers with some ingenious ploy and slink off to my favorite place in the woods. It was within the husk of a thick-girthed redwood tree whose insides had been incinerated by lightning. There was even a "door" just my size that the lightning and its subsequent fire had carved.

Once ensconced in my temple of solitude, I ceremoniously unwrapped the red silk where I kept my two special popsicle sticks. The flat slabs of wood, whose light brown color were mostly stained blue, were among my most precious possessions. I'd obtained them illicitly at a park in Santa Cruz during the one time in my early life when I'd managed to circumvent my mothers' strict dietary guidelines.

To begin my shamanic journey inside the hollow redwood, I cupped the tiny wands in my hands and blew on them for good luck. Next I touched them to the blotch on my forehead and the cross-shaped scar on my chest. Rapidly in the beginning, then with ever-decreasing speed, I rubbed my magic-makers together, instructing my body to relax ever more deeply. Adapting techniques from the meditation practices my mothers taught me, I compelled my inner eye to focus on a single image—not the bucrania or yoni mandala as my mothers might have me do, but rather on a heaven-blue popsicle melting in my hot mouth. Likewise, I applied the disciplined breathing exercise I'd learned from my mothers: *pranayama* they called it. Within minutes, without fail, I swooned and watched a new world drop over me like a falling net of gossamer light.

The passage I conjured thereby was like slipping from the waking state directly into a lucid dream, bypassing deep sleep and not losing my conscious awareness. I was no longer in the woods near the Sanctuary but in a streaming kaleidoscope of fantastic scenes—volcanoes made of mashed potatoes spewing warm chocolate rain down on fields of golden clover where fairies and I went on treasure hunts ... ladders made of diamond that stretched from the bottom of a peppermint tea river to cloud houses where friendly sphinxes carved medicine dolls out of magic black radishes ... talking eagles building me schoolrooms out of my ancestors' bones and teaching me how to ask trees questions. ...

In Melted Popsicle Land, I felt the total opposite of loneliness. Everything was alive, and everything wanted to play with me. Bees and ferns and rocks let me tune into their ever-singing thoughts. I could taste the sky and wake up the wind with a wish from my heart. The sun and moon themselves were creatures that loved me, and I loved them. I made many friends, from a magic dung beetle I called Khephra to a tall oak tree named Fortify to my beloved companion Rumbler, about whom I will speak more in a minute.

There was another amazing secret about Melted Popsicle Land: It was a giant magic television. What exactly did I mean by that? I barely knew what a real television was; my mothers had made it verboten on the grounds of the Pomegranate Grail. (It was a dangerous tool of patriarchal propaganda.) And aside from a few sets I had spied a couple of times in the window of a Santa Cruz store, I knew about the taboo objects only from my mothers' parsimonious descriptions.

Thus Melted Popsicle Land was free to be the kind of magic television invented by my imagination. According to this source, it was a terrarium the size of the woods. Its boundaries were formed by a circular force field that was invisible and impermeable to anyone not living in Melted Popsicle Land. Everything that happened inside was the television show. There was a broadcast tower arching over the staging area (though like the boundaries it could not be seen by outsiders), and this beamed out transmissions that only angels, fairies, spirits, and other magical creatures could receive.

I was the television storyteller who reported the action, who perhaps *made* the action occur by describing it aloud. My narrative was relaxed but nonstop. I barely kept up with the images and voices that streamed in and through and around me.

Sometimes my "stories" consisted of incantatory jumbles that were little more than spells:

Creep, creep, creep goes the girl. Gnaw, gnaw, gnaw. When no one was looking, when no one missed her, her teeth grew all the way in, all the way down, snuggly and iron-strong like the fangs of the wolfie wolf. Now she bites through the sweet jail of the mothers who hid her away. Chomps through the bones of the fathers who hurt her mothers so bad they had to build her a sweet jail. Goodbye, goodbye. To all, to all. She's off to school, her very own school. She's nobody's fool. She's cooler than cool. Begone, dead songs, begone.

Other times I "saw" and described real fairy tales with complicated plots and colorful characters. One of my favorite recurring adventures was a variation on the Rapunzel myth. It often began something like this.

Once upon a time, a wicked old warlock, king of the bad daddies, took his beautiful young son, Rumbler, and locked him away in the top of a tall tower with no doors or stairs. The boy was forced to live there with no other visitor besides his cruel father, who came now and then to bring him meager food and drink. Whenever the warlock arrived, he would stand below the single window high on the wall and shout up: "Rumbler, Rumbler, let down your hair."

I loved all my friends in Melted Popsicle Land, but Rumbler was my greatest delight. At times he was a co-creator, helping me decide where to go next and even telling part of the tales. More than that, I was convinced he was somehow indispensable to the ongoing adventure itself. The first time I met him was also the breakthrough moment I discovered the trick of gliding over into the fantastic realm I called Melted Popsicle Land.

It happened not long after my coronation ceremony at age six. Three of my mothers had taken me to a public park in Santa Cruz. While they were occupied setting out the food for our lunch, I sneaked away to spy on a strange family at a nearby picnic table. One of the three boys of the tribe saw me staring and offered me a blue popsicle. Up until that moment, I had never tasted ice cream in my life. (Pomegranate Grail's Commandment #137: The avatar must not be polluted with refined sugar.) To avoid having Vimala and company snatch my treat away, I immediately ran and hid under a picnic table as far away from them as possible.

I squatted there with my head against my knees, rocking gently and shivering with pleasure as I engorged my pure joy. It was the most strangely delicious thing I had ever tasted. The sweetness of an unfamiliar fruit exploded again and again on my front teeth and tongue and the roof of my mouth. Incredibly, its alarming hardness molted thick syrup. The shocking iciness provoked a hot, ambrosial spasm in my solar plexus. The treat was the same color as the sky, and I had an absurd flash that this was how the sky tastes high above the earth. The flavor of heaven.

Gradually I became aware that I was not alone. As the sweetness disappeared inside me I felt the presence of another body materializing—not exactly next to me; not exactly inside me; but both at the same time. It was as if there were two of us occupying a space that was big enough for just one.

"Who are you?" I beamed in the direction of this somebody. In response, I filled up with a feeling that was mine but not mine; it also belonged to a *him*. And this *him* was the same size as me, the same texture, the same bones and hair and heart—the same everything. I didn't exactly hear but sensed a voice that was like mine but lower in pitch. "It's me—Rumbler," my companion telepathized brightly. "Remember?"

I was licking the last sweet blue gobs of popsicle with both of our tongues as I tried to remember.

"We were together in the warm floating dark," he said. "Remember?"

A relaxing image rose from my heart, bobbing upwards. A memory? I was a small bird-fish suspended in gooey, salty juice. A fleshy cord emerged from my belly, rooted at its opposite end in a soft, gently throbbing wall. He was there with me, too: "Rumbler." A cord coming out of his gut lodged in the wall near mine.

"Rub the sticks together," I heard him say there in my cave under the picnic table. I obeyed. With him moving my right hand and me my left, I slowly swished the two popsicle sticks back and forth against each other at a right angle. After a few moments (or was it long minutes?), I heard myself talking aloud, seeing in my mind's eye and then murmuring aloud a story about clouds with happy pumpkin faces spitting out burning chairs which flew through a lemony sky and birthed giant flakes of snow shaped like hands. When I laughed with joy at this unwilled explosion of pictures, I felt his laugh inside mine.

It was the first, primitive outburst of a spectacle that would later evolve into a many-splendored institution. The biggest leap in its growth came a few days later, when I discovered my private power spot in the redwood husk. Ultimately I lived the stories, didn't just behold them; I traveled to strange astral tableaux, didn't just describe them. But one aspect of the ritual never changed: Stroking the popsicle sticks together was always the way I slipped over the threshold.

A couple of years later, when my mothers belatedly told me the uncensored story of my birth, I developed a theory that Rumbler was somehow related to or maybe even the same as the twin who had not survived the journey out of our mother's womb. By then, that historical fact was irrelevant. He and I were best friends, not brother and sister.

I had many other allies and companions inside Melted Popsicle Land: Firenze the Musical Sasquatch, Peekaboo the Hide-and-Seek Salamander, Snapdragon Dragonfly the Firefly who could spell out riddles with her blinking light, Jujubee the Angel Ghost Clown who brought me healthy candy, Itchy Crunchy the Beautiful Empress of the Trolls, G'Fretzus and G'Freckles the twin ticklers who always taught me new tricks about how to dream while I was awake, Sphinxie Spanky the Good Troublemaker, Jelly Kelly the Funny Bunny who showed me how to change my size and shape in the twinkle of an eye, and many others.

But Rumbler was my most special friend, and the one with whom I exchanged the most surprises. Sometimes, it's true, I couldn't actually *see* him. He was a kind of ghost who shared my body, a shadow whose spicy, aerated, mercurial texture moved around inside me. Other times, though, he lived quite distinctly outside of me, a vividly separate creature. Not exactly my twin: a little shorter than me, a little younger in spirit, a less furrowed brow and shorter hair. But his face, I thought, looked much like mine would if I were a boy, and his loping walk and strong, expressive hands were my doubles.

As I think back to those days now, I'm remembering the times he played the game "I Love You Honey, But I Just Can't Make You Laugh."

It would start whenever he thought I was taking myself too seriously. He'd suddenly appear hanging upside-down from a cactus-cloud or riding backwards on a fairy elephant, and with a totally straight face except for maybe a saccharinely sympathetic eyebrow he'd say, "I love you honey, but I just can't make you laugh." And I would of course immediately collapse in an implosion of guffaws.

I probably would have left the Earth at an early age without Rumbler and my home-away-from-home on the other side of the veil. My heart would have broken to death, or my subconscious mind would have invoked a disease like leukemia or muscular dystrophy to relieve me of my suffering. Melted Popsicle Land was a life-saver.

Not enough of a life-saver to allow me to forgive my mothers their sins against me, however. As I grew older, I became a rageaholic. Not that I ever showed it. How could I? I had no right. I had no excuse. I was showered with more blessings than any child in the history of the world. A multitude of spacious and beautiful homes in the country. All the toys and gadgets and books and companionship I could possibly want. Not just two doting parents, but seven, each of whom was— I think this even now—a highly accomplished, intensely expressive soul who would have been intriguing to me even if she weren't my mother.

And sweet Mary Magdalen, how strong and capable my moms were making me. How confident and radiant. I mastered algebra before my eleventh birthday and was sufficiently knowledgeable to discourse at length on quantum physics, English literature, and the shamanic tradition by age twelve. I could enact the entire ritual of the Eleusinian Mysteries, playing all the roles, and I knew both the intricate theory of the music of the spheres and the story of how Pythagoras had ripped it off from our ancient order. It's true I didn't know squat about the pantheon of Disney characters or the current Top 40 hit songs—pop culture was at least ignored and at most forbidden at the Pomegranate Grail—but I could compose duets for the violin, write complex and entertaining short stories, and perform forty yoga asanas with impeccable grace. Most precocious of all, I could meditate up a storm. My talent for concentration was heroic, my ability to induce alpha- and theta-state trance was legendary, and I had on numerous occasions provided incontrovertible proof of my power to read minds and perform psychokinetic tricks. Maybe someday you'd like to see me make the little bronze fox in the moon lodge spin around without touching it.

These last skills were handy in helping me execute the perfect punishment on my loving oppressors.

I remember the moment my brilliant plan first hatched. It was on the summer solstice shortly after my eleventh birthday. My seven mothers had convened the kind of Big Deal get-together they liked to do every six weeks, on each of the cross-quarter holidays of the year (solstices and equinoxes and the power points in between). Check-Ins, they called them. This was where they all assembled in one place with me, usually in the ritual room in my tower, to give me pep talks, evaluate my progress (sometimes with surreptitious tests), and gently pound into me reminders of the big picture I was supposed to be mastering.

The number-one topic on the agenda that day was the glorious and happy event that awaited me in the not-too-distant future: my menarche. It was not as if I hadn't heard the facts about the peach flower flow before. But this presentation was special. My mothers were uniformly adorned in miles of red silk gowns I had never seen before. Big scarlet circles graced their cheeks in apparent violation of the unspoken prejudice in our community against make-up. Their smell was unfamiliar, almost alien: what I would now describe as musky and sulfurous.

Vimala spoke in hushed tones of the mysterious transformations that would soon begin to work their magic inside my body. Sibyl regaled me with old myths and folktales about the origin of the marvelous gift that the female of the species had been blessed with. Artemisia told me of the deep awakening to holy gnosis she'd had on the day when she herself had crossed the threshold from girlhood to womanhood.

Not too many months later I discovered the other side of the menstrual story—how the phallocrats had always called our gift a "curse"—but on this occasion, the guardians of the Santa Cruz chapter of the Pomegranate Grail waxed with unqualified rapture about the joys and privileges I would soon know.

Fascinated as I was by their song and dance, I could not suppress my congenital urge to find some rib to tickle, some sacred cow to tip.

As always, I was two minds working simultaneously. One felt reverent gratitude for the soul-stirring show my mothers were putting on for me. The other was desperate for a laugh in the midst of all the sickeningly calm and poised solemnity.

Finally my searchlight imagination landed on a ripe spot: the complaint I'd been nursing forever and for which I'd never found a satisfying outlet. All those years I'd harbored my protest against the way I'd been carved into an idol, and all those years I'd never managed to retaliate with any act that matched, in its ability to inflict poetic justice, the unfairness of the wrongs I'd suffered. My little rebellious pranks—even the time I set fire to a dogshit-filled paper bag on Artemisia's porch, rang her bell, and ran away—were harmless, really, and usually ignored anyway.

And—who knows, maybe because I am an avatar after all, with a backlog of smarts and integrity built up over many incarnations, including one as Mary Fucking Magdalen—I never even considered carrying out any revenge that would stunt my own growth. Refusing to master algebra or Greek or temple dancing, in other words, was not an option. I may have wished from time to time that I could spend more time playing in the garden and less studying the esoteric myths of Persephone, but more often than not I was quite pleased to be in my classroom. I *was* hungry for knowledge and powers. I was driven by a fierce and almost impersonal ambition to be excellent at everything I did.

But now, finally, here on the summer solstice, I found a way to mess with my mothers' perfect program without hurting myself. As Cecily extolled the part that the metaphor of menstruation would play in the redemption of the planet, I decided, in a bolt of lucidity, that I simply would not menstruate. Would never even start. Would rejoice secretly in my heart as I watched my mothers' faces grow long and sad. Best of all, would pretend I was an innocent victim of the Goddess' inexplicable stroke of fate.

It's not completely honest to say I conjured up this revolution all by myself. Rumbler was there with me, spurring me on. That was a big surprise. Though I had had adventures with him in dreams, until that time he'd never shown up anywhere else outside the confines of Melted Popsicle Land. In fact, I'd become accustomed to believing that he was not able to contact me when I was in my mothers' realm. Their vibes were too thick and protective for him to penetrate. Or something.

Yet there he was, and right when I needed him, too. My heart was two hearts. I felt twice as strong as usual, twice as smart and brave. It wasn't like he gave me the idea to refuse menstruation; it was my own. But I think if he hadn't been there, I might have downplayed or ignored the brainstorm. He gave me the spark to act on it.

My (our?) plan was full-grown from the moment it bloomed. I would simply extend the power I had already developed to modify the autonomic functions of my body. For more than four years, my mothers had been teaching me to regulate my breath, slow my heart beat, and relax my nervous system. I'd done lots of biofeedback and could slip into the alpha state virtually on command. I'd practiced a technique which supposedly sped up the healing of my various childhood cuts and bruises, and my mothers were convinced that I'd become adept at it beyond their wildest expectations. In the past fifteen months, they'd even begun to teach me alchemical secrets they said had never been revealed to anyone under the age of forty in the history of their ancient order. Like for instance: how to digest my food so as to extract the *potable gold* that most people excrete in their shit. I won't gross you out with the laboratory details of how my doting mothers determined that I was succeeding at this magical task.

In that moment, with my red silk-clad mommies gathered around me on the summer solstice, I wasn't sure precisely what to do in order to postpone my menarche indefinitely. But I was absolutely certain I could figure out how.

I set to work the next day. As I'd been taught to do in the face of any difficult problem, I set up a three-pronged attack: analysis, meditation, and dream-quest. I studied up on the physiology of the female reproductive system till I could picture every detail of its operation. With my inner eye and proprioceptive nerves, I divined the specific shape and location of my own organs. Next I launched a series of meditations and prayers to plumb for the exact information I would need to carry out my desire. Finally, I devised a dream incubation quest.

There was a slight obstacle. Our ancient order teaches that meditation and prayer are at best useless and at worst rife with distortions when applied towards a goal that is purely selfish. And I firmly believed that, as I still do. Could I therefore twist and tweak the mission somehow so it would be morally correct? Something other than my petty and infantile rejection of my mothers' hopes?

The answer surprised me. It came in my very first meditation. The still small voice rising up from the supernal depths said, with no ambiguity, something like the following: "Unless you are completely united with the goal of serving as the avatar of the Pomegranate Grail, there is no use even trying to fulfill that goal. Therefore, you should either renounce the goal for good, or find a way to embrace it wholeheartedly—by any means necessary."

"By *any* means?" I asked the still small voice.

"The obstacle to passionate commitment is your feeling that an important part of your self is not being included in the mix," the still small voice replied unhysterically. "If the only way to include that part of you is through rebellion and rejection, so be it."

"So you're saying, basically," I questioned the voice further, "that in order to become the avatar, I should reject becoming the avatar?"

"Yes," soothed the voice, "at least as your mothers understand the role of the avatar. Who knows? The real avatar might be something very different from what your mothers imagine. And you'll never find out if that's true unless you wound your mothers' model."

I couldn't believe it at first. It was such a tricky thing for my still small voice to tell me. And yet it was speaking to me in the same direct and low-key tones I had long come to regard as a measure of its authenticity.

I had to make one more test. "OK, still small voice," I said with my inner whisper, "so in order to become an unselfish messiah working for the good of all humanity, I am not just being allowed but actually encouraged to be a selfish little brat."

"Now you're talking melodramatic nonsense," the voice signaled back. "It's not being a selfish brat to make a symbolic statement of resistance against an oppression that needs to be undone."

I had copped the perfect rationalization for refusing to menstruate, and it wasn't even a rationalization at all. It was a righteous sanctification. My meditations in the coming weeks, along with my dreaming mind's vivid replies to my incubation quest, gradually built up in me an understanding of the subtle visualizations I needed to practice in order to accomplish my goal. (Rumbler even showed up twice in dreams, once in a classroom where he lifted me up on his shoulders so I could get a look at a blackboard that was too high to read, and another time in a bathtub, where he washed moldy red bugs out of my hair.)

A little more than a month later, I knew beyond a doubt that I'd set in place all the inner adjustments necessary. On a cool August morning I woke up with the gift of a sign: a dream of a blood-red bull skull turning pale white right in front of my eyes.

More than five years later, I had still not acquiesced to nature.

From time to time, my seven mothers made efforts to get my flow going, though most were pretty timid. There were polite dress rehearsals and group prayer sessions and herbal treatments and trips to doctors and midwives. My moms were holding back from acting as hog-wild as they felt because they couldn't be sure my amenorrhea wasn't ordained by Goddess Herself. None of our scriptures or prophecies mentioned anything about the avatar not menstruating, but then again they didn't say she—I mean I—*did* menstruate.

There was also the fact that several of my mothers had dreams that could be interpreted as sanctioning my barren state. Vimala, for instance, had a doozy in which she watched me as I emerged from a cave dripping wet with a vulture on either shoulder—a sure sign that this was a vision directly from Persephone. As I strode towards my mother, she dropped to her knees as if in supplication. I handed her a large reddish egg and muttered, "Take, eat, for this is my body, which is given for thee." Cracking it open, she found it was empty.

The signs and portents changed, though, once I reached sixteen. Artemisia woke up sobbing on the summer solstice, having just dreamed of me collapsing in her lap and crying, "I want to learn the power of those who bleed but do not die." Cecily's twelve-year-old biological daughter Lilly had her menarche in July, and on the night after the ceremony both mother and child dreamed of me standing at the edge of a ritual circle with grief and longing, as if I wanted to come in but couldn't.

The garden that year was bizarrely and inexplicably unproductive, and even the fox and raccoons and deer and skunks were noticeably sparse. I felt the same as ever, at least in my mothers' domain if not in Melted Popsicle Land (whose name had changed to the "Televisionarium," as in television + terrarium), but everyone else seemed to think that I wasn't making as much progress in my lessons, and that I had suddenly become less wise in the advice I was so often called on to dispense.

As I look back now, I surmise that my evolving relationship with Rumbler was covertly messing with the collective mood of the Pomegranate Grail. Unbeknownst to everyone else—thanks to my perfect secrecy (and apparent ability to dissociate)—their avatar was indulging in an ever more intense and intimate exchange with male energy. True, the unknown polluter wasn't officially a human being, by normal definitions. But maybe that made his influence all the more profound. Rumbler was more beautiful and smart and interesting and fun than any imperfect boy could ever be. I opened my heart to him in ways I could never have done for anyone else.

Who knows? Maybe Rumbler and I would never have gone as far as we did if my mothers had granted me the time and permission to go on dates with actual guys. While Vimala and company were never shy about giving me the lowdown on sex—it was included in my curriculum—they were adamant that I would not even be able to think about romantic liaisons until I was eighteen. Even then—so I was brainwashed to believe—I wouldn't have much interest in such things; my destiny led in another direction.

Thank Goddess for Jordan and Elijah, the sons of Artemisia and Cecily, respectively, who grew up in large part in our community. Without their matter-of-fact presence in my life, Rumbler would have been my only break from unisex monasticism. But they were too different in age for me to brew up any flirtations.

No. If I wanted to go out on dates—if I wanted to improvise with the mystery of erotic attraction—I had only one choice: my best friend from the Televisionarium.

Still, it did not occur to me at first that he could be the solution to the strange longings that began to stir in me at age thirteen going on fourteen. Our timeless time together in the woods was filled with epic but innocent adventures, like journeys to see the Queen of Rats, who laughed beautiful stories for our ears alone, or leaps off the tops of our special tree, Fortify, whose supernatural help allowed us to fly over rivers of fire that we could not otherwise find.

Our first kiss came not in the Televisionarium but in a dream a few weeks before my fifteenth birthday. As the dream began, I was high above Rumbler, standing on a giant purple popsicle that was carved in the shape of a balcony jutting out of a purple popsicle tower. Gazing down, I could see him through clear water curled up in a ball at the bottom of a river. "Let's meet in the middle," he gurgled up to me as he launched himself towards the surface. Without thinking, I threw myself off the balcony. I fell in slow motion and felt a surge of sweetness welling up all over my body.

I landed safely on a boat that was also a bed. He was already there, acting as if he were just waking from a long sleep. "There's blood in your bed," I whispered to him, pointing to a red blotch on the sheet. "Yeah," he murmured back, "I just had my very first period. *One* of us had to."

He chuckled as he made the last comment and moved into a position where his hands were around my waist and his mouth on my belly button. Slowly he kissed his way up my abdomen, unbuttoning my white blouse as he progressed. At the center of my chest he said a prayer—"Dear Goddess, let me be the boy behind the girl, the man behind the woman"—as he ran his tongue along the two arms of my scar.

Finally his face arrived in front of mine. For a while we barely pressed our lips together as both of us hummed the song "Row, Row, Row Your Boat." Currents of heat were running down my legs and arms. Dizzying music was circling through my belly and pelvis. My hair felt as if it were as alive with sensation as the rest of me. Snakey strands floated out away from my head as if I were in zero gravity.

We stayed like that for a long time. My scary joy grew steadily bigger and wilder, until I wondered if I might die. I couldn't believe, didn't trust, how full I felt. Then, unexpectedly, Rumbler and I touched our tongues together and rolled them around the inside of each other's lips. Suddenly, all the jangly, fuzzy electricity that had been pulsing crazily around inside me became very lucid and pointed. From a lazily swirling sweetness I mutated into a well-organized grid of fierce bliss—

bliss that somehow felt as if it had an intention and will of its own. At the center of this grid was my heart, which was fluttering in a way that was both terrifying and gratifying. I wasn't sure if I was having a heart attack or the opposite of a heart attack—a heart expanse? Finally I felt an engulfing squeeze, then a delicious eruption that was simultaneously the taste of dark purple grapes and the sound of a cello and the smell of the ocean at dawn and the sight of an orange moon rising over a green hill. I woke from the dream awash in tearful rapture. The phrase "drenched in heart river" was echoing over and over in the back of my throat.

The dream was a taboo-breaker, an eye-opener, a hunch-generator. A few days later I smuggled myself into the Televisionarium bursting with a hypothesis I had never before entertained. Could my best friend and I give each other the same pleasure here that we'd had in the dream?

The answer was a thousand times yes. In the very first experiment, I danced with him cheek to cheek in an underground garden where giant, seed-laden sunflower heads burned like inexhaustible torches with blue flames. We jumped in mud puddles as we twirled and put four-leaf clovers on each other's tongues. When I dared to press my lips against his, he raised his eyebrows and laughed, "What revolution is this?" And when I picked him up and wrapped his legs around my waist, waltzing him around the diamond ladder as if he were my darling, he howled with shocked joy. "Bind me to you," he sang, spurring me on as he so often did, and I danced him over to an oak where the mistletoe hung down in fountainlike tufts. Using two such stems, we tied my left hand to his right. The kiss that began then did not stop until we disappeared together in a reverie of the thermonuclear ecstasy at the heart of the sun.

So began a new phase of our old relationship—infatuated courtship. It did not replace our epic play, only enhanced it. During the ensuing months, I sought him out in both dreams and the Televisionarium more often than I ever had before. I was not obsessed—one who was trained to be as balanced as I was is not capable of that state—but I was assuredly in love.

From what I could tell, our blooming union improved my concentration on the educational tasks my mothers pressed me so hard to master. I felt lighter, less resentful of my benevolent incarceration as the avatar. My need to inject humor into all the dry details of my rhythm had less of an edge.

And yet there was no mistaking the fact that my mothers' *joie de vivre* was declining as mine waxed. No doubt this had to do with their growing frustration at my failure to menstruate. What had been a rationalizable glitch in their master plan when I was thirteen or fourteen years old had evolved into a potential refutation of the master plan itself.

But in retrospect I am positive that my love affair with Rumbler was at least partially responsible for the ever-souring mood that climaxed just before the winter solstice seven months after my sixteenth birthday. What my mothers weren't consciously aware of, they were being affected by on subconscious levels. I was like a married person who was secretly cheating on my mate. A third party was mutating the chemistry of our community, and my mothers had no idea.

An almost hysterical undertone had begun to pervade the atmosphere of the Santa Cruz chapter of the Pomegranate Grail. Yet while this superficially suggests there was an overabundance of emotions, I noticed an increasing dryness in the way we all related to each other. There were fewer of the warm, pleasing surprises I'd come to expect from my interactions. Compliments seemed forced. The temple rituals lacked the full-bodied passion I'd grown used to.

The first two weeks of December seemed to be the most depressing I'd ever witnessed—not for me, of course: I was in love. Everyone else was miserable or down or dishwater grey. Vimala cried every day. No one wanted to cook. The pomegranate orchard had produced a pitiful harvest of tiny fruits.

On December 16, an emergency summit convened. Not only were my seven mothers in attendance, but all the other thirty-two members of the Pomegranate Grail who lived in the vicinity, as well as fifty-three grave-faced honchos from chapters as far away as Melbourne, Australia. There it was decided, after long, rancorous debate, that my problem had gone on long enough: It was time to fix it with a forceful act of ritual magic. This was by no means a unanimous decision; barely a majority, actually.

The next day I was installed, bed and all, inside a ceremonial circle

The world is crazily in love with you,
wildly and innocently in love.
Even now,
thousands of secret helpers are conspiring
to turn you into the beautiful curiosity
you were born to be.

Are you finally ready
to start loving life back with an equal intensity?
The ardor it has shown you has not exactly been unrequited,
but there is room for you to be more demonstrative.

For inspiration,
stay tuned to the Televisionary Oracle
and study the following passage from a poem
by the Persian mystic poet Hafiz,
as rendered by Daniel Ladinsky.

*One regret, dear world, that I am determined not to have*
*When I am lying on my death bed is that*
*I did not kiss you enough!*

Hi, beauty and truth fans, and welcome to Drivetime University,
coming to you LIVE from Persephone's Rehabilitation Center

for the Ecstatically Challenged, where we eternally strive to keep you in touch with the birth of your grandmother's grandmother, thereby flushing away any narcissistic self-doubt that might be threatening your ability to feel erotically aroused by silk, tigers, rainbows, umbrellas—and even the moon itself!

We're your naive and crafty hosts for Drivetime University—the slippery angels serving as temporary surrogates for your higher self—and we're proud to announce that this is a perfect moment. This is a perfect moment because the world is fresh, your soul is ingenious, and something very good is going to happen to you if you'll only tell us what you want.

So. What *do* you want?

What?

You want to know more about the Drivetime?

Unfortunately, it's almost impossible to convey to you the nature of the Drivetime unless you're already inhabiting the Drivetime.

Which might prompt you to ask, "How am I ever going to sojourn in the Drivetime if I don't know what it is or how to get there?" Excellent question.

Another way to formulate the riddle might be to imagine trying to construct a sensitive antenna with the help of the very same airwaves that can't be detected without that sensitive antenna.

But don't worry. We're not about to retreat into elitist secrecy or convoluted expertise. We won't imitate some know-it-all guru or careerist scientist eager to protect the power conferred on him by his specialized knowledge. That would be against our religion.

So let us take a stab at explaining. Without, we hope, becoming so literal that we emasculate the magic.

The Drivetime, please recall, is neither the Waketime nor the Dreamtime, but rather both at the same time. It's the place where you feel as if you're dreaming, but also wide awake.

OK, so then what exactly are the Dreamtime and the Waketime?

"Well," Nobel Prize-winning biologist Francis Crick might harumph at this point, "what you call Dreamtime consists of nothing more than the hallucinations conjured up during sleep as the brain flushes out metabolic wastes."

And Waketime? "Well," this macho thinker might pontificate, "what you call Waketime is the objective material realm we perceive with our five senses and measure with our instruments, or in other words THE ONLY REALITY THERE EVER WAS OR WILL BE, THE WHOLE TRUTH AND NOTHING BUT, ALL ELSE IS ILLUSION AND WISHFUL THINKING, DON'T TALK TO ME ABOUT YOUR FATUOUS INFANTILE NOTIONS OF SOUL AND ASTRAL PLANE AND LIFE AFTER DEATH!!!!!!"

The derisive curse "asshole" is not sufficient, we feel, to respond to this idiocy. Therefore, permit us to reach higher.

*Ass-soul.*

Don't misunderstand us, beauty and truth fans. We love science. We wouldn't want to have to live without antibiotics and computers and airplanes and velcro. We also love scientists, by which we mean the humble, curious, lucid, judicious seekers of objective knowledge who are eager to explore the possibility that there may be phenomena outside the reach of their theories.

But the ass-souls we're talking about, like Francis Crick, are not practitioners of science. They are priests of *scientism.*

*Scientism* is an intricate ideology supporting the disguised religion of fundamentalist materialism; an arrogant assertion that the scientific method is the sole arbiter of the ultimate truth; an absolute certainty that the metaphors of science deserve to trump all other metaphors. *Scientism* is an obsessive emotional investment in results that can only be perceived with the "five" senses, or repeated within tightly controlled experiments, or measured with instruments that have already been invented.

At least Judaism and Christianity have ten commandments. The zealots of scientism have just one: *Thou shalt have no other realities but the One True Consensual Hallucination known as Habitual Waking Consciousness.*

This shriveled dogma is now pandemic, though the shills for the cult of scientism would have us believe otherwise. They're fond of promoting the idea that ours is a scientifically illiterate society. And it may be true that the flock is laughably uninformed about the chapter and verse of the creed. Many can't name the planets of the solar system or say how many chromosomes constitute a human gene. But even the most simple-minded cult members cling with a fanatical fervor to scientism's core article of faith: *If you can't see it, it doesn't exist. If you can't see it, it doesn't exist. If you can't see it, it doesn't exist. If you can't see it, it doesn't exist. If you can't see it, it doesn't exist.*

Yes, there are infidels who *hope* that there's a heaven, and who nurture a yearning for the existence of angels or auras or UFOs. There are dissidents who ache to achieve confident belief in the healing power of prayer. But even these would-be apostates have so deeply internalized the canon of fundamentalist materialism that they literally can't muster a direct perception of the more ephemeral realities they long to contact, let alone carry on a lively communion with them.

Is it any great mystery that most people can summon no motivation to retrieve the adventures they have every night while asleep? According to Francis Crick and his fellow masters of reality, dreams have no inherent function or use, but are merely byproducts of metabolism. The events of the day, in this insane theory, are solid, substantial, and genuine, while night's experiences are entirely derivative.

The average victim of fundamentalist materialism doesn't ever have these conscious thoughts, of course. He doesn't need to. It's the ground of his being.

It's no coincidence that during the same week, both *Scientific American* and the *National Enquirer* published articles which came to the same conclusion: *Dreams mean nothing!* In one majestic synchronicity, gross tabloid superstition and brilliantly rationalized ignorance converged.

Woe is us. Our sadness in the face of this travesty is boundless. Not that we're going to challenge Francis Crick to a mudwrestle any time soon. We long ago gave up arguing with the enforcers of the One True Consensual Hallucination. Most of 'em are too damn fanatical and emotionally invested and, well, *unscientific.*

The science of the Televisionary Oracle reveals the coverup of the ages: that the Dreamtime is an actual place where you've lived most of your life as an eternal soul. It's the primal realm where you find sanctuary between every one of your deaths and rebirths—and to whose outer precincts you migrate every night when you sleep.

Isn't it curious to contemplate the fact that coming into this physical world is a kind of death? Whenever you materialize as a fetus in a new mother's womb, you begin your exile from your more ultimate home. When the alarm clock rings every morning, you recapitulate that death with less intensity, casting off your extra dimension as you shrink to fit this tunnelvisionary world.

In the face of our assertions, scientism's enforcers might sneer, "Prove it to us with concrete evidence. Either bring us back a broken tailpipe from a dream car, or don't bother us again." And even aspiring televisionaries might be forgiven if they mourn, "But how could we not vividly recall our return to the ground of our being? Why does the rich hyper-reality of our nightly swims in the four-dimensional bath seem so tenuous, flimsy, unreal?"

To which we reply: for the same reason you don't remember your birth, or your time in the womb, or the first two years of your life. Unless harnessed by arduous training that goes against the grain of everything you've been programmed to believe about the nature of reality since you were born, your conscious awareness doesn't have the conceptual framework to translate Dreamtime adventures into the language of the Waketime. You can't perceive what you can't conceive.

But here's the punch line, beauty and truth fans. You no longer have the luxury of forgetting where you come from. The Dreamtime isn't in trouble—how could it be?—but our *relationship* with the Dreamtime is. And that's a secret reason why the human race stands poised on the brink of collective suicide. We're all desperately lonely for our home. If we don't start rebuilding our access to it, we'll end up killing ourselves to get there. For the sake of all of us, then, beauty and truth fans, you need to recover your intimacy with the Dreamtime.

On the other hand, you can't afford to allow your love of the other side of the veil make you ineffectual in daily life. The point of the Drive-time revolution is certainly not a kneejerk reversal, overvaluing the Dreamtime at the expense of the Waketime. We seek to love and honor both realms, to fight for their reintegration.

To pull this off, Drivetime activists need to be as smart about the laws of the Waketime as the scientists are. And that's most difficult. If you've been cut off from contact with the other side of the veil, as most of us have been trained to be since birth, you're not prepared to deal with the consequences once the link is restored. Many new converts to the intoxicating attractions of the Dreamtime are tempted to lose themselves there. Widespread drug abuse can ultimately be traced to a lack of more measured approaches to spirit.

The high priests of fundamentalist materialism like it that way. It allows them to keep their con game going. They're eager to sell the fear that there's no way to function effectively in the Waketime if you have an intimate connection with the Dreamtime. Delusion and irrationality lie that way, they assert. They practically forbid the propagation of role models who both commune with the great beyond and maintain a robustly logical relationship with the here and now.

The Televisionary Oracle is a revolt against that blindness. It is the training ground for *homo drivetimus*, humans who can go both ways. Of course it's not the sole source of the teaching, beauty and truth fans—you don't need to raise us up as idols to replace the high priests of fundamentalist materialism—but we guarantee that if you stick with us for a while, you will learn to think like a scientist and explore like a shaman. You will have at your disposal both lucid analytical skills and soaring imaginative powers. You will be able to travel back and forth between the Dreamtime and Waketime with slinky grace— or even luxuriate in both at the same time.

Where do we start the work? Not with upgrading your grasp of the Waketime. You may not yet be an expert in manipulating the props of that realm, but it's unlikely you have any problem believing in the solid reality of those props.

On the other hand, there's a high likelihood that you desperately need a twelve-year course of instruction on the Dreamtime. The Televisionary Oracle can't fix everything immediately, but it has already started you down the path to what Plato called anamnesis—the recovery of the memory of your glorious origins. The very fact that you can make out what we're saying right now suggests that you've established a beachhead to reclaim your link to the Dreamtime.

Stay tuned to the Televisionary Oracle for more help, beauty and truth fans. And please begin keeping a pen and notebook by your bed so that you can record your dreams.

Now let's speak more intimately about the Drivetime.

First, consider the term *wormhole*. Originally it was coined by astrophysicists to assuage their fear that matter which is sucked into a black hole simply disappears forever. The hypothetical wormhole lies in the abyss of the black hole and serves as a short-cut connection to a distant "white hole," either in another universe or in our own, where it pours out like a fountain. The missing stuff, in this theory, doesn't die, but is conveyed elsewhere. A wormhole, then, has become for some scientists a religious allegory symbolizing magical linkage and eternal life.

In the age-old tradition of one mythology borrowing from another, we've gladly appropriated the term for our own purposes. The Drivetime, beauty and truth fans, is in one sense a wormhole between the Dreamtime and the Waketime.

Or, to steal from other mythic traditions, the Drivetime is the songline (Australian aborigine) or the shining path (Qabala) or the astral tunnel (shamanism) you inhabit as you flow back and forth between the two realms.

Let's go further. Let's say the Drivetime is the condition you achieve whenever you can see the ultimate unity of the wound and the cure ... the web you weave when you are loyal to both sides of any struggle ... the mood you conjure when you engage in Dionysian thinking, or what Freud defined as "bringing together the contradictory meaning of root ideas" ... the power spot you inhabit whenever you escape the digital tyranny of Yes VERSUS No and luxuriate in the sweet hum of Yes AND No.

Now try these Drivetime talismans on for size: organized chaos ... wild discipline ... reverent blasphemy ... self-effacing grandiosity ... fanatic moderation ... selfish gifts ... twisted calm ... garish elegance ... insane poise ... ironic sincerity ... blasphemous prayers ... orgiastic lucidity ... aggressive sensitivity ... convoluted simplicity ... macho feminism.

*Homework*

Discuss what is wetter than water,
stronger than love,
and more exotic than trust.

14

I'm a bad boy. It's past time for me to begin preparing for the show at the Catalyst tonight, but I can't fight off the compulsion to feed my obsession with Rapunzel just a little more.

I'm sauntering towards the home of Katrina, the one person I know who might be in possession of Rapunzel's phone number. She lives in the heart of the residential neighborhood north of the Catalyst, one of my most favorite places on Earth. I feel exhilarated here. Every half block or so contains a building that shelters the memory of some twisty, transfigurative liaison I've had. I salute the house whose backyard harbors the elm tree where I enjoyed a most gymnastic yet oddly lyrical tryst with the anarchist nymphomaniac Blade. There's the old Victorian that hosted my temporary hierosgamos with the linguist Luçienne, an androgynous beauty who was my wife in two previous incarnations.

Not every memory is a fond one. I shudder to see the apartment where one night Laurie and I wrecked our fine, long-standing Platonic friendship. We should never have made love at all. But if we did, it should have been with more kindness and care than we managed to summon for each other on that star-crossed occasion.

And then there's Eva. We were getting along so deliciously until the day I lent her my Chevy Malibu and she totaled it in a four-car accident on Highway 17. My trust and my lust both disappeared overnight. It stings to think about it now, but forever after I entertained a stupidly superstitious fantasy that she was bad luck.

But the good karma I incurred in these precincts far outweighs the bad. The saintly Cassidy lived here when I first met her, and we enjoyed our first mutual deep-tissue massage under her attic skylight. There's the house where I helped Kaitlin undo her ex-husband's curse on her sexuality. Three doors down is the cottage where Diane and I dedicated our tantric love-making to the magical project of getting Vaclav Havel elected president of Czechoslovakia. (It worked.)

A happy fantasy begins to bud. I theorize that all the intimate adventures I've enjoyed in this neighborhood have been lessons in a kind of sacred school. Now, finally, after all these years of studying, it's as if I've mastered the undergraduate work and am ready to move on to the graduate level. My advisor and master teacher will be Rapunzel, whose expert guidance I've more than earned with my diligence and devotion.

And to be honest, there *are* still a few holes in my education, which I'm quite ready for Rapunzel to fill. Like the following, for instance:

Theorem 1: What characterizes almost every woman I've ever loved for more than one night is that she looks good and smells good. Why the hell do I have to be such a looksist? (And smellist?)

Theorem 2: I'm afraid of women's anger and all too often run from it like a coward.

Theorem 3: I love to fall in love more than I love to stay in love. I'm addicted to the play of infatuation and the wonder of beginnings. Not that I've never had a committed relationship; just that my expertise is more in the realm of inspiration and revolution, less in the slow steady struggle which a long-term intimate relationship must be.

Hypothesis: Rapunzel's going to fix all that. I don't know how. I just have the unshakable certainty that class will very shortly be in session. Whatever I need to learn next, Rapunzel will provide the means.

I'm so high on this scenario that when I arrive at Katrina's house and find no one home, I almost don't mind. I leave a note on the door telling her I desperately need Rapunzel's number and address, and to phone it in to my voice mail as soon as possible.

A relaxed reverie cracks open as I lean against an old elm tree in Katrina's front yard. Images from earlier in the day begin weaving themselves into a collage, and the germ of a new song implants itself in the songwriter section of my brain. Maybe I could even do it as an improv at the show tonight. Fragments of potential lyric lines erupt first. *Graffiti in the ladies' room ... met the witch with the fairy tale name ... she crowned me with her underpants ... I kissed her boot reverently ... took a psychedelic journey with the magic goddess-pad....*

The song could start with me sing-talking in my growly low register over a funky bass line. Guitar and drums would kick in after the first verse, and I'd push my voice up to the next octave. The chorus would burst out, but slightly restrained, after two verses. Following that there could be another verse and chorus, leading into a bridge. I could have Darby, my co-lead singer, cut loose with some undulating background melody there while I interjected a percussive chant.

Uh-oh. A rude interruption breaks in. I suddenly have a nightmare vision of arguing with a record company executive on the fourteenth floor of hell. "Nobody wants to listen to a goddamn confession about menstruation, fer chrissakes," he's barking at me. "Least of all from a guy. You should keep the chorus melody, though; it's a great hook. Just drop the menstrual crap."

To borrow an epithet I learned at age ten while reading the dirty book *Candy* under the covers with a flashlight when my parents thought I was asleep: *Fuckshitpisscuntcock.*

In other words, the reverie's over. How can I generate the creative flow I was born to exude when there's that asshole bureaucrat pontificating in my brain? I must still be pretty far gone if he's able to spoil the artful fun inspired by Rapunzel.

I leave my sanctuary next to the elm and head back in the direction of the Catalyst.

If only. If only. If only the whole world could be, say, just twenty percent more like Santa Cruz. Nobody in Santa Cruz would ever ridicule my intention to write a song about menstruation from a male point of view. On the contrary. I would find abundant support, fierce encouragement, even adulation.

In minutes I arrive back at the Pacific Garden Mall, the downtown's main drag. Two gaggles of conga players and percussionists are performing for an audience consisting entirely of themselves. They're so lost in trance they apparently don't notice that their respective rhythms are clashing.

I stop in front of a store that I've nicknamed the pagan beauty shop. It has a whole range of fashion accessories for wannabe pagans and neo-tribalists, from crystal-tipped wands and athames to tit clamps and cock rings with ancient Egyptian designs to rentable costumes of twenty-two different goddesses. This evening, in the "performance window," there's a green-haired woman with a scraggly but unmistakable blondish-grey beard. Her supertight magenta bike shorts bulge comically, in places revealing the precise patterns of the cellulite beneath. She has the sleeves of her canary-colored satin smoking jacket pushed up as she tattooes the eyelid of a middle-aged woman who seems to be wearing Native American medicine rattles bound up in her hair like old-fashioned curlers. The woman receiving the delicate branding has another tattoo engraved on her substantial belly, a vast stretch of which is revealed between her violet harem pants and a battleship-grey, cone-shaped bra akin to the monstrosity that rock diva Madonna once sported. The belly tattoo shows the Goddess Isis entwined with the Goddess Persephone. I know they're Isis and Persephone because there's a tattooed caption below the image which reads "Isis mudwrestles Persephone for the right to make me CUM." Another image is etched into the woman's left arm, splayed vertically from elbow to wrist: a buffed Barbie doll with snakes for hair. She's wearing a martial artist's uniform and has a double-headed ax slung over her shoulder. The caption above her head reads "Tantric Mutant Ninja Barbie." I guess my earlier vision of creating a "Barbie of Willendorf" for Rapunzel wasn't as original as I imagined.

But I love this scene. I truly do. Not with *perverse* glee; not because of a decadent attachment to any old thing that happens to be vaguely odd. I love it because it's scenes like this that symbolize for me Santa Cruz's quixotic role as a nurseryland utopia—a big open-air performance art gallery and living museum of evolutionary mutations. What other town on this continent can brag that it has had a gay socialist feminist mayor? Where else can you find poems by Coleridge spray-painted on a highway underpass? Or shop at a store called "Art: Fifty Cents a Pound"? Or attend the "Christstock" festival, an only-half-satirical, three-day mini-Woodstock whose attendees all claim to be the reincarnation of Jesus Christ?

And what of this: Has my performance art campaign for the Santa

Cruz city council ever been matched by any other candidate in any other town in America? Has any other aspirant for political office ever claimed to channel the spirit of Thomas Jefferson and sought solutions to the homeless problem in lucid dreams and pledged to consult Tarot cards before making every important decision and called for holy mudwrestling rituals between liberal and conservative politicians as a way to decide intractable disagreements?

Where else besides this seaside paradise can you find a group of men who wear veils all day on International Women's Day? Or make the acquaintance of three different women painters who all claim to be channeling, in their own work, the spirit of Mexican painter Frida Kahlo? Has any other hamlet in the history of the planet ever passed an ordinance that made it illegal for businesses to discriminate in their hiring practices against people with nose rings or mohawk hairdos or ritual scars on their cheeks?

Now it's true that far less than a majority of the population of Santa Cruz County is composed of street-singing UFO abductees and parapsychology researchers who proudly breastfeed their infants in public and soap bubble-blowing artists who've developed their transitory sculptures with such grandiose craftsmanship that they tour the world doing shows to sold-out audiences. And for the majority of respectable, tax-paying, four-hours-of-TV-a-day Americans who make up the bulk of the Santa Cruz population, the data that make my heart glad are embarrassing. They would no doubt be repulsed if they ever heard my estimate that fully five percent of the adults in Santa Cruz have relationships with invisible friends.

But I myself am in full resonance with the eccentric side of this town. I beam with civic pride. I can't justify my illusion that the vegetarian astral-traveling conspiracy theorists and twelve-step, cigar-smoking, pagan bisexual folk singers are more spiritually advanced or psychologically healthy than everyone else in the world. I can only say that's what the playful, optimistic, I-want-heaven-to-be-here-now side of myself yearns to believe. My secret ambition is to take this Santa Cruz in me and find a way to give it to the whole world.

I browse on down the Pacific Garden Mall until I come to my other most favorite landmark. It's sorta kinda an art gallery and part-time cafe, but sometimes you can get your Tarot cards read here or buy odd occult knickknacks like "mojo bags" (hand-sewn velvet containers filled with talismans, crystals, straw fetishes, vials of essential oils, and other magickal stuff) or packages of sage (an herb that when burned is used for psychic cleansing). At least two people seem to live in the back rooms here. Like the pagan beauty shop, it's a hotbed of entertaining people and events that rarely fails to give me a seed idea for a new song lyric or poem.

I don't even know what the proprietors are calling the place these days. They seem to change the name regularly. I look around for a sign that might hint at its current alias, but all I see is a poster for an event that's scheduled here for tonight. It's an art opening for "The Eater of Cruelty."

"Take mad genius Antonin Artaud's Theater of Cruelty," the poster reads, "and insert a mutant *e*. What do you get? *THE EATER OF CRU-ELTY*. We find the treasure in the trash, the gold in the lead, the manna in the junk food. Sometimes the only way to get the good stuff into your system is to eat the whole disgusting thing."

This is spooky and exhilarating. Though Artaud's work has receded into near-obscurity in the last decade, he's one of my heroes, and a seminal influence on my performance career. And not only that. According to one of the early loves of my life, a woman who proved to me beyond a doubt that she had psychic skills, I was a friend of Artaud in one of my past lives.

The front display window of the storefront is filled with TV monitors, a scene which is also dear to my heart. My band World Entertainment War is well-known for the way we pack the stage with TVs, some tuned to whatever network or cable shows happen to be on at the time we're performing, some to rented videos. Lately I've been partial to using Disney's *Fantasia* and a documentary on the paintings of Matisse. "Too much entertainment," I sometimes proclaim to the audience as we arrive on stage, "because you're too much!"

The images appearing on The Eater of Cruelty's TV installation are of a different order than ours. The technology seems far beyond normal video. The almost three-dimensional vividness of the images surpasses the quality of a typical TV by several magnitudes. Their excruciating hyper-reality gives me a queasy thrill. The effect is exacerbated by the *cruelty* of the images. I mean, my band is famous for its shocking imagery, but The Eater of Cruelty makes us look like Sesame Street.

Example: In the midst of a vast stretch of snowy tundra, a wizened old pregnant woman with very little hair is joined at the hip, like a Siamese twin, with a teenage boy. She swings a double-headed ax at a ten-foot-high totem pole composed of the heads of well-known historical figures (all male), while at the same time she's breastfeeding a baby whose umbilical cord is still attached and being yanked on by a vulture wearing a pink tutu.

One of the monitors is itself highly anomalous. It's apparently made of stone and mud. Vines are growing out of cracks in it in several places. Among the hard-to-look-at but irresistible scenes lingering there is this: A creature that's simultaneously beautiful and hideous is puttering around the outside of a domed stadium at the main entrance of which is a neon sign in the shape of an equal-armed cross with a partially bloomed rosebud at its center. The sign reads "Mary Magdalen Memorial Stadium."

The creature's face is that of an attractive woman in her thirties. Her body, except for two phallic-shaped breasts that look like those of a human female, is a large vulture. The span of her wings is enormous, markedly greater than her height. She's using them as brooms or rakes, gathering trash and refuse into piles with majestic sweeping motions. Across the bottom of the "television" screen scroll the words "This Bud's for You, Uberwoman."

I can't resist going inside the building to explore what's behind all this. There's a series of circular black tables around the periphery of the room, each holding a stone and mud TV like the one that caught my eye in the front window. Near the back wall, a woman appears to be getting ready to speak or perform. A crowd of maybe thirty people sits on the floor.

The most striking feature about the performer is that she's apparently about eight months pregnant. The second most striking feature is that she bears an uncanny resemblance to Rapunzel. The bushy eyebrows are the same shape, though black instead of auburn. The flared nostrils. The gap between the front teeth. The high cheekbones and expansive forehead. About five feet, ten inches, same as Rapunzel. Am

I simply exhibiting the signs of extreme infatuation: Rapunzelizing the entire race of women?

I don't think so. She's a close match for my beloved except for a few details. Twin sister? Rapunzel herself in some kind of twisted disguise? Her black shag hair is ridiculously fat on top, which suggests that she's wearing a wig.

She's also wearing a gold contraption which is a near replica of the vulture headdress customarily worn by the queens of ancient Egypt. I know this for a fact because when I was a kid I learned all there was to know about vulture lore. The bald head and beak of the fake vulture bulge out from the top of her forehead, and the wings hang down like flaps all the way to her shoulders.

This would look almost regal if it weren't for the fact that she's also got a silly old pair of bulky black-rimmed eyeglasses with wing tips, and their lenses are tinted magenta. Her all-white costume is like an Indian sari. A stately, multi-tiered gold necklace, which matches the intricate engraving of the headdress, gives her the look of a mad sybil.

The third most striking feature about Rapunzel-Clone is that she has awakened in me a curiously guilty lust. Shouldn't the sight of her protruding abdomen cancel out the sight of her Rapunzel-like gorgeousness? Am I not breaking some taboo by sexualizing the carrier of another man's child?

Then again, Santa Cruz has a reputation for having the world's most single mothers per capita. An abundant and easy access to social services, combined with a fanatically supportive feminist community, has created a fledgling cult of young bohemian welfare moms—and another gang of cheerfully irresponsible and itinerant dads. The odds are fifty-fifty that Rapunzel-Clone's inseminator has already wandered on down the road.

I decide to listen to her spiel for a while, though I'm increasingly aware of my responsibilities back at the Catalyst. Finding a spot near one of the stone TVs, I squat. The screen next to me is more shocking than any in the display window. My first unconscious reaction when I catch it out of the corner of my eye is that it's pornography. But as I look closer, I see it's not exactly.

A naked pregnant woman on all fours is in the throes of strenuous labor. She's huffing manically, her muscles rippling involuntarily in exhaustion and duress. Her back end is facing me at an angle, and the crown of the fetus' head has split through her engorged vulva. There next to her, resplendent in a magenta bodysuit, is a woman who resembles the robust crone with grey dreadlocks I saw in the *Menstrual Lingerie Fashion Show*. I take the book out now to compare. Yes. It's the same person. Her name is Vimala.

Rocking and swaying like a saxophone player, Vimala is massaging the woman's back and stroking her thighs. The tiny brown wet feathered head bobs at the threshold; it pokes through and retreats twice. Vimala leans down close to it and blows gently, and in a slow-motion burst the tiny puckered face oozes free. With her left hand lightly grasping the head, Vimala sweeps her right index finger under the side of the baby's jaw and slips the chin out. There the reddish blue face remains lodged and suspended, between worlds, awaiting the next contraction.

And then the screen goes blank. After a few seconds, a looping cartoon appears. It features two recurring icons—my old friend the bull skull and the creature with the body of a vulture and the face of a woman. At times bull skulls emerge from the nipples of the vulture-woman; at other times twin vulture-women fly out of the eyes of the bull skull.

I feel queasy, shaken, in a light trance. The scene of the birth was provocative enough, but I think I'm even more disoriented because it was interrupted. I take a few deep breaths and lie down to try to quell my vertigo. As I cover my eyes with my forearm, I feel something skitter onto my midsection. Peeking out, I see that a woman in a black robe has airdropped a sheet of red paper. Everyone else in the room is receiving a similar gift. It turns out to contain the text of the little speech Rapunzel-Clone proceeds to give.

Her first words sound like a text that might be delivered by a television pitchman introducing a late-night infomercial or an HBO pay-for-view spectacle. On the other hand, she delivers it in a soft, lyrical voice as she opens out her arms in a majestic welcome.

"Live from the Drivetime. You're tuned to the Televisionary Oracle. Coming to you on location from your own future. Featuring continuous news updates about *you*. Brought to you by The Eater of Cruelty. Are you ready to lose your ridiculous omniscience?"

Huh?

Though I don't understand what conceit is informing this introduction, I can clearly hear that the woman's voice is a dead ringer for Rapunzel's.

Her next speech makes more sense.

"I hate to break it to you, beauty and truth fans, but your body's going to fail you one day. It'll utterly collapse and stop working. Your heart will shut down. Your genitals will go numb forever. Your brain will no longer whirl with liquid light.

"That's the bad news. The good news is that you're actually dying little deaths every single day. The inside of your body is a killing field where your cells ceaselessly give up their lives in service to producing the energy that keeps you animated.

"In another sense, your cells are tyrannical liquidators, immolating the food you pour inside you so that it might be radically transformed into useful substances. You're a slaughterhouse, beauty and truth fans. You're an uncompromising terminator who ruthlessly destroys the forms of the plants and animals and minerals that sacrifice their lives for you.

"So you're practicing death every day in every way. You're committing little murders with each breath you take, each move you make. In truth, you're so thorough and constant in your deathwork that you regularly disappear yourself completely. A few years from now, there will not be a single cell in your body that is here today. They all will have been annihilated in the ongoing carnage, replaced by new volunteers who in their turn will also perish while expressing their pragmatic love for you.

"Yet though your very survival depends on your mastery of burnt offerings, most of you have somehow managed to retain your innocence about it. If I asked all of you right now, 'Who in here is an expert in the art of dying?', I doubt I'd see *any* hands raised. I'm not criticizing, but mourning. Not condemning you to permanent ignorance, but exhorting you to awaken. If only, beauty and truth fans. If only you could own the hidden knowledge you harbor. If only you could bloom a continual stream of vivid meditations on the death that energizes you in every moment.

"But here's a secret: You can. You must. You will. Why? Because it's your best hope for surviving the ultimate death of your physical form. It's the foolproof way to learn exactly what you'll need to do in the moment of transition—when your body shuts down—in order to slip away with your soul's integrity and treasurehouse of memories fully intact.

"You must *practice* death, beauty and truth fans. If after your current body fails you want to be born again in a new body in complete possession of the consciousness you earned this time around, you must practice practice practice death. Not just instinctively and unconsciously, as you do now. But with the full participation of your intelligent will. In the bright light of day. With your courage and gratitude blazing.

"Practice death, beauty and truth fans. Not simply by noticing the destructive fury of your teeth as they rip apart the flesh you offer for sacrifice. Not just by contemplating your stomach's acidic assaults on this decimated material. Not just by tuning into the literal fires that rage in your lungs as they seize oxygen from the atmosphere. These visualizations are helpful, but for most of you they won't be enough to prepare you for crossing the abyss at the end of your body's days. That's because the processes in question have been going on since before you could talk, before you could even laugh or focus your eyes. They're too numbingly familiar, too woven into the unconscious fabric of your awareness.

"There is another kind of death that is pregnant with more viable meditations—if you're a woman. It typically occurs once in every orbit of the moon around the Earth. When you menstruate, a specialized cell in your body, the only type of cell capable of spawning a new creature, begins a quest for larger life—only to fail in its mission and disintegrate. This is a death that is more shocking to the body than digestion and oxidation, and therefore more palpable to your imagination. It even generates a symptom that in any other situation is a dramatic sign of rapidly ebbing vitality: loss of blood.

"Each menstrual death is potentially an initiation into the mysteries of the body's final demise. *Potentially*, I said. In fact only a shamanatrix trained in the techniques of The Eater of Cruelty has the skill necessary to extract the initiatory insights. Each month she steals a piece of the Other Side of the Veil and inseminates herself with its wisdom. Each month she becomes more and more pregnant with the secrets of death. Until one day—let's hope on a day before her body finally quits—she births not just a new vision but a new *version* of herself: an immortal soul capable of surviving intact during the traumatic exit from the body and the preparation for eventual re-entry into human flesh. Thus, she kills her own death.

"Now let me address those of you who might feel neglected by my last comments: the men. I want you to know that though you may never be able to enjoy the literal physiological experience of menstruation, it's not inconceivable for you to court a vivid metaphorical equivalent of it.

"Your success in this project may depend in part on your ability to remember when you were a woman. And I assure you with utter certainty that you *were* a woman. There was a period in your earliest life—indeed, in the life of every man—in which you were purely female. It was the first five weeks after you were conceived. That's because *every* fetus starts out female. Every fetus, in the beginning, has a clitoris, an Ur-phallus. It is only at the five-week mark that those fetuses destined to be males endure the spontaneous explosion of hormonal abracadabra that transmogrifies their clitorises into penises.

"Think back, men. Meditate back. You'll find those five weeks. And when you do, the gifts of menstruation may begin to become available. Perhaps we may offer you some help in this task with the next part of your program tonight.

"We'll get to that in a minute. First, let me say that what we're doing here now is but a bare introduction to the advantages of consciously dying every day of your life. If you'd like to know more, please sign our guest book. We will contact you.

"OK. Now we're happy to present you with a practicum that should allow you to begin putting to use the ideas we've spoken about.

"To begin, place yourself in a comfortable position. Relax and breathe deeply.

"Now bring your awareness to the inside of your abdomen below your navel. If you're a woman, do your best to locate the inner walls of your uterus. If you're a man, faithfully hallucinate that you feel a uterus.

"Imagine that a ripe ovum has just popped out of your left ovary and has begun its migration into your fallopian tube. You've ovulated. As if in time-lapse photography, follow that egg as it journeys. Let your mind picture this if you want, but more importantly, *feel* the sensation in the appropriate place in your body.

"Can you sense that there is a sentience in the ovum? It's more alive than any other individual cell in your body, even the unripe ova it left behind in your ovary. Without getting sentimental or anthropomorphic, pretend that this little fragment of you is a potential new creature, a proto-being that vibrates at the same frequency as the first chains of molecules that were shocked alive by lightning bolts in Earth's ancient primordial soup.

"It's important that you suspend any beliefs that might interfere with your ability to tune in directly to the actual living presence of this cell. What you're doing has no bearing on your political or religious notions about abortion, for instance. To worry that it does will only encourage your chattering mind to try to hijack this experience.

"Now imagine, as you follow your ovum in its travels, that it's a highly specialized essence both alive and not alive, both belonging to you and serving the agendas of an ancient instinct that has no interest in your personal needs. Become aware that the ovum is on a quest driven by a primitive longing to find a nest.

"Next, experience that perfect moment when its longing is satisfied. Feel its ecstasy as it nestles into the bed of tissue that has been prepared for it on your uterine wall. Exult in this homecoming—but not too long. In the ensuing moment, this inconceivably old entity launches the second half of its imperative: to be fertilized.

"Simmer in this sensation. A thing that is alive yet not alive, that's both you and not you, waits, yearning with a desire that's millions of years old, to become fully alive. Feel it waiting. Imagine its vivid instinctual intent, its utterly concentrated animal readiness. Waiting. And waiting. And waiting.

"And then visualize the moment when it gives up waiting. The exact second when it surrenders its lust to live and begins to wilt. Maybe your conscious mind is pleased there'll be no pregnancy. But a different mind in you, a primitive mind, feels loss and grief. Opens to the underworld. Falls down the hole. Feels the breath of death.

"Now imagine that as the ovum and its nest peel away from the uterine wall, they send a signal to your pituitary gland to secrete the hormone that will in turn detonate the ripening of a new follicle. Feel the signal. Follow the hormone. Tune in to the ecstatic twinge in your ovary as the cycle begins again. And wish yourself happy birthday.

"Meanwhile, remain aware of the dying that is simultaneously taking place in your womb. And wish yourself happy deathday.

"Imagine at this moment that you are between worlds. You're both alive and dead at the same time. Womb and tomb are conflating.

"And welcome to the Drivetime.

"Steep yourself here in the threshold, looking both ways.

"Now please visualize that you are the person you will be on the day your body dies. Pretend you're fully aware that these are your last hours on Earth. Don't worry about whether this is 'real' or 'imagined,' whether you're psychically viewing the future or merely fantasizing. Remember: There is a realm that is neither 'real' nor 'imaginary,' but both: a realm in between. The Drivetime.

"See where you are as you prepare for your adventure. Are you lying in a bed in a familiar place, or perhaps in a musty bed in a strange land? Look at your arms. Are there wrinkles and age spots, or is the flesh still smooth and clear? How old are you? Wiggle your feet if you can. Stroke your own cheek with tenderness. How does the inside of your body feel? Pulsing pain? Slow, dissolving serenity? Confusion and uproar? Resignation and excitement?

"Since this is wherever you imagine it to be, maybe you're not expiring in bed. Be frank. Do you think it's more likely you're going to die in an accident or during an earthquake or from a sudden heart attack? Or perhaps you've decided not to wait for death to overtake you on its own terms, but are going out to meet it. Can you see yourself standing on a beach, preparing to lose yourself at the bottom of the ocean?

"If you want, run through a host of scenarios, letting each tell you some quiet or spectacular secret. But at last settle on one. This is your last stand on Earth. The sweet spot where you will take your final breath. Become aware of how much you love yourself. Tune in to your amazement about how beautiful and strange and difficult and mysterious your life has been.

"See and hear and smell every detail of these closing moments. If nothing specific pops into your mind's eye, make something up. What color are the walls or the sky? What time of the year is it, what hour of the day or night? What are you wearing? Are there companions here with you? How do you feel about being separated from them?

"This last question may be the hardest. Leaving would be simpler if it weren't for these grieving souls begging you to stay. Look into their eyes now and say exactly what you mean. In this propitious moment, everything can change forever. This is your chance to banish suffering you've caused, to correct a thousand mistakes, to alter the entire meaning of your life.

"Or let's say that these are not your final seconds. Maybe you have an hour or two remaining. If you're dying of disease, your body is in full retreat from the fight. If you are to be killed in an accident, your subconscious mind is turning towards the Other Side as a dandelion swivels at dawn to follow the rising sun.

"Become aware, then, that your heart is in conversation with death. Consider the possibility that your passing from this world will be nothing like what you've ever believed, and that your real education begins now. Does it seem pointless to become a student in these waning moments, or can you glimpse the hint of a reason to become more alert than you ever have before? What if this is a great awakening? What if you're about to navigate an abyss as dangerous and exhilarating as the one you crossed in order to be born? What if there is another life on the other side of that abyss—a life as unimaginable as this one was in the moments before you arrived?

"Let's hypothesize that what you've heard is true: Your entire life can pass before your eyes at closing time. Do you want that? Say yes, and every experience you've ever had—every nuance of feeling, every amazing and trivial thought, every wordless memory of a memory— will flood through you in a vivid waking dream so compressed that only a person in your threshold state is capable of enduring it. Surrender to this extravagant blessing. For all you know, it's the fuel that ensures you'll make it to the other side with your self-awareness intact. For all you know, it's the key to a kind of immortality you never guessed the existence of until now.

"As you relive your life in this timeless time, we offer you our love in whatever form you need it, from tenderness to adrenaline. We pray that you will see what you could not see before.

"Spend as much time here as you need. We will leave you now for a while to muse and peruse."

"Imagine now that you have intimately experienced two kinds of death without having to endure the inconvenience of literally dying. You've zeroed in on that moment when the withering of one ovum triggers the bloom of a new one. And you've learned what your life feels like when you explore it from its last moments. Pretend that as a result you're now ready to wield death's purifying slash yourself—with love not cruelty; with joy not violence. You're sensing what it would be like to become an adept of creative destruction, a master dismantler of whatever threatens to kill your soul.

"Scan yourself now, searching for the hard, frozen fixations; the broken, frazzled obstructions; the angry, arrogant traumas. Track down the false hopes, short-sighted beliefs, and useless emotions that your death knows to be superfluous. Allow yourself to look at just one terrible truth about yourself; let yourself feel the suffering you've steadfastly refused to feel; come face to face with the ignorance you have nurtured most obsessively—the ignorance which, if demolished, would free you to become a more ultimate version of yourself.

"This is where you learn firsthand what the alchemists meant when they said, 'Dissolution is the secret of the Great Work.' This is the time and this is the place to use the Death Medicine on yourself.

"Continue breathing deep, hilariously sacred breaths. With each exhale, remember that your body is a furnace that destroys its fuel in order to live. With each inhale, imagine that enlightenment is not the accumulation of knowledge but the stripping away of amnesia. It's as if nothing can ever again be dangerous; as if not even time can murder you. You're better than dead. You're better than alive. You're dead and alive at the same time. From now on you will grow more ecstatically intelligent whenever you meditate on this: To the degree that you steal death's method and use it to invigorate your life, the specter of your own corpse loses its power to scare you."

15

If you know anything about quantum physics,
you'll understand why the treasure you've been longing for
has already been changed by your pursuit of it.
It's no longer what it was
when you felt your first pangs of desire.

Now, in order to make this prized experience yours,
you'll have to modify your ideas about it.

Fortunately,
you've come to the Televisionary Oracle
at exactly the right time
to get help in doing just that.

In Tibetan Buddhism's "Four Dignities of the Warrior's Path," which
the Televisionary Oracle has borrowed for its own use, courage and
ferocity are absent. In fact, the qualities regarded as essential have nothing in common with the training regimens of football players or Marines
or lobbyists.

The first dignity is translated in English as *meekness*, but that word
doesn't convey its full meaning. "Relaxed confidence" is a more precise formulation. A humble feeling of being at home in one's body.

*Perkiness*, or hard-earned, unabashed joy, is the second dignity. To
develop it, the warrior diligently drives out the self-indulgence of cynicism.

The third is *outrageousness*. It combines a delight in daring experiments with a passionate objectivity that is free of both hope and fear.

The fourth dignity is *inscrutability*, which demands a supple willingness to be unpredictable in carrying out one's moral vision.

The Televisionary Oracle
is brought to you by the state of mind
poet John Keats inhabited when he said,
"If something is not beautiful, it is probably not true."

16

I've been lying, beauty and truth fans. I've been riffing. What I described last time was my "menarche" from the standpoint of my smotheringly loving mothers alone.

But it wasn't real as far as I was concerned. By all the precepts of the Pomegranate Grail itself, it was a hypocritical fraud.

The more I thought about it, the more enraged I became. The so-called guardians of the ancient mystery school had committed a profane crime against their so-called avatar. They had desecrated the sacred meaning of my rite of passage into womanhood.

Let me explain.

From the time I was a young child, the figure of Persephone was at the heart of my spiritual training. She was like Jehovah for the Jews, Ahura-Mazda for the Zoroastrians. The Goddess, I was told, expresses Herself in countless names and forms, but the stories of Persephone were most important for this age and my mission. (Mary Magdalen was Her word made flesh, Her Jesus or Buddha, but that's another story.)

It wasn't until I was almost eight years old, while sitting in class on a spring day, that Vimala first shared the shocking news about my idol: Most of the people in the outside world knew only one tale about Persephone, and it was a terrible lie! According to this abomination, my Queen was a naive young girl picking narcissus flowers in a meadow when a big ugly brute of a demon-god named Pluto kidnapped Her, dragged Her down to his hellish kingdom through a hole in the ground, and made Her his prisoner-wife.

I burst into tears on the spot. I felt what a devout Catholic girl might feel if a foul tramp spit on her silver crucifix. The story wasn't true, I knew, but the fact that everyone believed it was devastating.

Vimala's intention in introducing me to this sacrilege was pedagogical. It was the formal beginning of her teachings about the loathsome sins of the fathers. The myths that I'd been raised on, she told me once I regained my composure, were the authentic and original ones. Persephone had reigned as the Queen of the Underworld eons before the patriarchy concocted the idiotic Pluto and superimposed his violent myth over the beautiful truth.

Not that She had been Queen since time began. When the world was still young—so said the teachings of the Pomegranate Grail—the realm of Tartarus had no ruler. The souls of the dead dwelt there listlessly, in ignorance and without guidance, waiting to be reborn. Meanwhile, in the brightly lit world above, Persephone was a maiden like me, steadily growing in wisdom as She mastered the skills She would need to serve as Queen. "When you're ready to seek the wilder, stranger path," Her mother Demeter told Her, "the shades will rejoice. You will be their Redeemer."

As Her body grew and changed shape, Her longing for mystery deepened, as did Her courage to claim the power that awaited Her. And when Her drive to know the depths matched Her power to navigate them, She menstruated for the first time. Awakened both to fertility and death, She began Her quest, beginning Her descent at a shrine inside a mountain near the city of Clitor, where the River Styx, the menstrual blood of Mother Earth, originates.

Now here's the key: She went willingly into the underworld, and under Her own power. *She abducted Herself.* She was not a resistant pawn dragged below to serve the agenda of a controlling monster.

Unlike myself. Unlike my own experience of first menstruation.

With hair-raising similarities to the hapless Persephone of the patriarchal story, I had been kidnapped. Taken against my will. Forced to do the bidding and obey the timing of a tyrant with intricate plans for my destiny. Was it any consolation that my ravager wasn't a Big Bad Daddy but my sweet generous mommies?

No. It was worse. It was a violation which ensured that any escape I made, any retribution I exacted, would arouse tremendous guilt in me. Nevertheless, I began plotting my strategy within days of the morning my blood first flowed.

My initial task was to remind myself of the lessons the still small voice had taught me when I first decided to prevent menstruation those many years ago. What lay behind my impulse to rebel was not merely juvenile pettiness. The stakes were much higher. I could not become the avatar unless I did it in my own way. And the ritual by which Vimala and company forcibly induced my first menstruation had reasserted their right and power to make me their puppet.

One menstrual period later, in early February, I formulated a plan to reclaim my independence and save my soul; that is to say, to *kidnap myself*, to slip into the underworld from a position of strength and under my own power.

I was in the menstrual hut, officially known as Persephone's Sanctuary, which is in the building closest to my home. It was just my second visit to the sacred precinct. Until my blood first flowed a month before, the place had been off-limits, as it was to all who had never menstruated—even the avatar.

It was after 11 P.M. I was in the large square adytum which occupies the heart of the top floor. Most of the other menstruators or postmenopausal crones were either meditating in the soundproofed chambers that line the west wall or already engaged in their dream incubation quests on the floor below. I had a strong psychic impression about the nature of the quest that Cecily was on. She was reaching out in the astral realms to her friend Priscilla, who lay in a coma in an Oakland hospital room. She was trying to coax Priscilla either to depart to the land of death or return to the living, but not stay stuck in between.

Also creeping into the corner of my awareness was the sound of a djembe drum rhythmically beating in the music room. Tuning in to the intention behind it, I sensed Calley. I fantasized or telepathically perceived (at that time, I didn't always know the difference) that she had launched herself on a shamanic journey not just through space but time. I felt her seeking out her Iroquois ancestors, hoping to sit with them as they practiced the dream-guessing rite, whose aim was to guess the dreamer's *ondinnonk*—the secret wish of the soul revealed in a dream. The murmur of a strange and beautiful word circulated at

the periphery of my inner hearing: *qaumanEq*. "What does that mean?"
I asked Calley with my thoughts. "Shamanlight of the brain," said a
voice that sounded like hers.

I forcibly turned my attention away from Calley and Cecily and all
the other souls filling up the Menstrual Temple with their passionate
night-time pilgrimages. It was good to know that my solitude here in
the adytum was in no danger of being interrupted.

I reclined in a black leather chair near the central shrine. The stars
shone clearly through the skylight above me. The sound in my head-
phones was a cassette called "Primordial Picnic," by a local Santa Cruz
band, Midnight Sex Picnic. Talk about music to menstruate by. Sly,
vulnerable, unpredictable, melodic, the band was looping me through
emotions that I'd never felt before but nonetheless recognized as if I
were returning to a home I'd forgotten I had.

When the song "Stronger Than Love" came on, I had a sobbing
meltdown. I knew the singer meant it to be a message to the demanding woman he loved, but my still small voice was singing it to my seven
mothers.

> I made it all up
> None of it was true
> I made it all up just to please you
> I gave it all away
> None of it was mine
> I gave it all away to try to reach you
> And I never fought in Beirut or Danang
> Never killed anyone to impress you
> I did not save the world
> I hope you'll understand
> It's not easy to prove that I love you
>
> Stronger than love
> I'll change myself for you
> Stronger than love
> There's nothing that I wouldn't do for you
>
> I'll turn into an animal
> Drive myself crazy

Light up like a bomb just to heal you
I'll sail submarines across the line of death
I'll give up my God just to heal you
Now I'm reading your mind
And I know you're behind
the freedom I feel to surrender
And it's stronger than love
more exotic than trust
I will prove that my love has no limits

Stronger than love
I'll change myself for you
Stronger than love
There's nothing that I wouldn't do for you
Stronger than love
I will explode for you
Thunder and lightning
fire and ice
money and fighting
all over the earth for you
Nothing is too good for you

Every day of my life for years I had stretched and twisted and pushed myself to become the perfect master my mothers yearned for me to be. At an age when most children were learning to tie their shoes, I was doing four hours of exercises a week to train my perceptions to be sharp and my memory photographic. When other kids were trying to decide whether Santa Claus was real or not, I was using meditation to build a sacred chamber in my brain that would literally house the Goddess Persephone and give me the power to commune with the fourth dimension on command. Every assignment my mothers had given me, I struggled to fulfill. Every time they criticized me for being less loving or discerning than I could have been, I worked to improve. I knew—I had been told over and over again—that it was all for a good cause, that I was being forged into a vessel of redemption for the entire human race. But why then did I feel more loyal and devoted to my mothers than to the human race?

In return for my service to their all-consuming cause, I had only asked my mothers for three things in all the years I was growing up. First, that I be allowed to have friends from outside the community. This they ultimately agreed to, though not without much dispute. Second, that I be allowed to form my own opinions about books written by "patriarchal criminals" before being bombarded with the Pomegranate Grail's official position on them. To this they eventually acceded as well.

My third request was hopeless, I feared, from the start. I wanted to hide or expunge the hideous brown birthmark in the shape of a bull skull that adorned the middle of my forehead. My mothers turned me down every time I brought it up, sometimes with a curt "never," on other occasions allowing for a discussion that made me hope it would one day be negotiable.

In the early years, I didn't know anything about how it might be possible; I just wanted it gone. But eventually I came to understand that there were people known as plastic surgeons who specialized in fixing problems exactly like mine.

When I was fourteen, I made an appointment with a dermatologist in Santa Cruz and hitchhiked there without informing my moms. I came back armed with information about how easy it would be to fulfill my desire.

Once she got over her horror at my sneaky behavior, Vimala said what she had always said: "Your mark is a blessing. It's the seal of an awesome ancient prophecy. It's the living proof that you are the avatar."

"But it's ugly," I said with uncharacteristic simplicity. "I hate it."

"We will not disturb the magic. We will honor it as a sign of your covenant with the Goddess. Your life's sacred journey requires you to honor your gift. The case is closed."

But there on my second sojourn in the menstrual hut, as I rewound the tape by Midnight Sex Picnic and listened again to "Stronger Than Love," the case opened back up again. The news arrived from a place so deep in me it felt as if I were touching the center of the Earth. It was delivered by a triumphant, bellowing, laughing version of my still small voice. "Scouring away your birthmark," it announced, "is the radical act of separation that will serve as your self-abduction."

Shock mixed with vindication. I had no doubt that I had just been given a blessing of the first order—a difficult, radical blessing, perhaps, that would be hurtful to people I loved. But a blessing nonetheless. Responding with a beam of gratitude in the direction of my still small voice, I promised to obey. By whatever means necessary, I vowed to obliterate my accursed stain as soon as I possibly could.

Close by, as familiar as my breath, I felt the shimmering endorsement of Rumbler. "Yes," he vibrated excitedly but humbly, as if not wanting to upstage my still small voice. "Yes yes yes yes yes yes."

I set to work two days later. My first task was to get a new, improved birth certificate. I had always looked older than my actual age, and I could pass for nineteen even then, a few months short of my seventeenth birthday. But I couldn't take the chance that my mature appearance would be sufficient to convince a plastic surgeon I'd reached the age of consent.

On a drizzly Valentine's Day, I drove to see my buddy Lena, a hippie punk chick who lived in downtown Santa Cruz. As a non-member of the Pomegranate Grail community, she was not high on the list of friends my mothers approved of, but on the other hand they didn't actively discourage me from seeing her.

Lena had a catalogue from an anarchist supply house in Washington state. It was full of helpful products and tips about how to avoid or cheat the government, declare yourself empress of an uninhabited island, or hunt small game with your bare hands after the apocalypse. There were also a few pages of contacts that promised assistance in acquiring a fake ID.

Lena didn't press me about why I was in the market for an earlier birthdate. She was content to accept my generic statement that it would be a handy thing to have. She agreed to let me use her address when I sent away for the stuff, and when I drove back to her pad two weeks later, a pile of pamphlets and books awaited me. I chose two from this group and mailed out my applications and fees. Within a couple of weeks I had received two extremely realistic birth certificates, one from Oklahoma and one from South Dakota, each with a birthdate fifteen months prior to my actual birthdate. I'd completed step number one successfully.

The second element of my plan was to decide what distant city I would run away to. There was no way I could pull it off while remaining at the Sanctuary. And staying in Santa Cruz would make it too easy for my mothers to track me down.

I narrowed the choice down to three places: Santa Monica to the south and Santa Rosa and Marin County to the north. I'd been to all three on trips with Vimala and some of the other mothers, and had a good feeling about each of them.

In Bookshop Santa Cruz I bought maps of each area. At the public library I found phone books from each area and xeroxed copies of the Yellow Pages listings for plastic surgeons, hotels, and boarding houses.

I didn't want to make my long-distance calls from the Sanctuary, since that would leave clues about my ultimate whereabouts on the phone bills. So I got a load of change and used the pay phone in front of the library. After an hour, I'd made my decision: San Rafael, the main city in Marin. There was a budget motel there which I had passed during my previous visits. It was on Lincoln Street, not too far from the main drag.

Many of Marin's plastic surgeons seemed to have congregated in nearby Greenbrae, a few miles away via bus. I called three of them and each indicated a willingness to take my case.

None of the receptionists would discuss specifics with me, but I knew from my earlier research that annihilating the repulsive brown stain would take at least a couple of surgeries six weeks apart. They would be followed by another few weeks' recuperation before the final step: sanding down the scar.

I was going to have to relocate for a minimum of ten weeks. Expenses for food and lodging, added to the cost of the surgery, could run as much as five thousand dollars. To be safe, I decided I needed at least six thousand dollars.

The next problem was how to raise such a sum. The million-dollar trust fund that Vimala and company allegedly had going for me wouldn't be available any time soon. Though my moms usually bought me anything I asked for, they gave me a mere one hundred fifty dollars a week in spending money. That wouldn't accumulate very fast even if I did become amazingly frugal.

No way was I going to get a job. Could I sell some of my belongings at a flea market? "Get a fine collection of genuine Goddess prayer cloths here, just five bucks apiece." That seemed tawdry. Same with the idea of hocking my belongings at a pawn shop. Too bad no one outside my little community knew I was a shining avatar and the reincarnation of Mary Magdalen. If they did, I could have hawked my doodles or old shoes for exorbitant sums.

I was tempted to surreptitiously start my "ministry" years ahead of schedule. The gospel according to my mothers was that the world wouldn't be ready for me and vice versa until I was twenty-five. But maybe in the meantime I could somehow figure out a way to get paid for doing psychic readings and healings. Besides the fact that charging money for my gifts was a big no-no, however, there was also the problem of where I would conduct my business. Bringing clients out to the Sanctuary was not a possibility. I could see about renting an office down in Santa Cruz, but my availability for appointments would be severely limited. With all my lessons, exercises, rituals, and duties, my moms had me on an extremely rigorous schedule which afforded me precious few breaks.

A brilliantly perverse solution to the fund-raising problem bubbled up in me one evening in early March. Wouldn't you know it was during my next four-day vacation in the menstrual hut? I'm sure it was no accident that I was having my first bout with severe cramps at the time. It was almost as if my plan emerged as revenge against the pain in my womb. As if I could punish it by allowing my fantasies to turn extra nasty. The weird thing was that I could have asked my mothers for herbs to alleviate the agony, but refrained. I didn't want to be deprived of my motivating power.

I was reclining in the same black leather chair in which I'd conjured up my epiphany a month earlier. Midnight had passed, and no one else was around. It was impossible to feel dreamy and meditative, however, since my insides were being meatgrindered through an electrified driftnet made of razor-sharp wires. Instead I stared at the altar in the center of the adytum and practiced cursing all the holy objects residing there.

"You goddamn fucking piece of shit," I prayed in the direction of the magic mirror, in which it was said you could divine the flaws in your soul you needed most to correct if you hoped to die well.

Gazing straight at the precious figurine of a pregnant goddess, a sixty-five-hundred-year-old artifact recovered near Pazardzik, Bulgaria, I hissed, "You bull-cocksucking, snake shit-licking, pig-fucking whore."

Words like these had never passed through my lips before, though I'd rehearsed them mentally from time to time after discovering a book on the anthropology of obscenities some years back.

I reached out and grabbed the deck of consecrated antique Tarot cards from their stand next to the mask of Persephone. The legends of the Pomegranate Grail asserted that they were created by Artemisia Gentileschi, a seventeenth-century Italian painter who was also a member of our order. I rifled through the deck until I found the Death card. I spit on it. "You limp-dicked eater of Goddess farts," I told the dancing skeleton depicted there beneath my pool of saliva.

Replacing the deck on the altar, I seized my next victim: the Pomegranate Grail itself. My mothers firmly believed this silver cup to be the very vessel which Mary Magdalen used in the menstrual eucharist rites she established in the south of France twelve years after she fled there following Jesus' crucifixion. And oh by the way, it was also alleged to be the container with which Christ served his disciples at the Last Supper.

Though I wanted to believe in the authenticity of the tales attached to this artifact, I had my doubts. Having read extensively about the Grail, I was well aware that there were many other claimants to the title of the cup used at the Last Supper.

As usual, it came down to herstory versus history; to my ancient order's version of the course civilization had taken as opposed to everyone else's version. Outside the membership of the Pomegranate Grail, there was probably not a Biblical scholar or archaeologist alive who would keep a straight face upon hearing the legends my mothers attributed to our sacred artifact. It looked old enough, for all I knew. But the scenes configured in relief on the side of the bowl were dramatically at odds with most conceptions of Christ's message.

The vessel was about eight inches in diameter and five inches high. There were four panels around the outside circumference, each separated by the figure of a pomegranate cut open to reveal myriad seeds inside. The image on two panels was of two snakes intertwined around an equal-armed cross with a rose at the center. The other two showed a man and woman in states of union. In one panel they were copulating in a seated position. In the other, they were fused, like hermaphroditic Siamese twins, and standing in a cauldron that appeared to be a larger version of the cup itself.

Back in January, when I first examined this object—which had been off-limits to me until my menarche—I was surprised. Why did one of the Pomegranate Grail's most sacred relics portray a man in such a prominent role? I don't mean to imply that my ancient order hated everything male. While my education placed a strong emphasis on the crimes of the patriarchy, I was always taught to adore and embody the beautiful qualities of the masculine archetype. My mothers insisted that in the glorious past, male and female lived in harmonious balance, bringing out the best in each other—and that they would one day be restored to that sublime symbiosis. In the meantime, it was up to us women to embody the beauty of both genders.

Still, I wasn't fully prepared for the shock of seeing the couples portrayed on the Grail. And yet that was only a prelude to the next unexpected revelation. Back in January, on my first day back in class after my maiden voyage in the menstrual hut, my mothers had unveiled a staggering secret about the nature of my work. I was here on Earth not just to redeem the menstrual mysteries, they informed me. It was also my task to regenerate the mythic template of *hierosgamos:* sacred marriage.

There was a catch to this glorious assignment, however. I was to forever remain a virgin—not in the contemporary sense of the word, as in sexually innocent, but rather in its ancient meaning: complete unto oneself.

"You will never marry," Vimala told me with an unctuous calm that I was sure belied the nervousness she must be harboring.

"I'm supposed to spread the gospel of hierosgamos without ever being married?" I protested, disbelieving.

"You must be the husband *and* the wife," Vimala proclaimed quietly. "To compensate for the egregious imbalance unleashed when patriarchy expunged Magdalen's role in the new covenant."

The next moment was a crucifixion, an intersection of joy and anguish. My heart filled with the bountiful image of Rumbler. I immediately guessed that my clandestine bond with him in the Televisionarium—a bond Vimala knew nothing about—was the sublime solution to her grotesque puzzle. Yet another part of me feigned ignorance of this secret and raged at Vimala's unfairness. "How dare she curse me like this?!" I fumed.

It was the ultimate insult in my mothers' drive to make me their puppet.

As I reclined now in the menstrual hut and seethed over these memories, cramps ripping at my center of gravity, I gazed down at the Pomegranate Grail in my hands. Sweet blasphemy welled up in me. "I ought to masturbate you with the devil's dildo," I murmured to the cup, "you slime-collecting, twat-mocking, garbage-worshiping scuzzbucket."

I took the thing and put it on the end of my stockinged left foot. I twirled it around a few times, then kicked it up in the direction of my head. It landed on top perfectly, as if I'd been rehearsing for days. I jumped up and broke into a temple dance. It, too, was blasphemous. Here it was two and a half weeks before the spring equinox, and I was doing a dance that was forbidden to be done at any time but the feast of Samhain, October 31.

I skulked. I waggled like a demented snake. I mimed sliding down a fire pole into the infernal regions. Only once did my two-thousand-year-old silver hat fling itself off, and I caught it before it smacked the ground.

Finally I strode up to the altar and gazed into the magic mirror.

"Mirror, mirror, on the shrine:

"Speak, you bastard,

"Give me an apocalyptic sign."

The bowl was crowning me in such a way that it half-covered my big brown birthmark. I jerked my head down so that the whole ugly thing showed, then jerked it up to turn me into a beautiful woman without a flaw.

And that's when the brilliantly perverse solution flew into my evil mind. Adrenaline shot through me as my mind conjured a future event. I would sell the slime-collecting, twat-mocking, garbage-worshiping scuzzbucket. I would locate a collector of antiquities who'd be so glad to get it that he wouldn't ask many questions. Thus would I raise the small fortune I needed to run away and free my forehead of its shame.

Thus would I once and for all show the ancient order of the Pomegranate Grail that I was its boss, not the other way around.

At 2 in the morning, I sneaked out of the menstrual hut down the outside stairs—being careful to prop the door open using a thick book—and made my way to my bedroom in the Magdalen Tower fifty yards away. There I retrieved my camera and returned to capture the relic on film.

17

Live from the United Snakes of Rosicrucian Coca-Cola

You're tuned to the Televisionary Oracle

Featuring continuous updates from the Threshold between Us and Them

Where everyone who believes in the devil is the devil

Where the archetypes are mutating
and so are you

Where compassion is an aphrodisiac
and all the commercials make you smarter

Where everything you know is wrong
and yet you still have as much power as fanatics who hate

Where there are always cherries ripening
in the smoke of burning rain forests

The scene: a mother and eight-year-old daughter at a restaurant. Peering earnestly at the waitress, the girl says, "I want a hot dog, french fries, and Coke."

The mother doesn't acknowledge this declaration. "My daughter will have the bean salad, plain yogurt, and grapefruit juice," she asserts.

Turning to the girl, the waitress asks, "Do you want ketchup with it?"

The girl beams at the waitress and muses to herself, "She thinks I'm real."

The moral of the story: Make sure that you hang out as much as possible with people like the waitress.

This experiment in adoration
is brought to you by Telepathics Anonymous,
a 13-step program for those who're never sure
where other people's feelings leave off
and their own begin.

Are you one of the millions of Americans
suffering from chronic psychic contagion?
Telepathics Anonymous offers living proof
that the Cult of Scientism
doesn't have a clue
about how human minds continually overlap.

As a get-acquainted gift,
the professional boundary-setters at Telepathics Anonymous
would like to present you with an omen
concerning the future of an illusion
you love a little too much.
Look for it exactly seventy-one hours and twenty-five minutes
from right NOW!

18

I force myself to open my dreamy eyes and sit up. The Eater of Cruelty
gallery is empty except for two lesbians speaking with their lips barely
an inch away from each other. Rapunzel-Clone is nowhere to be seen.

Checking my blurry watch, I see I'm scheduled to hit the big stage
in less than two hours, and I haven't even begun yet to conjure up the
conditions necessary to pull off a masterpiece of chaos therapy for the
audience tonight.

I stagger out of the place. My solar plexus is radiating superheated
ripples in all directions, my eyes are detecting all the elementals and
astral sprites they're usually blind to, and my heart is utterly purged of
waste.

As I trundle towards the Catalyst, I feel a mix of guilt and glee. I've
been uncommonly irresponsible. For the first time in I-don't-know-
how-long, I haven't spent the last four hours before a show obsessing
over my preparatory tasks. My stage props aren't in order, nor are my
various costume changes organized on the rack behind the stage. I
haven't done my yoga headstands and stretches, kundalini fire-breath-
ing exercises, or meditations on how to translate the special mojo of
this particular moment in time into specially-tailored shamanic tricks
that'll grab audience members in their guts. I'm very late if I expect
to be able to complete my usual routine of vocal warm-ups, improvisational drills, and practice in the art of falling apart. (It's always a
good idea to annihilate my self-importance and divest myself of all
my opinions before a show.)

All this feels overwhelming in light of the fact that my comrades and I have slotted a full two hours and forty-five minutes of entertainment tonight, including but not limited to money-burning, dirt-eating, puppet-fucking, and anarchist flag-desecrating. Also on the agenda are twenty-two beautifully outrageous songs scientifically formulated to blow minds, as well as an authentic sacred ritual (certified as such by a genuine native Slovakian-American goofball shaman, me), a radical new form of aerobics that requires participants to smoke cigarettes while doing half-naked jumping jacks, and the teaching to the crowd of a metaphysical cheerleader mantra based on both the linguistic theories and the political ranting of my hero Noam Chomsky.

It looks bad for the possibility that my ass will be fully in gear by the time these assignments come due.

On the other hand, I haven't felt this emotionally ripe in weeks. And I know from experience that that's an excellent omen. Any time I'm overflowing with googoo gaga, my acting ability soars, as do my improvisational skills. Ergo, I may not be as tightly-packed as usual, but I'm confident I'll make up for it with limber surprises and a stirring performance.


Two blocks from the Catalyst, I happen by a telephone pole bearing one of the posters I made to advertise our gig. I stop to admire my handiwork, at the same time remembering how humiliated I felt at having to putter around town on my bike putting them all up myself. That's what happens when you fire your corporate caretakers, your CBSs and Will Boehm Managements.

The image on the poster is of a television with a screen that's blank except for the words "Your Face Here." The text below the TV:

WORLD ENTERTAINMENT WAR
the West Coast's premier Jungian beatnik funk band
is throwing
AN AFTER-THE-END-OF-THE-WORLD PARTY
to celebrate the resurrection of your hopes and dreams,
which most assuredly will occur
if you show your beautiful face.

Wear pajamas, a bunny disguise, a skimpy bathing suit, formal wear,
or the costume of the person you'll be five years from now!

Prepare your polished or ridiculous
two-minute song, dance, joke, story, prayer, brag, stunt, or spectacle
in case we decide to stage a sprawling spontaneous version
of our Audience Performance Rites!

It all happens at the Catalyst,
Pacific Garden Mall in Santa Cruz.
Special guests will include
sexy Islamic celebrities, personal growth-addicts,
unoriginal sinners, image-looters,
Aphrodite's chosen people, and YOU!

For a measly ten bucks you'll be treated
to a radical form of musical therapy
that could make you one of the most creative people
who has ever lived

In two blocks I'm at the nightclub. I won't be able to get in the back
door at this late hour. The bouncers have no doubt locked it up. I'll
have to barge in through the front. Ahhh. A beautiful sight: There's a
long line of people waiting to buy tickets. Good chance there'll be a
sell-out tonight.

The ticket guy recognizes me and waves me through, as do the
bouncers just inside the door. I bolt for the stairway leading to the dressing room, shouting hey and doing little dances to acknowledge the
people that recognize me.

Once upstairs, I linger on the balcony overlooking the anteroom to
the dance floor. Out there the mood is already cranked up halfway to
pandemonium. Everyone in sight is holding a glass or bottle and ges-
ticulating like an actor in the play "Marat-Sade." This may be New
Age, super-feminist Santa Cruz, but the vistas of exposed flesh are still
vast and eye-popping. I don't deny myself the pleasure of gawking
(discreetly, because you never know when you'll be busted for doing
what you've been invited to do) at the cleavages and midriffs.

Mating games, though cloaked in nonsexist language and taking into account the critiques of leftist heroes like Howard Zinn and Susan Faludi, are nevertheless raging with the intensity of a college fraternity mixer. The buzz of myriad conversations, fueled by pheromones, is at jet-engine levels. Yum. I drink in the aromatic elixir of beer and sweat and cigarette smoke. (Do I also detect a tincture of marijuana in there?) Feels like home to me. I wonder how many orgasms will unfold later tonight because of what's foreplaying here now.

Up in the dressing room, all the band members are primping and costuming themselves. Keyboardist and back-up vocalist Amy shows me her recent addition, a cobalt-blue tattoo of an old Celtic design stretching around a strip of shaved skull from ear to ear. She's mixing goth with hippie styles tonight, long black funereal gown contradicted by a green and purple spangled vest and red leather army boots. Despite her talent for pulling off a royally bombastic stage persona with humor and elegance, Amy is one of the least pretentious people I know. There's not a femme fatale bone in her body. She's clear, trustworthy: an even-tempered friend.

That wasn't apparent, though, in the beginning. Amy was a precocious seventeen years old when I discovered her singing and playing flute in a primitive little performance art duo at the Louden Nelson Community Center. At our first meeting she arrived bedecked with enough jewels for the Queen of Sweden, her purple and green hair stiffly sprayed and splayed like peacock feathers, and dressed in gauzy sexy layers of black and red satin. I knew immediately she wanted to fall in love with me. But I forbade it. Couldn't indulge it. She was more useful to me as a versatile keyboardist, flautist, and singer than as an underage girlfriend. I soon became pleased with my restraint. Her versatile musicianship turned into the melodic glue that wove together the disparate quirky geniuses that comprised our band. While she unfurled on stage all the same glitz she'd invoked to try to seduce me, off stage she was earthy and wise.

My co-lead singer Darby is a ravishing earth momma-cum-diva, her long natural brunette shag and all-American good looks contrasting with her silver mini-dress and black fishnets. I'm sure that her voice tonight, as it is every night, will be a freaking miracle. Though I'm proud of my own singing and work hard on honing it, I'm always half-intimidated by Darby's seemingly effortless ability to send chills of awe down a listener's spine. With both the torrid robustness of a Janis Joplin and the savvy class of an Annie Lennox, she's a provocateur of rich emotion. Not that she has ever once acknowledged that her voice is in a class above mine. Like Amy, she's eerily unspoiled and easygoing.

I always laugh when I think of where I discovered her. Resembling a Nebraskan hippie, with cut-off jeans, birkenstocks, and red and white checked shirt tied at the waist, she was singing in an old shed at a Sunday afternoon party held for the teams in the softball league I played in. Even then, as raw as she was, her voice surpassed that of every white woman I'd ever heard.

George the guitarist is just as gorgeous as the two women. With his huge mane of black hair, bushy eyebrows, and big Greek leonine face, he's a charismatic king of beasts. He also has one of the most graceful characters of any man I know. Self-effacing, sensitive, and secretly compassionate as hell, he's very lovable. Sure, his inexhaustible creativity is linked to his inveterate pot-smoking, but that's not a problem. The world won't be running out of marijuana any time soon.

Tonight he's wearing an iridescent green waistcoat over a starched white shirt, black leather pants, and knee-high black boots that resemble the style of the men's men who live on the island of Crete. I fantasize that in dressing like this he's unconsciously paying homage to the father he never knew, a radical leftist Greek sea captain who was (so the story goes) mysteriously kidnapped by a cult of Turkish ecstatic dancers.

Rounding out the beauty contest up here in the dressing room is bassist Daniel, a strapping lad who unlike the rest of us always dresses on stage exactly how he does on the street, which tonight means he's donned a rainbow-hued Peruvian vest and purple Tibetan lama hat to go with his black jeans and workboots. Of all the people in the band, Daniel is the one with whom I get in the most scrapes. We usually disagree on matters of discipline—I want more, he less. But for all that, my run-ins with him average only three or four times a year—a tiny amount considering how much time we spend together. And I really do love him. He's a mad poet at heart, as tricky as me but not quite as enslaved by logic and reason as I can be.

As a musician, he's a wonderworker, magically blending a flowing, melodic sensibility with a telepathic instinct for the killer groove. He's one of those brilliant bassists who's too harmonically serpentine to merely serve as the understated rhythmic anchor. And yet as much as he explores orchestral flourishes, he never lets the beat wander.

Drummer Anthony, a.k.a. Squint, embodies the strange mix of lunacy and integrity the rest of us share, though he took a different route to earn it. Raised by a born-again Christian mother in a redneck town in central California (where he comes from, Denny's is the best restaurant in town), he was just thirteen when he began touring with a country band fronted by a gentleman cowboy who was trying to teach himself quantum physics. After years of nightclubbing, taking drum lessons with world beat experts, and doing stints with drone-metal bands, Squint landed a gig playing on the first two albums of Camper Van Beethoven, a band that achieved national prominence. When he joined World Entertainment War, he was already more famous than me.

Squint's rhythms are wild but precise; his passions fiery but righteous; his loyalty to the cause unflagging and ever-fresh. He won't even bother to wear a shirt tonight. This is wise, since he plays with such soldierly vigor that anything he wore on the top half of his body would be soaked with sweat after the first two songs.

I say a silent prayer to the Goddess to give thanks for these beautiful and talented people, who after all these years I still feel the most tender affection for. The bands I'd been in before this one were too often the worst mix of dysfunctional family and bickering co-workers. And before that, my collaborative group experience consisted of baseball teams crammed with posturing teenage macho jocks who would punch you out in a second if you were stupid enough to utter the prissy word "collaboration." To match the playful goodwill of the group energy I enjoy now, I'd have to go back to the pick-up baseball games of childhood.

Yup, the members of World Entertainment War, though not without flaws and annoying idiosyncrasies, are by far the sweetest-tempered, most symbiotically coordinated troop of humans I've ever encountered. Having previously grown accustomed to believing that it's the nature of *Homo sapiens* in groups to engage in endless politicking motivated by egotistical drives and hidden agendas, I feel as if I've happened upon a utopian mix that disproves my cynicism.

"Want a drag?" Squint asks rhetorically, offering me a joint in full knowledge I'll turn it down. I'm notorious for my abstention with the pot connoisseurs in the band.

In reply I hold up my own drugs of choice. First, there's a tall-necked Budweiser, which all my pot-smoking friends deride me for ever since NORML, the National Organization to Reform Marijuana Laws, exposed Bud's parent company as a big lobbyist for anti-pot legislation. Second, there's a styrofoam cup full of 7-Eleven coffee—a ritual necessity for all my performances ever since I was fifteen, when I first noticed the way it perked up my baseball skills.

"I've got everything I need right here," I announce. My formula is one bottle of Bud and sixteen ounces of the caffeinated stuff in the hour before the show, supplemented by one further beer and an additional eight ounces of coffee on stage. The beer isn't enough to get me drunk, which I certainly can't afford to be given how many tasks I have to concentrate on and coordinate while on stage. But it does serve as the mechanism by which I magically convert from a hermetic alchemist to an outrageous extrovert. Maybe someday I'll learn how to wangle that transformation without the aid of my caffeine and alcohol cocktail.

My artist friend and helper Marijka emerges from the bathroom and starts unbuttoning my shirt, the Menstrual Temple tunic that Rapunzel gave me way back when. Was it only a few hours ago? "Come on, big guy, strip," Marijka says. "Where've you been? We've got less than our allotted time to turn you into Jesus Pan."

"Jesus Dionysus," I correct her.

"Same dude, *n'est-ce pas?*"

She grabs her body paints and a chair while I prepare the canvas, my chest and abdomen. As I stand in front of her, she begins creating the image I've specified: not a Hallmark Valentine but a realistic, anatomically correct human heart at the top of which a flaming cross sprouts. Wrapped around the middle of the lurid organ is a band of crisscrossing thorns which in one place rips open the red flesh, causing a rain of blood to shower down on a single white rose. Marijka has rehearsed this painting on my chest twice in the past week, so it materializes swiftly now.

As she toils, my assistant Erica works on another part of my costume. First she fits the rubber goat ears over the outside of my real ones. They've been carefully altered to allow me to hear without any muffling. Then she slides on a plastic headband that's surmounted by two prominent goat horns. In recent shows I've been wearing my very long brown hair in a topknot, like a Samurai clown, but tonight Erica's brushing it into the Jesus-style.

When they're done, I slip off my shoes, socks, and pants, gleeful at the casual unisex atmosphere backstage which makes it no big deal for the men to change clothes in front of women or vice versa. Then I pull on the furry greyish-brown leggings and slippers Marijka has fashioned for me out of real goatskins.

"How do I look?" I ask Marijka.

"I'm reminded of a passage from Plutarch," she muses.

"You are?" I reply, surprised. "I had no idea you were a classical scholar."

"Actually, this is the only passage from Plutarch I know. I heard it from my ex-boyfriend, the Christ-phobic professor of ancient religions. Plutarch tells a story about a sailor on a boat in the Aegean Sea. It's during the time Tiberius is Roman emperor. The sailor hears a spooky disembodied voice say three times, 'When you reach Palodes, proclaim that the Great God Pan is dead.' It just so happens this is the precise moment Christianity is hatching in Judea."

"Yeah, well, I'm here to offer a bozo-ish cure for that tragic schism in the spiritual yearning of humanity."

"You're halfway there, big guy. Ready to materialize the fullness of the archetype on stage?"

"Let me go have a conference with myself first."

I lock myself in the bathroom. Closing the lid of the toilet, I sit down, bury my face in my hands, and begin my peptalk. Three years ago I would have been horrified to hear the blasphemous words I feel obligated to tell myself now. But after more than a year and a half of silly exile in the limbo of corporate hackdom, I have to ritually remind myself of what the hell I'm here for.

I AM NOT A ROCKSTAR. I HAVE NEVER BEEN A ROCKSTAR. I WILL NEVER BE A ROCKSTAR.

I affirm this aloud now in front of myself and the Goddess. I broadcast it from every synapse, driving it deep into my subconscious mind, as well as into the subconscious minds of any fans, music critics, record executives, radio programmers, or evil demons that might be working, advertently or inadvertently, to subvert my intention. I will never ever again place myself in danger of diverging from the One Righteous Path of My Destiny.

Am not a rockstar. Am not a rockstar. Am not a rockstar. Am not a rockstar. Am not a rockstar. Thus has it always been and thus shall it always be.

I'm not an inarticulate, barely educated elitist pretending to be a cultural hero disguised as a nihilistic outlaw.

I'm not a narcissistic vampire of mob energy who delights in staging onanistic, ear-numbing spectacles for eager-to-be-hypnotized voyeurs.

I'm not a smarmy opportunist sucking up to jaded cynics whose newspaper reviews might possibly pump up my stardom another octave.

I am not a sulking megalomaniacal celebrity squandering millions of dollars on high-tech hocus-pocus in order to record for posterity a handful of cliché-crammed four-minute songs that'll earn me enough money to buy my own private jet.

I am not a sexist dickhead bent on exploiting and relishing the misogynist traditions of rock and roll.

I am not the patriarchy's crowning achievement: the goddamn fucking hero; the all-conquering, greedy-for-glory, kill-everything-that-doesn't-adore-me and fuck-everything-that-adores-me, eternally adolescent ego.

I am not a rockstar. I have never been a rockstar. I will never be a rockstar.

But I *am* a singer. I love to feel the sweet, fierce, loud, moist sounds coalescing in my body and then rushing out of my throat in a wild but disciplined stream of loving voodoo. I love to move people to intelligent tears and gritty ecstasy with the power of my melodic words.

I *am* a dancer. I love stumbling around the stage like a slinky fool, whipping up the exalted emotions of a writhing, intoxicated crowd.

I *am* a pagan priest. I love to throw wild parties that are also sacred rituals, spiritual orgies disguised as rock and roll shows.

I *am* a dionysian bard and shamanic clown and guerrilla therapist. I love to channel coyote angel jokes from some higher part of my brain that I don't normally have access to—all in the sacred service of bringing the true goofy religion to my tribe.

I *am* a lover. I don't live to be worshiped, but to worship.

I AM NOT A ROCKSTAR. I HAVE NEVER BEEN A ROCKSTAR. I WILL NEVER BE A ROCKSTAR.

Amen.

Which leads logically to the question: Then how the hell did I end up signing contracts with two huge corporations that rank among the world's most ambitious perpetrators of the rockstar fantasy? Through what inconceivable sequence of events did I become a puppet for one of the most cartoony of all archetypes?

Yes, I owe myself an explanation. If I hate being a rockstar so frigging much, why did I marry my fortunes to: 1) the entertainment conglomerate CBS, and 2) WBM, the management company founded by rock demi-god Will Boehm? Am I a liar? A hypocrite? A self-deluded poseur?

19

You're tuned to the Televisionary Oracle
a pseudonym for a multinational corporation
composed of psychics, psychologists, and private detectives
who know more about you than you know about yourself

FAKE OUT

You're tuned to the Televisionary Oracle
a cover story for
time-travelers from the future
who are impersonating
the still small voice of your guardian angel

FAKE OUT

You're tuned to the Televisionary Oracle
entirely a creation of your imagination
and a repository for all your projections
about the caretaker
you've always wanted

FAKE OUT

You're tuned to the Televisionary Oracle
et cetera

For our first discussion on the history of spiritual pranks, beauty and truth fans, we turn to a performance by the renowned sixteenth-century physician Paracelsus.

First a little background on the man. Like Johannes Kepler, who was both astronomer and astrologer, Paracelsus was one of those rare scientists capable of living in the Drivetime. On the one hand he was a full-on, no-apologies alchemist who loved to commune with the spirits. On the other, he was an influential medical reformer who articulated a new model for disease. Previously it was thought to result from imbalances in the body's humors. Paracelsus replaced it with the theory that external agents attacked the body and could be driven out with chemicals.

He was named to the chair of medicine at the University of Basel in 1524. Soon after, he made a most astounding promise. He said he had discovered the Elixir of Life, the true Philosopher's Stone, and would reveal it to the students and faculty in a public demonstration.

On the appointed day, the hall of learning filled with curious but skeptical scholars. Before him on a table, Paracelsus set a large jar covered with black cloth. For three long hours he lectured on the First Matter, the raw material of the Elixir of Life. He quoted from Philalethes, who said that the First Matter is "a virgin who meets her wooers in foul garments." The Qabalists, Paracelsus noted, advised the seeker after truth to find the First Matter in "the stone that the Builders rejected." Even Pythagoras himself claimed the Philosopher's Stone could be made from a substance that the rabble look upon as being the vilest thing on Earth.

As the learned men grew impatient, shifting restlessly in their seats, Paracelsus finally circled to his climax. "Discarded daily as worthless refuse," he boomed, "eternally scorned and devalued, it is now ready, through my sponsorship, to receive its well-deserved due. In the bowels of the Earth have I found it. In the sewers and the gutters and the wasted places. And now, behold. The mystery is unveiled." Whereupon Paracelsus lifted the black cloth with a flourish and revealed . . . a pile of shit.

Instantly there was a storm of howling and stamping. Outraged, his colleagues denounced him as a fraud and exhibitionist. "If you knew how misguided you are," he shouted back, "you would make the sign of the cross on yourselves with a fox's tail."

Four centuries later, Carl Jung used dry, scholarly language to drive home the same point that an earlier performance artist, Paracelsus, had so amusingly made in Basel. The process of individuation and the awakening of the Self, Jung said, must begin by addressing the *shadow*— the disowned and ugly aspects of the personality.


This sneak preview
of the music of the spheres
is brought to you by
VULTURE CULTURE,
the fan club
for those specialists
that eat the rot
and transform it into fuel.
Like the ancient Egyptians,
we regard vultures as compassionate purifiers
sacred to the Goddess
because they process the rotting flesh of the corpse,
thereby expediting the soul's transition to heaven.

**20**

**D**efine your problem crisply and bluntly, my mothers have always taught me. Meditate on the truth that the universe is a problem-solving machine, and that you always stir up hidden forces to work in your behalf when you provide the universe with a beautiful problem to solve. Then relax with perfect confidence and make yourself available for the solution to find you.

Using this artful technique, I tracked down the collector of antiquities within a week. First I composed a precise description of the person I wanted, the nature of our interaction, and the money that would come my way. Next I incubated a dream about how to bring this person into my life. In two of my dreams that night I was hanging out in a certain cafe in Santa Cruz, Caffé Pergolesi.

My third step was to go do in waking life what I had done in my dreams. Stealing all the time away from the Sanctuary I could, I parked myself at Pergolesi and waited. During my third watch I met a forty-year-old antiques dealer who became obsessed with my ability to tell her what she was thinking and to prognosticate her future. In return for me providing these unofficial services (which ultimately led to her making three lucrative finds she would never have stumbled across without me), she connected me with an associate from Carmel who was seriously interested in the artifact I had to sell.

It all happened so easily, I couldn't help but interpret it as a sign to proceed with my plan. This helped quell the doubts that had begun to creep in about whether I was doing the right thing.

It wasn't the annihilation of the splotch I felt queasy about. Not in the least. That was a righteous quest I regarded as my birthright. But I was having trouble rationalizing the theft and sale of the Grail. I knew that for my mothers, it was precious beyond imagining. They believed it possessed a magical mojo that could dramatically enhance the link between Goddess and anyone who touched it. And though I was bent on waging a secret holy war with them, I also loved them with all of my surgically repaired heart.

My forehead belonged to me, which gave me the inalienable right to do with it as I saw fit; the Grail did not.

Unless. Unless I really *had* been Mary Magdalen in a previous incarnation. In which case the cup of destiny *was* mine.

So was I or was I not Mary Magdalen? Was I or was I not the long-prophesied avatar of the Pomegranate Grail? As was true of every other aspect of my life, I had always been of two minds about those questions.

My mothers never expressed the slightest doubt that I was the Chosen One. I'd studied all the hoary texts, and indeed it seemed that my story fulfilled every detail of the ancient oracle. And through the years I had found myself, in countless dreams and meditative visions (more than a few in Melted Popsicle Land and the Televisionarium), vividly acting out scenes from the life of a girl and woman I thought of as Mary Magdalen. Some of these scenes, it's true, I had read or heard about before my mystical extrapolation of them. But many others were unrecorded in the herstories of the Pomegranate Grail. No one, for example, could confirm or deny my assertion that I sometimes wore the foreskin of Jesus as a ring on the middle finger of my left hand.

On the other hand, my mothers had pounded home to me the dangers of hubris with the same relentlessness with which they'd programmed me to believe I was the exalted messenger of Persephone. My ministry would not thrive, they assured me, if I recapitulated the sins of the patriarchy—that is, if as a charismatic leader I felt I was better than everyone and thought I was immune to the laws of karma. They'd trained me, furthermore, to have a healthy (not knee-jerk) skepticism towards all claims of transcendent glory and authority. Mine was not a blind faith. While I loved sacred magic, I always made damn sure it was the real thing before I gave myself to it.

Under the guidance of my mothers—and maybe because that's the way Goddess made me—I became and still am a raging contradiction: a logical mystic, a faithful doubter, a scientific pragmatist powered by myth and poetry.

Was I Mary Magdalen? Was I the female messiah? The answer was *yes and no*. Not *yes* when I was in an inflated, thaumaturgic mood and *no* when I was in a hard-ass, realistic frame. The answer was always *yes and no*, emphasis on *and*. In other words, both *yes* and *no* were true at the same time. *Yes* being true didn't make *no* untrue, and vice versa.

Reincarnation was an objective fact; the exact same "spirit" that inhabited the form of Mary Magdalen was now animating my body; the Pomegranate Grail was an ancient mystery school that had secretly preserved the occult feminine mysteries during the dark ages of patriarchy; I was now preparing to finish the mission that was foiled two thousand years ago ...

## AND

Reincarnation was an unprovable theory; Mary Magdalen was a great teacher with whom I had tremendous resonance if not shared consciousness; the Pomegranate Grail was a source of healing inspiration even if it suffered from delusions of grandeur; and I was perhaps nothing more than a bright young girl being pumped full of projections by smart but frustrated idealists.

I had no choice but to apply this method to every self-inquiry. Was I a blessed exception with a special gift? Or just another narcissistic nobody in a world full of narcissistic nobodies? Was it my job to spread love and healing to everyone I encountered? Or else to ruthlessly destroy every illusion and prejudice? Should I strive to transcend or avoid every experience that brought me pain? Or should I embrace pain as my teacher and express gratitude for its power to motivate me? *Yes and no.*

As I contemplated the prospect of stealing and selling the Grail, I arrived at an exhilarating new edge. Though I had long felt a sneaky respect for my double-mindedness, this new application of the principle, in a situation that would have dramatic practical consequences, seemed to have ripened it into a new maturity. All these years I had borne the subliminal expectation that one day my contradictions would drop away and I would see with a unified eye and heart. Now I was finally ready to dispense with that infantile delusion.

I considered the probability that my double-mindedness was not a wounded state needing to be healed. It was a profoundly accurate reflection of the blessed nature of life on Earth.

*Crucifixion.* I understood that term in a fresh way. To be authentically and fully alive is to be symbolically crucified. No. More than that. To be fully and authentically alive is to be crucified without feeling tortured. Or else to be crucified and feel tortured, but exult that you have fully awakened to and accepted the heroic assignment of every single person who incarnates on this planet, which is to be eternally torn between heaven and earth, between spirit and body, between light and shadow.

Only the *inbetween* is real.

I saw that the doctrine of the crucifixion as transmogrified by the Christian church was half-baked. It lacked Magdalen's—my?—contribution. As usual, the patriarchy crippled the feminine element of the archetype, then overliteralized what was left, leaving a garish cartoon. "Jesus died for our sins"—what tired old redundant bullshit! Sun gods had already been getting sacrificially slaughtered for eons by the time my consort and I showed up.

You'd never know it by asking Peter or Paul, but Jesus and I actually had the intention of unveiling a fresh, new show. "Get this, friends," we intimated. "We're here to abolish the one-dimensional myth of the solo hero and replace it with the template of the divine collaborators. *Two* crafty souls together, male and female as equals, aiding and abetting each other's gutsy quest to live gracefully in heaven and earth at the same time."

The further implication of this innovation was that if there was indeed more than one god-inflamed avatar, why couldn't there be *many* more? We refuted the tradition of there being just one towering messiah who alone, among multitudes of plain old ordinary humans, possessed the key to the kingdom of heaven. Jesus and I were, in other words, the Great Examples, not the Great Exceptions. *Anyone* could master the art of being both god and human. Indeed, that was the divine plan.

I became drunk on this insight. It was by no means the first time I'd generated a unique philosophical eruption that fell outside the dogma of the Pomegranate Grail. But it felt bigger than any of my previous apostasies. It wasn't the result, as had usually been the case, of my polemical intellect straining to sharpen its claws. It was a creative distillation and apotheosis of my visceral life experience.

What if? I began to ruminate. What if there's more where this came from? What if there's a flood of new wrinkles primed to pour out of me? And what if these novelties, rather than being sour and irrelevant departures from the Pomegranate Grail party line, hail the emergence of a new covenant that will reinvigorate our ancient order? Maybe it was my job not merely to disseminate the neglected teachings, but to shatter the mold: to mutate and expand them.

If that were the case, I could think of no better symbolic act than to lose the Grail. Maybe it really was infused with mojo that could literally charge up anyone who touched it. But might it not also have the dubious power to keep believers locked into outworn ways of linking up to the Goddess?

I headed straight into the ironic hypocrisy at the heart of the Pomegranate Grail. The form of Goddess that its members worshiped above all others was Persephone, She who demands ceaseless change as the price of eternal life. And yet they had clung to the old principles, the old texts, the old prophecies for millennia. It was understandable, utterly forgivable: to be conservative and preservative in the face of the repressive horrors of the patriarchy. The sacred secrets could not have survived any other way.

But now *I* had arrived: the avatar of the Queen of Death; servant of She who lovingly breaks the old containers to make way for the shock of the new. There could be no doubt that I had been Mary Magdalen, because only the reborn Mary Magdalen could understand and articulate Persephone's latest dispensation: the radical logic of *yes AND no;* the annihilation—no, the transcendence—of the infantile *Us versus Them.*

"For what sort of mind wrestling with what sort of issue is the ideology of oppositionalism so useful?" wrote James Hillman, one of the geniuses I had discovered in my quest for wisdom beyond the canon my mothers had provided. "The heroic ego," he answered himself, "who divides so he can conquer. Antithetical thinking, found by Albert Adler to be a neurotic habit of mind, belongs to the will to power and the masculine protest."

I was without a doubt Mary Magdalen because I had mastered the perspective that allowed me to see I was both Mary Magdalen and not Mary Magdalen.

And since I was Mary Magdalen, the holy bowl was my personal prop to do with as I saw fit in order to advance the goals of the Pomegranate Grail.

My last night at the Sanctuary was the fourth day of the fourth month. I was in the fourth day of my fourth menstrual period. Four fours: a propitious omen to launch the new covenant. Numerologically, four means order, system, control, command.

I waited until the last entranced drummer retired from her shamanic quest in the music room (Sibyl was visiting her own death, guided by her astral vulture ally, Cronos) and until the questers in the sweat lodge shuffled off to the dream incubation chamber (Burgundy was hoping to receive a "medicine vision" that would relieve some of the paralyzing panic that had gripped her during her mother's battle with pancreatic cancer).

Shortly after 2:30 A.M., I tucked the Pomegranate Grail under my red silk-clad arm and left the menstrual hut via the outdoor stairs. With a flashlight I made my way to the place in the nearby woods where I'd stashed plastic garbage bags containing two leather tote bags full of essentials. I jammed my red silk robe and gown inside one of the plastic bags and stuffed it under a holly bush, then changed into black pants, black blouse, and black leather jacket.

It was here where my master plan almost got derailed. With a twinge of fear, my heart yearned and stretched in the direction of the burned-out redwood tree, a couple hundred yards away, which had hosted my ritual escape to Melted Popsicle Land and the Televisionarium for more than ten years. How long would it be before I could return to it? Would I be able to open the doors to the Televisionarium with the same ease from a new location in Marin County? Most pressingly, what would happen to my life with Rumbler? I had no doubt that we would continue to meet regularly in dreams; I was sure I would feel his comforting and arousing but elusive presence from time to time during my daily rhythms; but I felt less sanguine about the rendezvous we invoked with the aid of my ritual popsicle sticks.

As if in answer to an unformulated prayer, Rumbler surged into me right then. He didn't "speak." I got no specific message from him. But I felt enormously comforted. It was like getting a hug on the inside; like my heart filling up with "I'll Fly Away," a favorite old gospel song from childhood. Automatically, without willing it, I relaxed. My natural confidence returned. I felt united with my decision. Leaving the woods, I headed to the parking area at the other end of the compound.

I probably could have fired up the Honda without waking anyone. But just to be safe, I put it in neutral and rolled it silently maybe a hundred yards down our long driveway-road. Only when I was far out of earshot of even the guest cottages at the Sanctuary did I turn the ignition.

Forty minutes later I was enjoying coffee, scrambled eggs, and tapioca pudding at the Golden West in Santa Cruz—the same all-night restaurant where my biological mom and dad used to love to hang out. I wondered where they were at that exact moment. Magda was probably asleep in her little shack in Live Oak, a few miles from here. As for Jerome, nobody had heard from him for a few years, but I liked to think that wherever he was on the physical plane, his astral self was engaged in some righteous work with Joan of Arc or Anne Hutchinson or Jesus.

At 6:30 A.M. I left, drove downtown, and parked the car on Cedar Street. Then I hoofed it to the Greyhound bus station, where I caught a bus to San Francisco. I slept on the way, thank Goddess. My dreams were invigorating. In one I was planting lightning bolts in black loamy dirt near my redwood husk temple. In another I was inside a silver bathtub balanced on the crest of a tidal wave that was also a fountain.

The bus arrived in the big city around 9:30. Two hours later I was in a room at the Fairmont Hotel atop Nob Hill, showing Mr. Anthony Barso the relic he'd only seen photos of up till now. Elsa, my friend from Caffè Pergolesi, was also there to offer moral support. The tentative deal we'd arranged in the previous weeks was that Barso would pay me seven thousand five hundred dollars for the bowl: one thousand five hundred dollars up front as a deposit, and the remainder within three weeks, after he had a chance to run tests on it to confirm its age and authenticity.

Barso was not a demonstrative person, but I could tell he was pleased when he first touched my precious. On the other hand, he either didn't care that the bowl was the Grail, or pretended that he didn't. The age, the quality of the silver, and the unusual artwork seemed to be his main concerns. He indicated in a detached tone that he had seen this same group of symbols only once, and that was on an eighteen-hundred-year-old chalice.

By the time room service brought up our sandwiches, Barso was counting out seventy-five twenty-dollar bills.

The transaction was shady by necessity. We had a written document, but I knew there was no way I could enforce it if he really wanted to flimflam me. One favorable sign was the assurances I'd gotten from Elsa, who had known Barso for years and sincerely believed he wouldn't cheat me. Elsa was half in love with me; I could sense the same awed protectiveness coming from her as I'd felt so often from my mothers.

By 3 P.M. I was on a northbound bus for Marin County. As I crossed the Golden Gate Bridge, I pulled one of my new twenty-dollar bills out of the wad and rubbed it on my forehead in a silly act of sympathetic magic.

Somehow I had managed, until that moment, to ward off all thoughts of the grief I might be causing my mothers. I'd been aflame with visions of the scoured new face that awaited me. My imagination had also been toying with fantasies of what I would do if the chiefs of the Pomegranate Grail renounced and banished me. I couldn't believe they'd resort to that, but if they did, I was prepared to launch my own damn mystery school. It would be anchored in the old teachings but fueled by the epiphanies that awaited me.

Unexpectedly, though, as massive Mt. Tamalpais loomed to my left and sparkling Richardson Bay to my right, Vimala's devastation was pouring into me without any censorship whatsoever. I was not projecting or imagining what she felt. Her actual emotional state was being reconfigured in me. I'd had this experience before, but never at such a great distance (when had we ever been separated so thoroughly?), and never saturated with such anguish. I didn't know the thoughts that went with it. Had she already discovered that the Grail was missing? Surely this much pain couldn't have been stirred simply by my as-yet short-term absence. She couldn't possibly know yet that this was the beginning of a time of travail for her. Could she?

My master plan was vague on this point. Would I let my mothers know with a brief phone message that I was all right, even as I continued to hide my whereabouts from them? Or should I make a complete break, maintain utter silence, and require them to wander in limbo, terrified of what had become of me? The former would increase my risk of being found and would make it more difficult to carry out my grand experiment free of their vibes. The latter would be cruel but might be necessary if I hoped to sustain the resolve I'd need to transform myself.

By 5:30 I was checking into the slightly seedy but cheap and serviceable Villa Inn, about three-fourths of a mile from downtown San Rafael. My room had a kitchenette, and there was a coin-operated laundry room on the premises.

I loved the name of the motel. If you shoved together the two words in "Villa Inn," you got "Villain(n)"—the perfect hiding place for a renegade avatar.

No one in the world had any idea where I was, not even Elsa. I'd told her I was bound for Santa Rosa.


What I was looking for in a plastic surgeon was similar to what I liked in a gynecologist: a frank, earthy, voluble woman. The Yellow Pages were full of female doctors, and I began calling them on my first morning in my new digs. Dr. Lilith Elfland quickly emerged as the clear favorite. Her receptionist said they'd had a cancellation, and I could come in that very afternoon. Besides that, I liked her name. The ancient Hebraic heroine Lilith, much revered in the traditions of the Pomegranate Grail, was Adam's first wife, and a far feistier companion than Eve, the naive babe who replaced her.

A nurse led me into an examination room and wrote on a clipboard as I answered questions about my medical history and reason for my visit. Wanting to keep things simple, I didn't mention the heart surgery I'd had as a baby. I had my fake Oklahoma birth certificate in my bag, but she didn't ask for it.

Five minutes after she left, Dr. Elfland entered.

"Rapunzel, Rapunzel, push back your hair," she greeted me, throwing what I took to be a bemused glance at the spot where my bangs covered up my birthmark.

I was taken aback at her jocularity, and overcompensated by being much too quick to pin back my forehead hair with bobby pins.

"I don't think I've come across that name in thirty-eight years," she said, leaning against the edge of the metal-framed bed to face me. "Since I was six years old sitting on my mama's lap."

She was shorter than me, about five feet, six inches, and thin for a woman her age. Her black frizzy hair bordered on being an afro, and she wore no make-up that I could see—both unusual touches. I liked her immediately. My off-the-cuff telepathic scan registered her as smart and free-thinking yet kind.

"You know, I can't remember how that story ended," she continued, pushing beyond the boundaries of light introductory banter. "Her step-mother banished her from the tower, right? And sent her into the wasteland? Then what? The usual fairy tale BS about the handsome young prince saving her?"

"No, actually. More like the other way around. Rapunzel and the prince found each other by accident in the wasteland. Her tears fell on his eyes and cured the blindness he'd suffered when he jumped out of the tower escaping from the witch."

"Well, that's good to hear. A happy feminist ending."

"Yeah, except for the fact that the prince had made Rapunzel pregnant right before they got separated. Twins, it turned out. A boy and a girl. She had to give birth by herself out in the hinterlands, then raise them by herself on roots and berries."

"Booooo."

"Well, but there's this. Once she and the prince made it back to the home of his dad the king, I imagine she had all the childcare help she needed."

"Hooray."

Dr. Elfland moved close to me and examined my blotch. I liked the way she smelled. It was a natural, non-perfumy scent. Sweet earth.

"'Dysplastic nevus' is the name we experts call this phenomenon," she said. "What do you call it?"

"Splotch. Blotchy splotchy smirch."

"It's smooth and flat. That's good. Not likely melanoma material. Have you noticed any changes in it over the years?"

"No. I mean except that it's grown bigger with the rest of me. I think it takes up the same fraction of my forehead now as it did when I was young."

"So what took you so long? Must have been a difficult cross to bear."

I was shocked and pleased at her forthrightness. Should I respond candidly?

"Never had the money before now," I stammered. "My aunt and grandma finally decided to take up a family collection for me."

"Well, here's my plan, Rapunzel. A four-step process. Possibly five, but I think we can do it in four. First time we get together we excise half the birthmark. Local anesthesia. You'll be in and out of here in a couple hours. A week later we take the stitches out. Depending on how fast you heal, you come back in four to six weeks and we excise what's left of the mole. Same routine. Stitches out in a week. Third step is to re-excise the scar left from the first two surgeries. About six weeks later we use a machine to sand down any scar that's left."

"It's all outpatient?"

"Yup."

"And what does it look like when we're finished?"

"You've got a faint horizontal scar that looks more and more like a worry line as the months go by."

"How painful is it?"

"Not too. I'll give you a painkiller afterwards, but you may not even need more than good old Advil."

"When do we start?"

"Let's go check with the receptionist to see what's available. She'll go over the costs as well."

As we walked together up to the front desk, she had another surprise for me.

"Now how about this other name of yours? Blavatsky. Is that like Madame Blavatsky, as in the author of *Isis Unveiled* and *The Secret Doctrine?* Blavatsky as in one of the most notorious mystics of the nineteenth century?"

I couldn't believe she'd heard of the woman who, according to the somewhat suspect tales of my flaky biological father, was my ancestor. A plastic surgeon who was on speaking terms with theosophical literature? Though she'd used the wrong term. Blavatsky was an occultist and magician more than a mystic. She was too strong-willed to be a dissolve-the-ego mystic.

"Madame Helena Blavatsky was my great-great-great grandmother," I asserted with more certainty than I felt. In fact, my research into the life of my supposed foremother cast doubt on Jerome's claims. Blavatsky told some people she was unable to bear children, having suffered damage to her womb in a fall from a horse while bareback riding in the circus.

On the other hand, there's also the story that she had a child with the Hungarian opera singer and member of the radical Carbonari sect Agardi Metrovitch, whom she saved from assassins in a back street in Cairo—or maybe it was Constantinople. Her accounts varied.

I heartily wished it were true, that we were linked by blood. She was an improbably accomplished, colorful, and well-traveled woman. The erudite (if sometimes wacky) tomes she wrote synthesized Qabalah, Vedanta, and Mahayana Buddhism and were among the most influential occult books ever written. More than a few scholars of the Western Hermetic tradition view her as the mother of the occult explosion that began at the end of the nineteenth century.

At different times in her life, she had as spiritual mentors Swami Dayananda, Jamal ad-Din, and Thakar Singh—*the* leading reformers of Hinduism, Islam, and Sikhism, respectively. She survived a shipwreck off the Greek coast; dallied with secret agents in Central Asia; studied with voodoo priests in New Orleans; hung out with bandits in Mexico; toured Serbia as a concert pianist; worked as an itinerant spirit medium in her native Russia; set up shop as an importer of ostrich feathers in Paris; established the Theosophical Society in India; and traveled in Tibet at a time when it was virtually impossible for anyone, let alone a white woman, to penetrate that inaccessible place.

And besides all that, she had a wicked sense of humor. No less a judge of poetic justice than William Butler Yeats reported approvingly of her pranksmanship. Like the time she snookered a gullible disciple with a story of how the Earth is actually shaped like a dumbbell, having a twin orb stuck on to it at the North Pole.

She was also famous for her supernatural powers. Legends abound of her precipitating showers of roses out of thin air, clairvoyantly finding lost objects, and causing lamp flames to flare up simply by pointing at them. Yeats reported an eerie encounter with her cuckoo clock while alone in her house. Though it wasn't ticking and had no weights, its little bird suddenly emerged and whooped.

"Your feminist pedigree is certainly impeccable, then, isn't it?" Dr. Elfland said as we waited for the receptionist to get off the phone. "Rapunzel, the only heroine in the history of fairy tales to actually save a handsome prince. And Blavatsky, one of the most powerful, charismatic, and intellectually formidable women of the nineteenth century."

"Also the most madcap woman, maybe, who ever lived. Did you hear about the time she supposedly made little chunks of ice magically materialize inside the suit of a pedantic sycophant who was boring her to tears?"

"I'd like to have that ability."

The receptionist set me up with an appointment the following Monday morning at 9. Each surgery would run four hundred dollars, the dermabrasion one hundred fifty dollars.

I felt so excited, so brimming with energy, that I walked half the way back to my motel. En route, I decided to make a brief call to Vimala. Why not? She couldn't stop me now. I was master of my destiny. Compassion was a luxury I could afford.

I bought a blue popsicle at a convenience store and got some change, then picked out a pay phone at a gas station.

"Hello?" Her voice sounded frail.

"Vimala, it's me. I'm fine. Don't worry. I just need some time away." My voice was shaking.

"We need to work on this together, dear. Where are you?"

"I promise to take extra special care of myself. You know me. Ms. Responsible. I couldn't do something foolish if I tried."

"You're hurting me."

"I'm sorry, mom. I love you. I will be back, I promise you."

"When?"

"Not sure yet. I'll let you know next time I call. Bye."

That didn't feel good. I could already feel my resolve to go through with my plan eroding just a little. "Better not call again until after the first time under the knife," I thought.

For the next few days, I kept a low profile. Didn't want to make myself too familiar a face around town. Mostly bought to-go food and raw vegetables and ate in my hotel room. Hung out at a used book store called Mandrake's. There I ordered a tome I'd long wanted to dive into, Carl Jung's *Psychology and Alchemy*, and found an unexpected bonus by another Jungian—Marie-Louise von Franz's *Alchemy: An Introduction to the Symbolism and the Psychology*. On the front of the latter book was a crowned serpent swallowing its own tail.

On Monday, the day of the first surgery, I awoke at dawn awash in a joyously familiar scent: sage, pungent earth, moldering leaves, and burnt bark. As I rose out of the abyss of sleep, I realized that the redolence was wafting through my imagination but had no counterpart in the hotel room around me. Where was it coming from? Tracing back its origins, I remembered that I had just been dreaming of the hollowed-out redwood tree that was my meditation chamber back home. I had brought my seven mothers there to show them my other life apart from them. As they reluctantly sucked from the blue popsicles I had commanded them to eat, they were bewildered and distraught. I was triumphant and angry.

"You have never given me back myself," I told them. "I have had to take it from you. It has been hard and I am so angry at you it will take many years before I can forgive you completely. But now that I know how to become the queen I want myself to be, I can also be the queen you want me to be. And so I can freely say to you that I am your avatar. I am the reincarnation of Mary Magdalen, returned at the darkest hour to restore the long-lost balance of male and female so that apocalypse may be averted."

A few hours later I was lying on a table in Dr. Elfland's office, being prepped by her and the nurse.

"Now I'm finally going to bleed because *I* decided I wanted to bleed," I jokingly thought to myself as she injected the local anesthetic. "*This* is my real first menstrual period. My self-abduction. From a position of strength, and under my own power."

Dr. Elfland held my hand for a while. It was so sweet I felt like crying. But I held back.

"You have no idea how new this is going to make you feel," she said. "It'll be like getting to reincarnate without having to endure the inconvenience of dying."

I swooned a little. My heart was doing something funny. Almost as if skipping beats. Then it passed.

"You OK?" Dr. Elfland said sympathetically, perhaps sensing my discomfiture.

"Is it possible for the anesthetic to circulate elsewhere in my body?"

"No. Uh-uh. Why? Is there something going on someplace besides your head?"

"No. I'm fine."

"Next comes an injection of saline solution to expand the tissues," she said. By this time my forehead was pretty numb.

I flashed on the dream I'd had earlier that morning. For the first time I remembered that I'd stepped out of the sanctuary of redwood husk, leaving my mothers inside sucking on their blue popsicles. Some distance into the woods, I spied something I hadn't noticed before: a shrine. A large television in a black cabinet served as the foundation for a tiered wedding cake surmounted by a small, decorated Christmas tree. Bride and groom skeletons hugged the tree from opposite sides, their hands clasping. As I drew closer, I could see the image of a talking head on the TV: a sixty-ish woman who was a dead ringer for my great-great-great grandma Helena Blavatsky.

"Always pretend you mean the opposite of what you're saying as well as what you're saying," she squawked. "That's how you kill the apocalypse. Brag about what you can't do and don't have. Exaggerate your faults until they become virtues. Heal yourself by giving yourself more of the same germs that made you sick."

Her voice was simultaneously so sincere and so loony that I burst into guffaws.

"Ready to make history?" Dr. Elfland said brightly, interrupting my dream recall. "Or would you prefer to make herstory?"

"Herstory, please," I replied.

As she cut into my skin, I felt pressure but no pain. My heart began to do that odd skipping again, longer than the last time. Then it stopped, and in its place came a warm fountain of soft electricity. Was it psychosomatic? Suddenly I was flooded with jubilant feelings of love. It was as if a dam had been punctured. I felt possessed by the urge to tell Dr. Elfland how beautiful she was, what an exquisite creature that

Goddess had crafted in making her. And the nurse, too, same thing, and the receptionist at the front desk. And all my mothers and friends at the Sanctuary, and the bus driver who'd driven me here, and the hotel clerk, and Anthony Barso and Elsa, and the woman who sold me the von Franz book, and everyone I'd ever met.

It was not a longing to be loved, but a lust to nurture and praise and *give* love. It was unconditional and generic, a raging inchoate gush that made no discriminations about whom or what it wanted to celebrate.

"You look so happy," Dr. Elfland remarked as she began to sew the two sides of the hole together.

I made a cooing moan.

"No need to explain," she said. "I completely understand."

The worry I'd had about whether my heart was malfunctioning had passed. I fantasized that the palpitations were nothing more than my heart in the process of molting. What a concept. *My heart was molting.*

And it wasn't finished yet. Wave after wave of bliss welled up from my central pump. It was such a *physical* sensation. But because of its strong emotional content I had to believe it was originating in the invisible realm.

I wanted to call up everyone I knew and tell them how much I loved them. I wanted to sit down with them and listen as they told their life stories, give them advice about how to do what they came to Earth to do, kiss them all over.

"Phase one complete," Dr. Elfland half-whispered. "Rest here a while. I'll go get a bag of goodies for you to use in taking care of the new hole in your head."

My imagination drifted back to the dream again. It began to generate scenes that I didn't think were in the original but could have been. I found myself in a muddy pit behind the television shrine. Rumbler was there, garbed only in red bicycle shorts.

I made a formal bow to him, and he responded with two slapstick curtsies. I applauded him vigorously and he turned his face away in a bashful effeminate pose but then hocked and spit out the side of his mouth like a macho dude. I winked at him seductively with my left eye, and he cocked his whole face and winked his right eye in the gesture that means sharing a secret.

So began a dialogue of gestures in which I offered and he replied. I thumped my chest with my fist and thrust out my lower jaw, and he flashed the peace sign as he licked his lips nervously. I hid my face with my hands then took them away as if playing peekaboo with a baby, and he sucked his thumb. I jutted my hand out from above my eyebrows as if peering into the distance at him, and he flashed his middle finger as he unleashed a wolf whistle.

After a while I changed the rules. Lowering my head, I ran straight at him and butted him hard in the belly. He fell to the floor and licked the tops of my feet as delicately as a cat sipping from a bowl of milk. I pushed his head through my legs, perched on his back, and spanked him in a drum rhythm. He turned into a bucking bronco, vaulting his back up to try to throw me off. Unsuccessful, he gave up. He leaned back and motioned for me to put my feet on his shoulders and grab his head. I did. With a herculean thrust and a bellowing grunt, he stood up straight. I pushed myself into the standing position too, balancing on top of him. Both of us stretched out our arms. Then he delivered a little speech.

"Any tendency I might have had to worship my own pain more than everyone else's pain," he declaimed, "hereby disappears as I perfect my role as the avatar's beast of burden."

When Dr. Elfland returned, Rumbler and I were trying to do a whirling dervish dance without me toppling off him.

"How you feel?" she asked.

"Surprisingly good."

"There's no rush," she said. "You can relax here as long as you want. But we're done for today. I want to see you back here next Monday to take the stitches out. Here's a prescription for a painkiller. Which you may not need for more than a day or two. Call me if you have any questions or problems. I put a big old band-aid in your to-go bag in case you want to hide my handiwork from public scrutiny."

## 21

The Televisionary Oracle presents
ARGUMENTS WITH GODDESS!
Our trained Prayer Warriors are standing by,
ready to study the protests and complaints
you desperately want Goddess to hear.
Send your mad, rebellious, poignant, ingenious appeals and benedictions
to us now!

Be assured that our Prayer Warriors
have not only received extensive
training in the language of Goddess—
they have pull with the Supreme Being Herself!

That's right!
Every one of our Prayer Warriors
has been on speaking terms with Goddess for at least 10,000 years
(over the course of many incarnations, of course)!
And now YOU can have them working on your behalf!

The trained professionals at ARGUMENTS WITH GODDESS!
will study your pleas and telepathically relay them to Goddess
from the profound depths of their meditations
—in the most eloquent possible language—
within 72 hours!

Deliver your howl to <zenpride@televisionaryoracle.com>

Now it's time, beauty and truth fans, to test how receptive you are to further immersion in the Drivetime.

Please answer as many of the following questions as you can. Work with ferocious intensity and/or gentle reflection. Don't push on till you're exhausted, but try to come as close to total combustion as you can.

Be innocently truthful and spontaneously thoughtful, or else gratuitously sarcastic and recklessly flippant. If you find yourself responding with ideas that you used to believe but don't any more, abandon them and start over.

Take advantage of this rare opportunity to be creative and authentic for no reason. Don't save yourself for "something better."

1. What did you dream last night?

2. What image or symbol represents the absolute of your desires?

3. In what ways has your fate been affected by invisible forces you don't understand or are barely aware of?

4. Tell a good lie.

5. What were the circumstances in which you were most dangerously alive?

6. Are you a good listener? If so, describe how you listen. If not, explain why not.

7. Compose an exciting prayer in which you ask for something you're not supposed to.

8. What's the difference between right and wrong?

9. Name something you've done to undo, subvert, or neutralize the Battle of the Sexes.

10. Have you ever witnessed a child being born? If so, describe how it changed you.

11. Compose a beautiful blasphemy that makes you feel like crying.

12. What do you do to make people like you?

13. If you're not familiar with the Jungian concept of the "shadow," find out about it. If you are, good. In either case, give a description of the nature of your personal shadow.

14. Talk about three of your most interesting personalities. Give each one a name and a power animal.

15. Make up a dream in which you lose control and thereby attract a crowd of worshipers.

16. Name your greatest unnecessary taboo and how you would violate it if it didn't hurt anyone.

17. Give an example of how smart you are in the way you love.

18. What ignorance do you deserve to be forgiven for?

19. What was the pain that healed you the most?

20. Make a prediction about yourself.

***EXTRA CREDIT***

In the ancient Greek epic, Odysseus and his men become stranded on an island belonging to the sorceress Circe. In a famous scene, Circe uses magic to turn the men into pigs. Later, though, in an episode that's often underemphasized by casual readers, she changes them back into men—only they're stronger, braver, and more beautiful than before they were pigs. Tell an analogous story from your own life.

*Homework*
Discuss and act out the following:

To survive war, you must become war.
—Rambo

To survive love, you must become love.
—The Televisionary Oracle

22

I am not a rockstar. I have never been a rockstar. And when I launched my career as a sacred entertainer back in the mid-1970s, I was determined that I would never be a rockstar. My heroes were not Bruce Springsteen, the Rolling Stones, and the Doobie Brothers, but Jerzy Grotowski, Antonin Artaud, and the young David Bowie.

Jerzy Grotowski was author of *Towards a Poor Theater*. "The holy actor, by setting himself a challenge, publicly challenges others," he wrote. "Through excess, profanation and outrageous sacrilege he reveals himself by casting off his everyday mask, and thus makes it possible for the spectator to undertake a similar process of self-penetration. If the holy actor does not exhibit his body, but annihilates it, burns it, frees it from every resistance to any psychic impulse, then he does not sell his body but sacrifices it. He reveals the innermost part of himself— the most painful, that which is not intended for the eyes of the world. He becomes able to express, through sound and movement, those impulses which waver on the borderline between dream and reality."

That about summed up what I wanted to be when I grew up.

Antonin Artaud, second of my three male muses, was a visionary playwright who dreamed of creating a theater of cruelty. His choice of terms for his seminal theory was not meant to celebrate violence and sado-masochism. Rather, he imagined shocking, spiritually-rich spectacles that would be more real than real life. They would be cruel in the sense that they'd strip away masks, reveal the big lies, and drain the abscesses in the collective psyche. I wanted to stage extravaganzas like that: rituals that made everyone so crazy they got healed.

The third icon in my triumvirate was David Bowie, who had deconstructed and apotheosized rock stardom in his seminal work *The Rise and Fall of Ziggy Stardust and the Spiders from Mars*. His songs were the smartest of any in the rock genre that had come along since Bob Dylan. I loved how he mocked the institution of the rock star even as he exploited and enjoyed it. He was arch but tender, bizarrely ironic yet passionately innocent: a poet in a genre overpopulated with preening oafs. In my first two bands, compositions by Bowie were the only non-original songs we performed.

One December my girlfriend Layla and I drove to Atlanta from where we lived in Durham, North Carolina, to catch a live show by my third muse. Her uncle had not only scored us two tickets. As a friend of the concert's promoter, he'd wangled a couple of backstage passes for us. We had an excellent chance to meet Bowie in the flesh.

Irrationally, I took with me a tape of songs that I had recorded with my band Momo (a word borrowed from the French slang for "madman," used as a name by Artaud around the time he was sent to an asylum for the first time). I was hoping for a chance to give my raw treasure to Bowie—for what deluded purpose wasn't clear. To see if he could help us get a record deal somehow? To ask us to be the opening act for one of his shows?

Bowie's spectacle exhilarated me. With a hypnotized adoration I would not have given any other famous performer, I laid bare my psyche to be reprogrammed by his lyrics, singing, gestures, everything. I was the kind of blank-slate devotee that I had often ridiculed. And yet throughout the show I simmered with the joyous expectation that this was only the foreplay for an even more miraculous event: meeting my hero backstage.

Layla and I waited a respectful fifteen minutes after the closing song to accost him. His sweat had dried. He was eating a peach. With arrogant humility, I strode up to him, squatted so as not to tower over him, and handed him "Sacred Game," Momo's cassette tape of ten songs and poems. Hoping to appear wildly enigmatic and cool, unlike all the other groupies that normally sought his favor, I didn't say hi or introduce myself. Instead, I greeted him with chanted excerpts from Momo's composition "I Love America."

My nightmares predict terrifying and beautiful accidents of scientific research that will remove all germs from all money forever, giving rise to a generation of the greatest spiritual businessmen in the history of Disneyland . . .

For whatever reason—either he was impressed with my poetry or with the gall I showed by walking up to him so brazenly—Bowie engaged me in a conversation. Actually, he did most of the talking. I tried to sound smart by asking questions that fostered the momentum of his rap.

Over the course of the next twenty minutes, Bowie explained to me his theory of how America in the 1970s had much in common with Germany of the 1920s. An unruly form of music called jazz was on the loose back then, breaking down cultural inhibitions and catalyzing riotous eruptions of hedonism. In Bowie's view, the Third Reich's fascist clamp-down in the 1930s was in part a response to the chaotic repercussions of jazz. He likened this sequence to what he foresaw happening in America. The upsurgent music and culture of the 1960s, which had temporarily wilted under the relentless influence of dour Nixonism, would soon resurface in a tidal wave of jangly mayhem. A wave of anarchist bards would tickle and tempt the collective psyche into greater and greater acts of liberation. After a few years of this libidinous uproar, though, there would be an authoritarian backlash that would make the era of Nixon look like an age of enlightenment. Or so he prophesied.

I had never come across these ideas in any article about Bowie, and as far as I knew I had read every one of his major interviews. What if, I speculated, he had chosen to share these secret thoughts with only a chosen few, of which I was one? On the four-hour car ride back to Durham in the middle of the night, and with Layla's encouragement, the insane thought grew in my imagination that Bowie had recognized me as a kindred, if less developed soul, and had delivered unto me a special dispensation. I was to be his protégé, I fantasized; his younger brother in the cultural wars to come. As if in some magical blast of psychic insight, Bowie saw that I was destined to be one of the most elite of the anarchist bards. When the prophesied counterrevolution loomed, I imagined he imagined, he and I would evolve into the ultimate freedom fighters, singing and dancing and committing beautiful chaos with shrewd intensity. And our work would be all the more pure and effective because we would never get swallowed up by the system.

As I drove and Layla patiently massaged me, I hovered in an electrified state halfway between sleep and waking. One side of my mind was pouring forth extravagant scenarios of my glorious future as if I were stoned on red Moroccan hashish; the other side watched the unfolding panorama with cool objectivity and made sure I didn't drive off the road.

As we sped across the border of South and North Carolina and passed through Gastonia, the dawn still three hours away, I received a riveting revelation about what my next move must be. The vision arrived out of nowhere, unexpectedly, and fully formed. I was to relocate to Santa Cruz, California—a place which at that time I knew only by reputation as a wild hippie utopia—and ply my trade there. Nowhere else but there, my unknown spiritual source informed me, could my genius bloom. Here in the Deep South it could at best emerge only in sullen and distorted forms of expression.

Strangely, as this lucid waking dream erupted, Layla withdrew her kneading hand for the first time in a long time. I imagined that she sensed in that moment the beginning of the end of our relationship.

As indeed it was. A few weeks later, I dropped out of Duke University and headed for the West Coast on a Greyhound bus.

My ascent to the role of culture hero in Santa Cruz began at an open mike at the Good Fruit Company cafe. My song "Blasphemy Blues" and long rant-poem "Scare Me Smart" impressed a reviewer for a local entertainment rag, who described my contribution as a "mouth-waterin', id-ticklin', ass-kickin' communiqué from the collective unconscious itself."

Within a year, I had done seven poetry readings and performance art spectacles in cafes and maybe twenty others in guerrilla street shows. I'd also xeroxed and sold two hundred copies of my first homemade chapbook and practiced the art of compassionate demagoguery in a semi-regular late-night show, "Babbling Ambiance," on a local radio station.

Best of all, I'd cobbled together my first Santa Cruz band, Kamikaze

Angel Slander. When we played our first gig at a friend's party, our set consisted of five songs I had written with Momo, covers of two David Bowie tunes, and four brand new epics my bandmates and I had whipped up, including a poem with musical accompaniment called "The Prisoner Is in Control":

> I dreamed I saw drunken marines in Vietnam shouting, "These idiots have never even heard of Goofy and Mickey Mouse!" as they raced their golf carts through rice paddies and shot squirt guns full of napalm at everyone who seemed to need a dose of entertainment. I laughed. I cried. I ran towards the Lee Harvey Oswald Memorial Whorehouse, eager for consolation, but on the way was accosted and suavely raped by a pretty CIA tease. She made me shiver and sing, broke me down and stole my imagination. Thank God for that, though. It made me too woozy to pay attention when the President of Goddess-Haters hired ten thousand Hell's Angels to overthrow the democratically elected governments of Iran and Guatemala and the Dominican Republic and Brazil and Chile.

Meanwhile, out in the wide world beyond the borders of Santa Cruz, the first part of Davie Bowie's oracle in Atlanta was proceeding as prophesied. By the late 1970s, the rowdy, fuck-the-world spunk of punk music was in full eruption. I was appreciative of and sympathetic to the Sex Pistols and their ilk, though I felt vaguely superior to them all. Bearing (my delusion of) Bowie's seal of approval, I thought of my work as more subtle and intelligent than their simplistic and decadent dissidence. Sooner or later, I was sure, I would ride the punk surge to greater visibility, even as I distinguished myself from it with my more spiritual sensibilities.

There was only one factor darkening my growing exhilaration: grubby poverty. None of the music or spectacles I was creating earned me more than the cash I plowed into making them happen. And I resented life's apparent insistence that I was supposed to take time out from my ingenious projects to draw a steady wage. My enrollment at the University of California at Santa Cruz helped. For a few sporadic quarters I was able to garner government loans and grants in return for attending once-a-week poetry and creative writing classes. Monthly allotments of food stamps also aided the cause.

Despite assistance from the welfare state, I was still compelled to degrade myself with actual jobs. Among my humiliations were stints washing dishes at restaurants and posing as an artists' model and putting in time as a farm laborer in apple orchards. And even then I just barely made my rent, let alone being able to finance the kinds of accessories that up-and-coming mega-stars need, like a car and high-quality musical equipment.

I lived in a moldy basement with nothing but a temperamental space heater to warm my fingers as I composed rebellious anthems on my dinky electronic piano. On occasions I was forced to resort to a "performance art" trick, which was to hang out in cafeteria-style restaurants and scavenge the food that diners left behind. My wardrobe? Both my street clothes and stage costumes were garnered entirely from a warehouse called the Bargain Barn, which charged a very reasonable dollar per five pounds of recycled garments.

The proud shame I felt about my poverty was in marked contrast to the proud pride I sopped up as lead singer of my new band Tao Chemical. We were punky and funky and melodic and literate and politically polemical and spiritually aware all at once. In one of our shows we shared a stage with author William Burroughs, and on another occasion, I arranged for punk novelist Kathy Acker to call long-distance in the middle of a show to deliver an obscene screed. But the smart-ass, fuck-the-world trickery we had in common with those two malcontents was balanced by an equal devotion to messages of peace, love, and understanding. "Compassionate nihilism" was my description for our politics. We were New Age punks, a social category that as far as I knew had not existed before we invented it.

The name Tao (pronounced "Dow") Chemical was itself a masterpiece of contradiction. It derived in part from the multinational company Dow Chemical, which was the hated manufacturer of the Vietnam War's most nefarious novelty, napalm. The other meme came from the Chinese word "Tao," famous for thousands of years as the earthly embodiment of heaven's truth. Juxtaposing these two meanings embodied the esthetic by which the band was ruled: weaving together the opposites that seemed most alien; playing sacred in the heart of the profane and vice versa; redeeming the darkness not by avoiding it but by exploring it armed with light.

One of the first songs Tao Chemical wrote as an ensemble was "Post-Manhood." It was a seminal artifact of my career as a macho feminist.

> I fell in love with an amazon
> She's boss at bedtime
> I never have to make the first move
> Her pleasure is mine
> She says she don't like men or boys
> Then why's she like me?
>
> Some of my best friends are girls
> When they're acting like boys
> Some of my best friends are boys
> When they're acting like girls
> I'm post-manhood

"Post-Manhood" had a sweet, major-key melody that distracted even the most homophobic and sexist listeners from the controversial message. It embodied one extreme of our musical approach: wrapping confounding and confrontational lyrics in a pop package.

At the other extreme of our oeuvre were sardonic tunes that paid almost no homage to conventional song structure: no rhymes whatsoever, no typical verse-chorus structure, and not even a passing reference to (ugh) romance. Among these was "Scare Me," a response to Ronald Reagan's reign of affable terror.

> You have the right to remain silent
> You have the right to brainwash yourselves
> It's a free country
> You're free to be a slave
> You're free to be a proud voyeur of the friendly fascists' smiles

I did condescend, in the end, to composing one—but only one— love song for Tao Chemical, breaking the unwritten rule in the music biz that a minimum of eighty-five percent of a band's material must deal with the vagaries of amour. The first verse and chorus of "Romance Is a Sickness" went like this:

> I love the way that you use me
> Please ask me for more
> Let's have a wedding next June
> just in time for the war
> It sounds sentimental
> but I want to catch your disease
> I want you so badly
> I want to be you
>
> Romance is a sickness
> Romance is a sickness
> But I love you so

Tao Chemical was a supple vehicle that allowed me to scratch my creative itch just about any way I wanted. I was hot. I was radical. I was doing exactly what I was born to do.

On the other hand, I had made almost no progress in improving my financial lot. I had a plenitude of visions but a scarcity of long-range master plans. And I was almost utterly unknown outside a medium-sized California beach town.

I still didn't own a car, bought my wardrobe at the Bargain Barn, and cooked my rice-and-bean-dominated meals on a hot plate.

I trusted in the Goddess and believed the universe always conspired for the best, but had no idea where the specific money and help were going to come from to make my urges come to fruition.

And though I was a fucking legend in my own mind, the brute facts about my impact on the world were increasingly hard to ignore. Except for an infinitesimal mention of my music in *Option* magazine, my work had never once been reviewed anywhere outside Santa Cruz in a single music magazine or poetry review or performance art rag, not even of the "alternative" variety.

Before the devil's bargains I made with CBS and WBM almost two years ago, I had never caught the attention of or signed a single contract with any entity in the music business. The three records I made were all do-it-yourself productions done on budgets so low I had to donate blood to pay for one of them. Rock videos for my songs? Ha!

At least my poetry book, *Images Are Dangerous*, was not a vanity-press job. It was put out by Jazz Press, a legitimate and credible publishing company in Santa Cruz that had done books by established poets like Jack Marshall, Morton Marcus, and Deena Metzger. On the other hand, the book materialized mostly because I incessantly badgered the publisher, who was a friend of mine, and because I myself handled every step of the physical production of the book, including typesetting, layout, art design, and photostatting. It was accorded a favorable review in New York's tiny *St. Mark's Review,* but that was all.

*Images Are Dangerous* sold only about four hundred copies out of a total two thousand produced before the rest of the lot met an untimely end. The publisher fell way behind in the rent on the warehouse where he'd been storing my books and others, and during the eviction process the landlord relocated sixteen hundred copies of my pride and joy to the county dump.

At least my music cassettes had brisker sales: a whopping total of about two thousand, two hundred among the three of them.

I'm being sarcastic. Even by the samizdat-style standards of the indie record scene, that number was pathetic. I never had a deal with even a small distribution company, and so didn't have much power to get any of my precious creations in the hands of stores outside Santa Cruz. I can say with confidence, at least, that my work was played for a few weeks in more than twenty-five distant cities, from Schenectady to Chapel Hill. I have the proof in the form of playlists from tiny college radio stations in all those places.

The evidence was unambiguous. According to most of the standards by which success is measured, I had virtually no professional credentials. My fame was *extremely* local. The money I earned was miniscule. The artistic artifacts I produced were virtually unknown.

Maybe nothing embodied my chronic sense of abject humiliation more than a scene at an all-night Kinko's photocopy store one chilly October morning at 3 A.M. It was around the eighth anniversary of the launch of my career as a sacred entertainer. Though I had only crude, self-taught skills as a graphic artist, the task had fallen to me to create a poster for an upcoming Tao Chemical show. There simply weren't enough funds to hire a pro. For that matter, I barely had enough cash to order the two hundred or so flyers necessary to cover all the essential telephone poles, bulletin boards, and public walls in town. (A task I'd be handling myself later that afternoon.) I'd brought my penny jar with me, planning on looting it to pay the Kinko's bill.

As I struggled to assemble all the elements of the flyer in a visually appealing way, I kept an eye on the only other customer in the shop. It was Crazy Carl, the homeless prophet who always wore a pair of green baseball pants wrapped around his head as a turban. He, too, was working on his latest propaganda: one more in his series of telephone-pole broadsides wherein he detailed the CIA's collusion with Jehovah-worshiping UFOs in a sick project to use mind control technology to force every man, woman, and child in America to wet their beds every night.

As the years went by, David Bowie's prophecies in Atlanta detoured into the same ambiguous limbo as my brilliant career. Just as I was forced to re-evaluate my vision of being one of the anarchist bards on the leading edge of a national groundswell of feverish revolutionary culture, I had to accept the likelihood that Bowie had been wrong.

The counterrevolution had come, all right, but not in the way he predicted—not through anything so obvious as the arrest of dissidents or the suspension of the Bill of Rights. Instead, the "revolution" had been bought with Reagandollars and turned into an ingenious form of social control. The music of chaos, heresy, and disruption was now a lucrative product belonging to the Brobdingnagian engines of capitalism. They packaged it in such a way that it could never be truly dangerous to any institution. It had become a *simulation* of revolution. Spunky rebellious angst was confined to cartoony displays of generic rage at live concerts and on rock videos. Goaded by wealthy rock icons who cared not so much about overthrowing reality as basking in the perks of their fame, the kids spent a few hours pretending to be free-thinking outlaws, safely blowing off steam which might otherwise have been directed into staging protests about the widening gap between the rich and poor or organizing teach-ins about the deadly collaboration of American might with Salvadoran death squads or writing their congresspersons about the secret genocide in East Timor.

Rock and roll, owned and operated by the same corporate culture that became an invincible vampire during Reagan's swath of destruction, was the perfect smokescreen and diversion to drain off libidinous troublemaking and revolutionary fervor into mere fantasy.

The upshot to all this was that real wackos like myself—artists who weren't churning out the emasculated simulations of revolution formulated and sanctioned by the priests of Trickle-Down Economics—didn't stand a chance at fame and fortune.

In the wake of my depressing epiphanies, I retrenched. My imagination suffered a deflation, but I welcomed that as a sign of a growing pragmatism. Instead of trying to be a poet, musician, performance artist, raconteur, radio personality, graphic artist, writer, dancer, and actor, I decided to shrink a little—maybe just be a poet, musician, and performance artist.

I dissolved Tao Chemical and for a few years pursued a solo career. Using taped music and ambient sound as my accompaniment, I did shows in which I blended incantation, singing, and an approach to ritual that I called "shamanic performance." I was part-Patti Smith, part-Abbie Hoffman, part-minstrel. Years before MTV featured "spoken word" performances that brought the genre respectability, I recorded an album of songs, stories, prayers, and poems.

"Reality," I declaimed in one of the pieces, "is now nothing more than the sum total of the war between competing infotainment conglomerates."

> I have made the catastrophic discovery that it is legal to torture and murder people with entertainment. Your very body is a battleground for the World Entertainment War.
>
> The mass audience is in danger of total extinction through "enjoyment" and "education." An elite cabal of entertainment criminals has, through telegenetic engineering, created a telepathic analogue of the AIDS retrovirus that infects the human imagination, destroying its link to the Dreamtime.
>
> This AIDS of the imagination, which I call RAIDS, disguises itself as healthy signals and symbols. Its victims read-

ily drink it in, whereupon it devours their imaginations and substitutes the sterile and pathetic stories propagandized by the entertainment criminals.

Fuck the threat of war! The genocide of the imagination is at hand! You're lucky you don't have to live in fear of literal death squads, but you're not so lucky to be living in a country where death squads of the imagination are welcome guests everywhere you go!

Don't console yourself by choosing to believe I'm speaking metaphorically. This is not a poetic conceit. Actual electrochemical substances in your brain are being redesigned by the imaginations of the imagination-killers. And television is only the most obvious way they deliver their lethal payload.

If we don't stop them, there will soon be a single, monolithic, tragically inbred global imagination built around the favorite stories of a small group of American plutocrats and their media toadies. This black hole of insipidly dangerous images and sounds will bring the unholy perfection of totally destructive "peace." World War Harmony is the covert goal of the entertainment criminals.

23

Welcome to
Mary Magdalen's Monster Truck Rally and Tantric Cryfest!

Also known as
the Televisionary Oracle!

Coming to you on-location from your own dreams!

Featuring tantric voluptuaries
doped up on compassionate sex
and bent on wreaking revenge against the apocalypse!

Featuring infomania on how to change your mind about everything!

Brought to you by Yo Mama!

Your suffering is interesting and important, beauty and truth fans. No one can take that away from you. But we don't feel sorry for you. That's not our style, and it wouldn't help you anyway.

Our slogan is, *There are only two healers: death and ecstasy.* So as we flirt with healing you, we have to be sure we're always having fun killing off some worn-out part of you. If our words seem cruel or self-exalting or unlike what you've come to expect from healers, don't worry: They still work just as well. Better, in fact, exactly because we're not boring ourselves in order to figure out how to pierce your protective coat of narcissism. We just stay excited about you, and you do the rest.

We're effective healers because we never call ourselves healers. We don't allow our egos to appropriate and exploit that dangerous image. If someone accuses us of being healers, we deny it and claim to be poets or ritualists. Likewise, if someone admires us for being poets or ritualists, we deny it, professing to be guerrilla therapists or sacred janitors. We don't really mean any of it. We're just escaping from all the dangerous images that would force us to become parodies of ourselves—that would fool us into being more passionate about the impression we make on you than being who we love to be.

We know it has all been said and done before, but the difference with us is that we're not just out to manipulate you into giving us your adoration and money. We really love you unconditionally. Not sentimentally. Not ironically. Not as a joke or a con or with the disguised hope that you're going to owe us big-time. This is not a simulation, beauty and truth fans. It's real life.

We may tease, but never for our self-aggrandizement. We may prank, but never to get one-up on you or to jack ourselves up with fantasies that we're more spiritual than you. We really do want to be in your dreams helping you carry the garbage out of your nightmares.

The Televisionary Oracle
is brought to you by
the funniest sex
you ever had

Forty-five minutes after leaving Dr. Elfland's office, I was back in my hotel room, hoping to follow up on the feelings and fantasies that had overflowed while I lay on the operating table. I drew the curtains closed, took off all my clothes, climbed under the covers, and downed a tablet from my new supply of Vicodin. (Grand experiment: I had never had a psychoactive drug in my life.) There was a six-pack of ginger ale on the nightstand, and my journal was nestled close to me in case I was inspired to write.

I closed my eyes and imagined myself lying in the temple of my burnt-out redwood tree back home. Oops. I flashed on my popsicle sticks. Shouldn't I fetch them? They were stuffed in my leather bag in the closet.

I felt too woozy to retrieve them. Instead, I simply *envisioned* myself rubbing them together. What the hell. There was no way to recreate exactly the conditions I'd always needed in order to slip into the Televisionarium. Might as well experiment to see what worked here in exile.

I simulated the feeling of the crunchy leaves against my back and pictured myself looking up at the sky through branches. My usual relaxation exercises weren't necessary—my body was already limp— so I skipped right to the deep, fast breathing. The transformation was happening with amazing fluidity. I didn't have time to worry about whether or not I could do it. After a few minutes I easily invoked the melting sensation that was the final step over the threshold.

And then I was there on the other side of the veil. The syrupy gossamer web had dropped over me.

But this was different from any version of the Televisionarium I had ever explored back home. There were no unearthly iridescent colors, no talking animals, no volcanoes made of mashed potatoes spewing warm chocolate rain down on fields of golden snow, no diamond ladders that stretched from the bottom of a peppermint tea lake to cloud houses where friendly sphinxes carved medicine dolls out of magic black radishes.

Instead, I was in a junkyard inside a rust-red cave that was as big as a stadium. A rocky roof soared high above me, and everywhere I looked there were scraps and debris, some of it arranged into rough sculptures. In one place, a spiral tangle of decrepit window frames stretched around a central heap of shattered toilets, copper tubing, and televisions. Close to me was a giant claw-footed bathtub filled with baby dolls and human teeth, some of the latter still attached to shreds of decaying gums. Next to it, lodged points-first into a pile of mattresses, was a pair of red plastic scissors almost twice my height. About twenty yards away I could see two old Cadillacs, one pink and one blue, lying on their sides. They had both been bent in half by some powerful mechanical jaws and shoved together to form the approximate shape of a square. A mangled ferris wheel rose from inside the mass, and from its dilapidated skeleton hung scores of pajamas of all sizes and colors. Some of these were on fire.

The stench of the place was, I felt confounded to note, intoxicating. I mean it was terrible—a hot sulfurous melange of burning rot—and yet I couldn't get enough. When I first arrived, my fascination with the uncanny and overwhelming sensation drove me to inhale deeply again and again.

Out of a grotto in the brick-colored stone wall closest to me, there emerged a stage. Except for the fact that it was a rough-hewn structure whose foundation was composed of sections of tree trunks lashed together, it resembled a fashion-model runway. On either side of it were two totem poles, each constructed entirely of televisions crushed and welded together. Some of the screens, maybe fifteen altogether, were fully functional and showed looping scenes of different disasters. One featured the mushroom cloud of an atomic explosion. On others, there was an oil spill aflame on a sickly river, long rows of hospital beds with patients whose bodies were rupturing in torrents of blood, a monstrous tsunami inundating a beach town, and a mob of emaciated rioters invading barricaded condominiums to steal food.

My emotional state was a mix of shock and intrigue. This landscape, in its squalid realism, had none of the glamorous dreaminess I was accustomed to in the Televisionarium. In addition, I was not garbed in the luxurious silks and satins that were my usual vestments there. In fact, I was not clothed at all. For a few moments I contemplated the example of the ancient Celts who used to go into battle stark naked in order to intimidate their enemies. But in a place fraught with so much jagged unfamiliarity, I did not feel comfortable doing that. I made my way over to the ferris wheel, and, with a broken-off lawnmower handle I picked up on the way, plucked a lime green pajama bottom and orange and purple pajama top to cover myself.

Because I could see a person seated on the runway, I decided to head over there. As I pulled myself up onto it, I found an obese older woman seated on a bed that looked exactly like mine back in the motel room where my physical body lay. The same orange pillows were propped up behind her back, and the same orange and green striped bedspread.

The woman wore a homespun loincloth and a shawl, reminiscent of Mahatma Gandhi. On her head was a medieval-style jester's hat. Fishnet stockings reached to the middle of her corpulent thighs, where they were rolled up. There was a silver ring, some set with gems, on every one of her fingers. On her lap she had a large bowl from which she was eating shrimp, spaghetti, fried eggs, and chocolate.

Nearly surrounding the bed on the floor were colorful papier-mâché masks, mostly red and yellow, that looked like they'd been made by disturbed children. There were demented bunny rabbits, human-frog hybrids, alien babies, retarded bears, even a kind of waterfall face.

I studied the woman more closely. She had mesmerizing grey-blue eyes, crinkled light brown hair, high cheekbones, and a broad face with a wide nose. I recognized her. It was my great-great-great grandmother Madame Blavatsky.

"Well, I've been meaning to ask you, Queen Trashdevourer, what in Persephone's name are you doing to kill the apocalypse?" she said

to me abruptly in a gutteral voice full of phlegm. "How are you annihilating the armageddon that thrives in your and everyone else's heart?"

"My name's not Queen Trashdevourer," I replied.

"No, of course not. It is Rapunzel. Rapunzel Chucklefucker."

"Rapunzel *Blavatsky*, not Chucklefucker."

"Exactly. Certainly. Blavatsky. Like mine. But that doesn't excuse
you from answering the question. What the bloody hell are you doing
to kill the apocalypse? That is your job, right? The reason you came to
Earth this time around? Just look at this place. It is getting messier and
stinkier by the hour."

As she gathered a handful of eggs from her bowl and shoved it into
her mouth, she made a sweeping gesture with her arm to call my attention to the scenes around us.

I thought I knew what she was driving at, but I was annoyed that
she so presumptuously assumed I would play along with her outrageous use of language. "Kill the apocalypse?" It sounded ironic, mock-
ingly portentous: not exactly a tone I felt comfortable using in regard
to a subject as grave as the end of the world.

I heard noises from inside the stony cleft at the end of the runway.
A man and woman arguing?

"Sounds too violent for me," I said to Madame Blavatsky. "I can
barely bring myself to kill a fly, let alone an apocalypse."

"That's not what I heard," my great-great-great grandmother said.
"My sources call you the Slaughterhouse Savior. Annihilator of Armageddon. The Slayer of the Wreckers. She Who Murders Mass Death."

These terms offended me. Worse, they made my throat and gut feel
as if they'd been grabbed by a powerful hand. Before I was even conscious of being upset, a choking whine flew from my mouth.

It was embarrassing. Why was I overreacting so acutely? Maybe
because everything I'd ever been taught about myself had convinced
me that I was a peaceful lover of life, a force for healing and redemption in the world. I had never heard words like "murder" and "slaughter" used to describe me. In my vulnerable state they felt like an assault.

"Incinerator of Illusion," Madame Blavatsky continued in a majestic, mellifluous tone, not acknowledging my breakdown. "Extermi-
nator of Lovelessness. Liquidator of Suffering. Poisoner of Greed."

Now she was verging on caricature. I wondered if she was making fun of me, or testing to see how gullible I was. I was caught between an autonomous visceral distress and a humiliating doubt about whether my distress was unwarranted, having possibly been triggered by a sick joke.

I felt I was on the verge of not liking this woman.

"I'm a creator, not a destroyer," I managed to enunciate as I seethed. "I am spearheading a mystical conspiracy to restore the Goddess to her rightful place as co-ruler of heaven and earth."

This assertion helped restore my bearings, even though it was humiliating (albeit in a milder way) to be quoting the Pomegranate Grail, an institution from whose authority I was supposedly fleeing.

"But I ask you again," she insisted. "How exactly is the lovely art project you just described going to assassinate the apocalypse? How will you and your charming Goddess obliterate the beastly endgame that the bloody patriarchs are hocus-pocusing into existence with their relentless curses?"

Beginning again to believe that her obnoxious query was at least sincere, I forgave her a little. But I resented her insinuation that the role I had been prepared for all these years was a wimpy, ineffectual thing. As allergic as I'd been to certain aspects of my upbringing, I was proud of the education I had received.

In response to Madame Blavatsky's pressure, though, I had to make conscious a doubt that had long plagued me. Vimala and company had never been specific about the strategy by which I would foil the seemingly irrevocable drive of patriarchal culture towards mass annihilation. For a while I'd hoped they were saving juicy revelations about this matter until later. But as the years went by with no clues forthcoming, I increasingly suspected they had no master plan whatsoever. I grew numb and apathetic towards the whole project. It was all too fuzzy and abstract.

The sounds that had been brewing from inside the grotto in the far wall now emerged in the form of two dancers. It looked like Magda and Jerome, my biological mother and father. Neither of them made eye contact as they whirled around me and Madame Blavatsky.

They both wore vulture headdresses, the hooked beak curving down, along with black body suits that had an image of a skeleton on the front and back. Over this foundation, Magda was wearing a red satin merrywidow. Jerome had on a beige leather breechcloth.

Jingle bell bracelets, which they sported around their ankles and wrists, provided a cheery cadence. Their dancing was spritely and more athletic than I thought the real Magda and Jerome would be capable of. Or were these the real Magda and Jerome—I mean the Dream-time version of the real ones, their astral bodies? I was used to thinking that my experiences in the Televisionarium were objectively true, not merely products of my imagination. But I wasn't sure I was in the Televisionarium right then.

From time to time, the dancers who resembled Magda and Jerome joined arms, took swigs from metal flasks, then spit triumphantly in each other's faces.

All the while they sang:

> If I be dead
> or seem to be
> It means that death
> can't come for me
>
> And so I bleed
> Pretend to die
> And live again
> to kiss the sky

"Magda?" I called out at one point. She ignored me. I had to resist running over to hug her.

"Jerome?" He gave no sign that he'd heard me.

After a few minutes, the two dancers waltzed back into the grotto.

"I am waiting for some sign of intelligent life, Empress Cowdung," Madame Blavatsky said impatiently once they'd disappeared. "How. To. Put. The. Apocalypse. Out. Of. Its. Misery. Will you be getting a job as some Nelson Mandela-meets-Mahatma Gandhi politician who machiavelliates all the nuclear weapon arsenals into oblivion? Will you be building high-tech medical research labs to serve as our frontline of defense against nasty new successors to the Ebola virus and AIDS?"

She paused dramatically and turned to gaze at the TV screen where bodies were exploding in bloody gushes on hospital beds.

"Or perhaps you would prefer to buy and operate a chain of newspapers," she continued, "that awakens your celebrity gossip-drunk readers to the tragic fact that animal and plant species are getting snuffed out at a rapid rate unseen since the mass die-off sixty-five million years ago?"

"Well, I need to do some more meditation on this," I offered finally, trying to recover my composure. About fifty yards away, a massive piece of sculpted junk, a windmill made mostly of skis and crutches, chose this moment to collapse. As I strained my eyes to watch, I saw that some of its fragments fell upon a nearby pile of burning books. I wondered if I should go after the dancers who looked like Magda and Jerome.

"What are you waiting for, Queenie? Meditate the hell out of yourself right now. I've got time."

"It's been my impression," I began, "that the kinds of solutions you're talking about merely attack the symptoms of the blight. I'm all for people taking political action, but I myself have a different job."

"And tell me again what magnificent task that might be?"

"My role is to heal the sickness at the source—in the collective unconscious of humanity—through my teachings in the material world and my benevolent hexes on the astral plane."

"Oh, but that doesn't sound very crunchy, does it?" Madame Blavatsky chided. "It may be true in a wishy-washy way, but it is simply not crunchy. Nor very itchy, either. I think you will have to do better than that, Snow White. The patriarchs' apocalypse is a very hardy beast, and very dumb. It will not crumble in the face of just any old wishful thinking. We need something itchy crunchy, my dear. Something squawky twisty and punchy wacky."

"I'll just have to say," I muttered, exasperated at her persistence, "that at the present moment, to the best of my knowledge, I'm not doing anything to kill the apocalypse. Would you care to make a suggestion?"

"Ah! Excellent move! Most bumptious! I love to see receptivity in a sixty-six-million-year-old avatar. Fabulous omen! Lucky day!"

"Sixty-six million years old? You flatter me, grandma."

"Sixty-six million, twenty-two thousand, one hundred fourteen years, three hundred and eleven days old, to be exact."

"Now who's talking in a way that's not very itchy crunchy?"

"You got rid of one experiment gone bad, the dinosaurs. Pretty practical practice for the patriarchy, I'd say."

"You're making me feel crazy."

"Good. Good. It's about time. Those mothers of yours, Goddess bless them, neglected some crucial elements of your education. Madness, for instance. No way you will be able to massacre the genociders of the imagination without a healthy capacity for divine dementia."

I wrinkled my face up in a comically monstrous mask and flailed my elbows like a chicken attempting to fly as I sang "Somewhere Over the Rainbow" in the cracking voice of a wicked old witch. Then I squatted down to do a Russian Cossack dance as I alternately barked like a dog and shouted out, "I am a cabbage head! You are a cabbage head! He, she, and it are cabbage heads!" My sense of humor was returning.

"That is witty but not quite wise," Madame Blavatsky said coolly after my outburst ran its course. "The divine dementia I am talking about may sometimes require the enchanting idiocy you just exhibited, but more often it is inconspicuous to the naked eye."

"Give me a lesson," I dared.

"I already am, most certainly am right now."

"What we're doing now? This is what you call divine dementia?"

"That is correct, my dear. Otherwise known as living in the Drivetime. The realm that is neither the Dreamtime nor the Waketime, but both at the same time. You could say it is the wormhole between the two worlds. The tunnel of love. An excellent location for killing the apocalypse, by the way. Of course it would help if we could get a few million more wizardly people on the planet to master the skill of inhabiting this sly power spot. No question we could electrocute Armageddon in that case."

I immediately liked this notion of the Drivetime. Maybe that's where I was, I thought, and not in my good old Televisionarium. The landscape and garb were different, and so was my state of mind. I wasn't as far gone from my normal waking consciousness. I felt the same delightfully alien dreaminess as usual, but I was more grounded. The analytical lucidity of waking awareness was burning hotter in me, but without any loss of my imagination's fluidic potency. I was indeed in full possession of the powers of both Dreamtime and Waketime.

"So if you know so much about me," I said, "tell me more about myself. Am I, was I, really Mary Magdalen? Who is Rumbler? Is he real, or some split-off part of my own brain? How can my mothers be so smart and so stupid at the same time? If I'm sixty-six million years old, why I can't remember any details about my storied past?"

"For one thing, I am simply not allowed to reel off the story of your life so glibly," Madame Blavatsky said. "Though I can confirm once and for all that you were Mary Magdalen. Or rather you were and are and will always be Mary Magdalen. The past and the present and the future all happen simultaneously, you know.

"But for another thing, I have not actually been here with you for the duration. I arrived almost six hundred eleven thousand years after you. That is when you decided you needed a kind of secretary. Someone to remind you of your appointments—especially during your experiments with squeezing your vast primordial self into tiny little bodies."

"So I created you out of clay and my magic breath?" I said. "Or I had a romantic liaison with the sun and you were our baby?"

"No, ma'am. I was the very first offspring that popped out of what I currently refer to as the *Televisionary Oracle.* An ingenious creation of yours. Best thing you ever made. Though of course you did not call it by such a melodious term back then."

"Since that was before there was any such thing as human speech, right? So I must have given it a name that sounded like a waterfall or thunderstorm?"

"Its name in the beginning had a pronunciation similar to the sound of lightning striking a tree."

"So this thing you were born out of, grandma—what you're calling a Televisionary Oracle—what exactly was it, or is it? Does it still exist today?"

"Sorry, my dear forgetful one. Cannot yet describe it in a way you could intellectually fathom. The synapses you took on when you slipped into your all-too-human body do not yet have the spunk to even perceive it. You keep hustling up more meditation skills, though, and that will change. Eventually you will get linked back to your sixty-six-million-year-old brain. I promise. And I will be here for you when you are ready for that phase."

"How about giving a few hints."

"I can tell you that the Televisionary Oracle is a most excellent tool for expediting entry into the Drivetime—a kind of sacred machine for shamanic questers. In fact, it is how you got here today. Other than that I am afraid I cannot say much more just yet. I apologize. But it is your express directions, you know. Before you shrunk down out of your heavenly haunts and squeezed yourself into that tiny sack of flesh you are now stuck inside, you told me not to distract you with cosmologies and eschatologies. 'Keep me pinned to the details,' you said. 'Make me focus on the practical things.'"

"Such as?"

"Such as *what exactly are you doing to kill the apocalypse?*"

I had become aware of an emotion coalescing in the space between my heart and throat. It seemed to have been triggered by Madame Blavatsky's image of me "squeezing myself into the tiny sack of flesh I was now stuck inside." This was an unfamiliar psychic state, like what desperate longing would feel like if desperate longing were a good and happy thing. I was aghast yet pleased to tune into it. Was this what it felt like to be in love but denied the one you were in love with?

At the heart of this curiously comforting desolation was the ghost of a memory from when I was very young. It must have been from around the time I first started to talk, maybe about nine to ten months old. I recalled—for the first time ever—being in bed with my biological mother Magda.

We were alone together. The only two bodies that had ever existed. One body, really. Swooning and playing, rubbing and cooing, afloat under the gauzy purple blankets. I was tiny and helpless and hungry. She was hot and huge and soft and omnipotent. My mouth was our eternal link, stuffed full of her juicy fat breast. Sweet warm milk trickled forever down into my joy. Silver ocean of her voice drowned me every second. Smoky damp cave of her smell rescued me.

At some random moment in eternity, I paused in my gentle persistent sucking, partly to take a deep breath, but mostly to interrupt the calm joy of the flowing milk so I could incite once again the sharp ecstasy of it bursting afresh into my body. But wait. What was this? As I sighed and shivered, my whole self fluttering in anticipation of the renewed miracle, her giant hand repelled me. "Last time, sweetie," she singsonged sorrowfully but sternly. "No more. No more. Drink from bottle from now on. No more nursing. Time to grow up." And then she guided my confused mouth back to her enormous pulsing nipple. "Last time, baby. No more after this. Last time."

I may not have understood the words, but I felt the vibe with all my being. I realized exactly what was going on. Exile was looming. Separation and banishment. Grief and panic. Helplessness and pandemonium. She was trying to kick me out of the silken oceanic nest. Rip away the umbilical link for the second and final time.

Adrenaline shot through me. Acetylcholine surged through my synapses. At the core of my foggy bliss, the hard bright glimmering of a primal vow germinated. Was this the birth of my ambition? I felt then that everything I was, everything I would ever be, everything I would ever desire, must be devoted to avoiding exile from Her, the Great Goddess. I would learn every trick, discover every secret, penetrate every mystery, in order to preserve the picture of my angel feather love wriggling in her moist edible fire. I would learn to fly free outside of time and tell her a million stories about her beautiful self.

In the aftermath of that vow, my budding little ego, shocked awake by the threat of exile, mastered every nuance of the Great Goddess' needs. Part-telepathic adept, part-perceptive genius, I studied every one of Her smells, every gesture, every tone of voice, until I could predict precisely what feeling was coursing through Her and what response I should launch to make Her feel mirrored and loved and thoroughly delighted.

Whatever skills erupted full-grown in me during that moment of crisis, they proved immediately effective. She retreated from Her threat to cut off my supply of elixir. Not until I was taken from her by the bird-woman, Vimala, some months later, did exile finally claim me. But by then it was too late: My WHO AM I? had been imprinted with WHAT DOES THE GREAT GODDESS NEED?

To remember my atavistic desire was rapturous. Never before had I had a first-hand recollection of my early life with Magda. Vimala had told me a few stingy stories, and between the time I was eight and eleven I had had two brief and awkward meetings with Magda, but this was different. To be so much in love, to be in a trance of delight with the woman in whose body I had first come to Earth, was the recovery of lost treasure. A return to a paradise I'd forgotten I lost.

But as I fermented in this blissful recollection, it gradually gave way to melancholy, and then to anger. Without noticing the exact moment I passed the threshold, I found myself courting hysteria. I became obsessed with how Vimala had never told me I was adopted until I was eight years old. I fumed at how begrudging she had been about telling me the details of my first eighteen months of life. Where had I lived? What were my biological mother and father like? What was the full story of my separation from them?

My rage expanded as I thought of how it had taken Vimala even longer to inform me that I had had a twin brother who died in child-birth, and how unimportant she seemed to regard this crucial fact. I reeled as I thought of how grossly she and my other mothers had always underplayed my heart surgery, as if it were a minor detail that was irrel-evant to the project of engineering me into their little avatar puppet.

Worst of all, none of these traumas had ever been formally mourned, let alone acknowledged with alacrity and grace. Many far more minor events in my over-organized life had been accorded the honor of a ritual, but not the loss of my brother, my birth parents, and my natural heart.

"Hello? Is anybody home? Have you been possessed by the spirit of Helen Keller?" Madame Blavatsky was calling through the haze of my reverie.

"I'm too upset to kill the apocalypse," I said finally. "Right now I'm blinded by self-pity. All I can think about is how big a backlog of grief I have in me. And how angry I am at my supposed loved ones for never helping me unload it."

"On the contrary," said Madame Blavatsky. "You are killing the apocalypse even as we speak."

"No I'm not. I'm just a festering pool of narcissism."

"I am telling you, Excellency, that you cannot kill the apocalypse way out there until you kill the apocalypse way in here." She had her hand over her heart. "And you cannot kill the apocalypse way in here until you lovingly explode all the influences—both the terrible, demonic ones and the nice, loving ones—that would prevent you from making death your ally."

My heart had begun to rumble and career again, as it had back in Dr. Elfland's office. Was I on the verge of a heart attack? Had the surgical correction I'd undergone as a baby begun to fail after all these years? Adrenaline pulsed through me, either because there was a real problem or because of my fear that there was a problem. And yet as terrified as I was, a weird hopefulness welled up too. I could not help but entertain the irrational fantasy that my heart was shedding its unnecessary psychic armor; that I was blasting away the repressed emotions that had inhibited me from becoming myself.

"How do I lovingly explode my mothers' influences?" I asked in a whisper. "What does that mean?"

"First, feel the crash-awful feelings they muddled up in you. Drink them all the way down to the bitter bottom. Do not explain to yourself so wearily wise why you should not have the feelings, or complain to yourself about how you wish you would not feel them. Do not be consumed with the urge to blame or a desire for revenge. And do not, for Goddess' sake, bat around grandiose theories about how you came to be possessed by them in the first place. Simply marinate yourself in the stinging, sludge-like pain—the grief, the anger, the nausea, the helplessness. Allow it all to flood through you in all its hideous splendor. Let the feelings move you to lurch and gnash and writhe and twist for a good long while. At least until you realize there is no longer any need for you to pretend to be in control.

"The second thing you should do, Ms. Avatar Puppet, is *feel grateful* for having been given the feelings. And it is not enough just to *say* thank you. Find a way to sincerely feel your bravest, hungriest appreciation. It was the violations your mothers inflicted on you, you know, which are secretly responsible for you being here today, in quest of your true, love-it-to-death calling."

Slowly at first, then with increasing momentum, I was invaded by a perplexing riptide of diametrically opposed emotions. One strain in the weave was the same effusion of unconditional love that I had felt back in Dr. Elfland's office following my surgery. I overflowed with a wild longing to express my love for everyone I had ever met. Starting with my mothers' images, hundreds of faces streamed through my mind's eye, as in the instantaneous life review that supposedly flashes through the imagination of a person who's about to die suddenly.

It was as if the human body has, in addition to the drive for food, sleep, and sex, an instinctive but dormant need to bestow blessings, and I had turned on that primal reflex.

That was but one side of my conflicting mix of feelings. Just as strong as the pangs of fierce generosity was my howling incredulity at how terribly I had been wronged. I was on the verge of sobbing as I contemplated the sickening unfairness of being cast in the role of both treasured savior and hapless puppet. What an oppressive conundrum! I hated all those responsible for conjuring it—my mothers, mostly, but also everyone in the history of the world who had forged the tragic matrix that gave my mothers no other choice but to damage me as they did.

Neither of the two contrary uproars was more true or intense than the other. They coexisted in perfect balance, comprising a bounteous unity. I was a beatific saint and a growling monster. *Crucified*. Caught once again in the clutch of sublime torture.

*Only the inbetween is real.*

I did not wail. Nor did I cry or moan. Instead, I relaxed and giggled. I stretched my arms and legs out as far as they would go and I tuned into the curious inwardly spiral motion of the hot flashes in my belly. And then I gave in to a surge of shocking gratitude.

*Thank you*, I reverberated as I thought of my mothers' crimes against me. *Thank you* for forcing me to menstruate against my will, and for your confused and overwrought interpretations of the prophecies about me, because in this way you motivated me to discover the beautiful strategy of self-abduction. *Thank you* for refusing to help me erase my birthmark, because that forced me to seek the adventures and revelations I am enjoying now. *Thank you* for keeping so many important secrets from me, because that will spur me to be ruthlessly honest. And *thank you* for inspiring me to hate you, because it's through that hatred that I can understand in the most visceral way how everyone on the planet cultures a little apocalypse inside himself.

Madame Blavatsky had lifted her giant bottom off the throne and was now waddling down the runway towards the grotto.

"Follow me," she called out. "Not to Christ's Last Supper. But to Magdalen's First Supper."

I was hesitant to leave my ruminations—they were so sensually pleasurable—but I trod after her. Once through the mouth of the cave, we crouched down and skulked through a claustrophobic hallway. In a moment we arrived at a door that looked familiar, though I could not at first place it in my memory.

Once inside, I felt an even stronger rush of recognition, though my rational mind said I couldn't possibly have been here before. Madame Blavatsky had brought me into a run-down, matchbox-sized suburban apartment. The vomit-green shag carpet was ragged and filthy. The furniture was an ugly mix of dilapidated wood and scratched-up plastic. On the plasterboard walls were hung amateurish acrylic paintings of scenes from fairy tales, including "The Devil with Three Golden Hairs," "The Boy Who Left Home to Find Out About the Shivers," and "Rapunzel."

A playpen with a few broken toys was crammed into the tiny living room next to an old-fashioned television that was showing an animated cutaway view of the female reproductive system. A vacuum cleaner stood in the hallway to the bedroom. On the floor next to it was the bag of dust and dirt from inside the machine. There was a rip in it, allowing its contents to spill out.

"Welcome home, Rapunzel Blavatsky," Madame Blavatsky breathed.

What was she talking about?

"This is the spot you first came into the world this time around," she said. "Do you not remember? It is Magda's apartment. Though Jerome stayed here now and then, too."

A glimmer of memory told me she probably spoke the truth. This was the place on Wilkes Circle in Santa Cruz where I had lived until Vimala came and took me away. A welter of odors bloomed, as if my sense of smell had just turned on. The mildew on the wall was the strongest. From the tracks of brown streaks, I surmised that rain had leaked through the roof and watered the green patch on the yellowish plasterboard. I could also smell the lacquered blonde wood that comprised the broken-legged coffee table, wilted chrysanthemums in a Mason jar on top of the TV, and a grocery bag full of empty pickle jars next to the entrance to the kitchen. My grown-up mind judged these aromas as unpleasant, but some more primal sense swelled with sweet nostalgia.

"See that thing over there in the corner?" Madame Blavatsky said. "It looks like a television? It is in fact a Televisionary Oracle, heavily disguised of course. It is the generative power behind this Drivetime experience you are enjoying."

"You mean it's a *symbol* of the generative power?" I asked, confused.

"No, no. It is the actual *source* of your visit here with me. Although as I said, you would never be able to perceive it in its raw state—it would be invisible—so it has disguised itself as a television. Come with me now."

I followed Madame Blavatsky down the hall to the apartment's only bedroom. If this place was what she said it was, I was now in the room where I was born, where my brother died. Could it be? It was so small. There was only one piece of furniture here, a beautiful round wooden table, which stood in dramatic contrast to everything else.

The Grail cup I had sold—the beloved artifact of my adoptive mothers' ancient mystery school—was set in the middle. It was filled to the brim with a thick red liquid. Around it were platters filled with hot sliced turkey, cranberry sauce, creamed potatoes, corn chowder, artichokes, black olives, and strawberry cheesecake.

From under the table, Madame Blavatsky pulled a thin rubber hose and a red and black Supersoaker squirtgun. The latter was the size of a small rocket-launcher. With the tube she siphoned liquid from the Grail into the Supersoaker. When she was finished, she beckoned me to approach her. She brought the muzzle of her weapon up close to my mouth. I opened wide and she shot a dose inside. I couldn't place the taste. It was salty and smoky and slightly bitter. It didn't make me gag, but I was glad to have no more than one swallow. A pungent, astringent tang remained in my mouth for some time afterward.

"Take and drink of this," Madame Blavatsky intoned after she squirted, "for this is the Chalice of Your Blood, a living symbol of the new and eternal covenant. It is the mystery of faith, which will be shed for many, that they may attain tantric jubilation and kill the apocalypse."

She handed me the gun and gestured for me to feed her.

"But first, repeat what I said," she commanded, "only say 'Chalice of *My* Blood.'"

I did this. When I finished, she spoke.

"Here is how I plan to kill the apocalypse, Queen Grail-Stealer. I will help you build a global network of moon lodges. Sanctuaries to compassionately murder the death culture. Havens where it is always once upon a time, far from the nine-to-five crimes against the rhythms of sleep and love. Death to Pizza Hut! Long live Menstrual Hut! From Kuala Lumpur to Seattle to Tierra del Fuego, may all women everywhere get their four days of resurrection every month!

"And all men, too, for that matter. They need it even more than we do, do they not? Otherwise they just go on and on and on and on—their poor bodies do not have a built-in mechanism to slow them down like ours do—and they never stop to peer into the heart of their own darkness. Which is why they find evil *everywhere else* except in themselves, and create it *everywhere else*, and fight it *everywhere else*.

"Menstrual huts will kill the apocalypse. Four days of darkish down time a month will allow us all the regular breakdowns we sorely need. No more pushing and pushing until our shadows are forced to bite us in the butt.

"Like you always say, Rapunzel, everyone who believes in the devil *is* the devil."

Actually, I had never said that in my life.

"There is another way I am slaughtering the end of the world," she continued. "I am going to help you work on producing and promoting a global festival that will take the place of the apocalypse. 'Twenty-Two Minutes of World Orgasm' is what we will call it. I want it to martial some of the same climactic juice as the phallocratic *grande morte*, but sublimate it into a more *petite*, if still monumental, *morte*. Sort of an erotic version of New Year's Eve plus the Superbowl plus the original Woodstock plus the end of a big war. At the appointed minute of the appointed day—have not decided exactly when yet—I will help you try to get every single adult on the planet to maximize their bliss simultaneously."

She gestured for me to dose her again with the Supersoaker.

"One more technique for murdering armageddon I would like to testify about," she said. "It involves stopping the genocide of the imagination in *my own* imagination. Like for instance, right now I am imagining sex with candy bars ... and homeless oil company presidents digging for food scraps in garbage cans ... and a psychedelic mushroom cloud sprouting from the penis of a nine-hundred-foot-tall Christ ... and the Dalai Lama channeling Salvador Dali in testimony against Salvadoran death squads ... and Dionysus and Eleanor Roosevelt dramatizing the myth of Orpheus and Eurydice at a sacred shopping mall in Tadzhikistan ... and a new kind of aphrodisiac that stimulates compassion as much as lust."

Madame Blavatsky took the Supersoaker from me and shot it crazily at the walls. "Look out all you phallocratic ass-souls. Rapunzel and I will soon be spraying your decaying creation with bolts of the liberated imagination."

Then she placed the Supersoaker gently in my arms and addressed me. "Have I inspired you at all? Would you like to add anything to your previous testimony? What exactly are you doing—what would you like to do—to kill the apocalypse?"

"I think for now, if it's OK with you," I say, "I'm just going to start slow. I promise that to kill the apocalypse I will pick blackberries in the rain and dance around bonfires while singing freedom songs with mysterious friends. Amen."

If you dream of a three-legged dog
nipping at your leg just in time
to nudge you clear of a flowerpot
that has fallen off a third-story window sill,
it means
a dormant part of your genius is waking up.

If you dream you're a mute, wheelchair-bound princess
who inherits the war-torn crown of Slavonia
when your father dies
during rough sex with your stepmother,
the evil queen Katarina,
a terribly ambitious former prostitute,
it means
that in your waking life
you should seek out some high-quality boredom.

If you dream of having fat cells
from your butt
injected in your forehead
to smooth out the wrinkles
it means
you should go outside at night
and spit in the direction

of the heavenly body that's responsible
for the star-crossed fate you want to escape.

If you dream of gangs of wealthy feminists
fomenting sex riots
in order to liberate the political force
of the female orgasm,
it means
you're ready to master the art of thinking with your heart.

If you dream that you are naked
in front of a large crowd
and crying out, "Help me, mommy,"
it means
you should commune more
with the Televisionary Oracle.

We can't decide whether you remind us more of Captain Ahab
in his mad pursuit of Moby Dick or Sir Galahad in his pure-
hearted search for the Grail. Sometimes you seem irrationally obsessed
with an unworthy quarry that brings out dark though creative sides of
your nature. Other times your struggle appears to be a holy quest that's
forcing you to access the wild, smart goodness that is your birthright.
We suppose it's possible that both are true. Maybe that's exactly the
point.

The Televisionary Oracle
is brought to you by
the salt water in your blood
the medicine in your tears
and
the lightning in your brain.

26

My solo career as a humble bard was fun, but it was utterly off the media's radar screen. Even local Bay Area publications ignored my creations and performances. After a couple of years of anonymity, I grew antsy to return to the cultural wars with more intensity. I felt I wasn't living up to my potential.

There was one very auspicious development during my sabbatical from rock music, however. As I worked to refine my analysis of "entertainment crime," I felt I was making myself immune to its ravages. Maybe, I reasoned, I'd even become savvy enough to save my own soul no matter how symbiotically I joined with the corporate beast. I fantasized that I could remain a dionysian clown-priest even in the face of enormous record sales, splashes on the covers of national magazines, and relationships with hordes of lawyers, accountants, bureaucrats, and journalists whose values were as different from mine as the Dalai Lama's are from Bill Gates'.

Buoyed by this vision, I decided I would launch a band and snag a record deal perfectly tailored to my vision. I would trick the corporate beast into selling us to the mass audience with the very same machinery that I satirized and howled about. What a coup it would be. I would exploit the entertainment criminals for my success at the same time that I educated our fans about how evil they were. I would outwit their ability to turn everything they touched into neutered simulation, and bring the people of Earth crafty celebrations that inspired spiritual awakening and smart love. I would gain all the advantages of being a rockstar without turning into one of those ghastly monsters.

Thus was spawned World Entertainment War, my band and performance art support group.

Our songs wrote themselves. Our stage show evolved and matured with breathtaking artistry, and in close alignment with the vision I'd formulated from the beginning. I felt like a magician returning from exile, like an orphaned genius who'd finally found his long-lost family. Soon we were headlining weekends at the biggest club in Santa Cruz, the Catalyst. Next we made the leap to the greater Bay Area and built an underground following in grassroots clubs like Komotion and the Paradise Lounge. It wasn't long before we were headlining major venues like Slim's and the Great American Music Hall and the Kennel Club.

Finally, I felt, record companies were ready to hear what we could do. With nine thousand dollars from a benefactor, we crafted an eight-song masterpiece in a San Jose warehouse studio, working exclusively during the graveyard shift to save money. Soon I was sending out our newborn artifact, along with my poetic propaganda disguised as a bio.

WORLD ENTERTAINMENT WAR is as much fun as you can have during a riot. Rhythmically outrageous, melodically potent, vocally incendiary, this band of entertainment guerrillas incites its listeners to simultaneously think and dance and kick their own asses.

"Theater" is too wimpy a word for what happens at their live shows. Imagine instead a pagan revival meeting mixed with a dance therapy session and a cynics' pep rally and a tribal hoedown and a lecture at the "Anarchists Just Wanna Have Fun" Think Tank.

Likewise, "rock opera" is too pretentious a category to describe their new CD. Imagine instead a collage of eight killer songs interwoven with a conceptually rich musical tapestry of sly subliminals, hilarious media critiques, satirical commercials, and snippets of benevolent propaganda.

Soon the favorable reviews began to bubble up from both the alternative and mainstream press. One of the first was by Gus Stadler in the *San Francisco Weekly:*

They pack their songs full of enough heady words and phrases to fill a Greil Marcus-style rock critique. But World Entertainment War reminds us that smart music need not be the prisoner of rock academia. It's a stirring, entertaining band with a smooth, funky sound and a loose, punky attitude.... They succeed at wresting "smart" rock out of the critics' hands.

Shortly after we finished our eight-song album, a mysterious figure started showing up at our gigs and dropping portentous hints. Smart but evasive, half-Basque and half-Mayan, Daryl Stackman never looked me in the eyes and never appeared without his Mayan cloak draped around his shoulders or waist. "I'm gonna make you guys famous," he assured me. A little research about his background convinced me he was a legitimate, if modest, player in the music business. We agreed to let him represent us to the record companies.

A few weeks later, while World Entertainment War was doing a spate of gigs in the Pacific Northwest, I picked up a voicemail from Daryl.

"I signed a deal with CBS," he said. "We're ready to go. Forget that low-budget piece of junk you're trying to peddle. CBS is gonna give us a six-figure advance to do it up right."

All my previous records had been recorded at mediocre studios by inexperienced engineers in the middle of the night, which was the only time the rates were cheap enough for me to afford. But our first opus under the aegis of CBS unfolded luxuriantly in a state-of-the-art studio with a producer we loved and trusted. For weeks we spent thousands of dollars a day in a perfectionist zeal to get the exact sound we wanted on every song. CBS bureaucrats and bean counters were nowhere to be seen. We played and sang and composed and messed around according to no other specifications besides our own.

The CBS suits never meddled in the design of the cover art and insert for our CD, either. Which was saying a lot, considering the fact that the format I cooked up with our graphic designer was complex and voluminous: a foldout booklet which included a four-page full-color collage and four pages of lyrics and rants and poems.

Then there was the promo package. That's the stock info about a band sent out with every CD. Typically, this is either a facile grab-bag of smarmy clichés or a smart-ass, content-free assemblage of one-liners and soundbites. In either case, it's almost always penned by a record company hack. In our case, though, CBS made an exception. In an alleged bow to my writing skills and well-wrought vision, some vice-president or other made the decision to let me create the bio. No guidelines. No censorship. No questions asked.

I was thrilled. Gosh, I thought, those enlightened CBS folks are really on my side. I gave them a slightly edited version of a piece I'd written a few months previously.

Meanwhile, we of the World Entertainment War tribe also signed up to be managed by a company founded by rock demigod Will Boehm. Boehm may not have actually invented the San Francisco psychedelic music scene of the 1960s, but he was the guru who turned it into a world-famous, money-making institution. When we met him, his was a multimillion-dollar empire that had made more than a few musicians wealthier than the ancient kings of Babylon.

The relationship did not start through my instigation. Boehm found out about us accidentally. One of the many minions who worked at his vast corporate headquarters had seen us getting crazy at a San Francisco club called the Paradise Lounge. This spy reported to Will that he'd witnessed the second coming of the San Francisco music scene: a fresh eruption of the primal spunk that Will had exploited to launch his career a quarter-century earlier.

In his first and most dramatic act of seduction, Will invited me and guitar player George up to his private Valhalla in the hills of Marin County for a catered tête-à-tête. There he confided to us, in a tone as gushing as his tough-guy persona allowed, that he hadn't been as boyishly excited about any band since 1969. As he proudly led me past his souvenir cases, which included slippers once worn by Janis Joplin and a stuffed bear stabbed in the gut by the Rolling Stones' Keith Richards, he casually mentioned, "One day your jock strap'll be in here."

I was a skeptic in the beginning. I felt that if anyone was going to manage World Entertainment War other than myself, it would have to be a smaller company than Boehm's, more familiar with so-called "alternative" rock, and more in sync with my secret plans to forever be more of a dionysian clown-priest than a real rockstar.

But Will was unflagging. He booked us to open a show with Blues Traveler and cornered me in the dressing room to whisper more sweet nothings. ("I'm personally writing a letter to the executive producers at MTV," he said. "I'll contact REM's Michael Stipe, see if he'll plug you, help you. Let's try to get you a spot opening up for Soundgarden on their next tour. I'll make this thing happen no matter how long it takes.")

Later he summoned me twice to the inner sanctum at his sprawling offices in San Francisco for private confabs. By then he was selling himself as my mentor. ("I'd like to see you do a little less of the androgynous thing on stage. Be a warrior from the steppes of Russia now and then, a big bad daddy panther. And don't be so goddamned goofy all the time. You've got to make it easier for people to see you as Everyman. Put a hatrack on stage with five different hats. Change 'em from song to song. You've got the acting ability to change identities as fast as you need to.")

In the end, more than half-convinced he loved us for all the same reasons we loved us, I signed us up. "We're going to make you the Grateful Dead of the 1990s," he confided.

So there we were: under contract to be managed by a rock legend, having completed a fabulous album under the auspices of a conglomerate whose ability to distribute, promote, and hype our product made Goebbels' propaganda techniques look like the equivalent of a scraggly hobo walking a sandwich board down Main Street.

I might have been forgiven a bout of megalomania at that point. My master plan, I felt, was unfolding with impeccable grace. As a dionysian clown-priest plotting to slip the masses a big dose of poetic music that would delight their souls and martial their imaginations, I was about to strike a blow against the vicious homogenizing power of the entertainment industry. Against all odds, I had bamboozled the corporate beast into hawking us with the very same machinery whose danger to the imagination we so lyrically articulated in our music.

I can remember, when the recording process was freshly completed, envisioning the process by which the company's marketing team would make World Entertainment War a household name. I pictured Daryl

Stackman circulating around the central CBS offices in Los Angeles, piquing the interest of the publicity team and the marketing people and the distribution crew. "This is the Grateful Dead of the 1990s," he would rave about us. "We've got to make sure that every radio station, every music magazine, and every record chain knows that."

In a massive, coordinated assault, our CD and publicity package would arrive in the mailbox of every music journalist and radio programmer in America. All of these industry VIPs would soon receive follow-up phone calls from CBS publicists and independent agencies hired to promote our record. Our reps would try to arrange phone interviews with me on radio stations and in newspapers. To reinforce the impact, the CBS marketing team would buy ads for our CD in major music magazines and local newspapers.

Meanwhile, the distribution arm of the company would make sure that our product began appearing in all the record stores of North America. In the chains, like Tower Records, CBS would arrange for prominent World Entertainment War displays, complete with, say, a six-foot cardboard figure of a rainbow-uniformed, TV-headed soldier kicking her own ass.

But everything I just described never actually happened. Not even a little. From what I've been able to piece together in retrospect, less than four thousand CDs and cassettes ever made it into stores. MTV never called to beg us for a video. *Spin* magazine never called to implore me for an interview. A grand total of three radio stations put us on their playlists.

Why? I'll probably never know the exact story of how and why our luck finally expired, because researching the true feelings and actions of both Daryl Stackman and the CBS brass was harder than extracting a straight answer out of the CIA.

But I believe every conceivable scenario probably involves some or all of the following factors:

1. The marketing arm of CBS (as at all record companies) is only marginally in sync with the arm that signs and develops new artists. Just because some young turk gets excited about an act and brings it aboard doesn't mean the old boys are going to love it with all their hearts.

2. Daryl Stackman did something—or many somethings—to piss off the execs at CBS. He *was* a kind of weaselly, annoying guy, after all, who always seemed to be scamming even when he wasn't. With him as our representative, we didn't exactly have a master communicator and people pleaser.

3. As in the publishing and film industries, if a product doesn't explode into prominence within three weeks after its release, it's regarded as stillborn. The money people immediately decree that the thing has more value as a tax write-off than as a continuing cash drain for the marketing department.

4. Bureaucracies can conspire to sabotage greatness even when they're not trying to conspire. It's in their nature to be dumb and oafish.

5. When World Entertainment War, at WBM's urging, made a pilgrimage to Los Angeles to visit the CBS headquarters for the first time (after the record was already recorded), the execs saw that I wasn't exactly a spring chicken. A previously unheralded rockstar over thirty releasing his first major-label CD? Yeah, right. Not in this universe.

6. Perhaps in a previous incarnation I was a heartless highwayman who incurred so much karmic debt by robbing helpless victims that there was no other way for the cosmos to pay me back than by playing a really nasty trick on me.

Just kidding about that last one. I think.

The abrupt and brutal reversal of World Entertainment War's long good luck streak did not end with CBS' mysterious sabotage of our beloved CD.

One rainy autumn night, before Will Boehm could live up to his promises to me, he dematerialized. On the way back to his Marin home from a Huey Lewis show in the East Bay, the helicopter carrying him slammed into a utility pole in a driving rain. I woke up crying at 3 A.M., eight hours before I officially heard the news. In my dream, Boehm had come to me, holding his severed hands in the crook of his arms, and said mournfully, "I'm sorry. I can't finish the job."

I might have been able to love the music biz a little more if Boehm had survived. He was a pushy asshole, but he had soul, he had balls, and he was just enough of a madman to understand the full complexity of what I was trying to pull off. On the other hand, there was no way, in light of the passionless, bumbling strategies Will Boehm's lieutenants plotted for World Entertainment War in his absence, that I could survive the music biz, let alone love it. And even their sabotage looked positively benevolent compared to the cryptic evil perpetrated on us by CBS.

Yet I can't in good conscience condemn Boehm's lieutenants or the CBS executives to the seventh level of hell. They're merely the human administrators—hence, victims like me—of the same machine that came so close to mangling my metaphysical *huevos*.

Easy for me to say now. During the first flush of disillusionment with my two multinational allies, I came dangerously close to violating my pacifist Gurdjieffian-Buddhist-Qabalistic vows. In an embarrassing spectacle unmatched since I was four years old, I actually screamed bloody oaths at one of Boehm's lieutenants for fifteen minutes straight. (Sorry about that, dude.)

But the ripest target for my anger was of course myself. I could hardly believe that after so many years I had managed to sustain a level of naive idealism more appropriate for a kid launching his first garage band.

My spacy fantasy: that in a gift of love to Will Boehm's memory, the company that lived on after his demise would rise to the occasion, calling on previously untapped reserves of ingenuity to spread the word about World Entertainment War with an inventiveness and intensity that would top anything Boehm himself could have pulled off.

The crushing reality: Without the maverick charisma of Boehm pervading the place, his management team slumped into a glazed lethargy, carrying out cautious strategies by rote.

My deluded fantasy: that our music is so brilliant and unique and well-played that even the corporate drones at CBS would undergo a religious conversion in the presence of its redemptive beauty; that they would transcend their plodding, one-size-fits-all approach to marketing in order to come up with an imaginative strategy for making World Entertainment War a household name.

The scalding reality: CBS is a soulless assemblage of businessmen and bureaucrats committed solely to advancing the bottom line with products that slickly embody the cultural clichés *du jour*. It's true that from time to time there emerge in the lower rungs of the CBS hierarchy a few passionate idealists who yearn to unleash gifts of great art on the mass audience. One of them, after all, coaxed the big money people to sign us up in the first place. But he was probably axed from the company well before the divorce of World Entertainment War and CBS was final.

What was most humiliating, demoralizing, and downright unredeemable, however, was not the way the stinky brains of CBS sabotaged my baby. How could I expect them to be anything other than themselves? What hurt most was this: Ever-so-subtly, ever-so-creepily, I had begun to buy into the rockstar persona and lose my own private vision of how to pull it off. I had actually, I'm ashamed to admit, begun to do things I hated—sucking-up behavior I'd spurned all these years, craven acts I'd always felt were symbols of selling out.

I mean, it's difficult to have accomplished the feat of being nothing more than a cult figure in the Bay Area despite having performed highly original, well-executed music for more than a decade. My failure to become a mega-bestselling rockstar was actually a stellar accomplishment. I attribute it to the fact that I'd steadfastly refused to ham it up with radio interviewers who thought "genocide of the imagination" was a board game for five-year-olds; that I'd refused to tone down the quirks in our music in order to impress and yet not overwhelm the polite lemmings at music conventions; that I'd refused to change the lyrics to our song "Marlboro Man Jr." so as not to risk a lawsuit from the cigarette company; that I'd refused to make our music less melodic and chipper so as to pander to the pop-nihilists who dominated the "alternative" music industry; that I'd refused to spend every waking minute selling myself to the legions of promoters, radio programmers, booking agents, record company executives, and music journalists.

And yet when our CBS-financed record was finally released, I found myself, at the urging of WBM and CBS, bucking my own hallowed traditions. The gigs they booked for us were laughable: a poorly advertised concert at a cavernous auditorium in Ventura, California, better suited for productions of "My Fair Lady" than for World Entertainment War throbathons; a barely advertised show in sparsely populated Fresno at a tiny restaurant filled with rednecks who walked out when we played "The Wonderful World of War," our reverse paeon to the history of CIA-aided *coups d'état* all over the Third World; an off-the-map show in an obscure Los Angeles club that was so empty that the Mexican family having a birthday party in one of the back rooms comprised half our audience.

Did WBM or CBS place us with a real booking agency, one with the clout to ally us with touring big-name acts? No. Were ads taken out or promotional appearances arranged in any of the cities where my previous musical efforts had received airplay? Nope. Were we blessed with even a fraction of the funds Will Boehm himself had promised to lubricate our career? 'Fraid not. Or with even one one-billionth of the vast fortune megaconglomerate CBS had at its disposal? No chance.

Instead, I did interviews with a reporter for a college newspaper from southeastern Texas who wanted to know what my favorite flavor of Pez candy was. George the guitar player and I were invited to decorate the side window at a tiny San Francisco record store in the style of a World Entertainment War altar. The manager of the store took down our installation after three days because it was "too arty." Darby and I appeared on a cable-access TV talk show (probably watched by a total of forty people) side by side with a man dressed as a giant turtle who retracted his head into his shell and blew soap bubbles out, plus a woman wearing a diaper and bandaids across her nipples who could not only put her whole fist into her mouth, but could also sing "Swanee River" while it was in there.

The first shame was that we had placed ourselves in a position to let this happen. The worse shame was that we didn't rise up and follow a more righteous path, but endured it like well-behaved death-row prisoners.

And with every act I took to violate my own principles, the fortunes of the band sunk lower. The CBS record sold less than three thousand copies, a showing so dismal that only the most untalented, inauthentic, unseasoned bands could rival our failure. The CD got on the airplay list of only one major radio station, a renegade outfit in

New Jersey run by pagan warlocks. Mysteriously, after a long series of fabulous articles about us in the Bay Area media, we couldn't even manage a single review of the album, let alone a positive review. It was eerie, almost supernaturally improbable. It reminded me of those poor souls who have *reverse* psychic abilities. A statistically implausible percentage of the time, they're incorrect when they try to guess what card the psychic researcher is holding in his hand. That's what World Entertainment War had become. Our CBS project demonstrated more than a lack of good luck. It reeked with the most fetid, rotten, weirdly awful luck I'd ever experienced in my entire life.

Worse yet, I found myself one dragonish day actually contemplating what I'd have to do to compose a song with more of the standard pop formulas—a song that people would buy in droves.

27

The Televisionary Oracle
calls on
the spiritually suave,
erotically playful,
ironically tender,
divinely blasphemous
workers of the world
to seize the means of production
and use it to abolish all need for meaningless work.

This public service announcement
has been brought to you by
the smell of wet fox fur,
vanilla-scented candles burning in a cave,
and the soil of a Vermont garden just after the autumn harvest.

Although you'll never find an advertisement for Coke or Nike within the hallowed confines of the Televisionary Oracle, you will find lots of hype for more spiritual commodities, like disciplined freedom, orgiastic lucidity, and lusty compassion. Our flackery may be more sacred and uplifting than all the other hucksters out there, but the fact remains that we're still trying to coax you to "buy" our ideas.

There is one difference in our approach, however. We don't want you to become addicted to your need for the Televisionary Oracle. In fact, our ability to sell you our miracles depends on you being joyously rooted in the most ferocious self-protective instincts of your own free will.

With this in mind, we invite you now to participate in the Televisionary Oracle Sellathon. All you have to do is commune with the seven sexy oracles below, then choose the one that best suits your special needs at this unique moment. Tell us your decision at <zenpride @televisionaryoracle.com>, and we will arrange with the Fates to administer it with love and grace.

ORACLE #1: The word "imagination" doesn't get much respect. For many people, it connotes "make-believe," the province of children and artists. But in fact, imagination is the most important asset you possess; it's the power to form mental pictures of things that don't exist yet. As such, it's what you use to shape your future. Some people, alas, are lazy about using this magical power. They allow their imaginations to fill up with trashy images that are at odds with their deepest desires, and their incoherent lives reflect that. Other folks are very disciplined about what images they entertain in their imaginations. They tend to attract exactly what they need. What about you? How will you use your treasure in the months and years to come?

ORACLE #2: We hesitate to compare you to a nimble-fingered, sensitive-eared thief, but there's no better choice of metaphor: The task you have ahead of you bears a resemblance to picking a lock in the dark. Of course the treasure that's sealed away from you is actually yours, so it won't exactly be like stealing. Still, you won't be able to reclaim it with a forthright, no-nonsense approach. You'll have to be daring and delicate at the same time.

ORACLE #3: As an alternative to the oppressively stern, partially outmoded Ten Commandments, we have developed the Ten Suggestions. The First Suggestion is "Wash your own brain once a year—whether it needs it or not." There's no better time than now for you to heed this advice. The toxic build-up of junky thoughts in your grey matter has reached critical levels. One good thing about the Ten Suggestions— which distinguishes them from the Ten Commandments—is that they work by inducing your laughter instead of your fear. Guffawing loud and strong about your own shortcomings, for instance, is an excellent brain-cleanser.

ORACLE #4: In one of your past lives you were the genius who invented Pig Latin. In another, you were a nun who was expelled from your monastic order for wearing crotchless habits, whereupon you became an itinerant saleswoman of religious sex toys. In yet another incarnation you were the world's foremost collector of antique candy wrappers. All the talents you developed way back then will come in very handy as you meet the slippery challenges ahead.

ORACLE #5: Is the cosmos a great soulless machine? Is it a product of blind forces which just happen, through a prodigious number of stupendous accidents, to have conjured up the infinite web of miracles that surrounds us for billions of light years in every direction? Or is it more likely that the cosmos is the soulful "body" of a vast intelligence that lovingly micromanages every intricate detail of its unfoldment—an intelligence too colossal for our tiny brains to perceive, let alone conceive? We're sure you can guess our answer to that question. But we'd prefer to let you come up with your own. And there's no better time to do that than now. You're scheduled to catch a glimpse of the biggest picture you've ever been privileged to behold.

ORACLE #6: Do you know the distinction between actual compassion and idiot compassion? The idiot kind is the short-term fix we offer a suffering person in order to console him, even though it might encourage him to keep doing what brought on his pain. Authentic compassion, on the other hand, might at first seem severe—as when we refuse to buy into someone's habitual tendency to portray himself as a victim. If done lovingly, though, this more strenuous kindness serves as a wake-up call. We bring this up because you're now in a phase when actual compassion—though not the idiot kind—will reap richly selfish benefits for you.

ORACLE #7: Thinking of whipping up your very own moral code? Keep these guidelines in mind as you do: 1) A moral system is immoral unless it can survive without a devil; and unless it prescribes rebellion against automaton-like behavior offered in its support. 2) A moral system grows ugly if it doesn't perpetually adjust its reasons for being true. 3) A moral system becomes murderous unless it's built on a love for the sacredness of the vowels and the inscrutability of the consonants. 4) A moral system will corrupt its users unless it ensures that their primary motivation in being good is to have fun.

The Televisionary Oracle
is brought to you by
the reverie that inspired Blaise Pascal to murmur
"When one does not love too much, one does not love enough."

28

Up until the afternoon in the Marin hotel room following Dr. Elfland's first surgical swipe at my accursed birthmark, I'd always experienced my trips into the Televisionarium as radical breaks. The adventures I enjoyed there, while relaxing and invigorating, were utterly alien. I could find no way to translate them or make use of them back in the world I shared with my mothers. Indeed, it was as if I were two separate beings living two unrelated lives. To penetrate the veil between them felt violent, like a puncture. When I returned to earth from my cloud castles or peppermint tea streams, I often felt what I imagined it must be like to receive an electrical shock.

But my visit with Madame Blavatsky in the underground junkyard and Magda's slummy shack was nothing like that. I couldn't even say for sure it was the Televisionarium. I arrived in the strange land gently—not with a puncture, but in a rippling glide. The surroundings, the action, even the conversation were more like a hybrid of the Televisionarium and the material world, and I felt in full possession of both my sharp analytical faculties and my robust imaginative skills. In some ways the experience was like a lucid dream, as the Televisionarium had always been, but in other ways it was like lucid *waking*, or whatever you might call it when the daytime is infused with dream awareness.

Madame Blavatsky referred to this place as the Drivetime—a dimension that was neither the Dreamtime nor the Waketime but both at the same time. It was my first awakening to the possibility that a shamanic quest need not be a brief and grandiose stab, but might work more like a time-release capsule that distributes the medicine slowly over a long period of time.

My Drivetime guide also hinted that my entry there had been facilitated by a mysterious and primal "machine" which she called the Televisionary Oracle. From her cryptic comments, I surmised it fit the definition formulated by science fiction writer Arthur C. Clarke: "Any sufficiently advanced technology is indistinguishable from magic." Indeed, if Madame Blavatsky's assertions had any credibility, I myself created the Televisionary Oracle sixty-six million years ago, while in full possession of an archangelic potency which I have barely been able to tap into in my current incarnation as Rapunzel Blavatsky.

My departure from the Drivetime was a gradual ebb, like the tide going out. Long after the physical scenes had faded and my conversation with Madame Blavatsky had given way, I mulled over the events in a delicious hypnopompic state, engraving the details on my memory and letting them unveil further shades of meaning.

By 5 o'clock I had fully returned to normal waking consciousness. Or had I? In the back of my mind and in the bottom of my heart, I could still vividly feel the imprint of my sojourn in the Drivetime. Back then I would not have used the term "proprioceptive synesthesia," but it occurs to me now as I try to describe the sensation. It was as if inside my body there was a flowing current that was the texture of crumpled linen and the smell of sweet almond oil and the colors terra cotta and gold and the taste of warm lemony tea and the sound of a mysterious, lilting blend of Irish and Chinese music in a minor key. This internal stream was a palpable link—not just a memory but a living taproot—to the Drivetime.

I wanted to test its staying power. It was one thing to be lying alone in a quiet room, but could I remain in touch with my new secret while rubbing auras with folks on the street? I decided to take a walk down to Mandrake's bookstore to see if the weighty tome I'd ordered, Jung's *Psychology and Alchemy*, had come in yet.

All the clothes I'd brought from home for Operation Erasure were purposely unflashy. Now, from among the mass of drab colors and baggy shapes in the closet, I grabbed black jeans and a dark khaki green sweater. After gingerly covering my fresh wound with a large piece of gauze, I pulled on a black beret.

Half an hour later I stopped at a cafe. After a slow-motion communion with soup, scones, and tea, I trekked on to Mandrake's. Alas, *Psychology and Alchemy* had not arrived. But the clerk told me he'd just acquired a used copy of another one of Jung's alchemical treatises, *Mysterium Coniunctionis: An Inquiry into the Separation and Synthesis of Psychic Opposites in Alchemy*. Would I like to look at it? He led me to where he'd shelved it, and I sat down on a stool as I opened it up.

Turning to random pages to divine whether the book and I had any future together, I quickly found a couple of juicy parts. First there was Jung quoting Karl Kerényi: "'Basic to the antique mysteries . . . is the identity of marriage and death on the one hand, and of birth and the eternal resurgence of life from death on the other.'"

The second discovery, on another page: "In ecclesiastical allegory and in the lives of the saints a sweet smell is one of the manifestations of the Holy Ghost, as also in Gnosticism."

I'd never heard that one before, that the Holy Ghost smelled good, but I liked it. What exact odor, I wondered. I fantasized it might be like the sweet almond oil that I could still sense coursing through me, my link to the Drivetime.

In the spiritual beliefs of the Pomegranate Grail, there is a third party in a Trinity which also includes Jesus Christ and Mary Magdalen. "Holy Ghost" is not the name this character goes by, though, but rather "Mercuria"—feminine form of the phallocratic archetype "Mercurius." Like the Holy Ghost, indeed, like Mercurius in the alchemical tradition, Mercuria is regarded as a go-between or messenger, and sometimes as the spirit of the union between any two opposites, especially Jesus and Mary themselves.

Ha! On page 462, two paragraphs after the Kerényi quote, I found Jung saying, "Mercurius . . . is not just the medium of conjunction but also that which is to be united, since he is the essence or 'seminal matter' of both man and woman. *Mercurius masculinus* and *Mercurius foemineus* are united in and through *Mercurius menstrualis*."

"Now what the Hades does he mean by *Mercurius menstrualis*," I puzzled. As I was contemplating this delightful enigma, I became aware of a new fragrance. Had my sweet almond oil mutated? No, this smell was definitely on the outside of my body, arriving from an unknown source. I tried to describe it to myself. Like parchment on an ocean beach, maybe. Ancient but fresh. But also like the aromatic lacquered woodiness of a guitar, with a hint of moist carrots just pulled out of the rainy ground.

"Hey, Artaud," I heard a voice whispering. "Artaud. How are you?"

Looking around, I saw that someone had silently crept up behind me in the narrow aisle. It was this person who owned the delectable fragrance.

I say "person" because I could not immediately discern what gender the creature was. He or she was about five feet nine or five feet ten, and wore all white—work boots, baggy pants, an oversized man's shirt not tucked in, and a long cloth coat of the kind I'd seen worn by Sikhs. Breasts were not discernible, but they could have been cloaked by the abundant folds of white fabric. His or her face was a perfect hybrid of elegant male and witchy female. It was both noble and tricky. The thick, jaw-length flaxen hair and turquoise eyes reminded me of the style of the medieval Page of Wands, a figure depicted on a court card in the Pomegranate Grail's official Tarot deck. The person's age? I guessed mid-twenties, but I was not confident in that assessment. There was an ageless quality in his or her face.

"You talking to me?" I blurted out.

"*Mais oui*, Artaud. But I am not just talking to you. I am beaming at you. Gleaming my joy at having found you again after all this time."

His/her voice was, like the rest of him/her, exactly halfway between male and female. At this point I decided I couldn't tolerate the cognitive dissonance. Until further notice, I would think of this person as a him. I gazed at his throat, trying to decide if the swell in the middle was big enough to be an Adam's apple. Hard to tell.

"You must be mistaking me for someone else," I said, though I was in no hurry to drive him away. I hadn't had many social interactions in recent days and was a bit starved. I considered the possibility that he was just a dude on the make, but thought it might be fun to expose him. I rose to stand. We were the same height.

He took my left hand with his own and gave me what felt like a secret handshake.

"Remember this?" he asked slyly, his left eyebrow rising comically. *"Blasphème sacré?"* His middle finger stroked the base of my palm while his thumb thumped the top of my thumb.

French for "sacred blasphemy"?

"I'm your *bonne amie* (or did he say *bon ami?*) from last incarnation," he continued. "Not two lifetimes ago in Germany, but the one right before this one, in France."

"That's impossible," I said. "Last time I was on Earth before this was in Palestine, almost two millennia ago."

He held his head in his hands and uttered a "waaaaa," as if imitating a baby's cry.

"Wait here," he commanded. "Do not move. I will go retrieve some evidence."

I turned my attention back to *Mysterium Coniunctionis*, leafing to the index to glean where else Jung might have discussed Mercurius. Of the many entries under that heading, "dressed as woman," on page 442, caught my eye first. There Jung wrote that the hermaphroditic Mercurius was often dressed like a woman in the alchemical illustrations of the seventeenth and eighteenth centuries. Nearby that passage was another seed: "In alchemy Mercurius is the 'ligament' of the soul, uniting spirit and body."

In a couple of minutes the odd stranger had returned. He was holding a book called *The Theater and Its Double*, by Antonin Artaud.

"I imagine this will still sound familiar," he said. "It has been a long time, but you did write it yourself, after all."

"Are you suggesting I was this guy Artaud in my past life?" I asked, rising off the stool to face him more directly.

"I am not suggesting," he replied. "I am stating as a fact."

"But I have no idea who he was."

"We can do a hypnotic regression later. I'm sure it will all spill out."

"Can you give me a few hints?"

"You were a mad poet who liked to say that all writing was pigshit. *Merde du pourceau.* You were a tormented actor and a visionary playwright who lusted to kill and resurrect the theater."

There was that word "kill" again, being applied to me. But other than that commonality, the description of Artaud was so far from my self-image that I had to laugh.

"You were the genius that thought up the Theater of Cruelty, Artaud," he continued. "Probably had something to do with you having meningitis as a kid."

"Ouch!"

"A sick little joke there. Sorry. You did not mean *cruelty* in the usual sense of the word. Not the way I just used it. You did not mean *any* word in its usual sense. That is one of the things I loved about you so much. You would say *'pourquoi'* and really mean *'pourquoi pas?'* Or you would say 'animal yawns' and actually mean 'the sound of sap rising in the tree.' Here is how you defined cruelty."

He read conspiratorially from *The Theater and Its Double*. I could still smell his aroma as vividly as when it first bloomed, which was curious. Normally a scent hits in all its fullness, then wanes as you get used to it.

"'My cruelty is not synonymous with bloodshed, martyred flesh, crucified enemies. Rather, it is an appetite for life, a cosmic rigor and implacable necessity, in the gnostic sense of a living whirlwind that devours the darkness.'"

"Oh yeah, I remember writing that," I lied.

"You did not want the theater to be simply a silly diversion," he said brightly. "You hated how it had become a showcase for pitiful little catharses about personal ambition and sentimental love and social status. You wanted it to be a real religious ritual. You plotted and schemed to strip people of their defenses and terrify them with so much beauty that they could not help but get high."

"Yes, I was pretty cruel."

"Once a wacko high priest, always a wacko high priest?" he winked.

"I resemble that remark," I said, quoting one of my mom Burgundy's favorite lines.

"I was simply hoping to jar loose a memory or two from some of your *other* past lives," he said.

"Such as?"

"Such as Eumolpus, for one."

"Oh yeah, Eumolpus. I seem to remember being Eumolpus. That was when I was Plato's barber, right? Slight hunchback. Big broken nose. Bad teeth."

"No, ma'am. Guess again. Much further back than that. You have identified the right part of the world, at least. When you were Eumolpus, you were—how shall I say?—a self-made hierophant. You even started your own mystery school. Once every year you threw a sacred party, and once every five years a *really big* sacred party. Which was actually an occult ceremony. Which was also a riveting theater piece starring the Goddess Persephone and her mother Demeter. Remember? You called them the Eleusinian mysteries. They lasted long after your death, more than a thousand years."

Now that was a weirdly apt guess, I thought. Wrong, of course, but having a strong resonance with the truth. What would be the odds of a complete stranger guessing there was a connection between me and Persephone? If riffing about reincarnation was his game for picking up chicks, he was good at it.

"Oh, here is one of my favorite parts in *The Theater and Its Double*," he was reading again, "where you compared the Theater of Cruelty to alchemy. You remember you were also the sixteenth-century German alchemist Paracelsus, right? Listen to this.

"'Alchemy permits us to attain to the sublime, *but with drama*, after a meticulous and unremitting pulverization of every insufficiently fine, insufficiently matured form . . .

"'The theatrical operation of making gold, by the immensity of the conflicts it provokes, by the prodigious number of forces it throws one against the other and rouses, ultimately evokes in the spirit an absolute and abstract purity . . .

"'I believe that the Mysteries of Eleusis must have consisted of projections and precipitations of conflicts, indescribable battles of principles joined from that dizzying and slippery perspective in which every truth is lost in the realization of the inextricable and unique fusion of the abstract and the concrete. . . . They [the Mysteries of Eleusis] brought to a climax that nostalgia for pure beauty of which Plato must have found the complete, sonorous, streaming naked realization: to resolve by conjunctions unimaginably strange to our waking minds, to resolve or even annihilate every conflict produced by the antagonism of matter and mind, idea and form, concrete and abstract, and to dissolve all appearances into one unique expression which must have been the equivalent of spiritualized gold.'"

"Wow. I was pretty pompous, wasn't I?" I said with mock admiration. "Especially for someone who accused other writers of spewing pig shit."

"Yes. Exactly correct. But no longer, I think. This time around you have arranged for a personality that allows you to take yourself less seriously. Am I right? Same intensity, but more humor."

I found myself imitating the response I had made to Madame Blavatsky while in the Drivetime a few hours back. Scrunching my face in the ugliest expression I could manage, I danced like a chicken as I whisper-sung "Somewhere Over the Rainbow."

"No doubt we should get a theater group together," he said when I was done.

"Starting with a surrealist production of 'The Wizard of Oz'?"

"No. I do not mean the kind of theater group that puts on cute little plays. I am talking about radical rituals." He flipped through the pages of *The Theater and Its Double*, then read: " . . . by furnishing the spectator with the truthful precipitates of dreams, in which his taste for crime, his erotic obsessions, his savagery, his chimeras, his utopian sense of life and matter, even his cannibalism, pour out, on a level not counterfeit and illusory, but interior."

"Don't you think we should get to know each other better before we dive into such a serious commitment?" I said.

"But we have known each other for decades!" he protested. "Thirty-five centuries if you include our time together back in Germany and England and Eleusis. Do you not remember? Paris, June 11, 1923? The day we first met last incarnation? True, we both had different bodies at the time. But I recognized you the moment I saw you here in the bookstore. You cannot hide that—how should I describe it?—spasmodically rhapsodic soul of yours. Remember how you said, when you were Artaud, 'I am the man who has best charted his inmost self'? Well, it still shows all over your new face."

If this guy was making this stuff up, it was pretty entertaining.

"And how did you just happen to be here," I said, "in the same little bookstore in the same small city in Northern California at the exact same time I was?"

"Your wound," he replied. "As soon as you began showing up in my dreams with a bloody forehead, I knew that the real flesh-and-blood you was about to re-enter my life. In all our dream adventures up until recently, you see, you have always been a majestic and flawless goddess, not anything like a real human being. Our rendezvous have always been in archetypal landscapes—windswept battlefields and thousand-foot waterfalls and crystalline palaces. Last night, I dreamed I found you in this shabby bookstore with uncombed hair and dark circles under your eyes."

The implications of what he was saying were boggling. I could barely focus on sorting them out. For the moment, I obsessed on how he could have known about my forehead. Instinctively, I put my hand up and found there was a tiny corner of gauze jutting out from beneath my beret. So maybe that explained it. I'd inadvertently given him a clue to use in his confabulations, if indeed he was confabulating.

I longed to ask him more about his dreams of me. Had he really, as he seemed to be implying, had an ongoing series of adventures with me over a long period of time—comparable to my experience with Rumbler? But I wasn't ready to hear the portentous answer to that question just yet; if it were "yes," it would be too spooky.

"I would consider getting a theater group together with you," I said instead. "There's a slight problem, though. I have no experience as an actress whatsoever."

"Are you telling the truth? I find that hard to believe. I can plainly see a strong thespian streak in your physiognomy. But *de toute façon*, the more important question is: Can you bleat like a charging rhino? You could do that back when you were Artaud. Can you whirr like a cloud of locusts? And ululate like a beautiful young woman dying from the plague?"

"I can feel all those skills right on the edge of my memory."

"I have a very good idea," he said suddenly. "Shall we give you a crash course to help you get over your amnesia? I mean this very evening, a full-immersion exercise in the good old *le Théâtre de la Cruauté*? By the way, back in France I used to be Luçienne. You can call me that if you want. Or you may use my new name, Jumbler."

"Jumbler? What kind of name is that?" I said, not meaning to sound as shrill as I did.

"'Jumbler' is a name I gave myself eight years ago—in honor of my coming of age. It means I am the kind of person who loves to mix things up and put them back together in new combinations. What about you? Who are you this time around?"

"Rapunzel. Rapunzel Blavatsky."

Before I could expound, he reached out his left hand, and when I offered mine in return, he gave me the same secret handshake he'd applied before.

With his last announcement, the tide turned dramatically away from the interpretation that this character was merely a guy cruising for babes. First there had been his delectable aroma, which arrived just moments after I'd read about the Holy Ghost's sweet smell. Then he conjured up the scenario of me being connected in a past life to the Goddess Persephone, and confessed (I think) that he'd been dreaming of me for years. Now I'd found out that his name was one letter away from that of my magic companion in the Televisionarium.

I was torn about going along with the crash course he'd proffered. My imagination had become so excited by his improvisations that I was practically swooning. And wasn't this exactly the kind of adventure I had invited into my life by launching my apostasy against the Pomegranate Grail? But I worried that I should be more self-protective. I'd had surgery that morning, for one thing. And given the fact that I was an underage runaway, shouldn't I lay low and remain inconspicuous?

"Come on now, I will buy you these two books," he said, plucking *Mysterium Coniunctionis* out of my hands and heading towards the front of the store. I followed behind, hoping to find a definitive clue to his gender in the way he walked. There was the slightest swinging of the hips—more than most men I'd ever observed, at least, though less than most women.

My taproot to the Drivetime was surging deliciously again: linen and sweet almond and gold-tinged terra cotta and a spritely but mournful Irish-Chinese tune. There was no way, I decided firmly, that I was going to break the spell.

Suddenly Jumbler and I were pushing through the doors of the store and out into the warm spring evening. I was mad at myself for not noticing how he'd paid for the books. Had he used a check and been required to produce a driver's license, I might have seen his real name and gender.

We were headed down the sidewalk past a seedy vacant lot when he stopped, put down the books, and spread his arms up to the sky in an expansive yet formal gesture.

"Plato long ago recognized," he began, "that besides eating, sleeping, breathing, and mating, every creature has an instinctual need to periodically leap up into the air for no other reason than because it feels so good. I mean no offense, Rapunzel, but I would guess that you have not been attending to this need for a very long time. Seeing as how it is essential to our exercise, I implore you now to do just that. Nine times, if you would be so kind."

Surprising myself with my lack of hesitation, I did just what he asked. My first jump was a twisting pirouette in which I tried to imitate an ice skater doing a double axle. The rest were increasingly less disciplined and more careening. On the ninth I lost my balance and sprawled as I came down to earth. Having set down the two books he was carrying, he responded with sustained applause and a "Bravo!"

"Then on the other hand," he continued as I reassembled myself, "there is me, who has always recognized that besides eating, sleeping, breathing, and mating, every creature has an instinctual need to contradict himself at all times—since that is the only way to be like a god, *n'est-ce pas?* Again, Rapunzel—I hope you are not insulted—but my sense is that you have not had extensive practice in the art of smashing together the contradictions. Or rather blending them gracefully. I call this art tantra, and it is at the heart of the Theater of Cruelty crash course I wish to give you."

I had some knowledge of tantra—enough to know that contrary to its hip New Age transmogrification, it was an ancient magical tradition with far more to it than exotic sexual practices. My sense was that it aspired to create a union of opposites on all levels, and sacred copulation was merely one strategy among many to accomplish that. Still, I was unprepared for Jumbler's interpretation.

He took out a pack of Virginia Slims cigarettes from his shirt pocket and lit two, one for me and one for him. I had never smoked a cancer stick in my life, but I was willing to go along with the gag.

He launched into a series of strenuous exercises: ten quick sit-ups followed by eight push-ups and then a minute of jumping jacks. Through it all he puffed on his butt. Eager to please, I did the same.

"Excellent form!" he exclaimed at the end, gasping for breath. "Beautifully executed self-confutation!"

As I threw my cigarette on the sidewalk and stamped it out, he bent over to pick up something from the gutter. It was an empty, battered plastic bottle of Clorox bleach with the top off. He handed it to me as if it were a treasure.

"This is your reward for so faithfully taking up my challenge," he explained. "A priceless artifact from an ancient civilization. Long ago, this vessel was used in sacred water-purification rituals. All the reservoirs and aquifers of that once-proud land had been poisoned by pollution, you see, and only the potion contained in bottles like these could render the water safe for drinking again. I have rarely seen a better-preserved example. This will make a handsome addition to your home, if you choose to display it there. Or you will no doubt be able to sell it to a museum for a large sum. Accept it with my admiration."

I searched Jumbler's face for some sign of irony. But I was glad it wasn't there. I loved the inscrutable mood he had conjured up and didn't want it to devolve into a boringly literal conversation.

I put down my water-purification vessel and surveyed our surroundings to see if there were any gifts for me to offer in return. Awaiting my discovery was the gnarled knob of a root lying free on the edge of the vacant lot.

"And here is a token I want you to have in appreciation for how you've stuck by me all these centuries, Jumbler." I was trying to imitate his majestic cadences. "It's a precious goddess figurine from an even more ancient civilization, the peace-loving matriarchal society of Old Europe. As you can see, her shape is cast in the ideal of fertile beauty that prevailed back then: stocky frame with large, hammy buttocks and pendulous breasts. She was built for comfort, not speed."

Jumbler bowed deeply as he accepted my present. Just for fun, I did two exaggerated curtsies, pretending to extend the edges of my non-existent skirt. In response, he saluted me sharply with his right hand, and I couldn't help but salute back with my left, except with a goofy look on my face. Before I even realized the implications, he was scratching himself under the arms and jutting out his lower lip like a chimp—though in a somehow dignified manner—and I in turn stuck out my tongue and gave him the raspberry. Then he made the sign of the cross on his forehead with his index finger and stifled a big yawn, and I put my hands together in prayer and genuflected. He formally blew me a kiss, and I bared my teeth and growled. He aristocratically thumbed his nose at me, his eyebrows arched, and I replied by tilting my head to one side and holding my arms out in the offer of a hug.

By then I had become conscious of a memory from earlier in the day. While on the operating table in Dr. Elfland's office, I'd seemed to recall or maybe hallucinate that my dream at dawn had included a dialogue of gestures with Rumbler. It was an exchange eerily similar to the dance I was now doing with Jumbler.

I was paralyzed with an attack of self-consciousness. Jumbler didn't seem to hold it against me, though. He pointed his right index finger down at the top of his head and spun like a top, and when I failed to respond promptly, he retrieved our two books and simply resumed walking down the sidewalk, gesturing with a sweep of his hand. I picked up the valuable artifact he'd bestowed on me and followed along.

"Now be so kind as to tell me what the word is for that thing right there," he ordered cheerfully as we crossed Fourth Street, the downtown's main drag. He was pointing at a car that was stopped at a red light. I wasn't sure what the rules were for this part of the game.

"*Voiture?*" I said "car" in French, thinking maybe he wanted me to speak as Artaud would have.

"No, that is a rude dappled ganglion, my friend. Now tell me what that is." He was pointing at a parking meter.

"Uh. A black-market sphinx?"

"Better. Much closer than last time. Actually, it is a slippery loud fetish. But you are improving. What is this?" He was pointing at himself.

"Flaming milk tree?"

"Yes! Yes! Excellent! Now I want you to give names to everything else. Remember, it is our hallowed responsibility to invent words for everything."

"Cobalt mermaid serum," I proclaimed, indicating an empty baby stroller in front of a store. "Almond whirlpool medicine," I added, coining a fresh phrase for what was once a "mailbox."

"Coral hydrangea sap. Swampy opalescent lather. Pearly ejaculating heart. Eucalyptus anemone guard. Ovarian hawk cedar. Peachy porcelain mist. Beaded mushroom face." So I bestowed new names on what were formerly a window, a door, a sign, a garbage can, an awning, a cloud, and the sky.

"That was extraordinary work," he said, directing us to enter the door of a small market. "You show great potential in the art of naming.

That will come in handy in the latter-day version of the Theater of Cruelty, because in its domain absolutely everything must be blessed with a fresh name every day—sometimes twice a day."

This was no sleek 7-Eleven we'd slipped inside. It was a dingy, claustrophobic place with narrow aisles and dusty products crammed on shelves that reached the ceiling. The signs and packages were all in Spanish, though many had English translations. Cheap jewelry and watches were arranged in a messy display next to grimy bags of charcoal and disposable diapers that looked like they'd been languishing there for months. A riotous assortment of herbs, as if in a witches' apothecary, hung in small plastic bags adjacent to tall candles in glass containers that were painted with Catholic religious icons. Mostly there were foods, some of it exotic stuff I'd never imagined existed, like cans of curdled milk pudding and jars of deep-fried pork skin in brine.

Jumbler was filling a hand-held red plastic shopping basket. "For our sacred feast," he beamed as I examined his haul: a jar of *nopalitos,* or shreds of tender cactus; a very large jar of *pacaya,* which seemed to be the fruit of the date palm tree, whatever that was, though it resembled small octopi with long tentacles; a can of *olluco,* an "ancient Andean tuber"; Pulparindo, a hot and salted tamarind pulp candy; Extraño, popsicles made with jalapeños; and *rosa de castilla,* a bag of rose petals. He'd also gathered a can opener and three of the Catholic candles. Into the basket I threw a mini-pack of Advil, which I had already opened and swallowed without the aid of water. My forehead had begun to throb.

"Will that be all, ma'am?" the clerk asked Jumbler as he used cash to pay for these items. He either didn't hear her or didn't correct her.

So now at least one observer had cast her support towards the theory that my new companion was of the female persuasion. I asked myself whether it made a difference to me. Would I alter my behavior if I thought I was dealing with someone of my own gender? Maybe. Even though I was not yet sure if I was physically attracted to Jumbler, I wanted him to be male. There'd be more of a charge; the mystery would have an edge of uncertainty and risk. If he were a she, I'd instinctively feel more trust, and would as a result be lazier about advancing the mysterious game we were playing.

Jumbler had engaged the clerk in conversation. They continued to chat long past the time the money was exchanged. He seemed fascinated with the older woman's stories about her girlhood in El Salvador, the unusual bright green fabric she had bought for five dollars a yard at a garage sale, her granddaughter's communion, and several other nondescript tales that I tuned out. It all went on so long that I wondered if it weren't somehow supposed to be part of my "crash course."

At least this break had given the four Advils time to cure my head pain. But I was anxious to get back to our game.

"In the new Theater of Cruelty," Jumbler said as we exited the market, "I would like to suggest that one of our basic performance rituals should be to listen with smart sympathy to people whom everyone else considers unimportant."

So that's what he'd been doing.

"I like that idea," I said. "Though I'm not sure what it has to do with cruelty."

"It is cruelty *par excellence*," he exclaimed excitedly. "A radical rejection of widely held values. Going vehemently against the grain of all the habitual emotional reactions that fuel the daily grind. What could be more cruel than expressing compassion with concentrated intelligence? It is a living whirlwind that devours the darkness of angry superiority, knee-jerk dehumanization, and unthinking competitiveness."

"But there must be better ways to cultivate that kind of cruelty without boring yourself to death. I don't agree with the tired old tradition that being of service to humanity means sacrificing your fun."

"But I *did* have fun talking to the clerk in the market. Please know that I was not acting in the tradition of the bleeding-heart liberal, whose compassion is condescending and sentimental. I was not merely being nice to appease my own harassing conscience."

"What possible fun could you have had gabbing about all those inane subjects?"

"First, Rapunzel, I have my bodhisattva vow to guide me: *I will not accept liberation from the wheel of death and rebirth until I have worked to ensure that all sentient beings are also liberated.* So you see it gives me the sweetest pleasure to imagine that I am creeping closer to nirvana by helping the market clerk get there with me.

"And then there is my second vow, my Rosicrucian vow: *I will interpret every event in my life as a direct communication from God to my soul.*

With that as my guide, I find inspiration in the oddest and most unlikely places. As Carl Jung advised, I look for the treasure in the trash. As the alchemists recommended, I find the gold hidden inside the lead."

"And what great secret from the divine realm came your way courtesy of the boring clerk in the market?"

"Several. I will tell you one. When she described to me her granddaughter's first holy communion, she looked straight at you and winked and cocked her eyebrow three different times. I am not even sure she realized what she was doing; perhaps God was making His own expressions appear on her face. At that moment I knew without a doubt—perhaps God was also using her to communicate with me telepathically—that you too are in some way making your first holy communion. How I cannot say exactly. In my mind's eye, the image of the clerk's granddaughter kneeling at the altar turned into you."

I immediately flashed on my vision in the Drivetime earlier that day. Madame Blavatsky had initiated a ritual she called "Magdalen's First Supper." She'd filled the Supersoaker with the unidentifiable red liquid from the Grail and sprayed it into my mouth while repeating a mutated fragment from the Christian eucharist: "Take and drink of this, for this is the Chalice of Your Blood, a living symbol of the new and eternal covenant. It is the mystery of faith, which will be shed for many, that they may attain tantric jubilation and kill the apocalypse."

Jumbler had seen true.

We had stopped in front of a pawn shop. It was closed, but the lights in the window revealed a display with Easter themes. One rainbow-colored basket contained fake green confetti grass, jelly beans, a chocolate bunny wrapped in pink and yellow foil, and numerous necklaces with centerpieces of the crucified Christ.

I was aswim with two competing emotional states. On the one hand, I had become as soft and gooey as I ever got. My mothers had often experienced my melted heart, and Rumbler had certainly shared my most tender feelings in the Televisionarium. But I had never even come close to letting my guard down in the company of an actual male—if indeed Jumbler was a male.

On the other hand, my discriminating analytical mind was on full alert. (That this was possible, in light of my squishy state, was both delightful and unfathomable.) As close as I was beginning to feel to Jumbler, as much as I instinctively wanted to throw great heaps of trust his way, I was acutely aware that I knew almost nothing about him. Maybe there were grains of truth in his beliefs about me. Maybe he really did have some magical link with me that would be thrilling to explore. But my training as the avatar of the Pomegranate Grail demanded that I stay skeptical. Magical thinking serves you well, my mothers had taught me, only if balanced by scientific thinking.

My problem was how could I gather more concrete information about Jumbler without spoiling the mood he had created? I also thought it would be wise if I didn't let him control or initiate every aspect of our interaction.

"If you know so much about me," I finally said with as much poise as I could muster, trying to betray neither of my extremes, "why don't you seem to have any awareness of two of my most important incarnations? The one I had in Palestine almost two thousand years ago and the one I'm in now?"

"I confess that there are great gaps in my understanding of your destiny. I do not like this fact at all. It brings me pain."

"But how do you know so much about me in the first place?"

"I can give you three reasons."

"Please do."

"The first is that I remember my previous incarnations, or at least some of them, and in several of those I have been close to you. The second is that I am a true dreamer. That means that I know how to become awake while I am dreaming, and can discover secrets in my dreams about the waking realm."

We were standing at a red light waiting to cross the street. Just then three remarkable cars drove by in a mini-parade. They were old-style Mercury Comets, built in the 1960s. One was robin's-egg blue, one lemon yellow, one emerald green. With my recent meditations on Mercurius and Mercuria still fresh in memory, this vision lifted the levels of synchronicity to boggling heights.

Jumbler seemed to be hesitating or deliberating about the third reason he knew so much about me.

"And the third is," I jumped in, "you're good at making up strange stories about me that I have no way of confirming or denying?"

He took my hand, brought it to his mouth, and kissed it.

"No, my dear. The third is hard to explain in the limited vocabulary of the English language. If only you understood ancient Egyptian...."

The kiss and the reference to me as his dear and the vision of the Mercury cars and his gracious forbearance in the face of my taunt: All had conspired to make my knees feel weak, my solar plexus mushy.

Or, my skeptical mind said, maybe it had more to do with the fact that I had barely eaten all day.

"I am not your holy guardian angel," he began. "No incarnated human being can be anyone's holy guardian angel. But your holy guardian angel and I have affinities. We have what you might call conversations. She works harder to serve you than I do because you're her only job, whereas I have my own destiny to attend to as well as yours. But I am one of your great helpers."

"Do you know my other helpers?"

"Do you?"

"Earlier today I made the acquaintance of one of them for the first time."

"May I ask which one?"

"Madame Helena P. Blavatsky. Though I suppose I should mention that she was not exactly clothed in flesh and blood. I encountered her in a place called the Drivetime. Have you heard of it?"

"Of course. The wormhole between the Dreamtime and the Daytime. The songline that connects the two and is a hybrid of the two. But don't tell me you just discovered this wonder today. Surely you have known about it from an early age."

"I've called it by another name before now."

"Thank God."

"And what about Madame Blavatsky. Do you know her?"

"No, I regret to say that I do not. But then, as I said, I only know a part of your destiny's overall scheme."

"Do you know the part about how I'm the reincarnation of Mary Magdalen?"

For the first time since we met, Jumbler seemed to have become shy or evasive. He wouldn't look me in the eyes.

"I am going to take you to the holiest, most beautiful place in all of Marin County," he said with a weird fierceness as we passed a Pizza Hut. "It is very close now."

"I refuse to go to the holiest, most beautiful spot until you say what you have against me being Mary Magdalen."

"I am sure I will get used to the idea in time."

"But what's the problem? Aren't you happy for me?"

"It is just that if what you say is true, I have been kept in the dark about a very, very large piece of the puzzle."

"Who's the mysterious and powerful puzzle-master, anyway? Who's doling out these pieces so stingily?"

"You know," he said mournfully, "when you were dying—I mean when you were dying as Artaud—you refused to see me. I even visited the hospital, and you put your palms over your eyes and your fingers in your ears until I went away. But I forgive you. I forgave you then. In the hour when you died, a few days later, I woke up from a nap dreaming that you were wrestling a cloud for the right to block the sun."

"And why did I refuse to see you?" I asked.

"Because I loved you too much."

Up until this point, Jumbler had seemed superhuman in his glib mastery of the flow. He had been dashing, confident, relaxed. But now his face looked defeated. I felt sorry for him. My first impulse was to help him get back to the state he had been in.

"What does that mean?" I asked. "'I loved you too much?'"

"It means I loved you more than you loved me. And it was not the first time."

"You had a desperate unrequited crush on me when I was Paracelsus, too?" I said, trying to lighten his mood.

"Do not mock me, my dear."

"Maybe the problem started with you being my great helper without me being your great helper. That would create an imbalance of power, don't you think?"

"But I have never had the expectation that you should pay me back. My gifts must have no strings attached. I am a bodhisattva."

"But why shouldn't I be in cahoots with your holy guardian angel, as you are with mine? What if I wanted to give to you as much as you gave me? How could I be so narcissistic as to let our relationship be one-sided?"

"It is not right for me to ask for your blessings to rain on me, or even to yearn for you to be in my special service."

I felt a sudden rage. "Maybe that's why I was so mad at you," I cried. "Maybe that's even why I couldn't love you as much as you loved me: because you set it up so that I wasn't allowed to give you as much as you gave me. That was selfish of you, don't you see? It was cruel. You wanted to be the big giver, bigger than me, and you trapped me in the role of the receiver. You made me into the objectified idol so you could be the holy devotee."

I couldn't believe what I was saying. Where were these ideas coming from? It felt like I was picking up a centuries-old conversation with Jumbler. I was trembling with the bizarre familiarity of it all.

We had arrived in the parking lot of Goodwill, a store that sold recycled clothes and furniture and other miscellaneous stuff. Jumbler set his books and bags down near a dirty white trailer that was parked next to the rear wall. It was the back half of a large truck, which presumably housed raw donations before they were processed. At one end it rested on two pairs of tires, and at the other on thick metal stilts.

Jumbler's eyes were closed as he leaned against the trailer. The rapid twitching of his eyelids indicated that he was following a stream of inner images. I could well appreciate the state he was in and wanted to give it all my respect. When he tottered and started to slide down, I grabbed him as best I could to guide him. He ended up seated with his back against the tires of the trailer. I sat next to him with my hand on his knee. The smell of diesel fuel and motor oil was pervasive at first, but faded as my nostrils got used to it.

We remained almost motionless in that position for a long time, maybe half an hour. Now and then he would twitch or mumble as if he were asleep and dreaming of adventures. I felt, ironically, that I was extemporaneously fixing the age-old imbalance. All my energy was pouring into him unconditionally, all my attention. I had no inclination to tune into my own inner dialogue, but wanted to make myself available to him in whatever way he needed me.

After a long time, he spoke words that were intelligible. "All these centuries, I have been trying to atone."

"Atone for what?" I asked.

"Atone for my failure to make you my equal in the new religion we spawned. I did not make it clear enough how crucial you were. I did not work hard enough to wear away the resistance of the male disciples. And so our successors distorted everything we worked together to accomplish."

I could not for a moment believe that the person sitting next to me, as inscrutably magical as he might be, was the reincarnation of Jesus Christ. Yet that is exactly what his vision seemed to have told him. I was willing to play along with this fantasy, as I had been responsive to his other improvisations, but I regarded it as inconceivable that he could have been ignorant of this amazing facet of his destiny until now.

"The world was not yet ripe for me," I said simply. "But it is now."

Jumbler rose and stretched and gave an exultant sigh.

"Yes," he agreed. "And that is why I must declare an end to my compulsive atonement. It is time to stop feeling guilty and start letting you help me do what we set out to do so long ago."

He circled around to three big cardboard box-fulls of fresh junk that lay at one end of the trailer. Apparently some donor had deposited the stuff here after the store closed. Jumbler pawed through it purposefully until he found something he liked.

"Sumptuous carpets for the sanctuary," he announced, holding up an ugly green cashmere sweater and purple wool women's pants along with a grocery bag of other old clothes. "With these I lay the new foundation."

He crouched down under the trailer, which was a space about waist-high, and spread out the garments on the oil-stained asphalt. When he was done, he plucked two plates and some silverware from the boxes and arranged them on the "carpet." Darkness had fallen, but two lights outside Goodwill's back door provided dim illumination.

"Come, my dear," he cooed. "Let us build a tabernacle in the wilderness."

I was brimming with curiosity. What exactly had he experienced during his vision? Had he felt and used the psychic energy I'd fed him? Why was he so sure that the scenes he saw proved beyond a doubt that he himself was Jesus? (My training taught me to evaluate shamanic epiphanies with the same skepticism I brought to all raw data.) Had he received any revelations that filled in the gaps in his knowledge about my destiny?

But I decided to forgo this line of inquiry for the time being. Sooner or later, I promised myself, I would indulge, but for the foreseeable future I would suspend my desire to frame our adventure with my questions. I wanted to be in a fully surprisable mode, not as much in control as I had been all my life.

Over the next few minutes, I helped him fill the space beneath the trailer with other discarded goods. There were pyramid-shaped salt and pepper shakers, Christmas ornaments with angel themes, a hand-painted wooden egg within an egg within an egg within an egg, an Etch-a-Sketch, artificial sunflowers, a book of poetry by Sylvia Plath, a toy metal alligator, pipe cleaners, a rod and attached copper ball from inside a toilet, a roll of biohazard warning stickers, a troll doll wearing a doctor uniform, and a ripped print of Picasso's *Les Demoiselles d'Avignon*.

As a finishing touch, Jumbler lit the candles he'd bought at the market and placed the food around the two plates. An elegant if campy shrine now filled the cramped, dusty space.

Briefly, I worried that we might be caught by someone. But I reasoned that we weren't breaking any law. And though there were many cars whizzing by on the busy street where one side of the parking lot ended, we were well hidden from them by the trailer's double sets of tires. I hadn't seen any pedestrians in the vicinity since we arrived.

"It is show time, O Queen," he said then. "The sacred space is designed beautifully. The lighting is perfect. The mood is pregnant. So let us begin the ritual feast. Dessert first, of course."

He opened the box of Extraño, the jalapeño popsicles. Each one was a double barrel, with two sticks. As we sucked the cold yet hot green treats, he told me a tale.

"Long ago, near Hereford, on the banks of the Wye River in merry old England, there lived an odd little creature named Robin the Mouth. The people of the town could not remember when Robin had first appeared, nor how she had come to do the strange job that everyone needed done but no one else wanted to do. Sometimes she seemed to be a ghost flitting at the edge of their dreams—until that dire moment when they put out an urgent call for her flesh-and-blood presence.

"For Robin the Mouth was a Sin-Eater. That is to say, she took on the sins of recently deceased persons by ingesting food imbued with the last gasps of their departing spirits. Whenever a death occurred, Robin was called to the side of the corpse, upon whose chest lay a funeral biscuit and bowl of requiem ale. As she fed on this sepulchral nourishment, she pledged to pawn her own soul on behalf of the deceased, who might thereby find an unimpeded path to the kingdom of heaven.

"But there was a hitch. Have you heard the saying, 'No good deed goes unpunished?' Never was that more truly said than in regards to Robin the Mouth. The moment the Sin-Eater was paid, the corpse's relatives and friends chased her from the house amidst curses and threats, and often with sticks and stones as well. She was feared and hated for having such weird power to heal. And yet she would be asked to perform the same service the next time the community lost one of its members.

"Robin loved her job, despite its drawbacks. It was exciting to be so necessary during the greatest rite of passage of all. She was proud of how unique she was. Indeed, in time she grew ambitious to become even more unique. And when the opportunity presented itself, she began to innovate. No longer content simply to do as she was required, she ate the sins of those who were still alive.

"A wise, restless woman named Lethe was Robin's first experiment. How did it come about? A chance meeting between the two in the woods on All Hallow's Eve led to the discussion of forbidden topics and wild ideas. The Moon was conjunct Jupiter and Mars and Sun in Scorpio on that afternoon, and both women were in the darkly fertile time of the month when the blood flows. Surely these conditions invited them to plumb more deeply than either might have been normally inclined.

"The next evening Robin came to the cottage where Lethe lived, and the two conducted a rite that had never before been done.

"'Relieve me of my lapses, my malice, my thoughtlessness,' Lethe beseeched Robin. 'Devour my mistakes so that I may be born afresh.' And as Robin nibbled the biscuit and sipped the ale that lay on her chest, Lethe felt a great purification come over her, a release from the losses that had bent and twisted her destiny. 'This is high magic,' she exclaimed. 'You have made my heart light again. I feel endowed with the power to forgive myself.'

"In this way, Robin the Mouth discovered the rest of her calling. Secretly at first, she bestowed her gift on a few mavericks and odd folk. As she beheld the renewal she wrought, the burdens she lifted, she became emboldened to act more openly. That was her downfall, of course. If her healing had been barely tolerated before, now it became a menace.

"One spring morning, she ate the sins of the blacksmith's son, who then testified to all who would listen that he had been marvelously cleansed as not even the eucharist had ever done. Horrified, the townspeople went mad. Hunting the Sin-Eater down in her hut in the woods, they hurled sticks and stones at her with such force that she breathed no more.

"For in the end Robin was seen as a rival to Jesus himself. Was there not a perverse homology between their functions? In church, the supplicants ate the symbolic body and blood of Christ so as to have their sins absorbed and burned away by the devoured God. Robin, on the other hand, ingested the symbolic bodies and blood of the supplicants so as to take their sins into herself, that they might become closer to Christ.

"As I end this tale, my dear Rapunzel, I will ask you to guess what meaning it has for you."

The story had roused unfathomable emotions in me. They were huge and pungent but mostly out of the reach of my ability to articulate. The only words I could find that captured even a bit of the sensations in me were *triumphant sadness*.

At the same time, there was something dear and familiar about the Sin-Eater. I identified with her. I thought maybe it had to do with a theme I'd wrestled with for as long as I could remember: how risky it is to be a force for good; how delicate an operation it is to help people in a way that doesn't invite chaos and ruin.

Rocking gently back and forth, Jumbler was waiting for my reply to his question.

"Don't tell me you mean to imply that I was Robin the Mouth in one of my previous incarnations?" I asked tentatively.

"Not implying. Stating as fact."

"Antonin Artaud. Paracelsus. Eumolpus. And now Robin the Mouth. Anyone else I've been that I should know about?"

"Do not change the subject."

"I must admit I feel a certain resonance with Robin."

"You just ate her sins, by the way. I arranged for them to be contained in that jalapeño popsicle I gave you."

Almost unconsciously, I had begun to perform a gesture I'd done hundreds of times back home inside my redwood tree. I was rhythmically stroking two popsicle sticks together. Jumbler was doing the same with his.

"What were Robin's sins?" I asked.

"Her biggest sin was that she was too proud of her innovation. That kept her from being cagey enough to stay alive, which in turn prevented her from developing her new art to its utmost. Had she been able to continue, she would have become a master not just in swallowing but in thoroughly *digesting* the sins she ate. That was the special destiny she should have had, you see. Though there were many other sin-eaters in old Europe, most of them turned into pitiful martyrs by the time they reached the end of their days. They were hapless scapegoats, after all, not illumined Christs. They did not possess the soul force to process the demonic waste they regularly absorbed.

"But Robin had stumbled upon the transformative trick of Jesus: how to use the devoured psychic poison as fuel; breaking it down so as to neutralize its danger even as she tapped into the vital force that had been trapped therein."

"I don't understand what that means."

"The task the sin-eaters performed was not merely symbolic. The stuff they absorbed in the act of 'eating' was real. Not real, of course, in the eyes of those modern folks who believe the material world is all there is. But absolutely real according to most other cultures, which have always accepted the objective existence of a subtler form of matter—the stuff that composes the spirit realm."

"My people and I have always referred to it as the *prima materia*," I said, finally feeling a need to insert some of my own vernacular.

"But what the sin-eaters absorbed from their clients was not just any old kind of *prima materia*," Jumbler said. "It was the trashiest effluvia—all the most ignorant, unripe, nasty aspects of the departing souls."

"What Carl Jung described as the shadow," I interjected.

"Exactly right. Now for most sin-eaters, this was a horrible burden. They gradually became bloated garbage heaps. But Robin was unlike her fellows, who by the way were almost exclusively men. She had the shaman's skill of breaking down the garbage into its component elements, thereby gaining access to the libidinous charge at the raw core of all psychic energy."

Now I saw what he was driving at. My Goddess Persephone is renowned for her power to dissolve distorted and outworn forms, returning their constituent matter to its "virginal" state. In the tradition of the Pomegranate Grail, if not of the patriarchy, Persephone is the very archetype of the Virgin.

"According to the alchemists," Jumbler added, "*dissolution* is the secret of the Great Work."

"According to Jung," I said, "fabulous treasure lies hidden amidst the unlovely shadow." I was exhilarated to be able to contribute to the unfolding revelation with my own cherished beliefs.

"So you're saying that I—as Robin the Mouth—was a Christ-like character?" I continued. "I freed people from their sick karma without myself being infected by their gross poisons?"

"You were not a lost soul victimized by those you served. You were a skilled alchemist who thrived on turning lead into gold. Or at least you were headed in that direction. But you never arrived there. You got yourself killed before your work was done. Fortunately, now you are ready to pick up where you left off."

"I'm supposed to pick up where Robin left off *and* where Artaud left off? I'm going to be a sin-eater in the Theater of Cruelty?"

"Blend the two, my dear, and you get the next phase in the evolution of both the sin-eater and the Theater of Cruelty: *The Eater of Cruelty*. All we have to do to get there is take the Theater of Cruelty and add an extra 'e' after the 'Th' in 'Theater.' Theater of Cruelty transforms into The Eater of Cruelty."

I was seduced by the elegance and intricacy of Jumbler's theories about my destiny. Though they seemed at odds with everything I'd been taught, I struggled to integrate them. There was not necessarily a contradiction between being Mary Magdalen, I reasoned, and all the characters he had paraded out. None of his candidates were alive in the first century Anno Domini.

Searching my own experience for some link with the Sin-Eater and The Eater of Cruelty, I fell into a reverie about Madame Blavatsky in the Drivetime. I recalled the pungent, astringent taste of the "wine" she had shot into my mouth with the Supersoaker. That was certainly a cruel thing to imbibe.

The ritual we enacted there was, like the work of the Sin-Eater, a variation on the Christian church's eucharist. According to Madame Blavatsky, the holy nourishment we dispensed was a symbolic representation not of Christ's blood but of mine, Magdalen's. And what could be more cruel than drinking an avatar's blood?

Then I glimpsed an electrifying notion that had not occurred to me when Madame Blavatsky and I celebrated "Magdalen's First Supper" a few hours ago. The blood the Christians drink is that of their murdered god. Indeed, its potency for salvation derives in large part from the fact that the god agreed to be sacrificed. But what if the blood of the new eucharist is shed by a goddess who is renewing, not immolating, herself? What if the divine nourishment is *menstrual* blood?

It was beautifully logical, the perfect correction of the phallocracy's half-assed distortion of Jesus' and Magdalen's joint revelation. It was also blasphemous, an uproarious revenge that would deeply offend every Christian alive.

"Jesus died for your sins," I fantasized myself explaining on Easter Sunday to the faithful during a global TV broadcast designed to compete with the Pope's address from the Vatican. "You drink the blood he shed in his final act of love. But I, Magdalen, don't have to die because I can *menstruate* for your sins. I expire just a little bit, enough so that I can cleanse and renew myself, and then I return to menstruate for your sins again next month. Pretty elegant arrangement, don't you think? Wouldn't you rather have as your role model a divinity who doesn't need to be murdered in order to serve you? What?! You say that drinking menstrual blood is a cruel, disgusting thing to ask of you?! Well, I'll have you know that it's no 'dirtier' than any other kind of blood. It is far less gruesome, too—since no one has to die."

During my reverie, Jumbler had opened the food containers and filled our plates. The spread was dominated by what looked like a miniature octopus, though I knew it was *pacaya*, or date palm. Shreds of *nopalitos*, tender cactus, lay in a soggy heap nearby, as well as two pieces of *olluco*, the "ancient Andean tuber." The *pièce de résistance* was a flat strip of Pulparindo brand candy, a hot and salted tamarind pulp the size of an extra-wide piece of gum.

I hadn't eaten much all day, but as I gazed upon the feast Jumbler had prepared I was filled with a perfectly equal mix of hunger and repulsion.

"As we begin our cruel feast, my dear," Jumbler said, "I will ask you to feel empathy for every person in the world who is addicted to his or her signature form of suffering. This unique pain is comfortably familiar. It keeps them from being bored. It makes them feel special, and is in fact the lynchpin of their identity."

"It would be cruel to take away their anguish," I replied.

"It would be cruel to eat the cruelty they cling to," he agreed.

"You might have to resort to sneaky tricks in order to divest them of the feeling they love to hate."

"They might even despise you if they found out you were trying to steal their beloved suffering."

"Healing would be a dangerous act, both for the healer and the healed."

"You would have to be radical but discreet."

"Ferocious but friendly."

"Relentlessly tender and wildly disciplined."

"A living whirlwind that devours the darkness."

I picked up the yellowish white octopus, alias the date palm. It smelled like a cross between corn and lima beans. How the hell to eat it? Maybe twenty to twenty-five beaded, four-inch tentacles hung down from a short stalk. I gripped a few with my teeth and bit.

A chalky bitterness struck the roof of my mouth, followed by the taste of sour and rancid vinegar. With all my heart I wanted to spit it out but forced myself to press on. The texture of the tentacles was crunchy at first, but quickly turned into a crumbly mess of soggy granules. The acrid assault on all the tissues of my mouth intensified until out of self-defense I swallowed.

I immediately felt as if I were going to throw up. In an attempt to staunch the aftertaste, I took a bite out of the Pulparindo candy. It obliterated the previous imprint with a burst of unbearable flavor that was simultaneously salty and sweet and spicy hot and sour and chewy. It hurt my mouth too, but blocked the emetic urge. I swallowed it.

My face was puckered, my tongue sore, and I felt exhilarated.

"Bless you, my dear," Jumbler said as he took my hand. "You are indeed the tantric master I imagined." His touch was tender. It had a woman's suppleness. As he stroked my palm, I felt an impossible mix: sweet trust and a hot sexual rush.

29

Attention please.
This is your ancestors speaking.
We've been trying to reach you
through your dreams and fantasies and meditations,
but you don't seem to have heard us.

That's why we've been forced
to borrow the Televisionary Oracle.
So listen up.
We'll make it brief.
The fact is
you're at a crossroads
analogous to a dilemma
which has mystified our biological line
for six generations.
We beseech you now
to master the turn
that none of us have ever figured out
how to negotiate.
Heal yourself
and you heal all of us.

"I want to paint fat, pimply guys in muscle cars with as much panache as Leonardo da Vinci painted his Madonnas," mused our friend

Romney in describing her aspirations as an artist. "I want to invoke the elegance of Rembrandt," she continued, "as I create canvases depicting toxic landfills where pagan angels play catch with burning televisions as they scavenge for Pez candy dispensers." This is the spirit we'd like you to emulate in the coming months and years, beauty and truth fans. Be eager to find and even create beauty everywhere you go, no matter how little you have to work with.

The Televisionary Oracle
wishes you
bigger, better, more original sins
and wilder, wetter, more interesting problems.

I am not a rockstar. I have never been a rockstar. I will never be a rockstar.

Repeat a thousand times a day for the next thirty years. Get tattooed on the inside of my eyelids. Tell everyone I know to greet me with the chant "You are not a rockstar. You have never been a rockstar. You will never be a rockstar."

But now I return to the present. Release the weight of the past. Spiral back here to the dressing room bathroom at the Catalyst, and prepare to hit the stage for our big show.

In a few minutes I will stand under hot lights, amidst deafening sound, before nine hundred people. I will do this gladly. I will do this with devotion and gratitude, understanding that it is why I have come to Earth. I will not be a brooding, intellectual introvert but an animated, bright-faced extrovert brimming over with joy and exuberance. So help me Goddess. Amen.

I check my face in the mirror to ensure I've wiped away all signs of self-pity. Then I bound out of the bathroom, announcing "Time for the group hug."

George and Amy and Squint and Daniel and Darby gather. We form a circle, like in my old Little League pre-game rituals, and drape our arms around each other.

"What's the secret password?"

"WEW."

"And what's that mean?!" I bark.

"World Entertainment War!" the others chant.

"What's that mean?" I press on.

"Weave Extravagant Wobbles!" they cry.

"What's that mean?"

"Wild Epic Weddings!"

"And what's our ally?"

"Witches' Elegant Webs!"

"What's our war cry?"

"Wish Evolution Well!"

"What's our job?"

"Wash Every Window!"

"How do we get in?"

"Weird Entry Ways!"

As we perform our pep rally, we bend our heads down so that eventually the tops of all of them are touching. Meanwhile, our voices rise in volume until the final reply, when the force of the group sound flings our heads back and causes us to erupt in laughter. The rule is, everyone has to achieve an extended bellylaugh whether or not they're genuinely amused. Tonight, though, no one has to strain to reach the hallowed goal of total hilarity. All of us are feeling some version of the painful deflation and happy release that I feel, the result of declaring our independence from CBS and Will Boehm Management and returning to our scraggly roots.

"OK," I say, "let's go strap me in." All of us leave the dressing room. Amy and Darby head directly for the stage, while Daniel, Squint, George, Marijka, and I take the back way from the dressing room to the lighting booth, which is high above the back of the dance floor. Leaning against the wall outside the booth is an eight-foot black wooden crucifix: another exquisite piece of work by the multi-talented Marijka.

George informs our lighting director Manny and our video projectionist Gray that we're about to launch the show. Gray heads backstage to flick the switches that'll unleash the flood of images which will flow across the big-screen TV we've mounted behind the drums, as well as the other videos that'll appear on the five smaller on-stage TVs.

Marijka goes to the sound technician's booth, where she informs him we'll soon be ready, meaning that in a couple of minutes he'll turn down the taped music that has been playing over the house speakers since the opening band finished a half hour ago. Marijka also grabs my cordless headset microphone and returns to wrap it around my head without interfering with my Pan horns.

Glancing at the stage, I see Gray has already done his job. The giant TV screen is ablaze, through the magic of computer animation, with a scene of Eleanor Roosevelt being crucified on a cross composed entirely of thousands of Barbie dolls that have been glued together into a gnarled mass. Hundreds of pink Cadillac convertibles are parked around the cross, as if at a drive-in movie. Inside each car are moving human skeletons with televisions for heads. Most are talking on cellular phones while they engage in a variety of sex acts.

Daniel, Squint, George, Marijka, and I lug our crucifix down the stairway to the anteroom at the back of the dance floor. There we part the crowd and set the cross horizontally down on the ground. Ceremoniously, I lie on top of it. George secures my wrists to the horizontal arms of the cross with expertly knotted rope.

A gang of onlookers gathers to admire our spectacle. Though I make it a point to remain almost totally in character, keeping a serious, trance-like expression, at the last moment I wink at a cute girljock wearing a yellow jogging bra and mini-skirt.

My four helpers lift me and the cross up to their shoulder level, then carry their load like a coffin across the dance floor towards the stage. The spotlight is on us as we travel.

The titter and laughter of the audience subsides as soon as I declaim through my microphone:

> Performance is life! Entertainment is death! Long live the guerrilla therapy of our top-secret revolution! We will succeed where the paranoids have failed! We will take back the airwaves from the entertainment criminals! When you're too well-entertained to move, screaming is good exercise, so please scream along with me on the count of three. Are you ready? 1 ... 2 ... 3 ...

I unleash a giddy yowl, attempting to imitate the ecstatic exclamation I once heard a six-year-old girl named Allegra make as she leaped into a plastic swimming pool on a ninety-five-degree afternoon. The crowd is slow to join me, but eventually the shriek spreads. Finally, hundreds of different styles of scream coalesce in an apocalyptic caterwaul that raises goosebumps and makes me feel like I'm about to levitate through the sheer force of the room's vibration.

My butterflies have given way to endorphins. I'm feeling beatifically electrified and preternaturally relaxed. All eyes and ears in the place, maybe nine hundred people, are turned towards me, and I'm so excitedly at peace with what I'm going to do that I feel no pressure at all. A Buddhist might say I'm aligned with my dharma. An athlete would recognize that I'm in the Zone. In this state I can do no wrong, and yet it's the exact opposite of arrogant confidence. On the contrary, I'm empty. Humble. A big fat zero poised to do nothing more than what I was made to do. All the skills I've been programmed to develop since childhood—poetry, dance, song, jokes, making people love me—conspire now to weave themselves together into a single event.

Soon I'll be in the heart of a fuming maelstrom. The martial surge of one hundred decibels of electronically amplified music will be scouring away the accumulated dross of my monkey mind's infernal conversations like a month's worth of zen meditation. I'll be so happily given to the enormity of my assignment that I'll almost forget to breathe, yet I won't be able to afford that luxury because in the heat of the ritual, breath is the most crucial fuel.

Best of all, I'll be executing the appallingly arduous yet fun task of summoning for public consumption the same libidinous blasts I unveil in the private act of making love. It will embarrass and invigorate me at the same time. The expectations and longings of my nine hundred companions will swarm in upon me like a forest fire in a hurricane, commanding, "Be the million-year-old snakegod!" And I will obey. For two hours and forty-five minutes my collaborators will feed me squeals and shouts from their jiggle centers, operating me like a magic puppet, rousing me to dance across the stage in gestures I've never felt myself make before and may never feel again.

In one way I'll be the center of attention, and in another I'll be in a perfect position to be the biggest voyeur of all. No one would ever suspect that I'd have enough attention left over from my duties to spy on the people staring at me. But the forcefully expansive blessing of the revelry forces me to hold a hundred times more perceptions in my organism than usual.

I adore peering down from the stage, my entire body glazed from the exertion and the searing lights, and watching the uncensored faces of the crowd as they use the excuse of the spectacle to unshackle every repressed thought, every tortured question in their hearts. Bursts of telepathy spurt my way, as from a downed power line, and I love it. Right there in the midst of the pandemonium, a wide swath of raw data pouring into and out of me, I will sometimes home in on a specific broadcast radiating from a specific creature in the audience.

"I am the lowest of the low," I swear I telepathically "heard" during our last gig from a forty-ish hippie dancing near the front of the stage. "I abandoned my childhood friend on her deathbed," he beamed towards me. "Let this be my dance of atonement."

Meanwhile, back at ground zero, I'll be stretched as far as I can go: at the limits of what I can do with my muscles, my stamina, my concentration, my creativity, my precision, my everything. As each song demands, I'll sing beautifully or archly or with the savage power of a warrior in the heat of hand-to-hand combat, straining to remember to feel—not just *pretend* to feel—the meaning of the lyrics I'm channeling (even if they belong to imaginary characters portrayed in the songs rather than to myself) and to coordinate them with the gestures and dance moves that are possessing me, all the while remembering to inhale deeply and to interact authentically, not just automatically, with my bandmates. Between each song I'll decide whether we'll move on immediately to the next number or else wait for me to deliver a poetic rant that might either be a set piece I've rehearsed or an improvisation I invoke in response to some mood or current I sense in the crowd.

It's hard fucking work.

At 2 A.M., when I stagger off the stage, I'll sigh to myself again, as I have so many other times, that this is the feeling I most want to remember about my stay here on Earth; that when my body dies and my will-o'-the-wisp soul is negotiating its way through the Bardo planes, I will treasure most the exquisite blown-out sensation that comes from blending kamikaze release with practiced discipline.

Slicing a path now through the sweaty, smoky, boozy crowd, my four helpers and I are approaching the front of the stage. Gratefully, I drink in the welter of images flailing from the TVs on-stage. On the big screen, the huge feminine hand of God, sporting crimson nail polish and a sparkling silver band-aid bearing cartoons of snake priestesses, is reaching down out of the clouds to feed the crucified Eleanor Roosevelt a bite of a gingerbread boy. Meanwhile, the smaller TVs sport a documentary on Kandinsky's paintings, Disney's *Fantasia* (the scene where the mushrooms dance), the local 11 o'clock news (the funeral of a police dog), an educational video on childbirth, and a looped sequence that keeps repeating the scene of the guy in the film *Dr. Strangelove* who rides the falling nuclear bomb through the sky like a bucking bronco.

My helpers slide me and the cross to rest horizontally on the stage, which is maybe six feet higher than the dance floor. Then Daniel and George pull themselves up to join me and lift me and the cross to the vertical position. They lean me against a stack of amplifiers and drift out of the spotlight, where they take up their instruments and start playing an almost subliminal drone. I'm not hanging from the cross, though my arms are suspended from it. My feet are firmly on the ground. Pausing to make a panoramic gaze, I address the throng.

As of now, dear audience, you're being entertained by a hostage crisis.

As of now, you're experiencing a ransom note—a *designer* ransom note—which is also a major news story and a healing advertisement and a ticklish manifesto introducing you to the strategies by which you can prevent the global genocide of the imagination.

As of now, we, the peaceful soldiers of the World Entertainment War, have kidnapped ourselves and are holding ourselves hostage until you meet our demands. And we do mean *you*. We don't mean some friendly tyrant or criminally innocent celebrity. We are holding ourselves hostage until *you* meet all eight hundred eighty-eight of our demands.

Here are our first demands:

DEMAND #1: We demand an immediate three-week global boycott of all media. Consume no television, Internet, radio, movies, newspapers, or magazines! Return to the primordial silence for three days or else!

DEMAND #2: We demand that the word "asshole" begin to be used as a term of endearment rather than abuse.

DEMAND #3: We demand that the average length of an act of heterosexual intercourse in America—which is now an appalling four minutes—be required by law to be a minimum of twenty-two minutes.

DEMAND #4: We demand that all anchormen cry every time they report a tragedy on their nightly TV news shows.

DEMAND #5: We demand that *People* magazine do a cover story on "The Ten Sexiest Homeless Americans."

We have eight hundred eighty-three more demands, but there's plenty of time for them later. First we want you to know more about who we are and what we offer.

We are the World Entertainment War, sacred saboteurs dedicated to helping you learn the difference between your own thoughts and those of the celebrities who have demonically possessed you. Our purpose is to save your imagination from the poisons of the entertainment criminals.

On *their* televisions, the televisions of the entertainment criminals, crude storytellers called "journalists" terrorize you with nihilistic yet sentimental myths that seem to prove the lie, "If it isn't ugly, it's dishonest."

But on *our* televisions, on the televisions we control, aspiring bodhisattvas tell you funny stories about how to go crazy in the name of creation, not destruction. In *our* movies and websites and radio shows, holographic reruns of your happiest memories repeat continuously on instant replay, freeing up your libidos to become telepathically linked with thousands of psychoactivists who've already learned beyond a doubt that they are geniuses! Just as you are!

DEMAND #6: We demand the production of a major feature film based on our life stories. Also, a best-selling book, a weekly column in *USA Today*, and an appearance on the David Letterman show.

DEMAND #7: We demand that brilliant genetic engineers create a mutant bacteria that causes people to hate opinion polls.

DEMAND #8: We demand that you all live up to your full potential.

DEMAND #9: We demand that God be referred to on all future TV shows as a big black lesbian woman. We demand an end to the molestation, exploitation, and torture of God by the world's major so-called religions.

DEMAND #10: We demand an exposé of so-called nice people who cynically use honesty, cheerfulness, and openness to manipulate others into doing things their way.

We, the peaceful soldiers of the World Entertainment War, are supreme patriots! And when in the course of inhuman events you discover as we did that entertainment criminals are pouring trillions of dollars into making the world safe for America's most dangerous images, it becomes necessary to learn very intimately how everyone and everything worth loving—including our native land—is an inextricable blend of divine revelation and idiotic bullshit.

Therefore we hold these truths to be self-evident:

that everything we behold with our five senses composes but a tiny percentage of the twenty-six dimensions of ecstatic creation that God and Goddess freshly fuck into being every second;

that while there may be, for all we know, such a thing as "objective reality," it most certainly does not consist of the endless streams of pictures in our imaginations, which our arrogant egos mistake for the external world;

that therefore every "truth" you and I embrace with such certainty cannot possibly be more than a little bit correct, and to pretend otherwise is the only original sin;

that like docufiction movies and every nightly TV newscast ever done, like life itself, fact and creative storytelling are always blended together so seamlessly that there is no honest way to tell the difference; and that therefore our imaginations are our most sacred organs which create every story we see and believe in;

that we have the right to believe in any story we conjure up or believe in, but not to the point that we would hate or kill people who don't love our stories as much as we do;

that when an elite group of human parasites with obscene amounts of money and technology at their disposal try to trick us into believing that their stories are truer than everyone else's, it is our patriotic right and duty to become trickier than they are.

We therefore do uproariously declare World Entertainment War against all evil advertising geniuses, disinfotainment peddlers disguised as journalists, simulation experts specializing in the rape of our memories, fraudulently immortal celebrities bent on haunting our dreams with their empty souls, cartels of friendly father figures hawking pretty media viruses, and all other genociders of the imagination.

To defend our lives, our fortunes, and our sacred honor, we pledge to fight the entertainment criminals in such a way that we don't become like them.

DEMAND #11: We demand an affirmative action program that will make a majority of all Americans celebrities within five years.

DEMAND #12: We demand foreskin reimplantations for men who associate sex with violence because they suffered the trauma of circumcision within hours after they first came into the world.

DEMAND #13: We demand that brilliant American engineers create a machine for measuring emotional pain. We demand that moralists of every stripe use this technology to try to prove that their favorite victims suffer more than the favorite victims of other moralists.

DEMAND #14: We demand that you experience global warming in your pants.

DEMAND #15: We demand that somebody come and cut me down from this crucifix so I can teach everyone the fine art of kicking their own asses. NOW!

At this cue, Darby and Amy glide onto the stage, each armed with a black Navy Seal knife, and slice through the ropes that have kept me tethered. Meanwhile, the rest of the band breaks into the juju trance rhythms that launch our song "Kick Your Own Ass."

As Darby and Amy scurry to their microphones, I turn my back to the audience and begin demonstrating the proper technique. First I take both hands and rub the area that will soon be impacted. Next I thrust my arms up over my head as if preparing for a high dive, then wiggle the area below my belt, careful to give the gesture a masculine cast, like a male rather than a female stripper. Finally, in tune to the beat, I jump off the ground with both feet and thrust my heels forcefully backwards into the target area. Mission accomplished, I propel my feet back down, landing in time to avoid crumbling to the ground.

Meanwhile, Darby and Amy are singing and chanting:

Your body is bread in a holy war
Change     Change     Change     Change
My body is love in a holy store
Change     Change     Change     Change
Your body is God and I want some more now
Change     Change     Change     Change
My body is money and I'm spending it now
Change     Change     Change     Change

Kick your own ass
NOW!     NOW!
Kick your own ass
NOW!     NOW!

When they reach the lines commanding the audience to participate, I repeat my lesson with a twist. Facing right this time, I administer two boots to my rear end in quick succession, matching their explosive NOWs, then quickly turn the other direction and make two more stabs as they unleash the second set of NOWs.

As the song evolves, I show off every conceivable permutation of the holy gesture. By the end, all the band members except Squint join me in illustrating the technique. I'm ecstatic to see that well over half the crowd has joined our cause. It's amazing to provoke this much audience participation, but then that's our specialty.

"Now that you've disciplined yourselves," I proclaim to the audience as the song ends, "you have every right to ask for the world."

Amy switches the settings on her Korg keyboard to simulate a harp sound and begins playing in a hymnal vein. Soon she uses her other keyboard to add the reedy eddies of a snake charmer's flute. Meanwhile, Squint summons a sinewy rhythm, making his maracas sound like a rattlesnake tail. He's joined shortly by Daniel, who somehow makes his bass sound like a throbbing didgeridoo, and then George, whose churning guitar reminds me of a vat of chocolate cooking over an open flame.

Amy, Darby, and I sing in a whisper at first, chanting the same refrain over and over.

> Give me what I want
> Exactly when I want it
> Forever
> Now
> Once upon a time

Steadily the volume swells, and as it reaches ripeness, Squint pounces on his snare and bass drum, kicking the groove into overdrive. Now our chant becomes strident, an exultant cry for liberation. Many members of the audience have added their voices to the plea, even as they dance with abandoned minds, like those whose lives have just been saved.

When I sense the climax is complete, and the mood is ready to shift—and I hate to brag, but reading a crowd is one of my most infallible talents—I signal to the instrumentalists, who manage to pull off an impeccable ending followed immediately by the launch of the next song on the set list. It's a funky, percolating tune on which I sing lead:

I dropped out of kindergarten
to explore eternal youth
I talked back to Mr. Science
to defend eternal truth
I saw angels in my playpen
They taught me to kiss the sky
I unlocked all nature's secrets
Cross my heart and hope to die

I bailed out of Daddy's airplane
Fell to earth like angel dust
I broke into Caesar's Palace
looking for eternal lust
Every time I found a goddess
we had sex by accident
No one even tried to stop me
when I fired the government

I don't need no paradise
Living here is twice as nice
I don't need no therapy
Free of freedom
Free of me

In mid-song, I crane my head around to monitor the big-screen TV behind me, checking to see what scene is playing. Huge bulldozers driven by teenage girl ninjas in clown make-up are scooping away the cars full of the television-headed human skeletons. A gaggle of witches in conical hats is tenderly removing Eleanor Roosevelt from her gnarled crucifix.

I lucked into symbiosis
Worked my voodoo to the bone
Everything I love surrounds me
Never never am alone
I broke into kindergarten
to destroy the evidence
I danced backwards on the tombstones
to restore my innocence

I don't need no paradise
Living here is twice as nice
I don't need no therapy
Free of freedom
Free of me

On the big-screen TV, a beatific Eleanor Roosevelt is now sitting on a dragon-headed golden throne holding a phallic wand and sporting a new halo as big as a hula hoop. She's bestowing sloppy mouth kisses on a long receiving line of famous men from history, including Socrates, Charlemagne, various Popes, Napoleon, Teddy Roosevelt, Stalin, Nixon, Rush Limbaugh, Joseph McCarthy, and Howard Stern.

The band is hot tonight. No broken strings interrupt the flow, no extended tuning of guitars forces me to do shtick while waiting to return to the scheduled program. The moment "I Dropped Out of Kindergarten" is over, "The Triple Witching Hour" begins. As I light the thick green candle on top of the TV altar and pull out my wad of five-dollar bills, Amy and Darby croon the intro:

Fire and water
Earth and air
This is holy ground
Wall Street, Chrysler, IBM
Round and round and round

Audience members who've attended recent shows know this is their cue to purify their money karma. Quickly there's a gaggle of volunteers holding up their legal tender for me to dispatch. I sing the verse:

The Triple Witching Hour happens every now and then
When all the witches and warlocks on my block
Get in the mood
We cast hexes on the plutocrats
We laugh at their greed
We hoot and we howl and we dare God to make us rich
"Hey God make us rich!"

After another chorus and verse, the volume of the instruments drops way down as Darby and I do a call and response.

"Do you love money?" she sings. "Yes I do, yes I do," I reply, "by the light of the silvery moon." And then:

Do you worship money?
Yes I worship all the time by the light of the dreamy moon
Do you conjure money?
Yes I conjure all the time by the light of Hecate's silver moon
Do you burn money?
I burn it all the time by the purifying light of the moon

Some of the bills I torch are my own. Some are those handed me by the amateur performance artists in the audience. As I gaze out at the faces beyond the flames, I sense in many of them a fascinated repulsion and flabbergasted awe, as if I were incinerating an American flag and spitting on a crucifix at the same time. Others scream encouragement, egging me on as if I were conducting an exorcism.

Maybe seventy dollars have been turned to ash when there's an unscripted arrival. A tall woman has leaped up onto the stage. She's wearing a rainbow tweed jacket, unbuttoned to reveal a marigold bustier. Her lower half sports a semi-transparent chiffon wraparound skirt that reveals below it tight-fitting azure boxers with a pink camellia pinned at the crotch. Around her neck is a flask attached to a leather necklace.

It's Rapunzel, followed by a woman I don't recognize.

They stride right up to me, and I let a half-burned ten-dollar bill in my hand fall into a large bowl full of dirt on the altar. Our two roadies look at me apprehensively from the wings of the stage, wondering if they should intervene, but I wave them off. This is one interruption I'm going to try to integrate into the show.

Before I can figure out what they're up to, the strange woman kneels down on all fours behind me, and Rapunzel pushes me. I topple. Towering over me where I lie, she bellows gleefully, "The archetypes are mutating, Rockstar. See if you can turn *this* into fuel."

She squats down, pries my lips open with strong hands, and drops a thick gob of saliva into my mouth. I swallow it whole. She lingers, massaging the bones next to my eyes with a softly electrifying jiggle.

The spit and the jiggle have the strangest effect on me. My perceptual field shifts with a slide and a crackle, as if an angelic chiropractor had just manipulated my brain into perceiving a hyperdimension next door to the realm I usually inhabit. A crush of alien images cascades into my mind's eye—crocodiles dancing on their hind legs, a spinning weathervane surmounted by a vulture, not a valentine heart but the anatomically correct organ ejaculating half-liquid pearls from its aorta, sea anemones spiraling out of the horns of bull skulls. These scenes coexist with my view of the Catalyst stage, which itself is half-dissolving into a rippling gossamer curtain of liquid sparks.

Struggling to become accustomed to my new domain, I recall the technique of the whirling ballet dancer: To keep from getting dizzy, she compels her gaze to alight on the same fixed point during each rotation. The sight I choose as my focus is Rapunzel's beatific yet cracked grin, one side of her mouth raised higher than the other. Though the rest of her is at first distorted by my vertigo, gradually I can make out an impossible fact: She's removing her clothes.

"Thunderbolt," I hear her say (to me?), "let's go swimming."

"Namaste," I hear myself answer. "I greet the Goddess within you."

Then a further marvel unfolds, a miracle as shattering as if the Virgin Mary were descending from the ramp of a silver space ship with writhing purple snakes for hair and a wet t-shirt emblazoned with a bleeding rose. As I lie on the stage floor, Rapunzel pulls off my furry Pan pants, revealing my body to be fully primed for worship.

"You're just going to dive in cold turkey?" I hear myself asking her.

"Not really, dearest. I've been wading around you for centuries."

The next moment is impossible. My beloved, the Queen of the Menstrual Temple herself, lowers herself down onto my shouting cobra. I'm incredulous at how wet and ready she is. Instantaneously she's grooving on top of me with the improvisational playfulness of a dancer.

I flash on how voracious women are portrayed in porn movies and Islamic doctrine and Christian fantasies: as leering and menacing, oozing with twisted love. I shudder to think of all the clitoridectomies that have been inflicted in the sick name of reining in the libidinous urges of the descendants of Eve. A spontaneous prayer flies from my lips.

"O Goddess, thank you thank you thank you forever for the uninhibited joy and eagerness I feel in the presence of Rapunzel's uninhibited hunger. Thank you thank you thank you for scouring away from my body every last shred of the patriarchal fear of divine female ecstasy."

There's a time for love-making in which each partner is as concerned with the other's pleasure as with her own. There's a time in which the ebb and flow of desire from partner to partner follows a sweet, intuitive rhythm. This is not one of those times. My pleasure—I surrender to it with utter peace—consists wholly in reading the spiral of Rapunzel's drive towards delirious bliss. I want nothing more than to telempathically anticipate, beyond thought, the precise angle she wants to feel my lingam against her yoni, the exact spot she needs to be touched on her ass or back or ankles that will sluice the flow of kundalini to the source of her liberation. Does she want me to stay rock steady while she corkscrews and stretches and shimmies? Does she want me to lose control of my hips and pump her like a fibrillating heart?

Her dance atop me betrays no habits of movement. No sequence of squirms, shudders, and rotations is ever repeated. She's the best kind of prodigiously original artist—no contrivance, no self-consciousness. Hers is the deep orgiastic intelligence of nature eternally reinventing itself.

She leans down to blend her ancient mouth with mine, her primordial tongue. Tears that taste like seawater trickle down onto my face from her Neolithic eyes, triggering a reflexive gush of tears from me. I feel the soft prongs of her nipples massaging my chest, and become aware that she wants me to lift my knees so they're clutching her hips. She responds with a flurry of pelvic whirlpools, ratcheting my lingam back and forth from her cervix to her G-spot.

Sweat as thick as pear juice drips down from her neck and makes me glad. I can't stop drinking in the confounding sight of her acute jet pilot eyes drenched with what?—demonic compassion? savage vulnerability? How can anyone be so tender and so relentless at the same time? Many times I whisper, "My ... body ... is ... yours." As if in acknowledgement, Rapunzel performs the pompoir, rhythmically squeezing my jade stalk with her circumvaginal muscles.

Though I've been privileged with this tantric trick before, I've never experienced mastery like this. Her soaking, rippling, thousand-fold grip oscillates from delicate to firm, from a glissando shimmer to a furious suck, in an impeccably orchestrated rhythm. Warrior vulva. Shaman yoni. Gorgeous cunt that's fully awakened, relentless, and trained in militant playfulness.

Something like an orgasm begins to announce itself at the back of my head. Hers? Or mine? Or both together? My brain is a sky in which sexually excited particles of honey amber and iced rubies are gathering into storm clouds. My eyes are thick swarms of yellowjackets funneling into the heart of the pregnant thunder. Suddenly my legs spring out straight and taut, and every bone in my body stretches as if straining to outgrow itself. For a long time—ten minutes?—I am coiled stiff on the verge of a rapturous electrocution. And then I feel the spurt of lightning slam out of that sweet spot in the back of my head, wrap itself like hot oil around my spine, and plummet headfirst into the spongy gel of my scrotum. Instantaneously it swims a million tight spirals then spasms back up my spine like an eel on fire, burying itself in the nest at the back of my brain.

As if on cue, Daniel and George slip into a celebratory dirge, their dark and spangled flourishes pouring through drummer Squint's glistening fountain of cymbals as if to suggest the soul's journey after the death of the body.

Then, as Rapunzel and I trade a secret look utterly free of self-consciousness, and as Amy's flute gently pries open the top of every head in the room, there is for a moment the birth of a new emotion, alien to history yet communal property. No words exist for it in any modern language, though a delicious glimpse of its name emerges from the blend of "compassion" and "lust." It half-materializes, like an angel straining to burst through the dimensional veil.

31

You're tuned to the Televisionary Oracle
which will one day make heaven itself break open in your honor
revealing three 900-foot-tall angels with cracked smiles
playing your favorite songs through red plastic trumpets
while nearby a fluorescent green UFO flies loop-de-loops
and pulls a banner that reads
"We love you more than we love you"
and streams of gold confetti
fall from a cloud
shaped like your secret vision of paradise

Once upon a time. How it all began. The very first trickster, before all other tricksters, was a menstruator. Lilith to be exact. Adam's first wife, long before the docile Eve came along to take the fall. Lilith the Free. Lilith the Brave. Lilith the Master Purveyor of Holy Fun and Sacred Play.

The Moslems and Jews reviled her. "She doesn't come when we whistle for her," they whined. "She calls everything by its wrong name. Says our grave prayers are nothing more than smarmy flattery. For God's sake, she even uses our foreskins as jewelry."

The Christians were equally afright. "Succubus," they dubbed her. Monks were schooled to sleep with their hands crossed over their genitals, clutching a crucifix. "Every time a pious Christian suffers a wet dream," the old boys used to moan, "Lilith laughs."

Lilith! Let us sing her praises with chortling snorts. Let us celebrate her legacy with razzing guffaws. Lilith the Annihilator of Mediocre Desires! Lilith the Nourishing Source of Lovable Chaos! Lilith the Noble Asshole, scaring the shit out of all the mirthless ass-souls!

Lilith: the original woman who loved too much.

"Let me get on top," she badgered Adam. "You're missing my G-spot. You're boring me to tears."

But Adam was immune. Adam was outraged. "Missionary position or nothing," he bargained. "Cursed be the man who makes the woman heaven and himself earth."

"Plow me while I'm bleeding," she bitched back, giggling. "Lick me while I whistle."

"No way," spewed Adam. "You don't make the rules around here." (Dude didn't know what the ancient tantrics knew: that boinking a menstruator was like taking a genius drug.)

"Most of all," she dissed him with melodious snickers, "you hate my chuckle fucks; begrudge the way my orgasms and bellylaughs get all fluxed together."

That did it. He'd fix her. He wouldn't get it up. Couldn't get it up. "Get out," he decreed. "You embarrass me." Turning his gaze skyward, he croaked, "Dad!" and Jehovah thundered back in support, "Screech-Demon, begone!"

"Wha' the?!" Lilith mused. "Fuck 'em if they can't take a joke."

And so she split for cozy exile, shacking up with a horny crew of endearing robin hoods far from the scorch and belch of history. And the rest is herstory.

But as for history: There were never, no way, no more menstruating tricksters. A few phallocratic pranksters here and there, yes—driven by revenge and one-upmanship and the lust to humiliate. Tricks, my ass! Just war by another name.

Until now!

Until Yo Mama Persephone!

Praise goo and take a gulp! The archetypes are finally mutating—and just in time.

All hail the Menstruating Trickster! Nurturer of the Drivetime! Dismantler of the Apocalypse! Psychic Judge of the Invisible Government of Bloody Disneyland and Sacred Janitor of the United Snakes of Rosicrucian Coca-Cola! She who stands in the doorway between worlds and bellylaughs in both directions at once!

Your pain and the healing of your pain
are brought to you by
your intense desire
to tease out the dormant potential
in the person you love most.

32

Hunkered down in our home-made shrine beneath the Goodwill trailer, Jumbler and I successfully downed our cruel feast without vomiting: the bitter tentacles of the date palm, the salty sweet, beef jerkyish "candy" called Pulparindo, the sour and worm-like shreds of "tender cactus," and the mummified corpses of the ancient (and perhaps moldy) Andean tubers.

"And now comes the second ordeal that all must endure if they seek initiation into The Eater of Cruelty," Jumbler said. "This blasphemous yet sublime outrage will require us to assume the posture of beasts."

I scrambled to obey. The underside of the trailer was only about three feet above the asphalt. We had to hunch over while in the sitting position but had more room to navigate when we got on all fours. Jumbler and I were now facing each other, almost butting heads.

"Raise your fully-opened left hand to a location above and behind your buttocks. Concentrate all your lust for justice in that hand and prepare to smash it with great force against the target. But wait. Not yet.

"First, meditate for a moment on the terrible responsibility you are asking to take on. In seeking admission to The Eater of Cruelty, you are promising to be cruel to the forces of evil and ignorance without yourself ever actually *feeling* cruel. Bemused compassion *must* be your predominant emotional state as you dispense righteousness. Will you pledge, therefore, to fight to the death any hidden attraction you might have to the seductive lure of hatred?"

"Me! Me!" I called out. "I pledge to hate hatred."

"That is why you are being asked to spank yourself now," Jumbler continued. "Think of it as a pre-emptive strike, an immunization. By punishing yourself in advance for any hatred you may be tempted to entertain, you will steer yourself away from committing that original sin in the first place.

"Now let your left hand charge up with the beautiful cruelty of uproariously unconditional love. And spank yourself—for as long as it takes!"

Ow! The first few slaps hurt. But as I continued the relentless pounding, alternating cheeks, a slight numbness set in. A minute after I'd started, my body even found a perverse pleasure in the cognitive dissonance of being touched so forcefully without experiencing the pain that was implied by the fierce impact. But soon the accumulated shock of the battering began to unsettle me. The burning ache in my butt's nerve endings expanded into a kind of spiritual distress.

I found myself thinking of an experiment I'd heard about once. The test subjects were rapists. They were locked in a room and forced to watch film footage containing violence towards women. Every time a graphic scene came on, the subjects received an agonizing electrical jolt. In this way, they were deprogrammed of the power and gusto they'd unconsciously learned to associate with rape.

Would a similar approach work with me? I tried to recall times in my life when I had felt raging bolts of hatred. They were pretty few in number, mostly confined to the moments I had directly confronted Vimala with a demand to expunge my birthmark and she had refused. But I had to confess I was capable of another brand of hatred—sustained and calculating. The prize example was the way I had punished my mothers by refusing to menstruate. That was a five-year project in well-crafted resentment.

I conjured up those memories in vivid detail as I spanked myself with redoubled fury. Other scenes drew my attention, too, like the day of my coronation at age six, when I was possessed with the lucid realization that I was my mothers' puppet. In that moment I had first learned the majesty and potency of unrepentant malice.

"Left hand tired?" Jumbler said after a long time in which only slaps were heard over the roar of traffic on nearby Third Street. "Switch to the right."

Truly now it was becoming an ordeal. My leg muscles were shaking from a combination of discomfort and exhaustion. I thought I might collapse, and fought against it. The fact that I had to exert my will to prolong the torment made the torment even worse. I was both victim and torturer.

Now a new inner voice rose up, a dissident. It complained *why should I try to extinguish my hatred?* Hadn't it served me well? Wasn't it the dynamic motivating force that led me to discover the secret of self-abduction? I wouldn't even be having this mysterious encounter with Jumbler if I hadn't harnessed the fuel of my anger.

Unless. Could it be true what he said? Was it possible to invoke all my fighting powers without actually feeling hatred? Could I take aggressive action against injustice and ignorance if I was filled to the brim with love sweet love? That seemed insanely naive.

"Remember, there is a difference between grateful anger and dehumanizing hatred," Jumbler shouted above the din of our spanks. Was he reading my mind?

"What ... do ... you ... mean?" I yelled back in rhythm to my smacks.

"Grateful anger is *good* darkness. Dehumanizing hatred is *bad* darkness."

"More clues, please."

"Grateful anger flows when you have engaged and studied your shadow. Dehumanizing hatred flows when you have ignored and denied your shadow. One is fertile, the other hysterical."

A mathematical formula: I liked that. I assumed he meant the shadow that Carl Jung described. The unripe and unillumined corners of the soul.

"Grateful anger is when you feel thankful for the irritating people and sickening situations that have spurred you to clarity and righteous action. Dehumanizing hatred is when you are so in love with your terrible emotion that you forget what needs to be changed and turn yourself into your enemy."

Now I was really confused. Was my rebellion against my mothers good darkness or bad darkness?

"What about if the grateful anger and dehumanizing hatred are all mixed together?" I said. "What do you do then?"

Jumbler suddenly stopped spanking himself. Still on all fours, he crawled behind me and halted my participation in the ritual too. Instead of letting my hand down, though, he held it up in front of me.

"Winner and new champion of the spanking initiation, Rapunzel Blavatsky," he announced like a boxing referee. "Congratulations and blessings! No one has ever before asked the bedrock life-and-death question so early in the ordeal."

He let my hand down and bent over to whisper in my ear.

"The answer to the question, 'What do you do when the good darkness and bad darkness are all mixed together?' is this: You go out and launch a full-scale attack on that tricky old bastard God himself. Come with me. You are ready for initiatory ordeal number three."

Jumbler pulled me out from underneath the trailer. When I was standing, he seized my hand and took off running. My butt was throbbing, but it felt good to move so fast after being scrunched up. In a couple of short blocks we arrived at a large fenced lot. Inside was an electrical power-generating substation spread over maybe three acres, though it didn't seem to be in use. Among the maze of metal, there wasn't a buzz or a light or a human presence. I followed him as he climbed over the fence and dropped to the ground inside.

Heavy low clouds scudded along overhead and were about to swallow the gibbous moon rising over a highway overpass a few blocks to the east.

"Gather your ammunition," Jumbler commanded, picking up a big rock from the sandy ground.

"Take that, you lovable old asshole!" he screamed as he heaved his missile straight up. It fell to earth about ten yards in front of us.

"Aim for heaven, Rapunzel," he turned to address me. "Make a direct hit and God might be so intimidated, or perhaps impressed is the better word, that he will show you how to disentangle the good darkness from the bad. Then again, he might not. But in any case, it is good to apprise the Supreme Being that we know *it is all His fault*."

He collected three smaller projectiles and sent them soaring towards the night sky. In its descent, one rock pinged a transformer a short distance from where we were. The other two made audible sounds in the hard dirt as they nose-dived.

"The good thing about this command post," Jumbler confided in me as I scooped up two rocks of my own, "is that if the bombs don't actually crash into God, they will not hurt any innocent bystanders when they plunge back down."

My first effort was unimpressive, a shallow foray. I never lost sight of the rock's flight in the night sky. It plinked down meekly about ten yards away. Jumbler pounced on two fist-sized rocks and pitched them up with a relaxed fury. Again, two clanks heralded their arrival somewhere amidst the mass of metal that stretched before us.

I got a running start for my second launch. With a karate yell, I brought my arm down to the ground and then propelled my payload starwards as hard and straight as I could.

This time there was no chink of metal, no thud of ground. How could that be? I was sure I hadn't arced it so far that it landed out of earshot. My throw was almost perfectly vertical. Indeed, I was afraid it might hit one of us.

"Victory!" Jumbler shouted after another few seconds passed with no audible sign of my rock's descent. "The heavenly stronghold has been breached. Perhaps God himself has been dinged by the amazon's bombardment."

He grabbed both my hands and danced me around in circles.

"Even more important," he exclaimed, "The Eater of Cruelty is now open for business with its first two recruits. Initiation was wildly successful."

"But you didn't make a direct hit on heaven," I protested fondly.

"I did. I passed all three ordeals and you only passed two. Why should you get initiated too?"

"Because I was here to bear witness to your merciful assault, and that is just as crucial as the assault itself."

"OK," I allowed, "but only if I get to be the Queen of The Eater of Cruelty and you're vice-president."

"I do not want such a lofty position in the organization," he said. "If it is all right with you, I prefer the title of Head Janitor."

He shepherded me to the opposite end of the defunct power station. In a couple of minutes we were escaping over the fence. He bid me to follow him to a 7-Eleven that was within sight. Only then did I realize that we had left the Jung and Artaud books, as well as my empty Clorox bottle, back at the Goodwill trailer with the rest of the shrine.

"Shall we pick up some supplies at the sacred store over there and begin our first performance?" he asked, pointing at the 7-Eleven.

Suddenly I felt an uncontrollable urge. Too giddy to censor myself, I slinked up behind him and began tickling his sides. He squirmed and laughed at first, then launched a counteroffensive. He lifted me up on his back, locked his skinny arms around my legs, and carried me along with difficulty, breathing hard. I held on to his shoulders. We entered the store that way, to the alarm of the Pakistani clerk.

"No dancing in the store," he called out to us.

"We're not dancing," I said recklessly, "we're praying." I started murmuring the prayer-like thing Madame Blavatsky had had me chant during our Supersoaker eucharist in the Drivetime earlier that afternoon. "Take and drink of this, for this is the Chalice of My Blood, a living symbol of the new and eternal covenant. It is the mystery of faith, which will be shed for many, that they may attain tantric jubilation and kill the apocalypse."

This seemed to appease the clerk. It also caught Jumbler's attention.

"What does this colorful phrase mean—'kill the apocalypse'?" he said as he grabbed a box of envelopes, a package of ruled notebook paper, a bag of rubber bands, and two Bic pens. I leaned my face against the left side of his head. His hair smelled delicious, a kind of musky lavender.

"It comes from one of my other great helpers, Madame Helena P. Blavatsky. I told you about her earlier. She likes to ask me, 'What are you doing to kill the apocalypse?' She thinks it's the most important question in the world."

"But it cannot be the most important question in the world, because that title belongs to the one you posed before: 'What do you do when the good darkness and bad darkness are all mixed together?'"

"Maybe they're two different approaches to the same problem?" I said.

He plucked a box of small birthday candles from one shelf and old-fashioned razor blades from another. Soon we were in front of the cracker section. He knelt down and had me dismount from his back. I surprised myself by massaging his shoulders for a few seconds. Were we that familiar already?

He handed me the goods he'd gathered so that he could collect an armful of Cracker Jack boxes. I followed him up to the front, where he tried to pay with a fifty-dollar bill. The clerk frowned and refused to take the money. Jumbler returned the bill to his wallet, which I saw now was well-stocked, and produced two twenties, which were accepted. I noticed the clock. It was already 9:30. Close to my bedtime. I'd been up since 6:30.

In a minute, we were outside the store spreading out our haul.

"So what *are* you doing to kill the apocalypse, anyway?" Jumbler asked. He was using a razor blade to slice an inconspicuous slit in one side of the top of each of the Cracker Jack boxes.

"Today? Today I am killing the apocalypse by setting aside everything I believe in and forgetting all about myself so I can listen hard to you."

"And what about that head wound of yours? Does that have anything to do with killing the apocalypse?" He nodded in the direction of my forehead.

I instinctively turned towards the plate-glass front of the store, which we were squatting beside. Checking my reflection, I saw that a tiny corner of white gauze was jutting out from beneath my beret. Given all the running and jumping I had done, I wasn't surprised. I tucked the bandage back in.

"It's a long story," I answered. "And as I said, I'd rather hear your story right now. Later I'll tell you all the gory details if you want."

He had taken five fifty-dollar bills out of his wallet and folded them neatly in quarters. Now he was slipping one apiece into the Cracker Jack boxes he'd cut open.

"I will tell you one good strategy I have to kill the apocalypse," he said. "It is called mirroring. Do you know what that is?"

"Hmmm. Giving people images of themselves?"

"It would be better to say giving people *true* images of themselves."

"Yeah, I suppose most everyone is blasted nonstop with distorted and degrading images of themselves. Guess you couldn't call that mirroring. Funhouse mirroring might be a more accurate term."

"Exactly right. And I would say that is the prime reason why humanity finds itself on the verge of self-annihilation."

"Not enough mirroring, too much funhouse mirroring, is the cause of the apocalypse? How do you figure?"

"In Tibet, there are children who are identified at an early age as *tulkus*, reincarnated holy men and women. They are taken to monasteries and raised there by Buddhist monks or nuns who are absolutely certain of their divine nature. Day after day, year after year, these special children are told they are wise and compassionate beings who deserve to be showered constantly with devoted outpourings of love. And showered they are. Would you like to make a guess what proportion of these children grow up to be exactly what they are expected to be?"

"I imagine it's very high."

"Ninety-nine percent."

"But is that *true* mirroring or *inflated* mirroring?" I couldn't help but wonder what the implications of his argument might be for my own life. Hadn't my upbringing been similar to the tulkus?

Jumbler was on the verge of slipping fifty-dollar bills into eight more Cracker Jack boxes.

"Here is my point, my dear," he replied. "All children are born wise and compassionate beings who deserve to be showered constantly with devoted outpourings of love. Every single one of them would grow up to be a tulku if he were treated like a tulku."

"So true mirroring means never reflecting back a person's shadowy sides? Never criticizing or correcting? That doesn't sound right."

"Of course not. Take you, for instance. I have always loved you, and I will always love you. But if you agreed to allow me to mirror you, I would let you know, with all my most tender compassion, which of your unconscious habits might be preventing your full bloom."

I will always remember the next moment as a landmark because it was the first time in my life I had a visceral understanding of the word *swoon*. It was like in one of my dreams where I fall off a cliff and halfway through my plunge I figure out I can fly. It also felt as if the whole inside of my body suddenly billowed. In my mind's eye I saw a time-lapse film of the roots of an oak tree drinking in a downpour after a long drought.

When I opened my eyes again, Jumbler was writing on a piece of notebook paper. He didn't seem to mind that I hadn't responded to his mirroring. In a couple of minutes, he handed me the page.

"What do you think?" he asked. "If you like it, help me handwrite a few more copies. Or feel free to edit or expand it. I would like to make thirteen altogether."

The note read as follows:

> Dear Beautiful, Intelligent, Kind, Creative Creature:
> Though in the past you have often forgotten the truth about yourself, the fact is that you are an amazing gift to the human race. From now on you will never lose sight of that. Beginning today, your life will become an ongoing miracle of inspiration, bringing you a multitude of blessings you didn't even know you wanted. Ready or not, you must now learn to embrace the very success you've always been most afraid of.
>
> With all our love,
> Two Anonymous Celebrities

We worked in silence for a while until we had stuffed thirteen envelopes with a love note and a birthday candle. With rubber bands we attached each of these to a Cracker Jack box that was stuffed with a carefully folded fifty-dollar bill. A quick calculation put Jumbler's investment here at six hundred fifty dollars, plus the cost of materials.

As I stuffed the bundles into our plastic bags, he walked over to a skinny tree on the sidewalk and fiddled with the lock of a bike chained there. Returning with it, he said, "Here is our transportation."

It was a bulky one-speed bike with thick, well-worn tires. This was the vehicle of choice for a person with a wallet crammed with high-denomination bills?

"You ride on the handlebars," he said. "I will steer and peddle."

"Where are we headed exactly?" I asked.

"To your place, I hope. I would very much like to set up The Eater of Cruelty command post tonight. On the way there, we can drop off these offerings."

"Head north on Lincoln Street," I said. "It's about three-quarters of a mile from downtown."

I thought of what I'd told Vimala when I called her a few days ago. Don't worry about me, I said. I've always been Ms. Responsible. Couldn't do anything foolish if I tried.

And yet here I was on the night of my surgery, staying up past my bedtime and doing things that if not illegal certainly had the potential to draw the suspicious attention of law enforcement officers. Worse, I was bringing a stranger back to my motel room with me. A magical stranger, true, whose imagination thrilled me. But still.

High on the list of reasons to trust him was the fact that he hadn't leaked a single dribble of gross male carnality. Scoring with babes did not seem to be a shtick he'd studied. Not that I'd had a lot of previous exposure to that phenomenon, but more than enough to recognize its simple universal signs.

The truth seemed to be that I had to worry more about my own cravings. As far as I could tell, his passion for me was a platonic simmer. I, on the other hand, was a recent convert to the cult of swoon.

My imagination flickered with a scene of us doing a swimming dance together in the pool back at my motel.

Wait a minute. Was the pool heated? I didn't know. I'd never been in. If not, a night in mid-April would be unluxuriously chilly. Suspend that fantasy for now.

This dose of reality reminded me of a blunt fact that my conscious mind always had trouble acknowledging: I'd never had an erotic encounter with an actual male before. My extensive sensual play with Rumbler in the Televisionarium had filled me with rich memories of eros, however. Besides that, my sex education had been thorough and uncensored. I'd come of age armed with confidence about the subject.

But did I really want to have sex with Jumbler, as in sexual intercourse? I didn't know. First of all, I wasn't even sure I was attracted to him physically. With its weird blend of elegance and trickiness, his face wasn't aligned with the kinds of male beauty I'd identified as my type. And his body had a delicacy which, though not unattractive, wasn't a quality that had ever pricked my libido before.

Secondly, what I was sure I *did* want were silky, evanescent sensations like those Rumbler and I aroused in each other in the Televisionarium: the beyond-the-body rapture that came from flying together after leaping off the tops of magic trees or staring into each other's eyes until we disappeared into the taste of grapes and the sound of cellos and the smell of the ocean at dawn and the sight of the moon rising over a green hill in springtime.

As I contemplated these matters, a crushing collapse was dangerously near. For the first time it occurred to me that maybe the feelings I enjoyed with Rumbler were not possible to experience with an actual male.

By now Jumbler and I had traveled a rickety few blocks on his bomb of a bike. It was a miracle we hadn't crashed yet. I sat precariously on the handlebars, my hands grasping cold metal on either side of my butt. Facing out with legs dangling, I had to avoid contact with the front tire. Meanwhile, Jumbler struggled to pedal, largely blinded by my body. Two plastic bags full of stuff were wrapped around his wrists and hanging down heavily. Several times I shouted out a warning when it appeared he hadn't seen an obstacle we were about to crash into.

He took us back to our shrine beneath the Goodwill trailer, where we retrieved the books by Jung and Artaud, as well as my Clorox bottle. Here, too, we left the first of our Cracker Jack boxes and love notes.

"Anonymous gifts are much better than the other kind," Jumbler remarked as we remounted the bike and headed out.

"When the recipient doesn't know who the gift came from, she has no psychological debt to repay," I agreed.

"Even more importantly, the giver cannot use the gift to enhance his social status or inflate his ego. He is helpless to lord his generosity over everyone."

"Yes, I've noticed that people who're skilled at convincing you they're magnanimous are often masters of manipulation, too."

"Do you know what the German word 'Gift' means in English?"

"No."

"Poison."

"The story of my life!" I laughed. Then in a sudden burst of vengeful glee, I shouted out, "Mommies, Mommies, wherever you are tonight, *danke* for the *Gift* !"

"I want to hear more about where that comes from," Jumbler noted as he brought our vehicle to a stop.

"I plan on making a full confession in the near future."

"In the meantime, I have distilled my second answer to your question, how to kill the apocalypse."

"Which is?"

"Give anonymous gifts that no one can thank you for."

"I can see how that might be a recipe for a less crass culture, but I'm not sure I understand how it kills the apocalypse."

"Think of how much evil in the world is perpetrated by people who purport to be doing good. Think of all the murderous gifts history has been plagued by."

Jumbler's comment propelled me into a meditation I preferred to avoid. As an example of evil disguised as good, I couldn't help but think of the mangled religion the early fathers of the Christian church had fabricated out of the work Jesus and I had done. But I was shy about mentioning Jesus to Jumbler. I didn't want to get into a discussion about the implications of his apparent claim, earlier, that he himself had been Jesus in a previous incarnation.

"But the murderous gifts would be just as lethal if they were anonymous, wouldn't they?" I said instead.

"No, because the most destructive gifts are always those which are covertly meant to demonstrate the greatness of their givers."

A steady drizzle had begun, which would be unusual for April in Santa Cruz, though I thought maybe it was more common here in Marin. We had arrived on the sidewalk in front of a house. Jumbler skulked up to the porch and deposited a Cracker Jack box and love note in the mailbox, then hightailed it back to me.

"Quick, we must escape before our beneficiary spots us," he stage-whispered. We reassembled ourselves on the bike and barreled away to the next stop, a few doors down, where he performed a similar operation.

For the next half-mile or so, we delivered our boons as the rain fell harder and we got wetter. Jumbler chose the first four mailboxes, but then invited me to choose. This effectively exploded my unlikely hypothesis that maybe we would stop exclusively at homes where Jumbler had friends who were in on an elaborate joke being played on me.

We were almost to my motel and still had four undelivered packages. Our route along Lincoln Street had passed a lot of apartment buildings whose mailboxes weren't accessible. At this point I demanded that Jumbler switch places with me. Guiding the bike for the first time, I detoured down Brookdale Avenue, a short street parallel to Lincoln. It was packed with single-family homes.

As I unloaded the second-to-last package on a large porch, I noticed a face gazing out at me from a window in the front door. I scampered away down the stairs just as the door flung open. Having seen the danger, Jumbler motioned for me to abandon the bike and race away on foot.

As we ran, I heard what sounded like a baseball bat pounding on the wooden floor of the porch. "Next time I'll get my shotgun," a woman's voice yelled after us.

"Another good reason for keeping your gifts anonymous," Jumbler giggled when we'd made it back to Lincoln Street. "Some people hate you for giving them things."

"You just going to leave your bike behind?" I asked.

"An honorable sacrifice," he replied. "The first official loss of The Eater of Cruelty. May there be many such worthy losses in the future, all as easy to bear as that one."

As we pulled into the parking lot of my home, the Villa Inn, Jumbler and I were drenched. I remembered we still had one Cracker Jack box and love note undelivered.

"Uh-oh," I said, taking from Jumbler the bag that contained the last treat. "I hope we won't incur any nasty karma. Isn't it a sin when those with a lot to give don't get around to dispensing all their gifts? I think there are a couple stories in *Grimms' Fairy Tales* about poor souls like that."

"But I am bestowing this final treasure on you, my dear," he said. "What good is it to shower the whole world with our blessings if we do not grant the same favor to each other?" His teeth were chattering. The rain wasn't cold, but now that it had saturated us, we were.

We climbed the stairs to my room.

"But it's not an anonymous present," I protested. "Now I owe you one. You're probably already plotting how to use my debt against me."

It was a joke, but it reflected a secret truth. I felt that from the moment we'd met at the bookstore he'd done most of the giving and I most of the taking. And then there was that weird exchange on the way to the Goodwill trailer, when I found myself bawling him out for having tried to outgive me in every one of our lifetimes together—as if I implicitly believed all his stories about those lifetimes. At that moment, I truly felt that we were recapitulating an argument we had carried on for centuries.

"Then you will just have to present me with a gift of equal value as soon as possible," he said.

I put the key in the lock of room number 65, ushered us in, and flipped on the light switch. As always, the smell of this place was unexpected and inscrutable. It was partly stale cigarette smoke not-quite-overwhelmed by pine disinfectant. But there was also an entire musty-fresh kaleidoscope: lemon and mildew, perfume of violets mingling with formaldehyde, potpourris that were old when Joan of Arc lived. It made me think of the funeral of my mom Burgundy's grandmother in Detroit: shriveled-up ninety-eight-year-old crone packed amidst virgin white satin and lusty roses.

"Would you like some dry clothes?" I asked him as I turned up the thermostat. "You're free to select anything from my designer wardrobe in the closet. I'm going to take a bath." Since we were the same height, I was sure my stuff would fit him.

I grabbed my black velvet tights and long black velvet tunic and took them with me into the bathroom for after the bath. As I disappeared, Jumbler was examining the altar I had created on top of the television. Among other things, it included a wishbone, a postcard of a Miro painting, an Amnesty International sticker, pumpkin seeds, a prayer flag, a silver and black Persephone statue, an origami of a hummingbird, walnuts, my ceremonial wand and dagger, and a large rock on which I'd written a prayer in miniature calligraphy.

I felt a surge of pride that Jumbler would see this oasis of holy beauty I had managed to carve out of an otherwise ugly room. That was his specialty, right?

I wanted to come up with a return gift for him as soon as possible. Something from the altar? The prayer rock, perhaps? But as I waited for the bathtub to fill, I got a better idea. In the bathroom, hanging on the wall next to the sink, was an odd little artifact provided by the motel management. About four by twelve inches, it was a piece of material that blended the feel of paper and cloth. "Shoe Shiner" it read in blue print at the top, followed by these claims:

Will also
- Clean Your Razor
- Remove Cosmetics
- Clean Your Eye Glasses

Along the sides it said, "Compliments of the Management" and "Begin Your Day Bright and Shining."

It was a good gift—ordinary yet weird, versatile and anomalous—but I wanted to make it even better. I fetched a pen out of the drawer next to the bed and added to the list of what this magic item could do.

- Polish Funhouse Mirrors
- Wipe Out Poison From Gifts
- Prime Spanking Surfaces
- Mop Up Cruel Food Which Has Been Regurgitated

As I finished the alterations, I felt a twinge of pain, accompanied by a pinch of responsibility. It was time to attend to my head wound. I took four more Advils from my stash on the sink and assembled the supplies Dr. Elfland had given me.

In my small bathroom, there were two mirrors: a wide one over the sink and a skinny, floor-length one on the opposite wall. Since my arrival in San Rafael four days ago, I'd reserved all my self-observations for the latter. If I stood up straight in front of it, the top of its reflecting surface stopped at my eyebrows. In other words, it cut off the part of my body where the stain was.

Now, though, I felt compassion for the cursed blotch. It was in its death throes, after all. I could afford to be an indulgent caretaker. I stared into the mirror over the sink, removed my beret, and peeled away the bandage. Uhhhhgggg-ly. Swollen, red, stitched, Frankensteinian. I used cotton balls to gingerly apply some medicinal cleanser. It hurt, though not as much as I expected.

Then I got the bright idea to leave it naked and exposed. It would benefit from not being covered up with gauze for a while, I reasoned. Let it air out. Besides that, I had an urge to see how Jumbler would react to it. With all the apparently idealized notions he had of me, maybe he needed a dose of funky reality. I think a cowardly part of me was hoping to scare him off, too. That way I wouldn't have to worry about whether I should act on my erotic curiosity.

My bath was brief and efficient. I didn't want to risk amping up my sensuality any higher than it already was. When I emerged, fully dressed except for socks, I found him sitting at the round table in the kitchenette. He was making a sign on the back of the motel placemat he'd taken off the desk next to the TV. It looked like it would soon read "The Eater of Cruelty Command Center."

His waterlogged white clothes were in a pile in the corner. He had donned my only pair of pajamas, which were black flannel, and my only luxurious piece of clothing, an indigo cashmere robe. Without the frame of his boxy unisex white costume, he looked more feline, almost feminine.

Outside, the rain had become a soft roar. I was glad it had waited for us to finish most of our playtime before kicking in. It joined with the hovering steam from the bath to create an almost homey feeling.

"Here's my equal and opposite gift," I said matter-of-factly as I set the "Shoe Shiner" down in front of him. He looked at it, gazed up at me briefly, then returned his view to the gift.

"This is a masterpiece," he exclaimed with a quiet joviality. "Better yet, a spontaneously conceived masterpiece. Living proof that you are vivaciously attuned to the specific truth of the *eternal now*. Truly, no one deserves to be Queen of The Eater of Cruelty more than you."

He rose from his chair to face me and pressed his hands together in the gesture of prayer.

"And now," he said softly, "I request permission to kiss your crucifixion."

I nodded. He gently clasped my cheeks with his hands, then brought his lips to my forehead, kissing it five times: over my wound, under, to both sides, and then directly upon it. With the last, I erupted in sobs. To be able to share my age-old secret in the midst of its mutation, and to have it greeted with such intelligent tenderness, broke me open. Tears cascaded from my eyes and nose. A strange nectar welled up inside my mouth. My heart became a fountain, and the hot sweetness it gushed forth shot through the rest of my body in a branching slow-motion throb. In my mind's eye I saw an aerial view of a skyscraper imploding, its rock-hard skeleton and facade crumbling into billions of granules.

All my thoughts absconded, leaving my body free to act from its native wisdom. I leaned myself urgently into Jumbler, then pulled his face to mine and began to drink his mouth. My tongue undulated along the inside of his lips. I soaked in his surprising taste, a delicate honeysuckle. Streams of my tears flowed down into the mix, exciting me to spill even more.

As he responded to my swarming incursion, our bodies converged, our chests and bellies pressing together. Only then did I comprehend that I was embracing a woman. Her breasts billowed firmly against mine through the velvet and cashmere and flannel that separated them. But the extravagant dissonance did not short-circuit my passion; it only unleashed me further. Now, on top of my weeping, a wave of mournful hilarity struck, a rueful bliss that tempted me to howl or sing or make us collapse together on the floor. I resisted all of these. Through my blubbering laughter, I managed to carry on with the leisurely evolution of our grandiose kiss.

"I can guess why you are crying," Jumbler murmured in a quavering voice as we began to wheel lazily around the room in a demented foxtrot, "but what is so funny?"

"I just discovered a new way to kill the apocalypse," I said as I caressed her cheek with mine.

"Kiss all the bad guys the way you are kissing me?" she whispered as her open eyes brimmed.

"That's an idea. But I was actually referring to the fact that I somehow managed to turn a woman into a man for several hours."

"You did?" she said. She began to sniffle.

"Until a few minutes ago, I must confess," I babbled as my tears crescendoed again, "I was under a mistaken impression concerning your gender. But don't worry. It doesn't change my feelings about you in the least. In fact, I think it makes me feel even crazier."

Soon we were both embroiled in deep wailing sobs, our chests and throats heaving. I could not believe the volume of water that poured from us, or the soft violence of our convulsions. And yet we were both driven to keep kissing through the rising tumult.

The happy grief that had motivated my initial outbreak was expanding and mutating. No longer was I crying merely because I'd exposed my lonely secret to a smart playmate who had given me tenderness in return, nor because I'd had to make a sudden and shocking realignment of my perceptions about my playmate's gender. Those tear-jerking themes had become contagious, lighting up other sore points and hot spots within me. Now I was weeping in amazed excitement that this was the first person outside the Pomegranate Grail who had ever been completely real to me. I was weeping with gratitude that I was finally capable of becoming infatuated with an actual flesh-and-blood human. I was weeping in triumph as I ruminated on the increasingly stunning evidence that I'd done the right thing by running away.

And these were just a few of the epiphanies that were rushing forth, demanding to be wept for. I was spooked and curious at how wild my body felt. I was sad and thrilled at how rapidly I was changing. I melted with anguish and fear as I registered how severe a break I was making from my mothers and the Pomegranate Grail. My liaison with Jumbler was a dramatic upping of the ante in this divorce, not only because my mothers had decreed that I was not to seek any erotic connection before I was eighteen, but also because the lover I had chosen was an infidel, an outsider.

I cried, too, because I was feeling again, only more intensely, the poignant paradox Madame Blavatsky had taught me to feel a few hours ago in the Drivetime: gratitude for the inspirational violations my mothers had inflicted on me, for the ways they had forced me to find out my true destiny.

And why was Jumbler crying? I pledged to ask her when the time was right. For now, I could only guess. If she truly believed that in all our lifetimes together she had always loved me more than I loved her, then perhaps she was shaken to her root by how profoundly she had been able to touch me now, and how passionately I threw myself at her mercy. And perhaps she was crying because for the first few hours of our meeting, I didn't see her clearly enough to know that she was a woman.

Now and then, at the height of a fresh surge of lamentation, droplets actually launched themselves from our eyes, splashing down through the air into the confluence of moist flesh where we suckled each other. More often, a pearly flow trickled down our cheeks. However the elixir arrived, we welcomed it as a key ingredient in our kiss.

"In the fairy tale of Rapunzel," I whispered, "her tears have the power to cure the blindness of the prince. Do you have any blind spots that you would like me to cry on?"

We were still whirling dreamily around the room. During one sweep past the front wall, I had flicked the light switch off. Now, as we glided into the kitchenette, I doused the other. The space was lit only by the dim green glow of my alarm clock.

"I am so very close to healing an ancient split in my psyche," she said.

"Between?"

"Between being holy and having fun. For many lifetimes, I have tried to get them to originate from the same impulse. And now at last they are on the verge."

"So where should I anoint you with my tears?"

"Your tears need to reach the crucible inside me where I am trying to get my trickiness and my morality to mingle. It is a spot halfway between my heart and my navel."

"Then you must imbibe."

She licked the moisture from both my cheeks, then brought her lips just under the tear ducts of first my right and then my left eye, from which a seemingly inexhaustible supply streamed.

"Give me your potion, artful one," she sighed as she delicately supped. "Impregnate me with the secret of how to heal others with my pleasure."

I kept my eyes closed as she proceeded, working to visualize what it might mean for her to accomplish the synthesis she'd alluded to. Examples from the preceding hours immediately revealed themselves. The masterful way she had listened to the clerk at the Mexican food market, for instance. In one coordinated act, she had performed a kind service for the older woman and also used the occasion to do a magic trick which, she said, coaxed God to reveal a desired secret. But more than that. The entire series of fun events she had enacted with me was, I had no doubt, a holy ceremony that was as effective in invoking divine allies as any austere religious ritual could ever be. In fact, the more I meditated on it, the more I was sure that Jumbler was already a maestro in blending trickiness and morality.

"And now I will ask you another favor, dear Sin-Eater," Jumbler said, her lips poised again in front of mine. "As I pour all my sins into my tears, please eat them. Devour my sins, that I may be free of that which hinders my ability to become the most hedonistic servant of humanity possible."

As I set about my task, I visualized her tears filling up with any toxins she might be harboring in body or psyche. With my psychic eye, I saw oily vapors, wraith-like shapes, leaving their hiding place in her heart as they migrated into the tears that I was now disposing of. What specific bad behavior or negative habits might they correspond to in Jumbler? Excessive mysteriousness, perhaps? A tendency towards confabulation? I could not guess. But that didn't matter to me.

"If I was truly Robin the Mouth, the Sin-Eater, in a previous incarnation," I prayed silently, "let me tap into the powers I possessed then. Dear Persephone, help me melt down the torments and blights I'm absorbing, that they may become a source of beautiful raw energy for Jumbler and me."

As I sipped, Jumbler's sobs evolved into a half-rapturous, half-anguished moan, even as her tears continued to ripple.

"Do not stop," she whimpered. "It feels so real."

At the peak of her intensity, she let loose a breathy grunt and broke away from me.

"Ungggh," she said. "Got to lie down." She slumped over to the bed and lay down. "Come here," she commanded with a weak laugh.

"What happened?" I said, alarmed, as I slipped into position next to her.

"You made me come," she smiled, "in a manner of speaking."

"What manner is that?" I asked, confused but enjoying my confusion. My weeping, after a long copious run, was abating.

"You sucked down my sins so hard you brought on my period," she replied in a quietly maniacal voice.

"Oh. Sorry," I said, disappointed.

"Do not be sorry in the least," she said, shaking her head drowsily. "I have never felt so perfect in my entire life."

"You're lying," I cackled. "I hate people who call menstruation a curse, but it's not as if I ever heard anyone say it feels pleasurable."

"The onslaught of bleeding is always orgasmic for me."

Her streams of tears were following a different course now that she was lying on her side facing me.

"I'm flabbergasted," I said. "Flummoxed and flubadubbed." Delirium had begun to possess me, too.

"Not that I bleed all that often," she added with a cracked giggle. "Before tonight, it has been almost eleven months."

"Should I go out and buy you some pads?" I said, trying to force myself, against every inclination, to be practical. "I don't have anything here."

"No. Too late now. Let it flow. I apologize to your pajamas."

"But why has it been so long?"

Instead of answering, she grasped my head and pressed her whole open mouth around my mouth. It wasn't a kiss. She didn't flutter her lips or swirl her tongue. She simply held this pose and slowly breathed into my mouth, like a rescuer doing CPR. On her inhales, she maintained the seal, forcing me to exhale back into her.

To my surprise, I felt no instinct to pull away. As unnatural as it might have seemed to me in a more rational mood, I was enthralled with the searing intimacy of it all. From deep inside her body, warm, moist air wafted deep into my body. But it was more than air. Tasting and touching it now so vividly, its smoky persimmon amber, its maple syrup mingled with seawater, I had no doubt that it was thoroughly infused with her daimon, her life-force, the distilled essence of her most personal genius. And I returned her gift to her, suffused with my own concentrated potion. Now and then, one of us would unfurl a singing moan as we breathed out.

Gradually, I began to notice a fresh marvel. Or maybe it had been unfolding before, and I was just tuning into it. On her exhales, I saw but also felt a subtle ray of light streaming out of her teary eyes and into mine. There was an actual erotic sensation in my pupils, as if her dewy eyelight were a loving caress. As she inhaled, I sensed or maybe fantasized that she was drinking in an analogous beam from my gaze. *Dear Goddess*, I prayed, *I am making love*. Without stroking or churning or undulating, without doing anything more than breathing and looking, I was flooding with sexual pleasure. It sprang from my heart and my eyes as much as from my lowest chakra, and rippled out in pulsing spirals to the ends of me.

I swear that the very molecules of my lover's face began to vibrate and throb, until I imagined I was looking at an electrified cloud in the shape of an ever-shifting mask. The only constant, in her eyes, was a relaxed concentration mingled with mirthful excitement. She betrayed no restlessness, no distraction. There was nothing else we had to do, nowhere else to go, besides this. I felt utterly at home.

Our tears throbbed in celebration, tiny waves pulsing in rhythm to our heartbeats.

33

The Televisionary Oracle
is brought to you by
the Menstrual Temple of the Funky Grail

Purveyors of primordial gossip

Lobbyists for the Cackling Vulture Goddess

Sponsors of the Dream of the Month Club

Organizers of Zen Pride Week

Trainers of the sacred janitors of The Eater of Cruelty

The world's first think tank
for single mothers
and hedonistic midwives

A pack of anonymous celebrities
that conducts secret performances
designed to burn heaven to the ground

A multinational corporate band of guerrilla builders
fighting to stave off apocalypse
by erecting a global network of menstrual huts

A media coven
working to prevent the genocide of the imagination

As you glide closer towards invoking the exact intimacy you need, we'd like to offer you a few love spells.

1. While standing in a mud puddle and hugging yourself, dissolve a four-leaf clover on your tongue and visualize yourself riding piggyback on the one you love.

2. Draw a picture of copulating hummingbirds on a dollar bill and then tape it to a road sign on a street with a sexy name.

3. While standing on top of a mobile home wearing all red clothes, hurl a stolen meteorite as far as you can as you shout out the name of your beloved.

4. Using green food dye, write your initials and those of your beloved on a cake, then bury it in the woods along with your favorite book from childhood.

5. Forget all about trying to glom on to your perfect mate and instead make yourself into a perfect mate.


The doctor is sick.
Mommy needs some mothering.
The fire truck is on fire
and the therapist is crazy.
But don't worry.
The Televisionary Oracle is here
to help you use your nightmares
to become rich and famous.

34

I love to sleep. And when anyone else but me wakes me up for any other reason except for dream recall—especially the night after a show by World Entertainment War—I am very cranky. Several budding relationships of mine have foundered because my lover refused to respect the web of rituals with which I surround my sleep. The UPS delivery person has been trained never to knock at my door before 3 P.M., lest he be greeted by a dragon.

So as I am startled awake in the here and now, the day after last night's partially brilliant, mostly failed show at the Catalyst, by what sounds like rocks hitting my second-story bedroom window, I am immediately running hot with the adrenaline of anger. The clock reads a few minutes after high noon. Leave me the fuck alone. Go away.

The problem is, now that my body is radiating adrenaline, I probably won't be able to return to sleep anyway. But it's the principle of the thing. Another ping sounds at the window. Goddamn you to the seventh level of Dante's inferno. I don't care if you're Ed McMahon in tow with the Virgin Mary here to present me with a karmic credit slip good for release from the wheel of samsara and an eighty-five-million-year vacation in heaven after I die. You can come back when I'm good and ready to rouse myself. No matter how many rocks you throw, no matter how many knocks on my door, I will ignore you.

I shove my blue rubber earplugs deep into my ears and put one of my pillows over my head.

But the disturbance grows. I can't fucking believe it: the sound of a female voice through a bullhorn. My curiosity overwhelms my outrage. I take out my earplugs. The message is decipherable only in spots. But from among the jumble of chuckles, singsong words, and portentous sighs, I can finally make out a recurring phrase:

"Rockstar, Rockstar, let down your hair."

It occurs to me that I may be listening to a cracked variation on Grimms' fairy tale of Rapunzel. Before I can decide how to respond, a fresh interruption assaults me. It's my answering machine, which is on a shelf at the foot of my bed: I neglected to turn down the volume before I collapsed in bed last night.

Damn. It's my stalker, Patricia. She's the psychotic who calls, e-mails, and snailmails me with prolific devotion in order to keep me up to date on the latest developments in the massive conspiracy she's being victimized by—a conspiracy in which I am at the hub, along with the Queen of England, Bill Gates, baseball star Ken Griffey, the Holy Ghost, and the puppets of Sesame Street.

"Well, Mr. Sleazeball Scumbucket," she greets me, "you really kill me. I was at your show last night, of course. I wouldn't've even gone except for that dream I had where you said you'd get the Queen to chop off my little fingers and feed them to my cat if I didn't go. Why do you hate me so much? Motherfucking piece of garbage. Last night's show was a new low, even for a shithead drug-dealing asswipe like you. First you stuck all those subliminal curses in your stupid speeches. Gave me a rash on my thighs. If that wasn't enough, I had to deal with you getting your little friend the Holy Ghost to astral-project his big milky sperm right into my ovaries. Jerkoff dickweed. You hate me so much you'd even risk wrecking your inane little show just so you could torture me. Guess I showed you, Crudfucker. Didn't know I'm a wiccan voodoo priestess, did you? Used my mojo to grab a hold of that tall chick's mind and send her up on stage to mess with you. You looked so stupid when she stung my poison into you. I'm glad they had to carry you off stage like a bag of trash. I hope you're still unconscious. Now get this, you clucksucking jibberjabbering dunderstubber: I am not going to take your big dick in my mouth even if you do melt the Antarctic ice pack and flood my house away. Even if you do use your so-called poetry hexes to storm those meteors down on my head. And just keep in mind that the district attorney is a personal friend of mine."

Much as I hate to admit it, I'm entertained by this madwoman's rap. I keep listening to the end, even as the invader with the bullhorn outside repeats her absurd announcement. And besides, it's perversely comforting to imagine that I might have had some excuse, however preposterous, for my behavior at last night's show. I have *never* before blacked out during a performance, even in those three gigs, during my brief period of youthful folly, when I poured a blend of cocaine, Mad Dog wine, and pot into the holy temple of my body.

And yet, from the pissed-off though bemused reports of my fellow band members at 2:30 A.M., Rapunzel's magic gob of spit—or was it a knock on my head?—had plunged me into a daze so profound that I had to be hauled off stage and laid on a couch in the rear dressing room. For the first time in recorded history, World Entertainment War played for an hour and a half without me.

Even worse. My bandmates assured me that the fantastic love-making my darling and I enjoyed had in fact happened entirely in my own imagination. It was a damn fine hallucination, that's all.

The megaphone's lyrical crackle has died down. I'm about to drag myself to the window to investigate when I hear a sharp whap, like the sound of metal spiking wood. The whole wall of my house shakes. Next there comes a series of gritty clangs against the wall, beginning near ground level and ascending. My imagination whips up a picture of a woman climbing up my wall.

When a feminine hand lifts the window and reaches in through the curtain, I'm finally moved to sit upright and put on my glasses.

A tidal wave of auburn hair thrusts itself through the open window, some of it bound in two massive braids, followed by a vision of the woman with whom I've packed a year's worth of living and loving since I met her formally yesterday.

As the vision climbs casually into my red stuffed chair and removes her crampons, I record the details with the same concentration I devote to noticing my surroundings in a lucid dream: black tights beneath a purple silk mini-skirt; gold satin bikini top; red, white, and blue beaded vest with a picture of a baseball that looks like the planet Jupiter being hit with a bat by an angel or goddess in long white gown; and a silver beaded headband with a tail of yellow and red feathers trailing down her back.

But here's the shocker: Blooming out from beneath the nub in her bra where the two cups are fastened, there's a gnarly scar in the shape of a cross. Both marks must be five inches long. They're not manicured lines but textured gashes. Ouch.

"I was hoping you'd let down your hair or a reasonable facsimile so I could use it to climb up," Rapunzel says matter-of-factly. "I know it's kind of early for you, though, so I brought my mountain-climbing gear just in case. By the way, you've got some sleep in your left eye. Want me to get it out for you?"

In my embarrassment I don't answer but reach automatically to remove the accumulated fairy dust. Meanwhile, my fresh-from-dreams imagination is working hard to remember which of my already-extensive experiences with Rapunzel are not also engraved in her memory bank. The most important one, of course, was our fuck of the century, which she was not privy to.

Only two exchanges can I count on having been real in the traditional meaning of the word "real": the eternal moments in the women's bathroom, and the delivery, from her mouth to mine, of the elixir of saliva. Well, I guess I could count the "Eater of Cruelty" event I saw, where the pregnant woman I assume was Rapunzel in disguise gave her cracked little presentation.

When I tally up the extent of our objectively factual interactions, though, there's not really much to go on.

I can't help but notice, here in the bountiful present, that I have been given license to gaze at the veil guarding the mysterium. Rapunzel is surveying my room as she tugs off the crampons, leaving me free to lay my line of sight where I may. Her skirt is short, her legs are parted to facilitate the crampon-removal, and the view is clear all the way up. There in the crotch of her tights is not just a blank black screen onto which I can project my hallucinations, but an emblem of the bull skull, red head with silver horns. The sight of it causes me to involuntarily close my eyes, as if it were an instruction to go inward. Instantaneously, a picture erupts of the dream I had been having when Rapunzel's rocks first pinged my window.

I'd dreamt I was in a singles' bar talking with a really good-looking radical feminist gossip columnist about the art of hitting a baseball.

I was telling her that she had a politically savvy animal grace that would be very suitable for playing on the socialist libertarian baseball team I managed. And that I'd be willing to install her, without even a tryout, as my starting second baseman—in return for a favorable mention as a "sensitive man" in one of her future columns.

She was too drunk to understand what I was driving at. In a slurred voice she kept repeating, "If you sell your soul for art, make sure you get a receipt."

Rapunzel interrupts my reverie. "I must say, my dear muse," she begins in her dusky voice, "that I'm shocked by the advertisement on your curtains. Isn't it unseemly for a world-famous feminist pawn like yourself to so brazenly announce 'I want three wives'? Even if it is in Chinese?"

In the five years since I had a Chinese calligrapher paint the characters for "I want three wives" on my curtains, Rapunzel is the first to have ever translated the meaning.

I want to respond wittily. I want to say something like, "It's just my little private joke with myself. A reminder not to take my rabid feminism so seriously that I wound my masculinity." But I'm too garbled to actually get the words out yet. I'm still getting over my anger at having been awoken ... steeping in my dream ... settling into my delight at Rapunzel's divine presence ... wondering what the hell she meant when she called me her muse.

"If you're interested, I can interpret your dream for you," she offers.

"What dream?" I mumble.

"The one you just had, silly. With the radical feminist gossip columnist you were trying to seduce."

"How could you possibly know that?"

"Your dream is telling you," she says, "that it's OK to exploit your feminism as a means to try to pick up women—as long as you make lots of self-deprecating jokes about how successful and varied your love life has become since you've become an avowed feminist."

It's almost easy to hide the feeling of intimidation that wells up in me in the wake of Rapunzel's apparent telepathy. All I have to do is switch my attention to the lust that her telepathy has kicked into even higher gear.

Next instruction to self: Got to calm down. Pace myself. I'm yearning to ask her about her version of last night's on-stage encounter, but I must stall. If this budding relationship we have is a seduction, it is an arty, convoluted, inscrutable one. My moves must be crafty, not obvious.

She strolls over next to my altar and examines the place in my room I call the "Wailing Wall." There I've assembled a museum-worthy exhibit of artifacts that document those adventures with women that've caused me to wail, both in the old-fashioned sense of grieving and in its more modern usage as a description of a vocalist who sings with bluesy authority. There are photos of the Big Ones Who Got Away—the love affairs that never quite got consummated—headed up by the half-Italian painter Giulietta, whose series of "Burning Chairs Sailing through Yellow Skies" paintings, numbers 1–22, included one masterpiece in which I'm the model for the Greek mythic figure of Prometheus. The thing has hung here on my Wailing Wall ever since she presented it as a gift in lieu of having an actual relationship with me. As a rather vulture-like eagle nibbles my liver, I'm gazing at the sight of a red stuffed chair tumbling aflame past a choir of female angels flying in chevron formation through a bruised yellow-orange sky.

Tacked to the frame of the painting is the last postcard Giulietta sent before she absconded from my life. Therein she informed me that she could never risk consummating a relationship with me because every instinct in her body told her to have children with me and the only children she ever wanted to have were her paintings.

Rapunzel has got her back to me, examining a dream interpretation written for me by another Big One Who Got Away: Erzebet, the teacher of my dreamwork class. Five years my senior, she had written two books, *A Feminist Revision of Jung* and *Loving the Dream Body*. Both psychic and intellectual, brilliant and loving, feminine and feminist, she had a truly ambidextrous brain. I used to swell with pride as I fantasized how one day I'd make love with the goddess who had the most highly developed corpus callosum in the western world. But that day never came. Only when it was too late—when she had already married another man—did she tell me that she'd always hated the way I tried to turn her into a perfect idol.

"Who's the babe there with you in bed?" Rapunzel deadpans without turning around. She's referring to the seated, three-foot-long totem doll that's leaning against the wall next to me, partially under the covers. Bought for me from a local doll-maker by my ex-lover Cassidy, Scaramouche is made mostly of roots and vines. Her legs are coyote jawbones and her hair is dried greenish-brown seaweed.

"That's my imaginary girlfriend Scaramouche," I say, finally managing to recover some of my wits. "Actually, she's half-bird, half-woman—a harpy, to be exact. She probably doesn't look too lively to you right now, but she's a powerhouse in my dreams. Takes me places. Rides me on her back. Last night she flew me to be a contestant in a male beauty contest in the radical feminist secessionist state of Santa Cruz, formerly a city in Northern California. I got to hang upside down naked from the world tree while the judges evaluated my knowledge of how the Norse god Odin bluffed his way into Freya's good graces so he could steal the magic goo from her cauldron. It was a very successful night. The crones who ran the ritual promised me a role as breeder next time I come."

"You know, Rockstar," Rapunzel replies without a breath, "I truly wish I could adore your imagination. It is so close to but so far from my ideal. It's vivid and unpredictable and all that—which you already know so I don't need to tell you. But—and I truly hate to break this to you—most of the time you unleash it I feel like you're masturbating in front of me. I mean, some of the stuff in your rant at the Catalyst show last night was honest and engaging, but other parts sounded like fantasies you wrote to get yourself off."

"Is that why you pumped me full of some weird drug?" I ask.

She doesn't say a word, but merely grins and makes her eyebrows quickly flit up and down five times.

"And what's wrong with masturbation, anyway?" I say, taking a different tack. "Don't tell me you buy into the prevailing prejudice that female masturbation is liberating, sexy, and empowering, while male masturbation is pitiful, indulgent, and gross?"

"I have nothing against jacking off, as the male of the species has so eloquently named it. Some of my best friends are jack-off artists. I'm not even offended by onanistic displays of the imagination. In fact, some of my favorite patriarchal literary masterpieces are the work of jack-off artists. *Finnegans Wake* comes to mind. Most of Thomas Pynchon. John Ashberry. Dylan Thomas. Kathy Acker. Mark Leyner. Lots of their work reminds me of ejaculate spewed into heaven so high that it never falls to earth. It impresses but doesn't fertilize. You get the idea that the authors regularly got inspired to write by jacking off to a five-story-high billboard image of themselves."

"Well, thank you I guess for comparing my imagination to that gang."

"No. Don't thank me. Beg me to take it back. Cajole me to tell you my opinion about how you can learn to anchor your long, hard imagination in Mother Earth before spewing."

"I wouldn't mind going down in history as an artist the caliber of the ones you named."

"Here's the news, Rockstar. You can go down in history—which will be sputtering to an end here in a few years—or you can go down in *herstory,* which has a far more stellar future. You can be famous with the millions of amnesiacs who regard newspapers and magazines and TV news shows as oracles of truth, or you can be famous with the Goddess Herself. Which'll it be? You want to dribble away your kundalini in a fatuous attempt to perfect the art of the onanistic imagination, which phallocracy brought to its pinnacle long ago? Or do you want to plumb the mysteries of menarche for men, and be sanctified and certified as a genuine lesbian man, proud member of the Menstrual Temple of the Funky Grail?"

"Is it really so clearcut a case of either-or? Do I need to utterly purge myself of all wicked patriarchal onanistic memes before you will be my friend?"

"If you want to know a secret—don't tell any of my co-conspirators—I actually wouldn't mind if you preserved a healthy supply of those wicked patriarchal onanistic memes. They'd be spicy. Or maybe yeasty would be the better term. They'd be the leaven in my dough, oh yeah."

Rapunzel sings that last line, jacking up her attractiveness yet one more notch: Her voice is limber and expressive.

"Yeah," she continues, "those wicked patriarchal onanistic memes do have the tendency to keep all us fuzzy warm Gaia-worshipers from getting overly set in our nuzzle-comfy ways. Still, Rockstar, if it were up to me, I'd ask you to relocate your spermatazoic fireworks displays. Inseminate the wild blue yonder less and the good brown earth more."

All the while, Rapunzel continues to peruse my Wailing Wall. She seems fascinated with the most controversial artifact in my display: a photo of the fetus Cassidy and I aborted. We insisted the doctor let us take a roll of film so as to ensure that we wouldn't let the memory of the trauma slip into the realm of abstraction.

I am, of course, still in bed and under the covers, pyjama-less as is my custom. The whole time Rapunzel and I are talking, I'm thinking, I would fuck this woman in an instant. Just exactly like I did last night on the Catalyst stage. Or hallucinated that I did, rather. I'd fuck her with craftsmanlike devotion, sincere compassion, gentle insatiability. With my tongue and my hands alone if she's a lesbian and doesn't fancy penetrating cocksmanship. I'd fuck her as a woman fucks a woman if necessary, her clitoris rocking against my pubis bone.

I would fuck her any way she wanted. Up in a tree that thrusts dangerously over the edge of a cliff. Recovering from the flu with a grocery bag over my head. Dressed in a lobster suit lying in muddy turf at midfield during halftime at the Superbowl.

I would fuck her like a ballet dancer, wrapping her legs around me just below my waist and thrusting as I twirled her in figure eights. Like an egoless saint with telepathic powers, I would channel angelic hymns to sweet spots she doesn't even know she has. Like a Fortune 500 CEO, I would fly her to Cancún for breakfast and let her ride me cowgirl-style in a bed full of hundred-dollar bills.

I would fuck Rapunzel any way, any time, under any circumstances. Only if she would let me, of course. But then I wouldn't want her merely to *let* me fuck her. I'd want her to *want* me to fuck her. I'd want her to want me voraciously and uninhibitedly, and not desperately or neurotically. I'd want her to *lust* for me without even being tempted to surrender any of her sovereignty. No power games ever. I hate power games (despite the fact that Catherine MacKinnon and Andrea Dworkin and company insist that hetero men know no other way to make love). And yes, I'd want her to *love* me—not just because I'm a long-distance runner of a fucker, and a lyrical Buddha of a fucker, and a magnanimous poised servant (not a sniveling infantile slave) of her passions—but because I'm all those things and I *don't care* that I'm all those things. That I'm *accidentally* those things. That as a side effect of my intense devotion to the project of cultivating her inner male and facilitating the sacred marriage of her inner male and inner female, I just *happen* to be a long-distance runner of a fucker, and a lyrical Buddha of a fucker, and a magnanimous poised servant (not a sniveling infantile slave) of her passions.

"The other thing about your imagination," Rapunzel says, having the nerve to interrupt my fantasy about her, "besides the fact that it's so much like spermatozoa in outer space, is that a lot of the time you're just *pretending* to use it in service to the Goddess. This serves as a great cover story when in fact you're whoring your imagination out to a bunch of phallocratic demons."

Uh-oh. It's one thing when I criticize myself: I enjoy it; it's a hobby of mine; it invariably inspires me to be a better person. But I'm virulently opposed to being criticized by anyone else, even Rapunzel.

"For instance," she continues. "As feminist as you claim to be, you still have this pit-of-the-soul bias against revealing the totality of who you are. I believe the issue in question—which unfortunately is best summed up by a term that you rightfully deride as a sloppy buzzword—is *vulnerability*. You don't dare expose your softness or act defenseless or ooze a little tenderness—at least in your public persona and in your music.

"I mean, look at how you create yourself on stage—as a hard-edged, flaming visionary with a relentless passion for exposing hypocrisy. This is a true and beautiful part of you, but it's a fraction of the whole story. Anyone with even an elementary knowledge of physiognomy can look at your oceanic eyes and gentle mouth and tell that you're a deeply emotional creature who's kind and sensitive and eager to love and be loved.

"Have you ever—even once—allowed an ounce of those qualities to seep to the surface while you're on stage? No. Not that I've ever seen, and I've been to a lot of your performances. You may now and then speak sweet words, but your body language and vocal timbres belie them. You're chronically raging, declaiming, stomping, bellowing, ripping, ranting, flailing, and straining to smash through the edge of taboo. I guess you could call that emotion, but it's so one-note, such a small part of your total range. Most of who you are up there in the spotlight is a fiery spew of forceful ideas, not a cascading oracle of poignant feelings. Quixotic visions and nihilistic invocations, not the swampy ambiguities of life on Earth in the here and now. Have you ever written a single song in which you tell a story about how some person has affected you? In your between-song patter, are you ever anything but arch and inscrutable and godlike in your eerie wisdom?

"It turns out, I'm sorry to say, that you're just another goddamn fucking rockstar. You wield your imagination as a weapon to hide yourself from your audience. You use it to awe people, to stun their imaginations into submission so they'll always believe you are only and exactly who you tell them you are. Isn't that the supreme irony: You—who rail about the entertainment criminals that're genociding our imagination—are yourself genociding our imaginations. More softly, perhaps, but just as effectively.

"What a fabulously glamorous dionysian persona you have fabricated for yourself, and what a load of shit it is. Beloved of the Goddess my ass. You act like you're fucking embarrassed to be the gentle, emotional creature your feminine side wants you to be. You project yourself as this flaming, six-foot-tall erect penis, never ever radiating out pictures of yourself as a moist, welcoming, nurturing vulva. What a shame, and what a hateful lie. You ought to be ashamed of yourself for your hypocrisy. It's the scam of the millennium, King Penis Rockstar Unique Genius Superman Kill-Everything-That-Won't-Worship-My-Spurting-Seed trying to pass himself off as a propagandist for the Goddess. That, my pathetic liar, is what your imagination has accomplished for you."

As vicious as her rant is, she's delivering it all in even, almost sympathetic tones. Yet this discombobulates me more than if she were actually shouting. My emotional state has shifted with alarming suddenness. I'm actually starting to feel depressed, which is distressing enough, but it's made even worse by the fact that I feel bad about feeling bad. I'm disappointed in myself because the generosity of spirit I've felt since Rapunzel's arrival is so quickly degenerating into a feeling of manic deflation. I want to be holy for her, broad-minded and playful—not a whiny little squeak of defensiveness.

"The worst of it is this," Rapunzel starts in again. "The very things you're so good at have become your virulent enemies. The unique wisdom you've distilled from your wrestle with fame has given you a false sense of security, fooling you into believing that you're immune to the soul-killing dangers you've seen so clearly. You've created a public impression of yourself as someone who resists the phallocratic star-making machinery and fights against the cult of celebrity, and yet your identity is so ensnared in this role that you can no longer even write songs about anything else.

"Have you done *any* songs, even one, about your intimate relationships with women? Of course not, because they'd force you to deal with feelings that are irrelevant to the persona you want to project of yourself as the media warrior and macho feminist politico. Frankly, my dear, you've become little more than a propagandist. It's true you're a *benevolent* propagandist who happens to promote positions I largely agree with. But that doesn't mollify the sadness I feel for you. How tragic for you that you can't allow yourself to be or feel or express anything that falls outside the tight little boundaries of your propaganda. You're a master of the art of creating an impression. You're a skilled entertainer who knows how to move people with passionate ideas. But you're afraid to confess that you also harbor a sweet, less-strident side overflowing with ambiguous emotions that have nothing or little to do with your big ideas."

I'm beginning to detect in myself the blossoming of what I can only call grief. This seems like a disproportionate response, and I fight against it, but there's no holding it back. An ancient desolation erupts. I'm suddenly in touch with some usually sealed-off zone in my psyche that is packed full of anguished accusations against life. The dominant mantra is, "It's not fair, I don't deserve this." Behind it, feeding it, is the accumulated shadow of everyone in my entire life who has refused to recognize me for who I am, everyone who has withheld the love I know I deserve. I feel myself shaking, on the verge of nausea. My heart literally hurts. I feel hatred for Rapunzel.

"What's most pathetic of all," Rapunzel says calmly, continuing her incredible onslaught, "and the thing that really makes me sick, is that you confess you're aware of the obscene amounts of egotism that are hidden in your save-the-world shtick—and yet this seeming self-efface-ment turns out to be no more than a way to disarm people so they won't notice you're a megalomaniac. Every time you seem to say, 'I'm not really a flaming Bodhisattva oozing with righteous compassion, but just a regular guy with self-delusions,' you indelibly stamp your listeners with the suspicion that you are indeed a flaming bodhisattva oozing with righteous compassion. In fact, you're so eager to convince us you're a bodhisattva that you'll try to talk us all out of believing it—only after you've planted the idea in our heads in the first place, of course.

"I've got to hand it to you. You're a virtuoso at disguising your scam—surpassing even the evil genius of Mother Teresa, whose flim-flam I saw through from the beginning. I mean, there she was with her phalanx of public relations people informing the media of what high-profile act of sainthood she was going to commit next. The woman was a rockstar-style megalomaniac. She took great pains to portray herself as the most holy person on the face of the Earth. And yet you, sir, take the whole shtick one step further. You *call attention* to the fact that you're hyping your own benevolence; you make fun of your aspi-rations to sainthood. You can't be criticized because you criticize your-self. You render yourself immune to deconstruction. And the crowd goes wild. 'We love you, St. Rockstar.' The whole thing makes me want to puke."

Though I haven't taken drugs in many years, I may as well, right now, be tripping on bad acid. Though a tiny part of me is still laughing sweetly that Rapunzel apparently cares enough about me to be here at all, her excoriation of me has triggered the release of a fountain of toxic waste in my psyche. Welling up in my mind's eye is a series of memories from my most traumatic encounters with women. Every betrayal, every schizoid episode, every hellish emotion spews up through me now as if I were a fountain of psychic vomit.

There in the mix is the moment I confronted Cassidy in the light-ing booth at the Catalyst about my suspicions, and she confessed she'd been shtupping the coke dealer Carl. The nomination of Geraldine Ferraro as first woman candidate for Vice-President was unfolding on the TV in the background as Cassidy initiated, partly out of guilt and partly to get rid of me, a blow job. She rushed through it, carelessly scraping my jade stalk with her teeth, trying to get it over with as soon as possible. I found myself in the twisted predicament of receiving a half-tender, half-biting ministration from the traitor who at that moment I hated more than anyone else I'd ever hated.

Then there's the humiliating story of my ex-girlfriend (or should I say ghoulfriend?) Radinka, who fashioned herself as a "Zen decadent." That was a time in my life before I knew of the term from clinical psychology, "borderline personality." Half the time Radinka radiated a sweet poetic craziness and showered me with a quirky but tender love. The other half of the time she shamed me for having ambitions to be a successful artist and insisted that if I wanted her to stay in love with me I would have to abandon my music and poetry and either do nothing in particular all day every day or devote myself to absurd and meaningless rituals like licking her fluttering lotus every afternoon between 4 and 4:30 while she sat on the straw settee in front of the TV and watched "The Beverly Hillbillies." Except that one day I rose up in defiance at her crazy-making. I said I would indeed perform the usual ritual nibble, but this time with the TV turned off, thank you. Whereupon she angrily exploded—not in any performance art prank or imitation of psychos she'd seen in movies, but with sincere schizophrenia. (Not that I knew the difference at that time.) Grabbing my marble Buddha statue, she began to carefully and with much deliberation smash everything in her path. I didn't stop her. Some perverse (and possibly equally schizoid) part of me interpreted the scene as a glamorous romantic melodrama. Even more importantly—I rationalized like a lunatic—she was delivering a personal message from the Goddess that I needed to be less attached to my possessions. And besides all that, I didn't see how I could stop her without beating her up, and I had long ago vowed never to strike a woman.

I surrendered to her insanity, giving her license to keep raging. Before night fell, she had broken all my windows with a ritual flourish, muttering some for-all-I-knew satanic incantation before each shattering. When she was through exacting that punishment, she started a bonfire in the backyard, where she incinerated much of my wardrobe and a good portion of my library.

After ruminating through my galling memories of Radinka, I don't stop. I feel compelled to review every act of female treachery. I allow the eruption of every painful love memory that has been safely repressed. My throat's a mess of choking astringency. My heart is collapsing aridity. My solar plexus is a clenching stab. I summon the time Esther cruelly mocked the new pop anthem I was so proud to have just written, comparing it to the Snoopy theme song. The time Margo invited me to accompany her to Amsterdam, only to abandon me for a rich, chubby American lawyer halfway through, leaving me to discover the crime by accident as I returned unexpectedly early from a trip to the Anne Frank Museum to find them pumping each other in our hotel room.

Is it fair to count the wounded women I took under my wing who then traitorously rejected my attempts to fix them? Probably not. Most of them didn't *willfully* betray my efforts to help them detonate their dormant potential. Nevertheless, my memories are awash with the sting of all my failed reclamation projects. Like that ingrate Ariel, who took my money to enroll in community college and then dropped out after three weeks so she could go back to waitressing. And deceitful Sammi, who begged me to let her stay at my house for a while, neglecting to inform me that she was fleeing a jealous, psychotic boyfriend who would track her down and try to kill us both. And Trisha, who asked to borrow my car so she could go apply for food stamps but went instead to buy some methamphetamines. I only found out that's what she did because the car was stolen, and when the police came they found the bag of stuff.

As I gaze at Rapunzel, I'm fighting hard to remain objective, to not let myself be sucked down into the abyss of my dread. As saturated with anguish as I am, part of my awareness is split off into the understanding that it's inappropriate to blame it all on her. Without trying to suppress any of the crush of sensations in my body—the spiraling fury in my chest, the clutch of grief in my throat, the squeezing throb of bitterness in the back of my head—I also reach for some poised perception about her, free from my projections.

Strangely, in contrast to the part of me that wants to crucify her for crucifying me, there is another part of me that castigates the pitiful little wimp in me who's so hurt by it all, and who wants instead to see in Rapunzel an all-knowing Goddess delivering a pure oracle, a difficult gift, from beyond the realm of her human personality. This aspect of me longs to interpret every single thing she does, no matter how seemingly cruel, as a divine blessing offering me the guidance I've refused to receive from any other source. As if she were infallible, beyond reproach, inhuman.

I wish I could say that this is a fresh and spontaneous response to the innocent mystery of the moment, but it's really just another ancient habit of mine. Just another groove. For as long as I've called myself a feminist—since my epiphany at the hands of Robert Graves' *The White Goddess* at age nineteen—I've been slapping this type of exalted interpretation on the crazy behavior of all the women in my life. The morning after Radinka apocalypsed my windows, poetry books, and pants, I enjoyed a scintillating meditation which confirmed for me that the Goddess had indeed used Radinka to interrupt my dangerously waxing attachment to comfort.

So in my grand tradition, Rapunzel's rant has provoked a dual roar of blame and worship. She's the incarnation of the devil, the embodiment of life's refusal to give me everything I want, while at the same time she's the Sweet Mother who knows what I need more than I do. Just another variation on the trite old virgin-whore reflex, eh?

No. Wait. There *is* one difference this time. A part of me is amused by it all. Is detached. Is enjoying it for the spectacle that it is. Rather than ridiculing myself for my infantile narcissistic complaining, and instead of leaping to my automatic transcendence, I have the notion to regard both currents as half-truths that deserve criticism and compassion. And once this brilliant idea sets in, I notice that I'm relaxing my intense self-absorption. I feel ready to ask: Beyond the cacophony of my feelings and projections, who is Rapunzel really?

It occurs to me that she rightfully deserves a part, not all, of both my blame and worship. Though my feelings may be exaggerated because they touch the root of my alienation from life, they are not entirely hallucinations or projections. And yet I also see that most of who Rapunzel is right now is something I've never seen before in my life. Something for which my past experiences provide no context. My task is to behold her without prejudice, to climb out of myself and find out who she is free of the accumulated weight of my opinions and expectations.

As I contemplate how I should go about this, I'm drawn to her eyes. They periodically flash me an eerie knowing look, as if to reveal the eyes behind her eyes. It's a coordinated gesture: As she opens her lids wider, her eyebrows rise slightly, she draws her head up and back, and her arms open in a slight arc that seems to indicate both surrender and welcome.

I take this to be a higher and more beautiful form of self-consciousness—self-consciousness not as an awkward feeling of being out-of-sync but as a meta-communication, a nonverbal notification that her message to me is not just what it literally seems to be. This certainly dovetails with the fact that she has never raised her voice into sneering anger even once. I fantasize she's showing me that her apparent cruelty is a ritualized performance given in a spirit of love and concern. I speculate that part of her hates to be so mean but knows she must be in order to snap me out of my trance.

At the same time, I leave open the possibility that what she's feeling is just plain self-consciousness, the discomfort of telling a relative stranger intimate insights about himself. Maybe there's also a flawed part of her that's thrilled to be able to wield the power of inflicting cruelty.

Finally, plumbing to an even more refined intuition, I conclude that both varieties of self-consciousness are present, and that, furthermore, the "higher" one is not "better" than the "lower" one. They come together as an inseparable pair. They need and complement each other.

Likewise, the possibility that Rapunzel is giving me a valuable gift does not contradict the possibility that she's abusing me. She may be both a perfect goddess delivering a difficult enlightenment *and* an imperfect human egotistically relishing the intense impact she's having on me. Again, it doesn't make any more sense to say that one is "good" and one is "bad" than it does to suggest that the sunshine is my friend and the rain hates me.

A surprising urge breaks through at this point. I experience it first physically. The best way I can describe it is that a lid blows off the top side of my solar plexus. As if a fermenting host of images had been trapped within a boil or tumor in my belly and was now escaping like the upwelling waters of a fountain. My first impression is that this is a load of poison. But as the toxins stream from my solar plexus up through my heart, the sensation mutates. My surprising intuition is that my heart is turning the toxins into medicine. I'm reminded, in vivid physical form rather than the usual intellectual experience, of one of my favorite passages from an old alchemical treatise, *Book of Lambspring:*

> A savage dragon lives in the forest,
> Most venomous he is, yet lacking nothing:
> When he sees the rays of the Sun and its bright fire,
> He scatters abroad his poison,
> And flies upward so fiercely
> That no living creature can stand before him,
> Nor is even the Basilisk equal to him.
> He who hath skill to slay him wisely,
> Hath escaped from all dangers.
> Yet all venom, and colors, are multiplied
> In the hour of his death.
> His venom becomes the Great Medicine.
> He quickly consumes his venom,
> For he devours his poisonous tail.
> And this is performed by his own Body,
> From which flows forth glorious Balm,
> With all its miraculous virtues.
> Hereat all the Sages do loudly rejoice.

The biggest mystery to me is why I am focusing in on and following the unfoldment of these physical sensations. Unless I'm making love or meditating on my breath, it's very unlike me to tune in to the insides of my body. And to be somatically aware in the midst of a traumatic conversation is so unprecedented that I'm sure it's because Rapunzel is performing some kind of magic on me.

I feel the fountain of once-noxious medicine reach my throat. It shrinks into a hard, uncomfortable knot at first but then bursts apart into a fine, palliative mist that fills me with the same kind of sweet joy I feel when I'm singing a song I love. Meanwhile, a new upsurge departs from the very base of my spine and heads northward. Unlike the first wave from the solar plexus, this one's launch doesn't sicken me. On the contrary, it is the very embodiment of reckless virility. Molten, indomitable, pugnaciously blissful, it's like raw lust—until it filters through my heart. There, something alien is added to the old familiar texture. What? A tincture of bemused benevolence? A hint of the spirit of tender nuzzling? While its bellowing command to be satisfied is not emasculated in the least, its fire has been moistened; its crazed, impersonal relentlessness has accepted intimacy as an alloy. As this second eruption arrives in my throat, it awards me with a loopy sense of prideless confidence. I fantasize that there will come a time in the future when I will be able to say exactly what I mean all the time.

I have no idea where these subtle currents in my body originate: in actual energy shifts within my organs, or in flows of blood and hormone, or in twitches of my nervous system. I only know that they are palpable, and that as I allow my awareness to blend with them, they unleash a flow of gnosis. Images materialize, not in my mind's eye exactly, but in my heart's eye, and my solar plexus' eye, and my throat's eye. It's as if there are brains all up and down my spinal cord. And the information they're imparting to me is imbued with a humble certainty. It's nothing like the jerky machinations of what Zen Buddhists call the monkey mind.

The first message that erupts is that for the sake of my physical health and for the prosperity of my creative artistry, I must forgive all those women whose betrayals bubbled up in the wake of Rapunzel's psychic attack on me. Cassidy, Radinka, Margo, Esther, Ariel, Trisha, Sammi—every one of them. Not just forgive them through some Pavlovian reinterpretation of their actions as being inspired by the Goddess. Not just forgive them in an all-purpose, abstract pardon, lazily invoking an automatic prayer.

The message is that every single memory of violation that I harbor must be individually recapitulated and purified. I must recreate in my imagination the precise scene of me and Cassidy in the lighting booth at the Catalyst, with Geraldine Ferraro giving her acceptance speech in the background and the mixed look of disdain, guilt, and impatience on Cassidy's face. And then I've got to forgive her with intelligence and eagerness, not blankness and resignation. I'll work to understand what part I played in the unfolding of our destiny, and forgive myself. I'll surgically remove the memory from its original context, which was rife with my narcissism and ignorance, and transplant it into the part of my soul where I understand that love is the only law of success that matters, love ensouled by play, and that not just for Cassidy's sake but for mine I want to bless everything about her, the "good" and the "bad," forever.

Here is the cosmic joke I'm channeling from the mysterious intelligence that is snaking through my body below my head: In flushing away my resentment and accusations, I bestow a boon on my physical health. In pouring out my blessings, I invite the divine kundalini to flow in and inspire my creative artistry. In forgiving everyone who has offended me, I am doing myself a very great favor. I am loving myself.

Rapunzel is wrong. My desire to rake in glamour and glory, to get people to love me and give me what I want, has been only fifty-one percent of my motivation to act altruistically. Forty-nine percent of me has been faithful to the bodhisattva agenda because I love to see people healthy and happy.

And watch out, because I'm just about to turn the whole accounting technique inside-out. I'm on the verge of proving, with Rapunzel as my guinea pig, that there's a way to subsume both motivations under the same intention. I am going to show that being good to Rapunzel, being good to Cassidy, being good to anyone and everyone, friend and stranger and foe, is the ultimate trick in winning the game of life. Not just in the sniveling, passive Christian sense, because it's the nice thing to do, but also in the greedy pantheistic sense, because it's the one sure method for me to get everything I could ever want.

Forget the strenuous twelve-hour sitting meditations on the Zen planks; forget mastering the occult words of power and the greater banishing ritual of Western ceremonial magick; forget all the thousand-page tomes detailing the self-denials and contortions the human being must go through to obtain enlightenment. I say the secret of success is to bestow blessings. As I bestow blessings, I seduce the attention of all the best muses. As I bestow blessings, I relieve myself of the constricted, unplayful, dead-serious attitudes that repel the arrival of all good things. As I bestow blessings, I dissolve the energy blockages in my body that could turn into disease, and I attune myself to the secrets of immortality. In this mystery, selfishness and unselfishness fuse in a hybrid which is both and neither.

I can't say this aloud yet, Rapunzel, you gorgeous sphinx trickster, but I will as soon as you learn to trust me: I bless you, yes, because I want you to think the world of me and I want you to fall in love with me; but I bless you also because I want you to thrive and prosper regardless of what you'll do for me; and I bless you because being good to you is the same as being good to me even if you never speak to me again. They are all the same blessing.

I've been silent for a long time, having pulled my head under the blankets during my meditation. As I emerge again, I see that Rapunzel is examining what's probably the most embarrassing item on my Wailing Wall: a description of my fantasy of living in a big house in the Berkeley hills with three wives and our who-knows-how-many children.

"'Whose turn is it to be serviced by hubby tonight?'" Rapunzel reads. "'Or should we just simplify matters and sleep four abreast for a change?'"

Rapunzel looks up as I poke my head out. She breaks into a stunning, crooked grin. With regal silliness, she strides over to my bed and descends to her knees. She clasps my head, pulls it towards her and smooches me . . . on the nose. Weird. Then she's back up and sitting on the red chair.

Despite the subtlety of my meditations, when I finally speak I can't help but revert to my jive-talking, smart-ass persona. "Wow," I begin, showing at least enough restraint to speak in a humble whisper. "You divined all that shit about me just from studying my performances? Sounds like despite what you say, I don't really hide the totality of myself very well after all."

"I don't think of it as the 'shit' about you, Rockstar. I regard it as raw material of the finest quality. Valuable ore."

"Does that mean you're still interested in accepting my application to the Menstrual Temple? Is it time to schedule my menarche?"

"About all we've determined thus far, lesbian boy, is this: You're eligible and ripe to take the tests that could win you the right to kidnap yourself—thereby earning you admission to our holy order."

"When do we start? Raw recruit Rockstar reporting for duty, Captain Rapunzel."

"You'd better find out what the tests are before you jump so glibly in."

"I've been prepping for this moment since I memorized Robert Graves' *The White Goddess* at age nineteen."

"Your tests have nothing to do with accumulating more second-hand information, and everything to do with stalking gnosis."

"You mean you're not going to send a coven of witches to kidnap me on the night of the new moon and take me blindfolded deep into the woods to a ritual menstrual hut lined with murals of crocodile-headed goddesses where I'll be commanded to dance idiotic dances in celebration of my liberation from patriarchal dignity and then demonstrate my mastery of the secret words of power that open up all thirty-two astral doors on the matriarchal Tree of Life? And all the while the concentrated prayers of the coven will be swelling my ego larger and larger, forcing it to grow more and more intoxicated with its own dizzying power to share in these mysteries, until at the climax of the initiation ceremony my ego has become so huge, so undeflatable, that it overlaps the ego of the Divine Intelligence on all sides. In effect I will then have sneaked into enlightenment through the back door; not, as the Buddhists teach, by shrinking and shrivelling up my ego until it disappears but by puffing it up so big and strong there is nothing that it does not encompass."

"Our 'initiation,' if that's what you want to call it," Rapunzel replies coolly, barely acknowledging my riff, "begins not with ceremonies, but with very practical, very earthy tasks. I'll tell you the first few now so you know what you're getting yourself into."

"Shoot."

"Your first assignment is to dissolve your band World Entertainment War and quit the rock music business. Your second assignment is to get a job as a janitor."

"What's my third assignment," I reply after a stunned pause, "shave my head and starve myself of sleep and eat nothing but white rice and sell incense in airports to support the coke habit of the Big Boohoo of the Menstrual Temple? Or maybe you'd just like me to take out a life insurance policy that names the Menstrual Temple as beneficiary, and then gulp some strychnine-laced Kool-Aid?"

I can't believe she's serious.

"You have every right to be suspicious and resistant. I'd be disappointed in you if you weren't. Slavish devotion to authority is near the top of our ugly list. But we have very good reasons for asking these things of you. Though it's literally impossible for you to believe this right now, they would create wonderful changes in your life. They certainly aren't for our benefit. And besides, you have absolute freedom of choice. We're not begging you to join us."

Until this moment, I have been playing with Rapunzel. I have been riding along on the half-conscious fantasy that we are like sophisticated children enjoying a game, and that playing the game is more meaningful and important than any real consequences that might come out of it.

It's the story of my life. I always do this. It's one of my trademark assets, even as it's a signature flaw. Maybe it's because I'm a creative artist who has had a relatively trauma-free life. Most of my important decisions revolve around how to produce those simulations of life called songs and poems and performances. Imagination is the legal tender in my little corner of the world. My devotion to it makes it easy for me to act as if I'm still living in the land of childhood, as if everyone I encounter is eager and willing to join me in that land for as long as we're together. It could be the clerk at the gas station or my bandmates or my mother. I pretend or assume or theorize that they're all just a prod away from sharing my obsession with turning every experience into a tricky myth. Maybe they're normally entranced by the plague of literalism that stinks up the world, but when I touch their lives—so I reason—they'll play along with me for a while, as we might have when we were five-year-olds or before we were born, when we were angels.

Until this moment, I have been convinced that Rapunzel understands this perspective implicitly, and has accepted all of its rules. Now I don't know. I can still manage to interpret her "assignments" as gambits in a meta-game, but the consequences are more real than I would like. Couldn't she have asked me to do something more playful and mythical, like let her walk me as a dog on a leash downtown or find out what it's like to wear a menstrual pad and a crown of lilies for four days?

I've loved this flirtation with "menarche for men" from the "Menstrual Temple," which for all I know exists only in the imagination of Rapunzel. I do, after all, have a long history of being drawn to half-mad women whose imaginations so thoroughly bleed over into their "real" lives that it's often difficult to know what's objectively true about them. I guess maybe my attraction to the Menstrual Temple has really just been a stand-in for my fascination with Rapunzel's imagination. I'm not sure I have truly believed there is such a thing as the Menstrual Temple; or if there is, whether I would want to accept all the actual consequences of aligning my fate with its. I half-assedly assumed I was just playing out an especially amusing seduction that would lead me to Rapunzel's love, not some real cult that was going to ask me to make over my life.

But let's assume for a moment that there is an actual entity called the Menstrual Temple and a real ritual called "Menarche for Men." As intriguing as they sound, I can't truly envision myself throwing away my rock career to partake. What benefits might they bestow on me that could possibly justify such drastic action?

"Before I even consider your outlandish proposals, Rapunzel," I say finally, stalling. "I'm going to have to ask you to sell me on the advantages of Menstrual Temple membership. Do you have a brochure or something? A prospectus?"

"What if I told you the Menstrual Temple has a drug-free strategy to insinuate you into altered states that are so far beyond the lucidity and ecstatic intensity of any dreams you've ever had—and I know you've had a lot—that you will swear you've discovered a new dimension to live in? This dimension has all the fabulously erotic and kinesthetic adventures of the dream realm plus all the solid reality and recall of your waking hours."

"I'd be piqued, but I don't know if I'd be piqued enough to renounce one of the great loves of my life."

"And what if I told you that an even greater love of your life will remain unavailable to you until you graduate from World Entertainment War?"

"Could you find it in your cold cruel heart to give me a hint of what that bigger and better love of my life might look like?"

"I don't want to create any false impressions. The majestic gift that's awaiting your transmutation is so far beyond your current ability to conceive that any clues I might drop would be misleading. However, I will reveal this much. It would not be a lie to say that in the last hour you have been freshly delivered into the hint of a watered-down version of the majestic gift."

I can't help it if my heart and all the erotic nerves it's linked to leap to the conclusion that maybe possibly hopefully the majestic gift in question is Rapunzel herself—not just in the getting-to-know-each-other mode she's unveiling now, but in her refulgent splendor, primed by my love to engulf me with a sweet cataclysm of tender mercy. If I could believe that quitting World Entertainment War would annihilate obstacles that kept Rapunzel from signing on as my girlfriend, I would sincerely consider risking what was otherwise unthinkable. In the course of my romantic career, I have, after all, pulled off some extremely strenuous stunts and sacrifices in the name of love.

I recall the comical initiations Cassidy made me go through before she'd let me fuck her. Singing "The Impossible Dream" in crowded cafes, maintaining a .350 batting average in a softball league, shoplifting doll furniture for her from every toy store in town. Then there was that time—I almost forgot about this one—when she had me strip stark naked at 3 A.M. and ride my one-speed bike four miles straight uphill from downtown to the university—while maintaining a hard-on the entire way. She followed me, of course, in her yellow VW bug, to make sure I didn't cheat.

Performance art stuff like that, though, was fun and, moreover, an addition to my repertoire as an artist—not a subtraction, as Rapunzel is proposing. Sacrifice is a trick I've always been willing to try if and only if it pumps up the luster of my dionysian lovability.

"OK, Rapunzel," I say. "You've got me fermenting. But tell me this. Why oh why—I can't imagine why—is the price for these treasures you're teasing me with so unreasonable? How could my access to them require the destruction of my music career? It doesn't make any sense. From everything I can tell, your philosophy of life is to do what you love to do. Well, I love singing and dancing and being a Dionysian priest. I love being possessed by the snake god."

"I didn't say you had to stop singing or dancing and being a Dionysian priest, nor do I mean for you to divorce the snake god. My point is to get you to do what you love, only better. To figure out how to untangle your divine motivations from the diseased motivations, and then channel your wonderful talent into sacred pranks that will accomplish the only thing worth doing."

"Which is?"

"Ahh. Yes. More about that later. If and when you decide to kidnap yourself. If and when you commit to cultivating the states the alchemists call putrefaction and nigredo: melting down the half-sick, half-beautiful containers your libido inhabits, and returning for a time to what we affectionately call primordial chaos."

"I'm scared."

"That's a good sign. It means you're actually entertaining my proposal."

"But it's all so sudden."

"There's no rush. You know what the occultists say: The magician proceeds as if she has all of eternity at her disposal."

"I still wish there was a brochure you could give me to study. A prospectus. A holy tome."

"Those types of artifacts exist, but they're exactly what you don't need right now. You're overstuffed with intellectual knowledge and second-hand information. The most precious and instructive experience for you is what we in the consciousness industry call gnosis. Direct perception unmediated by other people's theories."

"So where can you steer me if I want to gather more data to help me make my decision? What should I do?"

"How about this? How'd you like to sample a class at our Dreamtime University? I can arrange for you, anytime you want, to get a fresh hot delivery, in your dreams, of infomania that'll be quite helpful to you as you carry out the prerequisites for signing up with the Menstrual Temple. When would you like it? Tonight?"

I'm skeptical. What is she, the most powerful psychic in America, able to induce a specific dream in my psyche on command?

"In fact," she continues, "I can absolutely guarantee that it'll be the most real dream you've ever had. The most detailed. The most voluminous. Not only have you never had a dream as long and rich as this one—you've never come anywhere close to remembering so much of any dream as you will of this one. It's as if the dream itself will give you a memory upgrade so you can remember it.

"And you should also know that there's plenty more where this superdream comes from. Membership in the Menstrual Temple has thousands of perks, but the privilege of communing with superdreams at Dreamtime University has got to be one of the biggest luxuries."

"Anything else?"

"Lots of treasures besides the ones I've told you about. I'll just mention one other one."

"Free tickets to the dark underbelly of Disneyland?"

"Nope. Better than that. An end to your low wages."

"This janitor job I'm going to get must be pretty lucrative."

"You'd be surprised."

Rapunzel is beginning to put her crampons back on.

"So does your offer to arrange a superdream for me have any strings attached?" I ask. "If I formally beg you for it, am I committed to do your will forever? I mean, if I agree to accept your fresh hot delivery, do I automatically have to quit the band?"

"Of course not. Think of it as a free sample. An introductory offer. You know, the first one's free, but the price goes up once you're hooked."

"OK. I accept. Now as to when I'd like it delivered. The band's got another gig tonight, and—well—I get into a pretty wacky state. Always have my beers and coffees. Always dance myself into exhaustion and absorb the id-charged projections of hundreds of people. My dreams the night after are usually pretty fragmented. So anyway, tonight wouldn't be a good time. How about tomorrow night?"

"You're on. By the way, do you know what 'rockstar' backwards is?"

"Ratskcor?"

"Yup. Rat's core. And now it's time for me to go."

"Can I get your phone number?"

"I'm afraid you'll have to wait for me to contact you. Too bad you're not already signed up to the Menstrual Temple, because then you could bypass the more mundane forms of communication and reach me directly through the Drivetime."

"And what exactly did you say the Drivetime is?"

"Next time, Rockstar. Gotta go."

She grabs the bull skull origami on my altar, the one she'd given me a month ago during the party at the newspaper offices.

"Maybe you're ready to receive the oracle I tried to handfeed you way back when. Why don't you finally open this sucker up?"

She flings the origami at me, climbs out the window, and scoots back down the way she came in.

I drag myself out of bed and peer out at her. The woman is fast. She's already ripping off her crampons. Soon she's scurrying out of my yard, brushing by the eight-foot-tall bushes that line the front boundary.

I lower myself down on the sacred spot on the chair where she'd been sitting and examine the origami. For the first time I notice on the back, in very tiny letters, the words "open me." Wonder how I missed seeing that until now.

Unfolding it, I find a text with print so small I can barely read it. I fetch the magnifying glass that came with my Oxford English Dictionary and discern the following:

The Televisionary Oracle

In the best-known version of the Greek myth, Persephone is dragged down into the underworld by Pluto and held hostage. But in earlier, pre-patriarchal tales, she descends there under her own power, actively seeking to graduate from her virginal naivete by exploring the intriguing land of shadows. Which of these approaches to higher (or should we say *lower?*) education do you prefer: imposed against your will or initiated under your own power? It really is up to you, and you should decide pretty soon. Maybe it'll help you make your decision if we tell you that according to ancient lore, the dusky realm to which Persephone journeyed is a place of hidden wealth.

35

This is how spells are broken:

by changing your name
every day for a hundred days

by bragging about
what you can't do and don't have

by telling nothing but lies for 24 hours

by staring at yourself
in the mirror
for hours

by confessing profound secrets
to people who aren't particularly interested

by forcing yourself to laugh nonstop for one hour

by acting with absolutely no ulterior motives

by dancing alone
all night
in slow motion
with your clothes on inside-out

by seeking out information
that renders your political beliefs irrelevant

by pretending to be dead
for three days

by burning down the dreamhouse
where your childhood keeps repeating itself

by communing with the Televisionary Oracle

A rtemisia went to her acupuncturist, Dr. Lily Ming, in need of relief for her menstrual distress. Ming gave her more than the usual array of needles, lightly pounding the nail of Artemisia's big toe with a small silver hammer for a few minutes.

"Why?" Artemisia asked.

"Good for the uterus," the doctor replied.

Indeed, Artemisia's cramps diminished as the doctor thumped, and she was not troubled by them for the duration of her period.

After the session, the usually taciturn Ming surprised Artemisia by disclosing a traumatic event from her own childhood. It seems that during the occupation of her native Manchuria, she was forced to witness Japanese soldiers torturing people she loved. Their favorite atrocity was using hammers to drive bamboo shoots through their victims' big toes.

The moral of the story? Dr. Ming has accomplished the feat of reversing the meaning of her most traumatic imprint. Can you do the same?

Your secret identity and your magical nickname
are brought to you by
*Dyke Punk Witch Talismans.*

These handsome, handcrafted power objects
have been carved exclusively
from the wood of the pomegranate tree.

Each features a secret compartment
that contains the last breaths
of some of the most famous wild women in history,
including Georgia O'Keefe, Virginia Woolfe, Joan of Arc,
Billie Holliday, Emma Goldman, Josephine Baker, Lou Salomé,
Bessie Smith, Anaïs Nin, and H.D.

36

At age nine, I began devouring the fossilized thoughts of all the dead white guys who still run the world from beyond the grave. My seven mommies believed that by then I had been safely brainwashed by my thoroughly matriarchal education. They wanted me to become familiar with the lies of the enemy. As I read the evil books, I was shocked, appalled, furious, incredulous—and rather well-entertained. My best guilty pleasure came from reading about how men down through the centuries had sought to jump out of their skins.

In Joseph Campbell's vision of myth, I found, the hero is typically a guy who braves dangerous ordeals all by his lonesome, though he may on rare occasions receive aid from a goddess. In medieval legends, a knight might obtain a talisman from his blessed lady before setting out on his Grail quest, but he sure as hell didn't bring her along to assist him. The history of shamanism is dominated too with stories of male explorers storming the astral plane ablaze with the macho glamour of solitude.

There is not only a dearth of women in the recorded history of humans penetrating the mysterium, but also an almost total absence of collaborative efforts.

I was already aware of this discrepancy at the ripe old age of twelve. By then I had read enough mythology and anthropology to realize how heretical my own jaunts into the other side of the veil were: I had a collaborator, Rumbler. True, he was as non-human as the goddess Athena, who gave the prototypical Campbellian hero Perseus a burnished shield to use as a mirror in his showdown with Medusa. But he was my equal and co-creator. We slipped into the Televisionarium together, and we shared the adventures there.

When my life with Jumbler got underway, I took my apostasy one step further. Beginning on that first night in the Villa Inn in San Rafael, high on pranks and tears and erotic thrills, the two of us, a loving couple, found a way to pull off a feat which as far as I knew no two flesh-and-blood magicians had ever done before: fly away together on a shamanic journey.

As the light from Jumbler's eyes caressed the light from mine, as our hot sweet breaths mingled in each other's lungs, as our almost unbearable pleasure mutated our brain chemistry out of its habitual groove, we disappeared into a gossamer net of shimmering light whose warp was gold and woof was silver. It collapsed gently around us, turning into a soothing, slow-motion tornado that soared and fluttered and finally set us down, many sighs later, in a dreamy landscape that seemed perfectly real. I never once lost sight of Jumbler even though the whole world changed around us.

We found ourselves lying on a grassy hill on a bright day with a very big sun directly overhead. There was an exuberant blend of smells in the air: spearmint, baking cake, varnish, brewing coffee. We were wearing the same clothes we had on back in the tear-stained bed.

"Doesn't this place look like a cemetery to you?" she asked with a matter-of-fact curiosity that made me laugh. How could she be so poised after a wild ride like we just had?

"It's rather festive for a cemetery," I said, trying to match her nonchalance. "Look at the prayer flags hanging from the trees. And the flower-bedecked floats over there. As if there's been a parade. Plus I smell all sorts of delicious aromas."

"Check out the women in their underwear dancing around the maypole," Jumbler said. "That's the wackiest lingerie I've ever seen. My favorite is the two floral shower caps attached to make a poofy bra."

"Do you mind if I ask you a stupid question?" I said.

"They're my favorite kind," she replied.

"Where are we?"

"I believe we must be having a lucid dream together," she said as she squeezed my hand.

"You mean I'm dreaming of you in my lucid dream and you're dreaming of me in your lucid dream?"

"No. We're dreaming the same lucid dream at the same time."

"But this can't be a lucid dream. Can it? I mean, my awareness is like it is in a lucid dream—I'm in full possession of my logical faculties—but the landscape itself is too solid. It's not fuzzy at the edges. It doesn't keep mutating."

"Yes," she agreed. "You're right. But don't you also feel that sweet, creamy meltingness of the astral plane? That floaty timelessness?"

"Yes."

"And don't you see things here that you'd only find on the other side of the veil? Like there's a herd of pink octopuses swimming in the air. Like the creature riding the centaur over there is half-woman, half-bird. Like all the gravestones have television screens in them."

I wanted to test a theory. Rising to a squat, I launched myself upwards with the intention to fly. In a moment I was high above the octopuses, swooping effortlessly. I sailed over to the top of a nearby pomegranate tree and picked two fruits, then whooshed back down to my old spot next to Jumbler.

"So if this isn't exactly a lucid dream," I said, breathing hard, "and it certainly isn't waking reality, what is it?"

"Maybe this is the Drivetime," Jumbler replied. "Maybe we're having a joint shamanic quest into the good old Drivetime."

"Is that possible?"

"I've heard of tantrically trained shamanic lovers being able to accompany each other into the *Dreamtime*," she said. "My teachers told me it was possible with a lot of practice. But they never said anything about two people getting into the *Drivetime* together."

"What if we're pioneers?" I bragged.

"We'd better start taking mental notes, just in case we are."

"Look at those huge women in bikinis over there," I marveled. "Dancing on the back of that Cadillac convertible. Must be three hundred pounds each. I like the hood ornament, too. I think it's a real vulture."

"I don't know if those are bikinis exactly," she said. "They look like they're round slabs of lunch meat sewn together. Wonder who their tailor is?"

"Do you smell—what is that exactly?—seaweed? And car tires?

And banana bread? It's weird how the whole palette of aromas keeps shifting."

"Yeah. I smell all that. There's also something like lipstick."

"Check out that long line of men wearing wedding gowns and pushing the shopping carts," I said.

"Wonder where they're going? Can't see the front of the line behind that hill."

"I'll go check."

I launched myself into the sky again and flew to reconnoiter. On the way I saw that all the shopping carts were packed full of brightly wrapped gifts. As I reached the other side of the hill, the procession's destination came into view. It was a tall, round, skinny tower whose surface was an intricate mosaic of red, black, and white tile. There was but a single window in the top floor, and no visible door. My heart leaped when I first spied it. It was virtually a duplicate of the tower pictured in a book I loved in childhood—the book that retold the Grimms' fairy tale of Rapunzel.

My next emotion was disappointment. Maybe this tower was evidence that the whole scene was nothing more than a projection of my unconscious psyche. I didn't want that to be true. I wanted this adventure to be an objective event, independent of my subjective fantasies.

I landed on the top of the tower and surveyed the scene. For as far as I could see, there was a single file of men in long white wedding gowns. The man at the front of the line stared up at me and began to shout, "Rapunzel, Rapunzel, let down your hair." Was he talking to me? I floated down to the window and perched on the ledge to look inside. No one was there.

"Rapunzel, Rapunzel, let down your hair," came the cry again. I climbed down into the room. To my relief, it looked like no place I had ever seen: evidence that tended to prove I wasn't merely making all of this up.

The bed was huge, round, and appointed with a red satin comforter and many black satin pillows. Lutes and hand-drums and flutes lay against a wall on a thick magenta carpet, along with a bowl of dark red cherries and figs. A richly woven tapestry hanging on the wall depicted a blue-skinned goddess with eight arms and long auburn hair. She was dancing atop a giant TV that had a scene of her dancing atop a TV. Among the objects in her many hands was a baseball bat and a baseball glove containing a pomegranate.

Next to the tapestry was a white marble altar. The intoxicating smoke of burning frankincense emerged from an aladdin's lamp. There was a bird's nest containing a single red egg which was noticeably rocking back and forth under its own power.

On the wall behind the altar was a round mirror. I peered into it. The reflection was not me, though in some ways it resembled me. The features of the face were the same. The hair was my auburn color but longer and thicker. However, the skin was blue like the creature on the tapestry, and there were patches of flames burning here and there on the skin—including that spot in the middle of my forehead. I switched my gaze away from the mirror and looked down at myself. Nope, my skin was still flesh-tone, and I was not on fire.

I stared again into the mirror. The blue girl there winked at me and blew a flaming bubble off her tongue. I laughed.

Outside, more voices had joined the lead man's. "Rapunzel, Rapunzel, let down your hair," chanted the throng. What should I do? Leaning out the window, I saw Jumbler flying towards me. In a few moments she floated in through the window.

"I thought you were coming right back, sweetie," she said brightly. "What's been keeping you?"

"I'm trying to figure out what to do about all those guys down there. They seem to want something from me."

"Come on with me. I met someone who's been asking about you. Maybe she can give us a clue."

"Who is it?"

"Says she's Madame Blavatsky. Your sixty-five-million-year-old secretary."

As we flew out the window and away from the tower, I could hear groans and cries of dismay rising from the men below. Just for fun, I blew several kisses down at them. Cheers and happy cries rang out. Many men fell to the ground and writhed, as if my long-distance smooches had struck them down.

Jumbler led me to a place near our original landing spot. The first thing I saw as we descended was a golf cart. It had a vulture figurine on the roof and sprouted two long poles in the back, at the top of which were "flags" that consisted of three pairs of plus-size white cotton underpants sewn together. They were partially unfurled in the mild wind that was blowing.

An obese woman with oiled-up, light brown hair smiled inscrutably from behind the steering wheel. She was indeed the vivid personage who had identified herself as my ancient secretary during my first visit to the Drivetime. Was that only a few hours ago? Seemed like weeks.

Madame Helena Blavatsky was attired in nothing but a huge white bra and panties. A number of rubber toy vultures hung from her garments, attached by gold safety pins through a loop at the tops of their heads. Our visitor also sported a tall, striped, stovepipe hat and was holding a large soft pretzel which she munched from time to time. Perched precariously on her dashboard was a can of Budweiser. She had an amazingly good smell that was perceptible even from a few yards away.

"Glad to see you went out and found yourself a real, live, fleshy, substantial creature to consort with, Queen Trashdevourer!" she beamed towards me. "Excellent addition to your apocalypse-killing repertoire. Not that I have anything against your friend Rumbler. But he is a little too chimerical to rely on for some of the more concrete work we have ahead of us. On the other hand, don't count the old boy out just yet."

She produced another can of beer from behind her seat, popped the top, and chugalugged.

"Now let me officially welcome you both to the Tantric Campus of Drivetime University," Blavatsky said, punctuating the "ver" in "University" with a prolonged burp, "for couples only. Not a moment too soon, either, what with the mass extinctions going on back on Planet Heavenandhell. Malkuth. Earth. Whatever you want to call it. We need all the collaborative kundalini we can get. Wink wink. Hint hint. Climb on board now, you love-buzzards. Time for class."

"But we haven't bought any of our school supplies yet," Jumbler protested archly as we both stood up. "Shouldn't we take notes?"

"This is all you will need," Madame Blavatsky said authoritatively, handing us each a giant pomegranate she produced from a pouch near her feet. "A Televisionary Oracle. Like all those sacred machines you see around the necropolis, only mini-versions. Open it up."

On closer inspection, I saw mine wasn't exactly a standard-issue pomegranate. It had about ten black seed-like buttons embedded in a row on one side.

"Press this one," Madame Blavatsky instructed, pointing to a button at the top.

I did, and a door popped open on the pomegranate's surface, revealing a screen that bubbled with images that at first glance looked pornographic.

"You just pour your thoughts right into the swirl," Madame Blavatsky said, "and it will converse with you, in a manner of speaking. You will hear its replies inside your head. It will feel very familiar and strange at the same time. Play around with it. You'll get the hang of it. Now get in the vehicle, please. Time is wasting. Oh, and here is your sacred underwear. Put it on immediately. You cannot do much learning without it. Or rather you *should* not."

She handed me and Jumbler battered grocery bags which we opened up as we got on board. My "bra" was fashioned out of two gold linen cups that were replicas of the Grail I had stolen and sold. My panties were white satin decorated with several dark brown blotches which were the exact shape and size of the birthmark I had worn on my forehead until very recently.

Jumbler's "sacred underwear" consisted of a flesh-colored leotard bearing a photographic likeness of breasts on top and a penis at the crotch. Laughing, she held it up to show me.

As we changed into our new costumes and rode over the grounds of the necropolis, Madame Blavatsky entertained us with an odd rendition of the children's alphabet song, a-b-c-d-e-f-g etc. She delivered each letter in a vocal ejaculation that was simultaneously a sung tone and a loud belch.

"That was a graphic example of profane entertainment," she proclaimed when she was done. "Though I admit that it is perhaps a slight exaggeration to equate it to the slick productions of Time-Warner or Disney-ABC or any of the other multinational narcissism-dealers that are infecting the mass imagination. But only a slight exaggeration. And it is an excellent context within which to begin exploring the other kind of entertainment—the sacred variety. Which, I am happy to add, is the foundation for the next step of your mission, Queen Chucklefucker. What you do *after* you kill the apocalypse."

After donning my sacred underwear, I gazed into the screen of my Televisionary Oracle. The scene I saw there can only be described as a sex riot. Hundreds of adults of all ages, universally naked except for red shoes and moving along in a slow, chaotic procession, were attempting to dance and copulate at the same time. They looked like Persians or Afghani. Though the men in the crowd were active participants, it was primarily the women who initiated and led the licentious improvisations. I don't mean to minimize the homosexual activity. There were men embracing men and women with women.

I tried what Madame Blavatsky had suggested: projected my thoughts into the swirl. "What meaning am I supposed to draw," I asked the Televisionary Oracle, "from this sex riot?"

The voice that spoke in my mind was female. Its cadences were stilted, as if it were using shorthand.

"Mass outbreaks of sexual bliss," it said. "You must help unleash them. It will end global flirtation with apocalypse. Explode boundaries through pleasure, not death. Blast apart tyranny of ego's petty vision and revive memory of divine origins through *petite morte*, not *grande*."

"And the implications of this for me and my mission?" I beamed into the swirl. "What specific actions should I take?"

"You are Queen Bee of Orgasmic Liberation," it glimmered back. "Not Queen Bee of Titillation. World already has too much arousal without release. You will replace pandemic of repressed teasing with revolution of brazen rapture. You are Great Juice Mother of Psychefunkapus."

"Psychefunkapus?" I asked with a mix of alarm and intrigue. "What does that mean?"

"Psychefunkapus: New Covenant of Primal Nookie; Rebirth of Once and Future Throbwiggle; Apotheosis of Slippery Boink; Coming of Fuckissimus."

"And tell me again what this has to do with me?"

"You are High Priestess of Global Jiggy Snake. Holy Empress of Planetary Oozeshimmer Revival. Sovereign Shamanatrix of Collective Flutter Magic."

Madame Blavatsky was demanding my attention with annoying pinches to my arm, so I had to promise myself to return later to my conversation with the Televisionary Oracle. She had driven us up to a large rock outcropping about three times our height. There was a giant television screen embedded in a steep, flat part of the slope, with long streamers of tied-together bras and underpants hanging down from large hooks on either side. A vulture was also perched on each hook. On screen, a talking head in suit and tie was pressing a headphone into one of his ears, keeping his eyes closed as he apparently listened to a message. He looked like an anchorman, complete with impeccable blow-dried hair and heavy make-up.

To the right of where Madame Blavatsky had parked the golf cart was a metal pole planted in the ground, at the top of which was a white box.

"Lesson one in Sacred Entertainment," Madame Blavatsky announced, "courtesy of the one and only Televisionary Oracle." She turned a knob on the box. The face on the screen opened his eyes and began to speak. The sound spilling from the box was surprisingly high-fidelity.

"Warning of imminent 'hype-ocalypse' and 'genocide of the imagination,' a team of self-described 'benevolent terrorists' calling themselves the 'Televisionary Oracle' is now in the third day of what they term a 'channeled *coup d'état.*' Two days ago they managed to seize control of at least a portion of the broadcast facilities of a number of major television networks. How exactly they accomplished this remains unknown, though they themselves have invoked the improbable term 'menstrual shamanic telekinesis' to explain it.

"Much of the regular programming on ABC, NBC, CBS, Fox, and CNN has been seriously disrupted. In its place the Televisionary Oracle has been presenting a bizarre hodgepodge of well-produced but controversial material, ranging from the mysterious 'Mary Magdalen's Monster Truck Rally and Tantric Cryfest' to the black comedic 'International Tribunal of the Multinational Narcissism-Dealers' to a kind of erotic telethon, the 'Kundalini Pledge Drive.'

"Less than an hour ago, we were contacted by one of the apparent leaders of the takeover, Rapunzel Blavatsky. She joins us now from an unknown location in Northern California. Welcome, Ms. Blavatsky."

"Dude, you are looking so good tonight I wouldn't mind licking whipped cream off your forehead."

Butterflies stirred in my belly as my doppelganger appeared on the Televisionary Oracle. She was an older version of me—how I might appear ten years in the future. I—she—was wearing a striped baseball jersey. The words "Menstrual Temple of the Funky Grail" were written in cursive across the chest. A smallish vulture was perched on her shoulder.

The anchorman ignored the joke.

"Until two nights ago, Ms. Blavatsky," he droned, "you didn't exist for me. That's when I saw you on the pirated CNN broadcast. I was confused at first. Why would someone with the media savvy to kidnap the airwaves then appear on those airwaves without a trace of make-up? You can't possibly be ignorant of the impact a close-up of a face without make-up has on the viewing audience."

"I wanted my new viewers to see the pimple I have here on my forehead," The Other Rapunzel said, pointing to her reddish bump. "If I make it difficult for them to attribute perfection to me right from the start, I might have a chance to prevent them from turning me into an energy-sucking monster they worship with all their hearts."

"Well, I have to say," the anchorman continued, "that pimple had a strong impact on me. As I fell asleep the other night, I could not take my mind off it. It was so big and ugly! And on such a pretty woman, too.

"Around dawn I had a strange dream about you, Ms. Blavatsky. I dreamed you had crawled into bed with me and my wife. You were lying between us, sexually arousing us with sweet words and tender touches.

"You murmured in my ear as you nuzzled it. You said something like, 'I predict Congress will pass new legislation decreeing that all Americans must be rewarded financially in direct proportion to how much beauty they create.' Then you were rubbing your feet up and down my legs and stroking my wife's breasts. 'I predict a Sufi real estate magnate will announce plans to build a chain of sacred shopping centers in the American heartland,' you said. My wife and I lay there for a long time while you pleasured us. The entire time you kept uttering more of your silly predictions.

"Just before I woke from the dream, Ms. Blavatsky, you had your right hand on my penis and your left on my wife's vagina. You were softly chanting, 'The apocalypse is dead! Long live the apocalypse!'

I am not exaggerating when I tell you that I have never felt so perplexed and yet so blissful in my entire life.

"Would you mind telling me your thoughts on the meaning of this dream? First of all, what did you mean when you said, 'The apocalypse is dead! Long live the apocalypse!'?"

The Other Rapunzel slowly stuck her tongue out to its full length before she spoke. It did not seem to be a sign of juvenile defiance, but a gesture akin to the depictions of the Hindu goddess Kali in her moments of arch ferocity.

"My greatest desire," The Other Rapunzel said finally, "is to kill the decrepit old patriarchal apocalypse in the hearts of the mass audience. That will clear the way for me to resurrect a fresh, new, sexy apocalypse. A sweet, aromatic apocalypse that restores the original meaning of the term *apocalypse:* revelation, a great awakening, second birth. Thereby eroticizing the same kundalini that the bad old daddies have been thanatizing all these centuries."

"And does that require you, if you'll excuse my irony, to make love to the mass audience in their dreams? As you did with me and my wife?"

"Think of me as a kind of succubus Santa Claus for adults," The Other Rapunzel said with a sly grin. "I bring a very special kind of blessing to everyone in the world."

"Now really, Ms. Blavatsky, do you expect me to take seriously what you just said?"

"I am as serious as the big old pimple on my forehead."

"Please don't take this the wrong way, but you sound like a deluded guru wannabe."

"Indeed, I am the most humble guru wannabe in the history of dreams. The most total nobody in a world full of nobodies. And as far as being deluded: I'm sure I am in my own lovable way, but do you know any other deluded fools who are capable of engineering a takeover of ABC, NBC, CBS, Fox, and CNN broadcasts?"

"Will you explain for us how you managed to accomplish that feat?"

"The rowdy ruby glissando of the silk lotus."

"I have no idea what you're talking about, Ms. Blavatsky. Would you care to try again?"

The Other Rapunzel stood up suddenly and ripped open her shirt, which revealed a bra surmounted by two rubber vulture puppet heads with their maws open. The real vulture on her shoulder flew off.

"I predict that compassion will become an aphrodisiac," she declaimed in a loud, laughing tone, her arms raised in a V-shape, "and charisma will replace cancer as the official national disease. I predict the networks will be required by law to show live childbirth in prime time every night. I predict supercomputers that will be able to converse with the Goddess. I predict that the launching of celebrity garbage into outer space will lead to miraculous breakthroughs of new sources of free energy. I predict that the Twenty-Two Hours of World Orgasm will usher in the amazing, thrilling, and just-in-time end of history—turning millions of entertainment victims into well-rounded, incredibly kind, sex-crazed geniuses—with lots of leisure time."

As I—she—finished her rant, she began to do a whirling jig, hands high above her head.

"End of lesson one in resurrecting the apocalypse," Madame Blavatsky announced with a triumphant chuckle as she turned down the volume on the speaker and peered at us with an expression that was both shifty and piercing. "Any questions?"

"So I don't have to just kill, kill, kill," I exulted appreciatively, glad for the apparent revelation that my mission was not merely as a destroyer, as she had insisted last time I saw her in the underground junkyard. "But how exactly am I supposed to go about resurrecting the good apocalypse?"

"Twenty-Two Days of World Orgasm, my dear," she said. "You will be hearing much more about that."

"Now I've heard three different versions of the World Orgasm thing," I noted. "Is it twenty-two minutes or hours or days?"

"Well, now, that is completely up to you, is it not? Seeing as how you will be the one to plan it and carry it out."

Madame Blavatsky revved up the golf cart engine and turned to depart. I could see that The Other Rapunzel had been joined on the Televisionary Oracle by women dancers wearing skimpy yet goofy clothes. Aluminum foil and Spanish moss and rainbow-colored clown wigs were common sartorial materials, as well as band-aids, flowers, papier-mâché, and plastic wrap. An older-looking Jumbler was one of them, though she was barely visible in the background.

"Well, I hope I get a bigger part in lesson two," the real Jumbler complained good-naturedly as we rolled away. "How come Rapunzel gets to have all the fun?"

"The Eater of Cruelty shall be the father of the new covenant," Madame Blavatsky replied with a portentous and scolding tone that seemed to misread Jumbler's jest, "and the Pomegranate Grail the mother. But you had better get used to the fact that the girlfriend you picked is Queen Bee, Sex President, and Chief Anchorslut of the United Snakes of Rosicrucian Coca-Cola. Believe in her, Jumbler. Help her. Most of all, get used to sharing her. She is the Global Initiatrix of Fuckissimus. The Universal Love Slave."

"Tell me more," Jumbler said to Blavatsky, which I thought was curious. Up till then, she had shown little interest in any conceptions about my fate that didn't originate with her.

"I cannot do that right now," my great-great-great-grandmother replied. "We have run out of Drivetime momentum for the moment. The two of you must return to the hotel back in the Waketime. There is a lot of work to be done, and we must pace ourselves. This is but Day Two of what we will in the future call the First Seven Days of Creation. You are not yet ready for full-scale immersion in the Drivetime."

Madame Blavatsky was weaving the golf cart across a densely packed section of the cemetery now, avoiding the tombstones but driving right over the flat grave markers. We were heading towards a giant Televisionary Oracle, the size of a highway overpass, at ground level on the far end of a field. Meekly I asked, "Is this safe?" The air smelled of mint candy and rum and cedarwood.

"Quickest way to get you back. Don't worry."

When Jumbler and I awoke on the morning after, back in the tear-stained bed at the Villa Inn, it was almost 2 P.M. We were dressed as we were at the height of the tantric exchange that had propelled us into the Drivetime: black flannel pajamas for her, black velvet tights and tunic for me. It took me a disappointed minute to adjust to the fact that I wasn't wearing my sacred underwear from Madame Blavatsky's necropolis.

We didn't groom ourselves with great care before making a foray to the crummy food market a couple of blocks away. We were barefoot and tousled and deliriously happy. It was amusing to witness the reactions of innocent bystanders as we foraged for our Ritz crackers, string cheese, lemonade, and celery. The latter was far from my favorite vegetable, but it was the only one in the store that didn't look like it had been invaded by rot.

I might have preferred our conversation during those first couple of waking hours to have centered on our excursion into the Drivetime. I wanted to compare notes and analyze the meanings of the experiences we had shared. And Jumbler did agree to a modest exchange that made it clear her experience had been identical to mine. It was not merely a creation of my unconscious mind.

Perhaps driven by Madame Blavatsky's parting words, though, she was mildly obsessed with questioning me at length about the story of my life as Rapunzel, which for some mysterious reason she knew nothing about even though she seemed so knowledgeable about my alleged other incarnations. I answered her inquiries happily, spilling out deep secrets about the circumstances of my birth, my upbringing as the avatar, and how and why I ran away. It was the first time I'd ever talked so much to an outsider about my history. My mothers had always forbidden such self-revelation.

Later, after we shared late-afternoon breakfast in bed, her interview finally ebbed. For a while we closed our eyes and were silent, my right leg and her left playing together.

"You are surprisingly receptive for such a flaming narcissist," she said suddenly.

"How can I possibly be a flaming narcissist," I replied, determined not to be offended though I had instantly gone rigid. Would this be our first fight? "All my life I've been trained—brainwashed, really— to believe that my life is devoted to serving all of womankind. More than anything, I want to be *of use*."

Nervously, I lurched away from her to the middle of the bed and began running my hands through the thicket of my hair.

"Yes. I see that. I don't mean to condemn." She glided behind me, lifted my tunic, and began stroking my belly with her almost supernaturally feathery touch. "But all that stuff is really just skin-deep, isn't

it? Your underbelly imprint is very different. And how could it be otherwise? You've never had any other experience except as a dearly beloved
object of devotion. Day after day for many years, women who cher-
ish you deeply have poured their life energy into you."

"I can't help that." I was annoyed at her even as she was arousing
a sweet warmth in my body.

"I know you can't," she said. "But what it means is that you have
never had the chance to feel wrenching, gut-level yearning for anyone
who makes you feel the way your devotees feel about you."

"Oh." Was it really necessary to discuss this now? I didn't feel like
defending myself, even though I had a good rebuttal: the memories,
which had surfaced the day before, of my relationship with my birth
mother Magda.

"And until you can add that primal emotion to the mix," Jumbler
continued, "all your service to the world will be one-dimensional. By
rote. Uninspired. You'll be a charismatic leader who's programmed
mostly to feel special about yourself, not to bestow great blessings on
other people."

I did not enjoy being told I was superficial, even by my beautiful
new lover. I got up from the bed and went to the mirror to check the
status of Dr. Lilith's slash in my forehead. As I applied some cleanser,
Jumbler continued.

"But I will say this, my dear. According to my tantrically trained
reading of your character, you actually possess equal potentials as
beloved and devotee."

"And will you deign to teach me the path of the devotee, O Great
Master Jumbler?" I said, daring to be sarcastic. "Will you lead me to
the feet of the alluring idol where I might immolate myself in the fires
of ecstatic surrender?"

"Gladly will I do this, O Great Master Rapunzel. Gladly will I offer
my humblest parts to be kissed by the beloved avatar." She stretched
out on the bed, arching her bare feet in my direction.

"Ah I see. You yourself are the solution that you are recommend-
ing. You are the beloved who will cure my flaming narcissism." I blew
her feet a kiss, then returned to the business of applying a fresh bandage.

"My goal would not be to expunge your sense of yourself as the
beloved one," she said. "Only to add an additional sense of yourself

as devotee. As I said, you have extravagant potentials for both. And I think both are crucial for your ascendancy to goddess-like power and splendor."

"So are you criticizing me or praising me?" I still felt slightly petulant. "Will you make up your damn mind?"

"I would like to quote now from the book that, with your help, I hope to write someday. It's called *The Dictionary of Tricky Love*. Please listen to the definition for the term 'radical intimacy.' Ahem. Radical intimacy is a virtuoso art that requires me and my freaky consort to master two seemingly contradictory skills: naming and nurturing the highest, holiest, best in each other, and thriving on the fact that our relationship will inevitably draw out and ask us to redeem each other's ugliest ignorance."

"So what you're saying is that the deeper you and I fall in love," I replied, "the more uninhibited we'll both feel about unveiling our worst qualities?" I had returned to the rumpled bed and was making grotesque faces just inches from Jumbler's face. "You'll get to spend lots of time with my inner gargoyles, and I with yours? And that's a good thing?" I grunted like a hippopotamus and licked her hand sloppily.

"It is a good thing," Jumbler murmured self-assuredly as she allowed me to chomp on her arm and shoulder, "because it will give us great ongoing practice at killing the apocalypse right down at the most microscopic levels."

"Yes, I suppose that's true," I allowed. "Each of us, even great masters like you and me, carry a little portion of the apocalypse within us." I got up from the bed and retrieved a black felt-tip pen from a drawer. Slipping the back part of my tights down a little, I drew an oval on my left butt cheek and wrote "The End" inside. This was rather forward of me. Despite our wonderful all-night trance-dance, Jumbler and I had not yet been naked with each other except incidentally in Madame Blavatsky's golf cart.

"Jung called our personal portion of the apocalypse the *shadow*," she said, taking the pen and drawing an oval on the sole of her left foot. Within it, she printed "Do not look at this" along with a picture of a single eye. "It's the unripe or wounded part of us," she continued. "It becomes evil only if it's repressed."

"So in radical intimacy," I replied, curling into the fetal position to stare into the off-limits zone she'd just created, "I get to practice killing off the apocalypse in you, and vice versa? Sort of a corollary to Jesus' plea to love thy neighbor as thyself. 'Love thy neighbor's shadow, and work with all thy tender adrenaline to summon its most constructive expressions.'"

"Hmmmm. I like that. But I was thinking more about how *I* will kill off the apocalypse in *myself* because I have such a high regard and attraction to you. And you'll do vice versa."

"So like when I suddenly turn into a jerk because my flaming narcissism has demonically possessed me, I'll rise up with a banishing spell. 'Begone demon, for I cannot allow you to trick me into hurting the feelings of my sweet groovemate.'"

I did the trick my mothers had always hated so much, which was to roll my pupils back so far in my head that only the whites showed.

"Yes, exactly," she laughed. "You won't just naturally assume that the demon to be exorcised resides inside *me*. Which in itself is so contrary to the style of the six billion apocalypticians on the planet that you might just shock armageddon into expiring right then and there."

"I catch your drift, Professor Jumbler. Or is it Guru Jumbler?" I saluted then prayed then bowed to her. "As Jung said, we tend to attribute to other people the very stuff we hate and fear most about ourselves."

"Radical intimacy means we kill the apocalypse at the source."

"So what is your ugliest ignorance, anyway, Jumbler?" I asked slyly.

"Wouldn't you rather have the fun of provoking me into accidentally leaking it at an unguarded moment?" she returned. "And there's also the possibility that I don't even know all the subtle varieties of my own ugliest ignorance. Maybe you can help me discover them."

"As long as I also always tell you how beautiful and wonderful you are, too, right?"

"Exactly."

The front half of Jumbler's body was on the bed while she knelt on the floor and held my feet, one in each of her hands. She placed her tongue on the top of the middle toe of my right foot and kissed and licked very softly and slowly in a straight path up the front of my foot all the way to the spot between my ankles. She repeated the gesture with my left foot. Then she returned to my right foot and began again.

This time she murmured a wistful tune as she proceeded. I couldn't understand the words, though I thought I detected syllables that sounded like Sanskrit. Whenever it came time for her to take a breath, she would keep her lips on my skin and suck gently as she inhaled. After she finished with this sweep, she performed the same operation on my left foot.

A third time she returned to my right foot. This time she added a new move. Instead of lightly sucking my skin on her inbreaths, she turned her head up and sipped the air. As she brought her mouth back to my foot, she made a delicate spurting sound, as if she were taking the essence of what she'd sipped and infusing it into my flesh. All the while, she kept singing her mysterious tune.

By the time she completed my feet and began applying a similar rhythm to my calves and shins, I was slipping into a most relaxed rapture. She continued with amazing patience, methodically but gracefully covering my entire body, removing my clothes as she wandered.

Then I was naked before her. It pleased me profoundly. I wanted to peel myself open for her, find ways to let her more deeply into me. I wanted her to wash over me, pour into me, turn me inside out and touch me in my oldest fantasies about myself.

"Come and find me," I sighed. "Surround me. Fill me. Engulf me."

A strange and wonderful feeling arose in the midst of this spreading expanse of surrender: a tremendous potency. It made no sense at first, and I held it at bay. How could relinquishing my will generate such strength? But as it continued to build, I accepted it, allowed it to billow. Confidence and authority surged through me crazily. I felt wildly powerful, as if I could do anything. This in turn cracked open a fresh intuition—a prophecy, really: that in the years to come I would indeed be called upon to take on assignments that would test me to my limits.

In the wake of this revelation, I wanted to plunge back into the Drivetime without delay. I longed to collect more clues about the destiny Madame Blavatsky had been unveiling. But I willfully held myself back. I didn't want to slip over to the other side unless Jumbler accompanied me.

"How can I give you what you're giving me?" I asked dreamily. "Let me rev *you* up too."

"You can't imagine how much you've given me by allowing me to worship you like this," she sighed. I could hear the other world in her voice. "More and more, I sense the truth of what Madame Blavatsky said about you. You *are* the Sex President. The Supreme Adept of the Fuckissimus."

"But I want you to come with me to the Drivetime," I insisted quietly.

"I'm almost there already," she said. "Lie on top of me."

I helped her take off her clothes. She lay down spread-eagled on the bed.

"Crucify me with your love, girl," she whispered. "With all your most furious gentleness."

I eased myself down onto her, matching her pose in every way except for my head, which was face down on the bed to the side of hers.

"Visualize that I am you and you are me," she said. "Imagine that you are me feeling Rapunzel's thighs on yours, and Rapunzel's breasts on yours, and Rapunzel's arms on yours."

As I obeyed her suggestions, we synchronized our long, slow breathing. Rippling swells of liquid velvet textures glimmered up and down the length of my body. Soon I felt like a syrupy slow-motion waterfall cascading into Jumbler and then spiraling back into myself.

So gradually I wasn't aware of the moment when I crossed over the threshold, I found myself in the Drivetime. It was a familiar yet strange place. I was lying down inside the husk of my old lightning-struck redwood tree on the grounds of the Pomegranate Grail. Jumbler was sprawled on top of me but just lifting herself off. We were naked.

The first thing I noticed was that the woods were missing. My redwood sanctuary looked and felt like it always had except for the fact that there were only a few yards of wild nature around it. Now it was inside a building with a high roof punctuated by a large skylight. In front of us a few yards away, visible through the "door" of the redwood husk, was a sizable image screen, maybe eight feet square, which I guessed was a Televisionary Oracle. At the moment, the screen was filled with a line of naked men snaking up to the back door of a red and black double-decker bus that bore a sign saying, "Global Initiatrix of Fuckissimus."

Suddenly, Madame Blavatsky's stout form trundled in front of the screen, blocking my view. She was clad in a black conical witch's hat, pearl necklace, red cashmere mini-slip, and burgundy satin bra. The latter was far too small for her corpulent breasts.

Smoking a cigarette and chewing gum, she was sitting on a giant red tricycle that had a basket attached to the handlebars. Her saturnine face peered in at us.

"Wake up, sleepyheads," she snorted. "It is high time for your next Drivetime University class. But first put on your sacred underwear." She removed her gum so she could stuff her mouth with a spoonful of what looked like mashed potatoes from a bowl in her basket. Then she hurled a bunch of clothes towards us. It was the same stuff from before: for me, the Grail-shaped bra and the panties decorated with replicas of my birthmark; for Jumbler, the flesh-colored leotard painted with the realistic likeness of breasts and a penis.

I put on my costume and strode out of the redwood husk to survey my surroundings. It was a cross between a temple, a toy store, and the studio of a sculptor who uses junk as raw materials. I saw three majestic altars crammed with elaborate candelabra, big bouquets, and tiny, brightly colored UFOs, some of which were hovering in mid-air. A giant metal and wood scarecrow with glowing eyes and many arms was clapping in rhythm to a guttural melody that was flowing from her mouth. Next to a "garden" of fantastic Salvador Dali-like flowers and vegetables made of painted dishes and kitchen utensils, a miniature roller coaster reeled along a wooden track. Its cars were filled with puppet versions of fanged Tibetan deities and crones.

"Where are we?" I asked Madame Blavatsky.

"Glorious Universal Diddlemaster," Madame Blavatsky replied, taking another spoonful of mashed potatoes from her bowl, "I am glad you asked. You are on the grounds of the Menstrual Temple of the Funky Grail, the mystery school with which you will replace the Pomegranate Grail. We are visiting the future again so as to further instill in you the confidence you will need to oversee the many mutations it will be your fate to initiate."

Jumbler had joined me as I stood with Madame Blavatsky.

"We did it again, baby," she grinned as she took my hand. "We're pioneers of Drivetime collaboration."

"You must be a very skillful tantric magician, my love," I said admiringly, kissing her on the mouth.

"I am not nearly as experienced as you might imagine," she replied, "although it's true I have received an extensive education. But I swear I have never before done a shamanic journey together with anyone to the Drivetime. You and I must have a natural talent that we bring out in each other."

"I'd like to claim a bit of credit, too, if you don't mind," a familiar voice called out from behind us. I turned to behold a shocking but welcome sight. Rumbler was walking towards us. "It's not as if Rapunzel is a virgin in these collaborative out-of-body experiences, after all."

He strode over to Madame Blavatsky and handed her a blue popsicle. She seized it eagerly and began to slurp. Then he glided over to Jumbler and me and offered one to both of us. I took mine and hugged him, unable to speak. After a moment, I partially broke away, grabbed Jumbler, and pulled her into a three-way embrace. I was aware that neither of them knew who the other was—I had included only a bare mention about Rumbler when I told Jumbler the story of my life—but I fantasized that both of them loved me so much they would just naturally love each other.

"Looks like I'm overdressed," Rumbler said as we finally dissolved the hug. In contrast to the skimpy attire Jumbler and I had on, Rumbler was dressed like an actor I once saw playing Robin Hood in a movie: bright green linen tunic with a rough leather belt, deerskin pants and green wool cloak, and leather boots.

I was still having trouble making intelligible sounds. Cognitive dissonance ruled my brain. The first impossibility was seeing Rumbler in this place, the Drivetime, which was so much more like the daytime world than the Televisionarium landscapes he and I had always frequented. We were not lying beneath a lemony sky right now, afloat on an ocean of geraniums where giant flakes of orange snow that tasted like butterscotch fell on our delighted tongues.

The second impossibility was being with Rumbler in the company of an actual flesh-and-blood person from my waking life. In all my years of consorting with my male playmate, there had never been such a crossover. Our companions in the Televisionarium were creatures like Firenze the Musical Sasquatch, Snapdragon Dragonfly the Firefly, and Itchy Crunchy the Beautiful Empress of the Trolls. My shamanic travels and my life in ordinary waking reality were strictly segregated.

"I'm Rumbler," he said to Jumbler, reaching out to shake hands. "Rapunzel might prefer to tell you I'm her muse or animus or her vivid imaginary stand-in for her dead twin brother, but I like to think I have an objective existence aside from her."

I had rarely heard Rumbler be so wryly self-conscious. Back in the Televisionarium, he was usually such a *creature*—given instinctively to the feral poetry of the moment.

"I have to say that I can see a bit of a family resemblance, though," Jumbler said. "Which is not to say that I don't believe your version of the truth, too. It is the Drivetime, after all. Whenever contradictory statements pop up here, you can be sure that both are accurate."

"And you are who?" Rumbler asked her. "I mean, I know who you are, but I want to hear your version of who you are."

"I'm Jesus the Hermaphrodite Clown, also known as the Wealthy Anarchist Burning Heaven to the Ground. Rapunzel might prefer to tell you I'm her teacher or servant or fool, but I like to think of myself as her sexfriend."

Jesus the Hermaphrodite Clown? What was that about, I wondered.

But Rumbler looked delighted at this nonsense from Jumbler. I was glad, because I wanted them to get along. But I was nervous, too, because—well—shouldn't they be jealous of each other? I didn't want them to be, and since they lived in different dimensions maybe the usual laws of human nature didn't apply.

"Do you know Madame Blavatsky?" I asked him, trying to find a way to proceed. I gazed over at her. She was busy smoking her cigarette and devouring her popsicle, but she took a moment to give the thumbs-up signal to me with her cigarette hand.

"I'm proud to say," Rumbler replied, "that Madame Helena Blavatsky—who, I should note, suffers from the same indignity as I do, being imagined by you as a split-off aspect of your own psyche rather than an autonomous spirit with a life apart from you—Madame Blavatsky has called on me to help administer your next crash course at Drivetime University. Aren't you going to eat your popsicle?"

I was studying his face. Though it had not been so long since our last meeting, he looked older and stronger. He'd always been the embodiment of sensitivity, but now he emanated even more kindness than I remembered. A more mature, vigorous kindness.

"Let's go climb into the Drivetime University classroom, shall we?" he exhorted. "Come on, Jesus. You too. Madame Blavatsky, you want to sit in?"

She shook her head and mumbled, "Maybe later."

Jumbler was contentedly licking her popsicle, seemingly empty of her usual restless initiative. If there was any jealousy flickering here between Rumbler and Jumbler, it was well-hidden.

"You doing OK?" I asked Jumbler as we strolled.

"I'm on a mysterious tantric jaunt into the Drivetime with the lyrical creature I've loved for millennia. Couldn't get any better than this."

As we sat down inside the redwood husk, Rumbler arranged the three of us in a triangle with our legs splayed out, each person with a foot touching a foot of the other two.

"First off, I want you to know that in order to expand my service to your mission, Rapunzel, I have been tending to my fellow men with a new intensity lately," Rumbler announced when we were in place.

"Men as in generic name for humanity?" I said, feigning dismay. "I thought you were free of sexist language, dear."

"Men as in literal guys. Dudes. Fathers and brothers and sons. Who, by the way, gave me a message to send to you." Rumbler blew two kisses, first in the direction of my navel, then towards my face.

"All the men in the world just kissed me?" I asked, holding my hand demurely to my face.

"No, no, no—not all. Just the lesbian men and macho feminists. A very select group, unfortunately. By Madame Blavatsky's calculations, it represents point zero two percent of all men."

"OK, Rumbler," I said, exulting in the giddy sensation of feeling crisply logical in the midst of crazy fun. "Let me suspend my disbelief here for a moment and accept your implication that you have somehow been in communication with—how many would it be?—480,000 adult males all over the planet?

"Overwhelming majority are in North America," Rumbler noted.

"So let me ask you: How did you get elected to be the representative of this elite group?"

"You are so modest, Rapunzel," he replied. "Of course I got elected because of my close association with the Queen Bee of Orgasmic Liberation. Because I was the first male-type creature to be benevolently infected by the Global Initiatrix of the Fuckissimus."

"Rapunzel's mothers would no doubt be skeptical," Jumbler broke in, "to hear that half a million men are having erotic fantasies about the high priestess of their Goddess cult."

Ignoring Jumbler's kibitz, Rumbler moved to a kneeling position and prostrated himself so that his forehead rested on his outspread hands a few inches from my crotch. "My fellow men also wanted me to convey the following request."

"Yes?" I said expectantly, glancing over at Jumbler. She seemed bemused. Her hands were stroking her inner thighs and she was sporting a grin.

"Rapunzel, Rapunzel, let down your hair," Rumbler said with a histrionic stage whisper. "Pull us all the way up to your menstrual hut, so that we can learn to menstruate too."

I cackled hard, the result of being both incredulous and entertained. "I see," I finally managed to sputter. "You lesbian men and macho feminists are envious of how we women have cornered the market on the glamorous fun of bleeding out our genitals. And you're overwhelmed with yearning for the right to feel bloated and crampy and crabby four days out of every month."

Jumbler's shoulders were shaking with laughter. Brazenly, she reached over and applied a teasing spank to Rumbler's upturned butt.

"We men want to master the art of regular self-abduction," Rumbler continued seriously, not acknowledging the humorous effect of his previous statement. "We want to learn how to die a lot of little deaths so we don't have to get crushed by huge annihilations."

"Hey Rumbler, what's in it for Rapunzel to let these guys climb up into her menstrual hut?" Jumbler blurted out mischievously. I was grateful, wanting to stall for time while I tried to digest what Rumbler was talking about. It certainly seemed connected to the tower and the long line of men in wedding dresses from our previous foray into the Drivetime.

"Rapunzel can't kill the bad apocalypse without us," Rumbler told Jumbler quickly and calmly. "She can't resurrect the good apocalypse without us."

"That's not what my mommies told me," I protested halfheartedly. "My mommies said the male of the species is a lost cause. A drain on our resources I shouldn't bother with. According to them, I'm not even supposed to get married."

"Your mommies are wise and good and strong," Rumbler said solemnly. "We bow to them with reverent devotion. But they don't know everything."

"But neither do you, of course," I shot back affectionately. "Why should I listen to your advice?"

"Besides the fact that it was revealed to me by your eternal secretary, Madame Blavatsky, it also resonates with everything you know about yourself. All your instincts, for as long as you can remember, have told you to be inclusive, not separative. To embrace the contradictions, not reinforce their enmity. Preaching to the choir is not your destiny, Rapunzel. You need to expand your audience. A lot."

"Why haven't you told me this before?"

"Couldn't meet you in the Drivetime till you kidnapped yourself. Them's the rules. Couldn't reveal the missing secrets till you rose up against the old ways and started making your own traditions."

"By the logic you're espousing, Rumbler," Jumbler interjected, "Rapunzel would try to translate the esoteric wisdom of the Pomegranate Grail into a New Age self-help book and tour the world making personal appearances. 'High Priestess of Ancient Mystery School Reveals Ten Practical Ways for Both Women and Men to Make the Menstrual Mysteries Work for Greater Health, Wealth, and Happiness.'"

"Not a bad idea, actually," he replied.

"Well then, I hope Drivetime University has a marketing division," Jumbler retorted, "because the education of our Supergirl here has probably not included much training in that area of human knowledge."

"Actually," Rumbler said, "there *is* a marketing division of Drivetime University. A whole phalanx of marketing teachers awaits Rapunzel's arrival."

"I can't believe we're talking about this," Jumbler marveled. "It's certainly a day for firsts. My first joint shamanic trip into the Drivetime. My first shamanic conversation ever about marketing."

"Has the dissident propaganda you're preaching been approved by Madame Blavatsky?" I asked Rumbler, dubious. "Is this all an official part of my Drivetime University curriculum? Especially the part about adding men to the choir I preach to."

"My Damn Latchkey!" Rumbler shouted. "My Damn Latchkey!"

As my eternal secretary puttered up to the doorway of the redwood husk on her oversized tricycle, she was wiping her mouth with the back of her arm.

"You require my august presence?" she gurgled.

"My Damn Latchkey," Rumbler said to her, "your ineffable ward here is wondering if I speak with your authority when I counsel her to upgrade her marketing skills and reach out to the masses. She's particularly scoffing at my hint that she should invite some selected men to join her exclusive girls' club."

"You do not have to physically fuck *all* the men," Madame Blavatsky growled. "Spiritually you do, of course, in the Drivetime. But physically only a small fraction. What was the figure I worked out? Point zero two percent of point zero two percent. Not that many, really, as long as they are the right men. That should be good enough to infect the whole global gang of phallus-bearers."

I was apoplectic. "*Fuck* them?! What are you talking about?!"

"It will certainly not be fucking in the patriarchal sense of the word," Madame Blavatsky said blandly. "But the specifics about that will be revealed a little later. For now, think of your task as a kind of mass mercy-fucking. For the good of the planet."

"Shouldn't I be at least a little concerned about what's good for *me?*"

"To the tiny little ego into which you have stuffed your vast primordial self, it sounds extreme. But remember, Queen Giggleshtupper, this is one of those decisions you yourself made while ensconced in the more eternal perspective, if you know what I mean. I am merely serving as your secretary. Reminding you of your agenda."

"I told you to remind me to turn myself into a kind of glorified sacred prostitute?" I laughed with disbelief. "I, the avatar of a mystery school that has only accepted women as members for millennia?"

"There is no better way to set the healing infection in motion," Madame Blavatsky said with curt certainty, taking a sip from a bottle of wine, "than to administer the tantric yoni juju directly to a few elite contagious agents among the beloved enemy. It will make the Drivetime aspect of your work far more effective. Besides, you will have plenty of time to get ready. The earliest possible launch date for you to become Global Initiatrix of the Fuckissimus would be five years from now."

"OK, Rumbler," I said, setting my not-quite-finished popsicle down on a brown leaf, "time out." I lifted his head up off the ground and looked him in the eyes. "I've come to enjoy Madame Blavatsky in the short time I've known her, but I don't know how much I trust her. Your word, on the other hand, I swear by. So tell me. Are you and Blavatsky sincerely offering me a new dispensation about my life's mission, or is this your idea of a prank?"

"It's a trade-off, Rapunzel," he said. "The men will come to you to be filled up with the mysteries of menstruation, and you will exploit their openness in order to infect them with the Psychefunkapus meme. They get something and you get something. Remember what I said. You can't kill the bad apocalypse without them. You can't resurrect the good apocalypse without them."

"Just as long as you don't try to tell us," Jumbler fired in, "that she needs these men for personal reasons; that only a male can bring out the real woman in her. That kind of scripture tends to make me subject to projectile vomiting."

"You have my word," said Rumbler. "I won't say that. But I will say that she needs men in order to reach her full potential as an avatar. No way around it. The bad apocalypse *will* occur unless she infects the male of the species with the Psychefunkapus meme."

Jumbler stuck out her tongue and gave Rumbler a long, hard raspberry.

"And tell me again what the Psychefunkapus meme is?" I asked.

"Lust globally, fuck locally," Rumbler said.

"Meaning you should desire every halfway attractive person you encounter, but only make love to your committed partner?"

"That's one way to interpret it."

"What are the other ways?"

"Get in the habit of cultivating a tender, appreciative lust for everyone. And I do mean *everyone*. Convince yourself with brilliantly rational arguments why it makes total sense to overflow with hot-blooded compassion for all of creation. And I do mean *all* of creation—the wetlands and the libraries and the hummingbirds and the highways. And then infuse that well-crafted, unconditional generosity into the love you give to any imperfectly beautiful consort you actually fuck."

"Sounds strenuous."

"At first it will be. After a while it will become second nature."

"Jumbler," I said, placing my hand on hers, "I need your counsel. Speak freely, please."

"I'm afraid this is coming dangerously close to being just another in a long line of history's famous megalomaniacal fantasies, my dear," Jumbler said with a hint of an emotion I had not yet seen in her—disgust. "Not L. Ron Hubbard or Allah's prophet Mohammed or Mao Zedong as the One True Way, but Rapunzel Blavatsky. Just because I love the way your mind works and share all your values, my dear, doesn't mean I want you to be the resplendent saviour that everyone in the world needs to worship or even fuck in a non-patriarchal fashion, whatever that means. 'Global Initiatrix' is another term for 'Fascist Uber-Guru' if you ask me."

"Please, Jesus," Rumbler said to Jumbler with a hint of defensiveness. "It's poetic license. We're playing with caricatures. We're making fun of ourselves. Of course we're not proposing that Rapunzel purge all her competitors and rule the mass imagination alone. But neither do we want to repress all thoughts about the danger of that fantasy taking root in the back of her lovely mind. That would surely make us fall prey to the poison we want to avoid."

"Yes, I understand that principle well," Jumbler admitted. "It's the heart of the tantric teaching. Whatever darkness you ignore will always sneak up from behind and bite you in the ass eventually."

"Rapunzel is not the Great Exception," Madame Blavatsky croaked as she rocked her tricycle backwards and forwards and scooped what looked like deep-fried shrimp out of her bowl.

"Exactly," said Rumbler. "She's merely the Great Example, a role model who shows how it's done. I call her the avatar, but everyone who lusts globally and fucks locally is a potential avatar, too. The goal is six billion masters of Psychefunkapus."

"But she must still be a charismatic superstar," Madame Blavatsky added. "That is the only way she will get enough recruits for Twenty-Two Weeks of World Orgasm."

She pedaled her tricycle in a half-circle so she was facing away from us. "Hop on, Queen Sexlaugher," she called over her shoulder. "Let me take you back to your kidnap of the airwaves. Come on—you too, girlfriend. You too, Rumbler."

I climbed aboard the step on the back of the tricycle and held on to Madame Blavatsky's shoulders. Jumbler was able to squeeze on, clutching my waist. Rumbler jumped up on the handlebars, barely keeping his butt from sinking down into the food in Madame Blavatsky's basket. We took off with difficulty, but soon picked up speed.

Peddling furiously, Madame Blavatsky took us out a door and into the woods. She proceeded down a narrow paved road that cut a swath through strange buildings. There was not a single rectangular shape among them—ziggurats, tepees, domes, and pyramids predominated—and they appeared to be made out of giant rubies and amethysts and topazes and emeralds. Next to each front door, which was lozenge-shaped, was a neon sign. "The Eater of Cruelty" read one. Others said "Feminist Orgy Network," "Center for Tantric Janitorism," "Telepathics Anonymous," and "Drivetime University Presents: How a Global Network of Menstrual Huts Can Stave Off Apocalypse."

After a few minutes of traveling down this road, we began to hear the hubbub of a large crowd. Soon we came into view of a huge structure that towered over the landscape. It was a stadium. Madame Blavatsky wheeled us inside through tall double doors.

The place was packed with a sea of people, most of whom were wearing only the skimpiest clothes. It was shocking to see so much flesh all at once.

At the opposite end of the stadium was the biggest Televisionary Oracle of them all—maybe a hundred feet square. Dominating the screen was a person who looked like me, only about ten years older: same as last time. Dressed in a green and black tweed kimono and sporting the same pimple on her forehead, The Other Rapunzel was in a television news room with several large video cameras on gurneys and numerous TV monitors. There was also a black altar surmounted by a huge bird's nest, around which a number of lingerie-clad women were kneeling. With a huge, translucent squirt gun, The Other Rapunzel was shooting streams of thick red juice into their mouths.

Madame Blavatsky shooed us off her tricycle and dismounted herself, bidding us to climb a dais and sit down next to her on a circular rug with a mandala design.

"I love all of you," The Other Rapunzel thundered in a voice that felt like an earthquake. "You know that, right? In fact, I love you *more* than I love you. And that's why, unlike every other journalist, scientist, politician, priest, celebrity, or teacher you've had to deal with all your life, I'm going to confess my biases upfront. I'll tell you that my body feels pretty strange right now—sort of like a dizzy sow stuffed with junk food.

"It's the first day of my period, you see. I'm three sizes too big for my body. The only thing that's keeping me from biting the heads off small animals are four tablets of Advil and two bottles of Sierra Nevada Pale Ale.

"Right now it's a real struggle for me to maintain my usual high standards of compassionate objectivity. For all I know, I'm not succeeding. For all I know, my tender wisdom has been twisted off center just enough to have turned me into just another hypocritical phony.

"I don't think so, but I wanted to warn you.

"Take this as a disclaimer, then: Question my authority and expertise with the same rigor as you would the anchormen who feed you your regular doses of the daily newzak or the high priests of the American Medical Association or the strong men who embody your personal ideal of competence.

"Although of course none of their ilk would ever have the courageous self-knowledge to admit that the state of their bodies might be subliminally mutilating their truths. Alpha males rarely recognize that their 'logic' is in secret service to their repressed emotions, which always leak out in physical symptoms.

"But I'm sorry to sound so hateful. For my sake as much as yours.

"Every time I conjure a compact meme of poetic logic that's crammed full of bile, I risk turning one more pocket of my brain cells into a slimy imitation of the ancient disease called phallocracy. And whenever I do that, I aid and abet the apocalypse. Which is the exact opposite of my mission.

"Therefore, I hereby retract my vicious emotion. I do not renounce my objective analysis, but I do retract the nastiness I wrapped it in.

"I do not hate you evil advertising geniuses who turn everything into money-colored shit. I do not hate you satanic Christians who fear the human body. I do not hate you fatherly journalists who exult in selling us every last detailed story of murder and mayhem as if it were a blessed treasure.

"In fact, I love you all. I love you *more* than I love you. At this very moment, I am sending tender telepathic regards to deadbeat dads and wife-beaters everywhere. I am beaming sweet gobs of kindness in the direction of arms dealers and psychotically emotionless middle-aged men in lab coats speaking in know-it-all cadences and every last macho politician spouting football metaphors to illustrate how much fun it is to destroy the English language.

"I celebrate all of you with the same lucid joy I rain down upon all the people who help me and agree with me.

"I must confess that I did not master this technique willingly.

"Frankly, the Goddess Persephone forced me into it. She proved to me that the only way to overthrow the goddamn fucking phallocracy—which is also our only hope for killing the bad apocalypse and awakening the good apocalypse—turns out to be ... to love the goddamn fucking phallocracy.

"Ha! A thousand times ha!

"But wait a minute.

"Dangerous ground here.

"Don't want you to get the idea that this is a repackaged version of 'turn the other cheek.'

"I am not saying be nicey-nice to the bad daddies while they stick voodoo pins in the globe.

"Fight them with all your heart and mind and soul, yes; pull out every trick you have to thwart their mad rush towards collective suicide; but just make sure that you don't infect yourself with their poison. Swear that you will never dehumanize them even if they dehumanize you.

"Smash the phallocracy with sympathetic grace!

"Feel gratitude for the clarity it invokes in you and for the self-corrections it forces you to craft.

"Kill it with sweet kindness.

"Love it to death."

The Other Rapunzel paused. For a moment the throng was virtually silent. Then a rolling cheer broke out. It soon grew so loud that the dais began to vibrate beneath us. Parts of the crowd began to chant, "Kill your own death! Kill your own death!"

While The Other Rapunzel had been ranting, my three viewing companions had moved closer to me. Madame Blavatsky stood behind me, playing with my hair and massaging my scalp. Jumbler and Rumbler had made me into the centerpiece of a sandwich. They each sat facing my side with their legs wrapped around me. With one hand Rumbler stroked my belly and with the other my back, all the while kissing my shoulder and whispering a wordless tune in my ear. Jumbler caressed my thigh and butt as she butterflied her lips along my neck.

In addition to a cascade of erotic feelings up and down my body, the touch of these six hands and the sound of the crowd's happy vigor stirred a curious sensation in the center of my brain. It felt like something was hatching: a ticklish irritation mixed with blissful release. I had an urge to scratch myself there.

Gradually this prickly opening made me alert to some fresh layer of meaning or substance in the sights and sounds around me. It was as if a new perceptual apparatus were awakening. It didn't duplicate any of my five senses but was a blend of them all—and more. As I tried to explain to myself what was happening, I flashed on Helen Keller's reputed ability to "smell" an approaching storm hours before its arrival.

I could hear the honeysuckle fragrance of the light streaming from The Other Rapunzel's eyes on the Televisionary Oracle. I tasted the grainy texture of the crowd's buzz with the soles of my feet. Madame Blavatsky's head massage precipitated a serpentine trill of trumpets on my tongue. The hatching place behind my eyes surged with chiming fountains of incandescence. Was I merely hallucinating? Or was I extracting the secret quintessence of this world, which I had previously been numb to?

In the course of my explorations with altered states of consciousness over the years, I'd developed a special fondness for dreams in which I was dreaming. Now, the memory of that paradoxical condition provided a small bit of reference for the supercharged state of my sensorium. It was as if there were a more essential Drivetime within the Drivetime, and I had slipped into it.

"I have one other thing I want to say to you," The Other Rapunzel boomed above the tumult, and in response the crowd gradually shushed.

"Now that we have formulated a strategy to wriggle out of our predicament," she murmured, as her tone became lower and more intimate, "let's talk about your third eye. Or maybe you'd prefer to call it your second nose. Whatever you wish. Your pineal gland. The thousand-petaled lotus. The philosopher's stone. The one part of your body that might someday give you direct perception of—not merely second-hand gossip about—all the places the scientists don't believe in and therefore can't see. The one part of your body that can abolish time and survive death and dream while awake and fuck everything alive. P.S. to astrophysicists: It can even locate the universe's so-called dark matter.

"At the Menstrual Temple of the Funky Grail, we refer to this joy jewel as the Televisionary Oracle. Everyone who has ever lived has owned one. Only trouble is, it's dormant in most people. They live and die without ever using their birthright even once. That tragic loss is due mainly to the fact that you can't turn on the Televisionary Oracle all by yourself. No matter how smart you are, no matter how holy or rich or selfless or famous you are, you just can't get the Televisionary Oracle up and running without the divine intervention of Our Lady of the Vultures: the Primordial Menstruator, Yo Mama Persephone Herself.

"There is a fairly reliable way to enlist the Goddess' help, though— maybe even seduce Her into slipping you a massive dose of grace. Can you guess what it is?"

The Other Rapunzel stopped her rant, as if making room for a response.

Of the thousands of people in the stadium, Jumbler spoke first. "Become a tantric fucknut," she shouted out at the top of her lungs, "and direct your fucknut energy up to your pineal gland."

"Yes! Excellent!" The Other Rapunzel exclaimed, beaming, as if she had heard Jumbler.

She took a moment to shoot a stream of liquid from her squirt gun into her own mouth before resuming.

"When you circulate your sexual energy away from your genitals and up towards your heart and head—ideally using not just your heroic willpower but also your naked compassion as a pump—you show the

Goddess you're ready to collaborate with Her in switching on your Televisionary Oracle. As a reward, She may take custody of the nerve currents you have sprung loose from their confinement down below, and shepherd them in just the right way into your sleeping power spot. In Her own good time, if you continue your work faithfully, She may shock awake the magic organ, allowing you to tune in to the data-rich splendor you've always been missing.

"Then you can join the Goddess at will in the wormhole between the Dreamtime and the Waketime."

As the crowd burst into a new round of frenzied approval, I remembered—or rather recapitulated—a scene from my life as Mary Magdalen. This was not happening in some finished past, but *now*. I was in the company of Jesus on our sleeping mat in a room of my family's home in Bethany. It was before dawn. Through the window I could see the Morning Star hanging low in the sky, and above it a crescent moon. We sat facing each other, blissfully conjoined in the hierosgamos. As he moved in me, I picked up the alabaster flask containing the spikenard and anointed his head. Then he ceased the undulation of his hips and allowed me to take the active role. Holding the flask, he crowned me with an equal measure of the sacred unguent.

As our mouths met to consecrate the blessing, other lives began to stir in my mind's eye. I remembered or rather *was* Eumolpus, leading frightened neophytes into Persephone's subterranean labyrinth at Eleusis on a September morning. I was Robin the Mouth, devouring a cake from the chest of a dead man as his relatives looked on. I was Antonin Artaud, alternately struggling and soaring from the effects of the peyote I'd ingested in a Mexican hotel room.

And then I was Rapunzel Blavatsky as I would be further on along the thread of time. A million memories from the future exploded simultaneously in the hatching place in my brain—events that from the standpoint of eternity, I realized, had already occurred or were occurring now and always. I saw myself returning to the sanctuary where I had grown up, scoured clean of my blotch and accompanied by Jumbler, to fight for my right to transform the Pomegranate Grail into the Menstrual Temple of the Funky Grail. I relived the arduous process of building the ever-expanding network of menstrual huts all over the world. I paraded down the streets of many cities with my "Funeral for the Apocalypse" spectacles. I revisited the entire process by which I prepared myself to initiate selected men into the menstrual arts and bless them with the gift of the hierosgamos. I remembered every kiss—with Jumbler and everyone else—and every dream class, every Drive-time excursion, even every meal. Our kidnap of the airwaves, our murder of the bad apocalypse, the celebration of Twenty-Two Weeks of World Orgasm: I remembered the future in every detail, all the while communing with the Televisionary Oracle, the sixty-six-million-year-old, hyperdimensional, organic "machine."

37

Live from the Gleamtime

You're tuned to the Decompositionary Miracle

Your reliable source
for communiqués
from the Clandestine Indigenous Revolutionary Committee
in Charge of the Ingenious Liberation of All People of Earth

Featuring the antidote for all the other antidotes

Reflecting the face you had before you were born

Featuring good arguments
for why
you should change your mind
about everything

Here we are again, beauty and truth fans. Your personal diplomatic representatives to the Queen of Heaven. Lonely lovers of all sentient beings and all-around global village idiots.

As you can see, we've set our hair on fire—don't worry, it's treated with flame retardants—while juggling ancient goddess figurines unearthed in Çatal Hüyük as we balance atop leather medicine balls in our glass slippers and snakeskin underwear. All for you. All in the quest to seduce you into knowing exactly what you want.

So what *do* you want, anyway, beauty and truth fans?

What?

You want to know what *we* want?

Well, to be truthful, our greatest desire is to become anonymous celebrities with enough access to your imagination that you will allow us to *daimonically* possess *you*. Not *demonically* possess you, like the entertainment criminals.

What's the difference?

The English word *demon* refers to an evil spirit, while *daimon* is an ancient Greek term meaning a personal guardian angel or a supernatural being that serves as an intermediary between humans and gods.

When entertainment criminals *demonically possess* you, they extirpate your imagination and replace it with their own decadent simulation of an imagination.

When we eaters of cruelty *daimonically possess* you, on the other hand, we devour the fake imagination that the entertainment criminals have infected you with. We then serve as kick-ass guardians at the threshold of your awareness, preventing the entertainment criminals' poison from slipping into you for as long as it takes you to establish a reliable link to your own best teacher—the ingenious angel in your own higher brain.

The Televisionary Oracle
is brought to you by
Breakfast of Amazons cereal.

Made
from organically grown artichokes, pomegranates, wild rice,
and the purest menstrual blood available,
obtained exclusively from authentic, initiated shamanatrixes.

Try it with Virgin's Milk,
the alchemical elixir
formulated especially to synergize

with the unique flavor
and healing effects of Breakfast of Amazons.

Or eat it right out of the box.

Breakfast of Amazons cereal:
for those who like their eucharist blood
to be untainted by the murder of a god.

S ince long before I was a soldier in the World Entertainment War, I have loved to dream. Every night I feel a thrill as my head impacts the pillow, knowing there's a good chance I'll live through at least one story that will be far more interesting to me than any Hollywood movie.

This has been true as far back as I remember. My love affair with adventures on the other side of the veil began early. I still have the three pages of three-holed, blue-lined, loose-leaf paper on which I wrote down my dream of a trip to the planet Venus when I was eight years old. (It was a successful journey; I was greeted by thirteen girls who covered me with kisses and fed me chocolate candy and gave me magic baseball cards.)

As I muse now upon this innocent passion, I can't help but think I was born to be what other cultures have called a shaman. It's immaterial whether I explain it as a genetic predisposition or the result of past-life karma: Without stimuli or encouragement from my family or teachers or anyone else in my early environment, I was drawn to explore a world beyond the one my senses perceived. My quest was naive and self-taught. Though I managed when I was in fourth grade to find a few scientific books on dreams in the local library (the New Age had not yet sprouted), all I had to go on was instinct.

At age seventeen I discovered psychedelic drugs. They offered me a different entry into the realm I'd previously accessed exclusively through dreams. Powered by this new tool, my attraction to the other side of the veil leaped to a higher octave, and I became even more committed to recording my sleeptime excursions. Beginning then and continuing till the present, I have kept a notebook and pen next to me virtually every single night of my life, even while crashing on the floors of friends' crowded apartments. At a conservative estimate, I've remembered and recorded thousands of dreams. Bookshelves full of old dream journals prove it.

Upon leaving my parents' home and arriving in college, I confirmed my growing suspicion that the educational system had tried to conceal a secret of great magnitude. Readings of Eliade and La Barre and Joseph Campbell introduced me to the paper trail documenting the existence of other realities besides the narrow little niche most people regard as All There Is. Their work in turn led me to the literature of Western occultism, whose intriguing material was written not by academics but by experimenters who had actually traveled into the great beyond.

The myriad reports were not in complete agreement, but many of their descriptions overlapped. The consensus was that the other side of the veil is not a single territory but teems with variety, some relatively hellish and some heavenly. Among its many names: the Dreamtime, Fourth Dimension, Underworld, Astral Plane, Collective Unconscious, Afterdeath State, Eternity, Bardo, Hades, and Realm of the Archetypes—to name a few.

There was another issue on which all the explorers agreed: Events in those "invisible" realms are the root cause of everything that happens down here below. Shamans visit the spirit world to cure their sick patients because the origins of illness lie there. For Qabalists, the visible Earth is a tiny outcropping at the end of a long chain of creation that originates at a point which is both inconceivably far away and yet right here right now. Even psychotherapists believe in a materialistic version of the ancient idea: that how we behave today is irrevocably shaped by events that happened in a distant time and place.

As I researched the testimonials about the treasure land, I registered the fact that dreams and drugs were not the only points of entry. Meditation could give access, as could specialized forms of drumming and chanting and singing and dancing. The tantric tradition taught that certain kinds of sexual communion can lead there. As does, of course, physical death.

I wanted to try all those other doors except the last one. Pot, hashish, and LSD were very good to me (never a single bad trip), but their revelations were too damn hard to hold onto. As I came down from a psychedelic high, I could barely translate the truths about the Fourth Dimension into a usable form back in normal waking awareness. At least in my work with dreams I had seen a steady growth of both my unconscious mind's ability to produce meaningful stories and my conscious mind's skill at interpreting them. But my progress was almost nil in the work of retrieving booty from the holy places where drugs took me.

The big problem was that unlike the other techniques on the list, the psychedelic substances bypassed my willpower. Their chemical battering ram simply smashed through the doors of perception. No adroitness was involved on my part, no craft. One of my meditation teachers referred to drug use, no matter how responsible, as "storming the kingdom of heaven through violence."

Gradually, then, I ended my relationship with the illegal magic that had given me so much pleasure. Instead I affirmed my desire to build mastery through hard work. Dreamwork, meditation, and tantric exploration became the cornerstones of my practice. In time, I learned to slip into the suburbs of the mysterium via song and dance as well.

I must confess, however, that in the many years since I swallowed my last tab of acid, my plans have not borne the fruit I hoped they would. Even my most ecstatic lucid dreams and illuminated meditations, I'm afraid, do not bring me to dwell on the other side of the veil with the same heart-melting vividness once provided by my psychedelic allies. Even my deepest tantric love-making and music-induced trances fail to provide the same boost.

Until recently, that is. Two nights after Rapunzel eased herself in through the window of my upstairs bedroom and delivered her crushing invitation, I had the "superdream" she promised me.

"Super" isn't a strong enough modifier, really, to describe how far beyond a dream it was. Though my long practice of cultivating my dreams has made them strikingly rich and detailed, not one has ever achieved such resplendence as this thing, which Rapunzel apparently delivered to me through some telepathic means I can't fathom. It was of a far higher order. A previously unknown species.

The first miracle was that it satisfied my deepest fantasies. By that I mean I experienced something like the metaphysical version of an orgasm. When I awoke I felt utterly at peace, more at home in the world than I can ever remember.

The second miracle was that the texture of the dream was way beyond the flamboyant palpability of even my best lucid dreams. The things I perceived there seemed more solid and fully realized than any of the props of the physical world. It's as if I were able to revel in a symbiotic blend of the highest, finest awareness I've ever achieved in normal waking consciousness and the deepest, most elemental awareness I've had in drugs or dreams.

The best part: I remembered it all. Every detail of this excursion remains with me now.

As the superdream began, it was late afternoon. I was lying down with my face in the grass. The engulfing sexual fragrance of the earth was so intoxicating I couldn't pull myself away for a while. Then I felt a tickle below my navel. Upon investigation, I saw that a short, scrubby weed had pricked me. There was no pain, but a little blood.

I raised my head to look around. The air and light were—and I know this sounds crazy—*drinkable*. As I inhaled, I felt I was supping a delicious azure nourishment, sweet and filling.

I became curious about where in the world I was. Nearby I saw a garden where enormous pumpkins and tomatoes were growing. Behind it was a three-story pyramid composed entirely of smoked bronze-colored glass. I could also see two thick reddish towers, each four stories tall. My attention was drawn by a large green envelope hanging from the branch of a birch tree next to the garden. I pulled it off and opened it. It read as follows:

## MENSTRUAL LINGERIE FASHION SHOW

Dear Janitor,

You're hereby invited to come be our sovereign shaman!

A sumptuous sanctuary has been specially reserved for you at the world-famous Moon Lodge on the grounds of the Menstrual Temple of the Funky Grail—all expenses paid!

All the cranberries you can eat! (And plums and egg-plants and cherries and pomegranates and fish eggs! Yum!)

Use of a full-service sweatlodge and the ecstatic meditation technology known as the Televisionary Oracle! (Ten years of uproarious discipline earned in one short week!?)

Lectures on fucking in the Fourth Dimension from the renowned menstruating shamanatrixes of Dreamtime University! (Guaranteed to improve your physical appearance, not to mention your soul's smell!)

Hundreds of sacred toys and games to mess around with in the Dragon's Playhouse! (And be assured that you will not find your foreskin hidden away inside a pagan dollhouse wrapped in quetzalcoatl feathers and the fat of a wild dog!)

Your fortune told and told and told till you probably won't want it told any more! (Your past prophesied, your future corrected, your relationship with death sweetened to an almost sugary sheen!)

Bonus! As a free introductory gift you'll receive tips on how to kill the apocalypse—designed with your unique, spiritually sexy needs in mind! (Guaranteed to make you famous with the Goddess, too!)

Don't dawdle! Come as soon as you can! Dangerously compassionate luxury is calling to you!

Directions to the Moon Lodge: Cruise over to the metal stairway that looks like a fire escape, and ascend to the door on the fourth story. Knock three times, pause, knock three more times, pause, knock three times, and when someone answers, say this: "I am a holy cabbage-head! I have more supernatural powers in my whole body than you have in your little finger! You must give me something valuable in return for all the pain I have crafted for myself!"

Feeling most delighted, I followed the directions on the invitation. When the door opened, I was greeted by an androgynous person. Her thick flaxen hair, which looked like a helmet, evoked the aura of a tomboyish Norse goddess. Witchy yet elfin, extravagant yet tricky, her face was *loud*. She was wearing a baggy, V-neck, black silk blouse and black silk pants.

Actually, I recognized her. She was the woman who had jumped up on stage with Rapunzel during World Entertainment War's show at the Catalyst—the prankster who got down on all fours behind me so that Rapunzel could easily push me over.

After I delivered my cabbage-head rap, this leprechaun warrior placed her left foot on top of my right. She lifted up my shirt and pulled down the waistband of my shorts a little. I saw the same thing she did: A red ooze was still trickling from the wound below my navel. She swiped her finger down to capture a daub and then brought it to her mouth for a lick.

"Pure menstrual stigmata! Hooray!" she exclaimed. "Consecration by the Goddess!" I felt an inexplicable burst of pride.

"From now on your home must be everywhere," she said as she patted me sympathetically on the shoulder. "Your names must be legion. Your dates of birth must change daily, and your horoscope must be a fluctuating medley impossible to interpret by anyone but a well-integrated owner of multiple personalities. Your body must be a five-dimensional hologram telepathically in touch with all sentient beings simultaneously, as it was before the Big Bang bonged."

As she gave me this strange pep talk, she led me down one hall, passing several closed doors, then another, at the end of which was a room with an open door. We went in.

The floor was black and rubbery. The walls and high ceiling were dark red. Hundreds of lit red and black candles lined the periphery of a room maybe seventy feet square. There were several pomegranate trees in big pots, and next to one was a seven-foot-tall scarecrow with many arms. She was composed of a metal skeleton and a skin consisting of vines. I knew it was a "she" because pendulous eggplant breasts hung down from an armature composed of branches woven together. Lodged in her belly was a TV that was animated by two fetuses, as in a sonogram. Her face was a jet-black mask with blinking red lights for pupils. Her hair was a tangle of electrical wire, knotted shreds of fabric, and tree roots.

As we passed it, a crackly voice emanated from the creature.

"What did the scarecrow say?" I asked my host.

"'Come be our sovereign janitor shaman.'"

She escorted me to an area in a corner enclosed by three huge, free-standing TV screens. Here there were five beds, each swathed in a red comforter and topped with copper-colored pillows. Tapestries hung on the walls. They depicted an eight-armed, blue-skinned goddess with long red hair. A round lapis lazuli table stood in the horseshoe space formed by the beds. It was piled with hot food on silver trays.

"Help yourself," my host said.

I filled two plates and a bowl. There were grilled sweet potatoes, a thick orange soup, broiled salmon, wild rice, corn on the cob, Greek salad, and pecan pie. I was thrilled.

"While you eat," she said, "maybe you'd like a story."

From under a clutch of pillows on one of the beds she slid out a thick black loose-leaf notebook and handed it to me. Then she turned and walked away, leaving me alone. I got comfortable on one of the beds and opened the notebook. It had a long title. *The Heroine with a Thousand Ruses: The Autohagiography of a Close Personal Friend of the Sly Universal Virus with No Fucking Opinion.* Its author was Rapunzel Blavatsky.

"Dear Rockstar," read a note paperclipped to the first page. "Feel free to plagiarize this story of mine for your next art project. If you do, though, try not to take too many liberties with it, please. Remember, good writers borrow; great writers steal. Love, Rapunzel."

The food was delectable—I can think of no comparable taste treat in my repertoire of memories from waking life—and the manuscript was so vivid that it became like a dream within the dream. It told the tale of Rapunzel's birth, and how she was the avatar of an ancient mystical order.

Was it a true story? I hoped so. But even if it weren't, this intimate view of how her mind worked made me feel close to her. I felt I'd broken through to see the real, *personal* Rapunzel for the first time. Not my glamorous projection. Not my mythic wish-fulfillments.

Just before finishing the third chapter, I was interrupted by the arrival of a small crowd of women, including Rapunzel herself and the leprechaun warrior from before. They were dressed in a bizarre melange of goofy costumes, as if they'd raided a costume store right before Halloween. Rapunzel, for instance, was wearing a mauve silk sari that was lovely except for the fact that it had several large rips in it, baring patches of skin. She was also sporting an orange mohair vest and a bright blue cowboy hat.

"We want you to be our menstrual king," Rapunzel said as she sat down beside me on the bed and slapped me playfully on the face with light strokes. "We want to give you the key to slipping into Crazyland at will."

"Get the key to Crazyland, get the key to Crazyland," the other women chanted together like a chorus. They were hopping up and down, bouncing randomly around the space.

Rapunzel lifted my shirt and pulled down my shorts as the leprechaun warrior had done. The trickle of red was still there. She swiped her index finger over it and brought the blood to her mouth.

"Holy communion! It *is* the real thing," she exulted. "Menstrual stigmata! Who'd've thunk it? Our very first recruit and he just happens to be bleeding one hundred percent genuine menstrual blood. Like no man has bled in more than six thousand years! Who else wants a taste?"

The women lined up, tittering excitedly. I was nearly paralyzed with excitement and bewilderment. Though I was a bit concerned about the continued bleeding, I decided it was worth it if it garnered this much attention.

Rapunzel held open my shorts while the first petitioner, a pretty, young, big-boned blonde with wild blue eyes and a bikini made out of the yellow plastic streamers that police put around crime scenes, reached in and partook.

"You'll help us out, won't you?" she told me while she licked her finger with a dreamy, slit-eyed look that I couldn't help but interpret as seductive. "You know how much we need you, right? Come live with us. Make us all very, very happy. Please?"

I nodded, though I wasn't sure what I was agreeing to.

The next woman in line reminded me of the Mexican painter Frida Kahlo: dark, bushy eyebrows joined in the middle and a face like a beautiful ocelot. She sipped her share of my scarlet flow, then addressed me. Her piercing brown eyes were just inches from mine. "The pandemic muzzling of the female libido has got to stop," she said. "It has turned the tender, poignant penis into a berserk cosmodemonic doomsday machine. Do something about it, Mr. Janitor

Shaman. OK? Starting here. Starting now."

She bent in closer and gave me a juicy kiss on the lips. "Lust globally, make love locally," she added before stepping away.

The next supplicant, a petite and very attractive black woman with glasses and lots of nervous energy, wanted to lick directly from the source.

"Pull 'em down farther," she told Rapunzel, pointing to my shorts. Rapunzel peeled the waistband down to my crotch, and the woman pressed her lips against my small but seemingly inexhaustible wound. I relaxed as best I could as she puckered and sucked.

"You can sleep with her most of the time," she said to me as she finished, pointing at Rapunzel, "but save something for the rest of us, OK? She deserves your best, but we deserve your second-best." With this she laughed.

Before turning to make way for the next in line, she pointed at her belly and breathed, "Not going to trust anyone but the menstrual king to fertilize this womb. You know what they say: One spoonful contains enough sperm to populate the entire planet."

The next woman in line looked familiar. Where had I seen her before? On the one hand, her body was that of a well-wrought thirty-five-year-old. She had relatively broad shoulders on a petite form, with narrow hips, low body fat, and sinewy muscles. On the other hand, I guessed her to be in her sixties—possibly older. Besides the grey hair, she had major forehead wrinkles and crow's feet.

Then I remembered where I had seen her before—twice. The first time was in the picture book titled the *Menstrual Lingerie Fashion Show.* There her name was Vimala. The second time was on a strange TV at the gallery where I heard the Rapunzel lookalike deliver a rap about practicing the art of death.

Now, like the previous supplicant, this curiously young-looking crone bent down to drink directly from what I had finally come around to believe was my "menstrual stigmata."

"Mmmmm," she sighed in the direction of Rapunzel. "I love the virgin ooze of a menstrual king. It's been so long. Too long. I am proud of you, dear. You have conjured up the perfect male consort. Well, maybe not the *perfect* one. But the best that could be expected under the circumstances."

"Thanks, Vimala," Rapunzel replied with a chuckle. "Had to start somewhere, I guess, huh?"

As Vimala left, the Norse leprechaun sat down on the bed, taking the side opposite Rapunzel. "Mind if I have seconds?" she asked expectantly.

"He'd be honored, Jumbler," Rapunzel answered for me.

Jumbler partook of my gift, then snuggled close to me as Rapunzel did the same on my other side. Both had their arms around my shoulder.

"You can have your cake and eat it too," Jumbler whispered in my ear. "We'll give you the hand of the queen *and* the hands of all her court as well."

"Not to mention the key to slipping into Crazyland at will," Rapunzel breathed into my other ear. "All you have to do is place your creative skills in the service of the Menstrual Temple. What do you say?"

I could feel the soft contour of both their breasts on my upper arms. To my right, Rapunzel's thigh and navel showed through big holes in her sari. The smell of her smoky velvet musk penetrated me to the bone. To my left, Jumbler's small but perky breasts were clearly visible as her baggy, low-cut blouse gaped open. I felt my imagination attuning itself to her fragrance of orchids.

I became aware of an emotion trying to form itself in the space between my heart and throat. It was an unfamiliar one, maybe what emptiness would feel like if emptiness were a good and happy thing. I could almost sense the texture of a word echoing out of its midst: *vacate* or *vacancy* or *vacation* or *vacuum* or *evacuate* or the Spanish *vamanos*.

Barrenness but buoyancy. An exhilarating desert. Vacation in the void.

As I bobbed and floated in this desolate yet welcoming white sky, I passed through the ghost of a memory from when I was very young, well before I could talk, maybe just a couple of months old. I was in the lap of a person, my grandmother I think, who over and over again was hiding her face behind her hands and then suddenly peeking out. I was sure of it: This was the moment in my life when I first laughed. Unable to use the sculpting power of language to create my world, barely able even to perceive the boundary between a face and the air around it, I found something funny; I invoked a gift of pure amusement *ex nihilo.*

The next thought that sprouted from the emptiness had no obvious connection to the previous impression. I found myself mulling over the fantasy of writing a story about the adventures I'd had since meeting Rapunzel—possibly borrowing from the manuscript I'd read earlier. The first scene would take place in the Catalyst bathroom. The second would be the vision I had while sprawled on the sidewalk in front of the Catalyst. Maybe. I didn't know the sequence exactly. The story was shaping itself in me; I could feel it. I imagined that my work would be like that of an amanuensis, a transcriptionist.

Would I really do such a thing as I was imagining? In many ways it went against my artistic instincts. If there has been one constant in my highly miscellaneous career as a creator, it's my allergy to the personal and the emotional and the intimate. Narcissism and egocentricity have been my taboos. Confessionalism repels me. I've been secretly proud of how steadfastly I've avoided mining even the most interesting events of my idiosyncratic history. Instead, politics and myth and dream have fueled my art. I've been like a surrealist anthropologist from Mars throwing out jokey analyses about the weird customs I observe.

And now this: an inspiration to indulge in the most excruciatingly personal narrative imaginable. I was embarrassed even to contemplate the shameless images that were already welling up. And that was exactly what was so exciting about it.

The superdream ended there. Long after I awoke, I lay in bed reliving every detail. Eventually my thoughts turned to a meditation on whether Rapunzel was really responsible for delivering this wonder to me, and by what mechanism she could have done it. That's a crucial question, after all, in deciding how to respond to the deals she proposed during her invasion of my home.

This I know for certain: The superdream was the Grail I've been stalking all these years. It allowed me to inhabit the other side of the veil with a piercing lucidity that I have not been able to muster since I gave up drugs.

There is also another delightful prospect the superdream has inspired me to fantasize about: What if it is a prophecy, or at least a foreshadowing, of an encounter with the Menstrual Temple that will actually happen in my waking life? What if Rapunzel transmitted or incited this scenario as a way to dramatize what awaits me when I receive the "menarche for men" she promised?

When I finally ended my ruminations on the dream and got out of bed, it was to find William Blake's *A Vision of the Last Judgment* on my bookshelf and reread one of my favorite passages.

> This world of Imagination is the world of Eternity; it is the divine bosom into which we shall go after the death of the Vegetated body. This World of Imagination is Infinite and Eternal, whereas the world of Generation, or Vegetation, is Finite and Temporal. There exists in that Eternal World the Permanent Realities of Every Thing which we see reflected in this Vegetable Glass of Nature. All Things are comprehended in their Eternal Forms in the divine body of the Saviour, the True Vine of Eternity, the Human Imagination.

In the wake of my landmark incursion into the paradisiacal enclave of the Dreamtime, greedy fantasies have been welling up in me. Do I dare imagine it's possible to drench myself in this deliverance at will? That I might gorge on this orgiastic catechism nightly? Could it be Rapunzel has established some telepathic link to my subconscious mind—a link that will allow me to drink deep draughts of this rapture again and again?

I am achingly tempted to do the unthinkable—if that's what it would take to earn this gift. Not to sell my soul, which is too expensive even for the devil to buy, but to sell my *ego*. To unload a big chunk of my megalomania. To dissolve my band World Entertainment War and quit the rock music business.

The joyous feast of the superdream, after all, is not the only offer on the table. How did Rapunzel put it when she made her visitation to my abode? She implied that my romance with World Entertainment War would seem like a crush in kindergarten compared to the mysterious love that awaits me if I renounce my precious band. "It would not be a lie," were her exact words as she shimmered like a vestal virgin next to my Wailing Wall, "to say that you have been freshly delivered into the presence of a watered-down version of the majestic gift." What else could that mean besides a relationship with Rapunzel herself, which was also strongly implied in the superdream? At the moment she spoke those words, nothing new besides her auroral splendor and its cathartic effect on me had freshly penetrated my sanctuary.

Take the promise of regular dips in the enchanted precincts of the Dreamtime, and add to it the hope of becoming betrothed to the embodiment of beauty and truth who has already broken my heart open with scary blessings, and there's a temptation so blindingly irresistible that I can't possibly indulge any fears that it would destroy me.

That last thing I said is oozing so much childlike idealism and romantic bombast—typical, typical—that I'm blushing. If I ever stage another "Lousy Poetry Reading," as I did once in my bad-boy days as a performance artist, it'll be statements like that which will deserve the spotlight.

The fact is, though, when you take into consideration the disenfranchised part of myself the Jungians call the "shadow," I'm too complex a schemer to actually live up to my childlike idealism and romantic bombast. That's why I've decided to be realistic in my response to Rapunzel's challenge.

I've concocted a covert strategy that I believe will allow me to gobble up my cake and maybe possibly hopefully have it too.

At the very least, it's such an evocative prank that it'll no doubt inspire an entire album's worth of songs.

It wasn't easy to convince the band we should risk my scheme. In fact, when I called them all together at my house last night, they were initially aghast. They gave me the same kind of mushy resistance I've met in the past when I've proposed other radical experiments designed to mutate our course. But in the end they bought it. Did they have a choice? My mind was made up. And besides, they've seen ample examples of the successful outcome of other loony inspirations of mine.

This is what I proposed. We'll carry out an extended performance art experiment which will appear to signal the demise of World Entertainment War, but which will ultimately multiply our mystique a thousand-fold—and pave the way for an explosive rebirth.

The first step is for the five of them to send a press release to all the newspapers.

"World Entertainment War's lead singer and conceptual master-mind," the blurb'll say, "has announced he's leaving the band in order to devote himself full-time to his role as a member of a radical feminist religious cult.

"Though he has indicated he's not at liberty to reveal the complete picture of his new mission, he has allowed us to divulge these facts: 1) The name of the cult is the Yo Mama Brigade. 2) His work there will consist of mastering the arts of the 'Lesbian Man' through ascetic service to the neo-matriarchy and by pursuing a hands-on study of the tantric version of chaos theory. 3) His 'ascetic service' will consist mostly of cleaning the toilets and washing the dishes of Goddess-worshipers, as well as a host of other janitorial tasks. 4) He has renounced all further contact with the media, which he dismisses as 'universally infected by the entertainment criminals' conspiracy to genocide the global imagination.'

"We regret that this transition means," the press release will go on to say, "we must abandon World Entertainment War's good fight. As of today, the band is no more. Its founder's departure breaks our hearts too badly to try to salvage a wounded version of our former selves.

"Perhaps when the dust clears and the rest of us have had some time to think, we'll formulate a new cadre of musical freedom fighters and return to the battle. But for now we must grieve the decision of our inspirational leader, and hope that this difficult and courageous move brings him closer to the core of his quest to become the ultimate prayer warrior. It has always been his unflinching devotion to his soul's truth that has fueled World Entertainment War's mission, and we can only admire him for upholding his tradition, even if in the short run it derails our highest ambitions.

"On the other hand, having whispered all those sweet nothings, we now have to be honest and confess the rest of what we feel. Goddamn him. Goddamn that moody, whimsical narcissist. How dare he fling himself off our muscular young stallion in mid-race? Is there something we're missing here? Some essential fact he's not telling us? Far be it from us to question His Worshipfulness' inscrutable fate, but what the hell is he thinking? We can't believe his new friends are so eager to psychically castrate a masculine role model who does so much good for the world. And we cannot fathom how this proudly independent thinker could have been so utterly brainwashed as to go along with their program for his life.

"To our fans—our extended family—we apologize with the biggest shit-eating mournful frown we can summon. We hope to hold a wake for World Entertainment War in the near future. Stay tuned for an announcement."

In my heart of hearts, of course, I have no intention of euthanizing my beautiful offspring, World Entertainment War. Just the opposite. I intend for this maneuver to up the ante of our fans' emotional invest-ment in our fate, and to seduce thousands of new melodrama addicts into our sphere. A couple of months down the line, when I come out of retirement and reconvene the band, newly invigorated by my sojourn with the Menstrual Temple, World Entertainment War's Mythic Quo-tient will have skyrocketed. If I know the way my creative process works, I'll also have conjured a whole rock opera's worth of new mate-rial based on the twisty tales I've just lived through. We'll go into the studio and record an irresistible new CD.

Granted, it's not as grandiose a publicity stunt as blowing my brains out with a shotgun like some rock stars I've known; nor is it as titil-lating (if hackneyed) as punching out a journalist or overdosing on heroin or romancing a naughty supermodel. What it lacks in predi-gested gossip-worthiness, however, is compensated for by its stark orig-inality. No rock star, not even a semi-famous one like me, has ever abdicated the throne to take on the monastic life—let alone a *radical feminist* monastic life. If I do say so myself, it has fair potential as a sto-ryline for a Hollywood movie.

I don't regard this as being deceitful towards our fans. For one thing, I really am suspending the band's operations for a while. For another, I sincerely want to hook up with Rapunzel and her crowd, and the truth is that she has made the dissolution of the band and a job as jan-itor conditions for accepting me.

Beyond that, I have for a long time regarded my art as consisting in part of translating the themes of my complex inner life into a rela-tively accurate, if simplified, public image. My job, in other words, has definitely NOT been to let my public image be sculpted by the one-size-fits-all machinery of the rock business; NOT to leech off a fake version of myself by fitting into the generic archetype of the famous rock star.

Rather, I've wanted to lend my creativity and spiritual awareness to the task of revolutionizing the whole act of persona-making. My hypothesis has been that maybe a celebrity's public image can be more than a hyped pack of pretty lies; that maybe I could shape, through artistry, an outer package that quite precisely reflects the spiritual intentions that lie inside.

One upshot of this line of thought is that I've concluded I sometimes have to fudge a little on the specific details in order to tell the bigger truth. Another implication is that my life really is, essentially, a story. It is not an assemblage of objective, incontrovertible data. It is a swarming fiction composed of endlessly permuting levels of truth (often contradictory), any one of which I can choose to highlight or downplay at any moment to create an entirely novel version of my history. There's no difference between my life and the story I proclaim to be my life. In the end, I *am* a performance art project.

I'm reminded of the children's picture book that consists of three groups of pages assembled vertically. The top group of pages has thirty different heads, the middle has thirty different bodies, and the lower has thirty different legs. At any one time the mongrel personage you have before you can be built from, say, the clown face on page one of the top group plus the soldier body on page eleven of the middle group plus the ballet dancer's legs from page twenty-seven of the bottom group.

The story—or rather the *stories*—of my life resemble that children's book.

So I've rationalized with exquisitely lyrical logic why our performance art experiment is not deceitful towards our fans. Can I manage the same feat in relation to Rapunzel?

Well, she specifically said I didn't have to leave the music business forever. And she did not say exactly how long it might take for me to, quote, untangle my divine motivations for singing from the diseased motivations, unquote. Two months might be enough, for all I or she knows. And I figure I want to let the first part of my prank simmer at least two months before launching it into its next phase. Besides, I really do want to be free of the day-to-day demands of the band for now so I can make myself abundantly available for whatever Rapunzel and company have in store for me. I can't imagine any feistier fun. And after having had to reconnoiter the music accountants' and music bureaucrats' sections of hell in the last few months, I richly deserve to indulge in such feisty fun. An artist needs regular doses of fertile chaos.

Best of all, it's one hundred percent guaranteed that my imminent adventures with the gorgeous sphinx trickster will generate a spate of killer works of art.

I am as sure of that as I am of the solidity of the bedraggled mop and bucket full of slopwater I am gazing at here in the kitchen of India Joze restaurant in downtown Santa Cruz at 1:30 in the morning.

It's my third night on the job as a janitor. Shreds of moldy tomatoes dangle from my hair. Dirty cake frosting clings to the sleeve of my khaki Sears work shirt, as well as rotting eggplant pulp blended with the pulverized fragments of a dead insect. My matching khaki pants, new just a few days ago, have already absorbed so much grunge that the cuffs have permanently turned the color of crud.

I'm ecstatic. Maybe I won't be in a week, but for now, I'm awash in infatuation with my role as a total nonentity. I'm living the dream of any egomaniac who has ever loved the Buddha: to be as empty as the moment between the ticks of the clock; to be stone-cold, dead-dumb, flat-out unimportant, the biggest nobody in a world full of nobodies.

For years I've allowed my ego to sway and groove to the rhythm of its cute hallucinations of grandiosity. I am, after all, the spiritually savvy rockstar fueled by feminist lust, right? I am a hip philosopher for the proletariat of geniuses, the postmodern bard who channels the most entertaining brand of crazy wisdom that's ever held down a regular spot on the periphery of the mass media.

And oh the crushing weight of it all. To be chronically teetering with top-heavy self-importance yet pretend that I'm naught but a humble seeker. What sublime guilt! What messianic sneakiness! What ineffable tomfoolery! What lousy stinkin' graceful fragrant logic!

Now, though, for going-on-three nirvana-crammed nights, I have been scoured of all such bullpuckie. With each used tampon I've had to fish out of the clogged toilet with my mini-roto rooter, my innate hubris shrinks. With each crop of shattered drinking glass fragments I gingerly harvest from the sink, my treasured invisibility grows.

Tonight I wept with unironic joy as I scraped away years-old gunk with a putty knife from a corner behind the bread table. "I am nothing!" I laughed aloud as I marveled at the perfect gnosis. Not a single soul will ever know I carried out this secret act! And even if they did, they wouldn't be in the least impressed by it! I did it, indeed, because there was absolutely no reason to do it. And in that moment, as the gummy green-black slag responded to my earnest ministrations, a liquid thunderbolt of love blasted through me—I mean a tangible elixir of blessing from the Grandmother of Us All. The Goddess saw! And rewarded me! I felt it! I swear I sensed Her nectared presence! Her fiercely sweet touch! And hallelujah I deserved it! Because for once in my life I was wildly free of all lust for results. I had lived, if only for an instant, outside of karma.

Here's the best part: I'm not even being paid for busting my ass six hours a night. In fact, I'm *spending money* to earn the privilege. In carrying out Rapunzel's assignment to get a job as a janitor, I wanted to be as free of attachments as possible. I didn't want to give anyone the false impression I was interested in a long-term commitment. Nor did I particularly want to call attention to my new role from someone who might know someone who knew me.

My solution was to stroll over to my favorite restaurant in the wee hours a few nights ago. When the janitor came out to the street at about 2:45 to hose down the rubber mats in the gutter, I engaged him in conversation.

"How'd you like a little paid vacation?" I offered.

"Huh?"

"I've got a proposition for you."

"Listen, I ain't into gay sex."

"It's nothing like that. What's your name?"

"Dave."

"Well, Dave, my friends call me Rockstar. And there's a little performance art project I want to try which involves doing exactly the kind of work you're doing. Thing of it is, it's important that I do the job completely off the books."

"You're fuckin' crazy."

"No, Dave, I assure you I've never felt more lucid in my life. Here's what I propose. Do you work here every night?"

"Five nights a week."

"Here's what I propose. You let me do your job every night for, I don't know, let's say your next fifteen nights. And in return I will pay you five dollars an hour for every hour I work. So in other words you'll get to collect your regular salary from India Joze plus what I provide."

"I still think you're fuckin' nuts. But I'd think about it if maybe I knew you better. I mean, what's to stop you from stealing stuff from the restaurant and then my boss'll blame me?"

"I'm perfectly willing to make you feel totally comfortable about that, Dave. If you want, you can hang around during my entire shift and monitor me as I work. You can sit back and watch TV or read while I slave away."

"Well. I don't know. I mean I guess so. You want to start now?"

"Perfect. You can show me everything you do so I can take over full-time tomorrow."

I became Dave's apprentice for the next four hours, and as we parted at dawn I handed him twenty dollars. I met him here last night and gave him his thirty dollars right away. He hung around for an hour before giving me the keys and taking off. Tonight before I came to work I got a call from him saying to start without him, that he'd come by at dawn to pick up his nightly wage. So here I am alone, blissing out on the stench of the fermenting meat littering the stove I'll be cleaning next.

Or should I stack the chairs on the tables in the dining areas and sweep and mop the floor? Or maybe ply my craft on the sinks and urinals in the men's bathroom? There are so many thrilling acts of self-abnegation, I'm almost paralyzed with my freedom of choice.

For now I think I'll just kick back, chill out, and meditate on how pleased I am with my fascinating life. All is proceeding with sweet synchronicity. The band's press releases should be arriving en masse at media outlets later today. No doubt there'll be a flurry of inquiries on the World Entertainment War hotline by nightfall. Despite the bit in the press release about me refusing all further contact with the media, I just might get back to a couple of journalists if I think they're capable of helping me promote the mythic angle of this experiment.

Suddenly I'm overwhelmed with the urge to bellow out "I Know Nothing," one of the last tunes World Entertainment War and I wrote before my "retirement." It's actually more of a rap than a song.

A continuous peekaboo game inherent in nature
The big bang began in an upside-down mirror
The universe has a condition resembling dyslexia
But as quantum physics demonstrates
There's nothing to fear

I know nothing
I agree with everything
I love everyone
I am not myself

Are we really nothing more than antimatter holograms anyway
Do we communicate via telepathy with our future selves
Are there mini-black holes even now invading our bodies
Is it true there's too much energy and we'll all go to hell

I know nothing
I agree with everything
I love everyone
I am not myself

I feel the editor's scissors closing in on these thoughts
I feel the editor's scissors closing in on these thoughts
I feel the editor's scissors closing in on these thoughts
I feel the editor's scissors closing in on these thoughts

The goddess Juno Februata
is said to have conceived the god Mars
by communing erotically with a sacred lily.

The Virgin Mary
achieved her gravid state
with the help of a dove,
and the Greek hero Attis
started germinating in his mom
after she ingested a pomegranate seed.

Now you,
beauty and truth fan,
through the magic of the Televisionary Oracle,
have the power to become pregnant
with a brilliant brainchild
through mystical union with a six-pack of beer.

JUST KIDDING!

You won't need any mind-altering substance
to conceive the divine inspiration you're ripe for.

Communing with the Televisionary Oracle
will work just fine
all by itself.

You are now wrestling with a subliminal message. BMW bouquet protector feast. On a conscious level, you may not know what the hell we're talking about, but your subconscious mind will record and remember all the mutant joy contained herein. Slamdunk peak-experience blueprint. Your dormant genius has already begun to stir, ensuring the genesis of love spells that will dispel the black magic you've wreaked on yourself. Pain-reliever flushed cheeks lucky dog dream-treasure. That's why we have utmost confidence that you will soon discover the power to kill your own death. Moist hot laughing bloom.

This sacred subliminal commercial
is brought to you by
The Committee for Surrealist Investigation of Claims of the Normal
(CSICON)
which is now seeking evidence that "reality" exists.
Send proof to:
zenpride@televisionaryoracle.com

40

I'm back. It's me, Rapunzel. The chick with the seven mommies and the invisible twin brother and the forehead that used to have a blotch and the impossibly grandiose reputation to live up to.

I'm coming to you now from a new, improved version of my life. The Pomegranate Grail has married The Eater of Cruelty and brought forth an offspring called the Menstrual Temple of the Funky Grail. The rigorous schooling of my mothers has blended seamlessly with the tantric trickery of my freaky consort Jumbler and the uproarious training I've received at Drivetime University. And the old schism between my outer and inner worlds has been healed.

In this new life of mine, five years after I kidnapped myself and erased my blotch, I have become the avatar of the ancient mystery school on my own terms. Sacred fun and erotic prayer are the esthetic ethics at the heart of my reign. My mothers' love steadies and nurtures me as my freaky consort's love challenges and inspires. I have figured out how to have my cake and eat it too.

How did I pull it off? The better question would be, how could I *not* have pulled it off given how much help I've had: an eternal yet earthy secretary who keeps track of the master plan I've been working out over the course of countless incarnations during sixty-six million years; a soul twin-shaman brother-doppelganger muse who has lubricated my travels to the other side of the veil since I was six years old; a lover and best friend who is an unpredictable, multi-gendered genius with tantric training and an inexhaustible supply of brainstorms; and the Televisionary Oracle itself, the sacred "machine" that always reveals to me exactly what I need to know exactly when I need to know it.

There was a rough patch back when Jumbler and I first returned to the Pomegranate Grail six months after I'd run away. My mothers wanted to blame all my crazy new notions on her bad influence. Besides, they had long ago decreed, drawing their authority from the Pomegranate Grail's prophetic tradition, that I would never marry, and they had difficulty accepting how thoroughly Jumbler and I had already woven our fates together.

But the Televisionary Oracle guided me every step of the way through the crisis. I had already seen in abundance how practical its wise and often wacky revelations could be, but that was the first of many times it helped me come up with creative solutions in the face of intense conflict with people I loved.

The breakthrough was, of course, when my mothers agreed to become my students so that I might teach them how to personally access the wonders of the Televisionary Oracle. Once Vimala, especially, began accessing the secret identity of her own "holy guardian angel," my battle was won.

For more than four years now, not only my mommies but the entire worldwide membership of our ancient mystery school have fed on the funny medicine of the Drivetime. As a result, their individual evolutions have sped up just as mine and Jumbler's began to during the First Seven Days of Creation back in the tear-stained bed at the Villa Inn. Yesterday Vimala confided in me that she has become more herself in the last four years than she did in her previous forty years.

And yet in a sense, the last five years have all been prelude for what is to come. Since Jumbler and I first discovered the tantric practices that allowed us to milk the Drivetime for all it's worth, we have been preparing for today's coming-out party.

It was all spelled out near the beginning. Day Four of the First Seven Days of Creation brought the revelation that the Menstrual Temple's inaugural blast into the wider world would materialize right here and now, a little after noon on the first day of May, known by us funky pagan tantrics as the holiday of Beltane.

Strange but true. Jumbler and I divined way back then—are living

out the divination in actual waking life and broadcasting it to wherever you are—that the most profanely holy spot on the planet, the
grossly sublime vortex where beatific splendor is most thoroughly interwoven with trivial squalor, resides in a women's lavatory in a nightclub
on the main street of a small California beachside town called Santa
Cruz. That's where the vision of the Menstrual Millennium is hatched.
That's where we're staging the "Kill the Apocalypse" festival, which
is also the official public launch of the Televisionary Oracle.

In the initial scene of that original Drivetime University revelation,
which is being fully materialized in physical reality right now, Jumbler and I are in that grubby little lavatory, getting ready with a private
ritual.

To an untrained observer, the ambiance here may seem less than
ideal for such a pregnant moment. The place stinks, and it's ugly. The
dingy yellow-white walls are marred by idiotic grafitti, and the mirror
is cracked. Our nostrils twinge with the fragrance of stale bleach and
the fresh droppings of our prized pet vulture, Yo Mama Death, who's
perched on the top of the stall.

Only a precious few thousand initiates truly understand why this
is the epicenter for the most intimate revolution in history. May that
all change in the prankishly reverent future that awaits us.

In a few minutes Jumbler and I will go outside to the street in front of
the Catalyst to meet my public, which has gathered for the joyous
funeral procession I will lead down Pacific Avenue to the Evergreen
Cemetery in Harvey West Park. But right now we are building a guerrilla shrine next to the sink to summon forth the divine allies whom
we want to bless our event.

Next to the sink, there's a bouquet of chrysanthemums, flowers for
the dead, and a large silver chalice filled with what we like to call
dragon's blood. Around them we've arranged these items: a miniature
Mexican candy sculpture of a pink-hatted skeleton pushing an ice
cream cart; an inkpad and rubber stamp that says "GENIUS"; an
unopened package of freeze-dried "Astronaut Strawberries"; a small
oil painting of the Goddess Persephone wielding handpuppets resembling me and Jumbler; a bowl of pumpkin seeds that I saved from the

first jack-o-lantern I carved when I was five years old; a hammer painted lavender and decorated with drawings of bees and unicorns and snakes and bull skulls; a fossilized vulture egg; and the Menstrual Temple of the Funky Grail Tarot deck, in which all the human figures are wearing menstrual lingerie.

To be honest, I'm already crying. Not continuously, but in short bursts, which is a good sign. It means I'm tapping into the sexiest zones of the Drivetime, but not with such overwrought intensity that I'll be a blubbering mess for the duration of today's event.

Jumbler is sniffling a stream, if not a raging river, herself. I wouldn't be surprised to see it swell as the day goes on. She has never had to share me so wildly; never had to witness, let alone assist in, me giving others the riches I give her. It's not that she's resisting this breakthrough. I'm in awe, in fact, of how generous she has made herself in the face of this new phase of my work. Still, I can't help but be aware that her heart is breaking, too.

My own heart is not exactly a stronghold of serene stability. I'm at the threshold of harvesting the fruits of my menarche. I mean my *real* menarche—not the literal spilling of virgin menstrual blood that was induced by my mothers—but the self-abduction I plotted and carried out by myself.

"Remember back at the Villa Inn when you first started telling me all the contradictory stories of how you grew up and where you came from?" I ask Jumbler, wanting to take the edge off the portentousness of this, the party we've been planning for so long.

"That was, I believe, on Day Three of the Creation," Jumbler says sweetly. "When we branched out from Ritz Crackers, string cheese, and celery, and also got some corn chips for our only meal of the day. You were so cute, the way you wanted so much to believe every last crazy thing I said."

"But remember how pissed off I was at you when I finally realized you were dumping a heap of pretty lies on me? Rat-bastard." I speak this last curse with a honey tone and loving grin. "Condescending to me like I was a gullible child."

"But you suspected even then that it was for your own good, freaky.

And as you know now, it wasn't all pretty lies. Quite a bit of raw truth mixed in there."

"First you said you were motherless. Said your father was a born-again Christian satanist general at the Pentagon who kept you locked in a cage your entire childhood. Fed you nothing but grits and chicken gizzards and black-eyed peas. Made you perform ridiculous assignments in order to get permission to go to the bathroom, like reciting the Periodic Table of Elements."

"Which is why I'm such an idiot-savant to this day. Want to know the atomic mass of tungsten? It's 183.85." She arches her left eyebrow like a mad scientist but somehow makes the rest of her face go blank.

"Ten minutes later, totally straight-faced, you were telling me you were a coddled child genius whose mom and dad gave up their careers so they could devote themselves to your education. You enrolled in Duke University when you were ten years old."

"Hmmm. Doesn't that have a certain resemblance to the biography of someone we both know and love, initials R.B.?"

"Yes it does, goddamn you," I say as I take the "Genius" rubber stamp and decorate Jumbler's right arm. "How dare you claim the right to be more megalomaniac than I?"

"I would have done anything to help you, my darling. Anything to liberate you from your enslavement to excessive factuality. It was choking off the growth of your myth-making skills, therefore preventing your full flowering as the avatar of feminismo."

"And then there was the tale about how you were brought up by deathologists. Your mom ran a hospice and a graveyard and collected black-market skulls and black-market orchids. She taught Kubler-Ross everything she knew. Your dad specialized in guiding dead souls through the Bardo realms during the first forty-nine days after they departed their bodies."

"Every bit of every one of those stories was an absolutely true hallucination," she says as she dips her finger into the dragon's blood and creates a simulation of my old birthmark on my forehead. I don't resist. These days I'm no longer sensitive about the blotch that was once upon a time my worst curse. Besides, I'm pleased she wants to have fun.

"My favorite version of your life story is one you didn't even tell me until Day Five," I murmur, feeling almost romantic. "About how you were a so-called 'magickal child,' conceived by four men and four women on a tantric commune. How they meditated their four sperms and four ova into the womb of one woman who was only really one-quarter your mom but they never told you which one she was."

"Though later I was blessed to learn your diabolically precise anamnesis technique, my dear," Jumbler says, "so I was able to recover all my preverbal memories. Jacinto was the mom who physically birthed me."

"You're welcome," I say, creating two streaks of dragon's blood warpaint on each of Jumbler's cheeks. I also break open the Astronaut Strawberries and offer a few to Yo Mama Death. "And I'm very grateful for your service on my behalf, how you disabused me of the curse of literalism. 'Hello, I'm Rapunzel Blavatsky, international spokesmodel for Heroically Unified Multiple Personalities, also known as HUMP. We're dedicated to overcoming negative stereotypes about people who live too many different lives to be contained within a single personality.'"

"The universe is not made of molecules; it's made of stories, my dear," Jumbler singsongs, repeating her favorite mantra. "But shouldn't we be finishing up? The masses are awaiting our arrival, and here we are chatting about old times."

"Ever since then," I press on, not quite ready to leave the intimate space for the spectacle brewing outside. "I've been in love with your idea of how two people who are standing next to each other can have such wildly clashing internal schemes of reality that for all intents and purposes they live on different planets."

"Yes, and who would have thought that a breeder chick like you and a hermaphrodite queer like me could ever have ended up inhabiting Znipwof Arksty together. Or I forget, what's the name of our planet again? Zwofpin Starkty? Pozwinps Traksty? It seems to keep changing."

"It hurts my feelings when you call yourself a queer hermaphrodite," I complain, truly perturbed. "That's just so damn reductionist." I'm wondering if this is a passive-aggressive leakage of the sadness Jumbler promised me she would suppress tonight.

"Just a temporary, extremely relative truth," she says, "provoked by the reckless emotions of tonight's historical turning point."

"Well, OK," I pout, looking in the mirror to wipe away the dragon's blood Jumbler anointed me with. I survey her face for any signs of grief writhing just under the skin. "But before we go, address this question for me, please, Jumbler darling. I know we've discussed this to death, but it's my ritual duty to ask what you have to say about it here in the heat of the moment, when the flip is about to flop."

I push my shoulders back, stomach in, and chest out, simulating the formal posture my mothers used to make me assume during the "Confront the Guardian of the Threshold" portions of my childhood rituals of initiation. "Is it really one-hundred-percent ethical," I say with mock solemnity, "for me to use our sacred tricks to get people to come live with us on *our* planet? What gives us the right to invoke the full power of the Televisionary Oracle to seduce *anyone at all* into imagining that our confabulation is truer than all the other half-truths out there?"

"Because we're the only soldiers in the world entertainment war," Jumbler sighs with a soupçon of boredom, "that blaspheme our own deities. Now come on, let's wrap this up and go meet our blind date with destiny. Pray with me."

I follow Jumbler down as she kneels and prostrates her forehead on the scummy floor. As if aware she's a participant, Yo Mama Death unleashes a nicely timed raucous shriek.

"O Persephone, Great Cackling Goddess," Jumbler intones, her voice muffled by the proximity of her lips to the concrete, "You Buzzard-Lipped, Bottom-Feeding, Garbage-Gobbling, Puke-Drooling, Beady-Eyed Slimebag: We pray that you give us the wisdom to always pretend we mean the opposite of what we say as well as what we say."

"O Musty Queen of the Dead," I continue, "You Overseer of the Underworld's Grotesque Cornucopia, You Weirdo Purveyor of Lipstick and Bullets and Glamour and Poop, You Creator of the Stagnant Water and the Funny Words We Thought of While We Were Standing Knee-Deep: We dare not claim the hubris to burn anyone else's flags or spit on their fetishes unless we're willing to burn and spit on our own."

"O Sacred Gargoyle of Beauty and Truth," Jumbler chimes in, "You Dumb Fast Infinitely Plump River of Electricity, You Sluggish Smoldering Lump of Angel Fat Left Over from the Big Bang, You

Ingeniously Seductive Maggot Who Loves Inventive Tragedy and Sophisticated Superstition, You Cool Furnace That Incinerates the Props of Our Nightmares Much Too Slowly: We pray that You will always break us open with juicy secrets about how to die a little now so we don't have to die a lot later. Shatter us with moist clues, Goddess, about how to slough off what worked for us yesterday so that we may conjure what'll work best for us tomorrow. Turn us inside-out with terrifying opportunities to kill the phallocratic model of death and foment the menstrual model."

"Halle-fucking-lujah, comrade," I say, lifting myself from the floor. "Let's go careen."

Carrying Yo Mama Death and our grail of dragon's blood, Jumbler and I slink out of the bathroom into the atrium of the Catalyst— just as we did in the Drivetime University class five years ago. Out here, recreating that prophetic adventure perfectly, are hordes of revelers packed wall to wall, spilling out into the street, waiting to join us in the celebration.

We push our way outside, then boost ourselves up on the lead float of the funeral parade. Stretched between two maypoles on the back end of the float is a clothesline from which hang many pieces of freshly consecrated sacred lingerie and a banner that reads "Kill the Apocalypse with Love."

Two richly adorned beds surround a gold casket, which is open, revealing the contents: a replica of "Little Boy," the atomic bomb dropped on Hiroshima; a loose-leaf notebook which contains xeroxed copies of the prophecies of Nostradamus and the Bible's Book of Revelations; a television with a giant band-aid on it; a bumpersticker with a quote from Jung, "The present world situation is calculated as never before to arouse expectation of a redeeming supernatural event"; a foot-tall sculpture of Jesus crucified on the cross, blood dripping down his face; the "Armageddon Bra," a lingerie item which has built-in sensors to warn of fiery objects falling from the skies (missiles, asteroids, UFOs); and a totem pole featuring the faces of Julius Caesar, Columbus, Napoleon, Stalin, Charles Darwin, and Dan Rather.

Lingerie-clad female models are lounging on the beds. Though a couple of them are voluptuous young things, most have rather ample asses and abundant body hair and less-than-perky breasts. I know and love all of these beauties well. Every one is a member of the Menstrual Temple of the Funky Grail.

My favorite model, of course, is my ancient mother Vimala, face as old as the Mona Lisa's great-grandma. She's wearing purple cowgirl boots, a lacy red bra, and a purple leather mini-skirt. Over her shoulder-length grey dreadlocks, there's a tall crown of inflated pink and purple balloons tied together in the shape of a vulture.

"Hi, mommy," I beam, patting her on her crown. "How's your bad self?"

"My bad self is positively sparkle-dark," she replies. "And by the way, I love your latest creation."

She's pointing towards the giant Televisionary Oracle screen which is set up on one side of the float. It reveals a panorama I finished programming only yesterday.

The view is from a flock of vultures, as if the camera were mounted on the belly of one of the birds. For a while they fly uneventfully over an eight-lane highway on which no traffic moves, though there are numerous abandoned vehicles everywhere, including cars, ox carts, tow trucks, baby buggies, catapults, fairy godmother coaches, chariots, milk wagons, and even a Trojan Horse. Winding as far as the eye can see, always remaining inside the "walls" formed by the wreckage, is a thick train of men trudging doggedly towards the setting sun. Each is pushing in front of him a wheeled version of the golden casket that appears on the lead float of our parade.

The vultures veer away from their path over the highway and spiral down towards a field just to the north. Now we see a labyrinth cut out of a vast field of waist-high grass, at the center of which is a stupendous oak tree with a door in its trunk. The birds maintain a holding pattern just above the top of the grass and beyond the reach of the tree's longest branches, wheeling clockwise.

As they pass the door, we can see a sign on the front which reads:

Menstrual Hut of the Cackling Goddess
Formerly Pizza Hut of the Corporate God
Under New Management

The labyrinth is constructed in the fashion of the sacred labyrinths of old. That is to say, it's not a maze rife with dead ends and confusing turns. Rather there is just one unambiguous though convoluted path to the center. Everyone who enters will eventually reach the center if they walk patiently onward.

Now here's my favorite part: I've designed this Televisionary Oracle in such a way that anyone who beholds it sees a likeness of himself or herself meandering through the labyrinth.

As this part of the program comes around, there are a few gasps from audience members who've been watching attentively.

"Whoa. How can that be?" someone calls out.

"Fucking amazing. How do they do that?" another voice mutters.

This is a tease. The scene stops here and begins again with the vultures soaring over the marching men. Later, when the funeral parade reaches the graveyard, I'll let this sequence continue with the rest of the story.

I turn away from the scene, gratified at its craftsmanship. I like to think it's entertaining despite the fact that its message is covertly sacred—and covertly sacred despite the fact that it's entertaining. In other words, it embodies the esthetic ethic that has been my obsession these last five years.

Standing up and stretching, I grab my cordless microphone from a mike stand. I'm ready to get this show on the road.

"How are your bad selves today, beauty and truth fans?" I bellow. The response is more a swell than an explosion, so I try it again, gazing up into the azure sky and beckoning to the crowd.

"I said, how are your underworld selves today, beauty and truth and garbage and death fans?" This time a pleasing roar billows up.

The sea of faces is not yet as vast as I'd hoped, though. While there are growing numbers along the procession route ahead of us, I see very few people back along the line of vehicles that snakes down Pacific Avenue towards the beach.

"You ready for the immortality cheer, everyone? Ready to chant the mantra that gets you in the mood to live forever? Let me hear you say, 'I die daily.' Shout it with me now, sex and death fans. Celebrate it with me. I die daily. I die daily. I die daily. I die daily."

The hair on the back of my neck sprouts as hundreds of voices join me in intoning the prayer I've only heard in the privacy of my meditation chamber or the bed I share with Jumbler.

I wait a moment after the last echoes die away, then resume my address.

"Welcome to the party that will launch the murder of the apocalypse!" I shout as I slowly turn three hundred sixty degrees. "Today, we begin imagining the canny actions that'll crush the pandemic of pop-nihilism. Today we start creating a world in which prophecies of boom and zoom will be more fun and interesting than conspiracies of doom and gloom."

People are looking at me quizzically. What I just said was not perhaps the most entertaining way I could have conveyed what I meant.

"We bring you glad tidings, beauty and truth fans," I continue, still half-improvising. "The archetypes are mutating. All the flips are about to flop. Very soon, YA YA will actually be YA YA. YA YA will no longer be NYAA NYAA. Very soon, you'll know exactly how to ask the Greatest Mystery of All what the fuck it wants from you—and you'll really get an answer."

"Why am I so handsome and talented but I can't get a girlfriend or a job?" some male voice heckles loudly, enough to rouse ripples of laughter from those close enough to hear him.

"Have faith, love and justice fans," I continue. "Have delirious, orgiastic, perverse faith. I promise you that compassion will become an aphrodisiac. There'll be feminist supercomputers that can talk to the Goddess. Your daily wage will be directly tied to how much beauty and truth you bring into the world. Best of all, there'll be a global network of menstrual huts and dreamwork salons for that cranky time every month when you know you'll just die if you can't go blissfully mad."

This last spiel goes over much better. Confusion has given way to amusement in the faces I can see.

I congratulate myself for being so sensitive to the mood of the crowd. The meditation exercises I've done with my acting teacher Gail have slowly but surely fine-tuned my raw charisma. (I like her definition: A charismatic person is not just someone who has personal charm, star quality, and animal magnetism, but who also is interested in other people and makes them feel good when they're around her.) My Drivetime University lessons with the showman shaman Madame Blavatsky have had a lot to do with my growing skill in playing with group energy, of course, as have the performance art shows I've been doing in the Waketime under various disguises.

There has been another influence in recent months as well. I've had the benefit of studying the live shows of a certain local rockstar, the chief boohoo of the World Entertainment War band. Whether he's the best entertainer in the world, I don't know—probably not, since he's not monumentally rich and famous—but his techniques for captivating the imagination of an audience resonate with those I aspire to master.

"Kill your own death!" someone shouts brightly from the crowd, providing me with the gratification of hearing one of my own slogans mirrored back. I imagine that she is among those who read the two newspaper articles about the Menstrual Temple that appeared in the days before the event.

"Exterminate the apocalypse with unconditional love!" screams a male voice, offering a variation on the theme that I couldn't have said better myself.

I signal to my driver Sonia, and our float begins to creep slowly forward. The crowd's hubbub swells in response.

"I'm your host, Rapunzel Blavatsky," I say to the crowd, "and I'm proud to announce that this is a perfect moment. At this perfect moment, one hundred trillion lascivious feminist vibrations are beginning to pour through each and every one of you like a permanent orgasm, annihilating all blockages to your divine charisma and jostling loose an abundant flow of creative ideas. Sooner than you think, your unique genius will be unleashed, allowing you to express all of your true potential!"

An electric wave of gleeful cheers erupts. Five floats back in the parade, the Menstrual Temple's house band, Feminist Orgy Network, begins the opening strains of "Soundtrack for the End of the End of the World."

I should confess that I stole one—well, actually two—of the lines in my last spiel from the guy in World Entertainment War.

I gleam over at Jumbler as I draw the mike away from my mouth. Then, grabbing her hand, I initiate our famous "water-buffaloes-making-love" rhythmic grunt, which she takes up too after a moment's hesitation.

I can't imagine even being alive today, let alone presiding over this grand opening, without the presence of Jumbler in my life.

She's the only one who busts me in the ways I need to be busted. Everyone else is a little too enslaved to their belief that I'm a divinely inspired superstar to be of much use to my project of continual self-dismantling.

Ever since I returned from exile four and a half years ago, my mothers have done a great job shedding their fixations about me. But it's just not within their power, I'm afraid, to critique me with the fierce ingenuity I need in order to die every day. It really helps to have a collaborator who's adept at homing in on the exact deaths I need.

Not that Jumbler is a non-stop debunker of all things Rapunzel. What makes her so credible in purging my bullshit is that she's equally adept at recognizing and drawing out my idiosyncratic brilliance. These seemingly contradictory skills, which I have never known any other person be able to wield, have been my privilege to enjoy from the first days of our relationship. And they have been crucial in my ability to become myself—to fulfill the promise of my self-abduction.

But it's not as if I have merely sucked up Jumbler's contributions with regal narcissism. One of her great gifts to me has been her ability to arouse my passionate, reverent attention to *her* needs. I'm devoted to serving her devotion to herself, just as she is to mine. In this way, I've overcome an imbalance in my psyche that made it easy for me to be the beloved one but hard to treat another flesh-and-blood human as the beloved. (I've always been a master of paying homage to Persephone.)

I'm grateful, too, for the psychological skills Jumbler has helped me cultivate. Dealing with difficult feelings has been at the heart of our "radical intimacy" all these years. Not only do we not hide or manipulate; we grow closer through our difficult honesty. I tell her the godawful truth about my dark toxins and she listens with equanimity. It's the same going the other way. Shadow-stalking, we call it. We've toyed with collaborating on a book by that very name.

But Jumbler's gifts go beyond even all these wonders. As Madame Blavatsky prophesied on the First Day of Creation, Jumbler's "The

Eater of Cruelty" has been the "father" of my revisioned mystery school, just as the Pomegranate Grail is the mother. Jumbler has been my collaborator. We've extensively explored the Drivetime through the power of our tantric meditations; we've stalked revelation there, gathering raw materials to use in building the new covenant; back in the Waketime, we've exhaustively discussed the meaning of our visions and put in motion the plans to translate them into material reality.

I'll list just a few examples. The idea that the sacred could and should be playful: It originated with Jumbler but came natural to me, and I helped take it places Jumbler couldn't imagine by herself. The theory that menstruation is a central metaphor for an understanding of death that could save the world from extinction: It was implicit in the teachings of the Pomegranate Grail, but I couldn't have brought it to fruition without having my brainpower supercharged by Jumbler's brilliant, sensual devotion. The notion that spiritual women should find a way to aggressively celebrate sex, thereby seizing the authority to redefine its cultural expression: the Menstrual Temple's strategy for doing this grew directly out of my response to Jumbler's tantric mastery.

It's no surprise, then, that a part of me feels desolate, even a little guilty, as I contemplate the hurt I must unleash on my beautiful companion. But most of me is completely united with my fate. From the time its contours were first revealed during the First Seven Days of Creation, there has never been a single contradictory omen to call it into question. Jumbler herself, the one person with most to lose, has steadfastly counseled me to carry out the mandate.

Beginning tonight, I am linked to the whole world with the same intimate connection I've previously shared only with Jumbler. It may be a poetic exaggeration to say that from this day forward I am officially the Global Love Slave; nonetheless, there is a huge grain of truth in that title.

Even more problematical for Jumbler, tonight will bring my first literal sexual encounter with a human being other than her. As Madame Blavatsky put it on Day One of the First Seven Days of Creation, I will begin "administering the tantric yoni juju directly to one of the elite contagious agents among the beloved enemy." I will set the healing infection in motion.

The funeral parade has been continuing to proceed slowly up Pacific Avenue. I gaze back to take in the spectacle. On the float directly behind us, Sibyl, the oldest member of the Menstrual Temple, is filling a large iron cauldron with paper and objects that she is gathering from people along the route.

"Give me a written statement or symbol of your most heart-rending anguish," she's saying over her microphone, "and I will conduct a ritual of purification during which I will burn that statement or symbol to ash as I pray for your deliverance. This may not extinguish your pain completely, but it will conjure a healing that you will be able to feel the benefits of within days. Guaranteed by the Televisionary Oracle!"

Behind Sibyl is our one and only Cadillac convertible. Three of the Menstrual Temple's beefiest babes, Tara, Wendy, and Alana, are sitting on the back of the car wearing, aptly enough, bikinis made from round slabs of baloney sewn carefully together by our excellent seamstress Dagmar. Given the fact that each of them tips the scales at over two hundred twenty, a lot of lunchmeat has been sacrificed.

The three bathing beauties are handing out party favors to the crowd, among which are "Owl Pellet Dissection Kits" (includes actual owl pellets, plastic forceps, magnifying glass, and bone sorting chart) and bumperstickers that read "Daily Dream Work Prevents Genocide of the Imagination" and "Own Your Shadow Or It Will Own You." Every now and then they're also sneaking in a select few "Unconditional Love Certificates." These precious documents assure their owners that the Menstrual Temple's Prayer Warriors will conjure a flurry of fierce petitions to the Goddess Herself in their behalf for a given hour in the near future.

Dancing women, faces hidden by skull masks, are weaving around the floats. They're clothed in black body suits with the image of a skeleton on both the front and back. Over this foundation, they wear red satin merrywidows, silver lace bras and panties, crotchless emerald silk leotards, and other lingerie. Jingle bell bracelets adorn their ankles and wrists. Now and then some of them sing a chant I heard in the first vision of Madame Blavatsky:

If I be dead
or seem to be
It means that death
can't come for me

And so I bleed
Pretend to die
And live again
to kiss the sky

After the bathing beauties, the next float back in the procession is the home of "Shotgun Marriages of You to Yourself." It features a garlanded gazebo and life-sized papier-mâché figures of a tiger bride and wolf groom. Indigo, the Menstrual Temple's only ordained Unitarian minister, is offering to officiate the wedding of any audience member who is brave enough to tie the knot with his or her own "bad self."

I can make out a heavy-set man standing next to Indigo on the float, presumably undertaking the ceremony that she and I created for the occasion. I imagine with satisfaction how she's prompting him to repeat the vows that will bind him to the magic of self-respect. "I will never forsake you," he'll promise himself. "I will unfailingly bless you with all the love I am capable of summoning." And at the climax of the rite, Indigo will say to him, "I now pronounce you Husband and Wife."

As I've been contemplating the wedding float, an amusing fantasy has sneaked up from my subconscious mind. In the parlance of the tantric code Jumbler and I have developed, I am seeing in my mind's eye a vision of myself *shepherding a tender thunderbolt*. From the perspective of the English language, though, I am holding a hard cock. It vaguely belongs to a specific male who will soon be playing an interesting role in my master plan.

This is, I reiterate, happening in my imagination. I have never actually done such a thing in waking reality. My dear disembodied Rumbler and I messed around a lot in the Televisionarium when I was a teenager, although even there I never partook in what Rumbler has recently become fond of calling "wang dang doodle."

It's also true that Jumbler is not just a woman. With her amorphous

414

gender—testicular tissue mixed in with a uterus and ovaries, plus a rather sizable pearly root (tantric code for clitoris)—she's a little bit of a man herself. And I have enjoyed thousands of erotic exchanges with her: marathon eyegasms, shamanic bellylaugh climaxes, crown chakra fluttergasms, and so many other varieties of bliss it would take eons to catalogue them with the detail they deserve.

Still, by most standards, I am a virgin in the realm of heterosexual sex.

And I have most definitely never held an actual erect penis in my hand.

In a few hours, that changes. Later tonight, to celebrate the ancient feast of Beltane, the May Queen will consort for the first time with a May King. The Chief Shamanatrix of the Menstrual Temple of the Funky Grail will take as her temporary husband a man who has been initiated into the mysteries of menstruation. I emphasize the word *temporary*. In my role as Global Initiatrix of the Fuckissimus, I plan to draft quite a number of temporary husbands in the coming years. Through it all, however, Jumbler will remain my freaky consort.

I should be clear, though, that I do not intend to be merely a nirvanic vessel of the Great Goddess during my direct engagements with tender thunderbolts. I will not be motivated purely out of duty to the noble goal of killing the bad apocalypse and resurrecting the good one. Carnal curiosity is a feeling I am most definitely not ashamed of.


I gaze with pride and joy back at the funeral parade snaking behind me. Almost everything I dreamed of has come to fruition. All the floats seethe with spooky but uplifting rituals which the crowd can't help but yearn to participate in. In addition to the themes I've already named, there's the display representing the "Proud to Be Humble" contingent of the Menstrual Temple, a group which for one dollar will kiss volunteers' naked butts (or fully clothed if they're too modest) while listening intently to them brag about anything their heart desires and asking them good questions to spur them on.

Behind that one is the "Videomancy" booth, where Burgundy, our resident oracle, is responding to seekers' requests for divinatory advice by flicking on a good old-fashioned (battery-operated) television (not a Televisionary Oracle) at just the right cosmic moment to capture the random phrase on a random channel that will supply the necessary guidance.

There are two roving Menstrual Temple therapists who aren't confined to a float. Anna and Firenze are wearing T-shirts that advertise their special services to anyone in the crowd who asks: "Casting Love Spells on Yourself" and "How to Read Your Own Mind." Now and then they also sneak in stage-whispered promos for "How To Stop Thinking About Yourself All the Time."

Krista, five floats back, is giving "Emergency Dance Lessons for the Ecstatically Challenged." The rhythmic, writhing strains of Feminist Orgy Network provide her soundtrack.

Near the end of the parade, though I can't see them right now, Calley and Goolagaya are demonstrating "Laughing Sex Tantra" with the help of the Menstrual Temple's answer to the inflatable doll, our eight-armed, ten-foot-tall scarecrow with a fully functional Televisionary Oracle in her belly. A little later, as we draw closer to the cemetery, the two chortling sexperts will begin initiating audience members into the mysteries of the reverse striptease, the art of playing strip poker with the sacred Menstrual Temple Tarot deck, and many other tantric specialties I've cooked up during my explorations of the Drivetime these last five years.

Among the performance art spectacles here today, I muse with pride, there are no crucifixes bathing in vats of urine. No chocolate-smeared comediennes jamming yams up their butts or tattooed torture experts lancing their chests with sharp steel rods (ho-hum) or midgets with strap-on dildoes smashing piles of televisions with sledgehammers. Ours is mischief after another manner.

Though I should confess that it's not entirely original. There is another artist, the self-proclaimed "demonically compassionate" lead singer of World Entertainment War, who seems to have tapped into the same vein of sacred blasphemy that I have.

I grab the microphone and command the crowd's attention. "I'm ready, beauty and truth fans," I proclaim. "Are you ready? What do you say we start heading towards the crux of this lovely crock of bull. The question behind all our other questions. The holy probing fun that shatters all weak-hearted conceptions. Help me out here, my dears. Lead me unto rosy red temptation. What chant is the Goddess horniest to hear? Where do all our explorations lead tonight?"

"What exactly are you doing to kill the apocalypse?" yells the crowd, spurred on by all the menstrual lingerie models here on the lead float.

"What?" I say. "What artifacts are you using to chill the cops' lips?! What does that mean?"

The cry goes up again, more forceful and precise this time. "What exactly are you doing to kill the apocalypse?"

"Oh, now I understand you. 'What exactly are you doing to kill the apocalypse?' As in, 'What progress are you making in your all-out war against the silliest form of death?' Though to be truthful I hate to even dignify it by calling it death—it's such an insult to the concept."

I glance over at the Televisionary Oracle screen here on the float. It's the scene of a mushroom cloud sprouting from the end of Jesus Christ's erect penis, as if in an ejaculation, then breaking away from his body and floating skyward, only to morph into a giant psilocybin mushroom, which billows and blooms and bursts into a rain of thousands of smaller mushrooms. They fall to earth, where they are welcomed into the upturned mouths of women of all races wearing lingerie over their khaki soldier uniforms.

"So who's first to testify today?" I call out. "Which of you beauty and truth fans wants to name the murderous love you're invoking to slaughter the goddamn fucking end of the world?"

I'm not worried if there's no one brave enough in the audience to leap up on the slowly-moving float and take a shot. There'll be no dead time. All the menstrual lingerie models lounging on the beds have prepared spiels to deliver.

For a moment it looks like a middle-aged woman carrying a toddler is about to come forward, but she chickens out. I turn around and wink at Monika, the youngest member of the Menstrual Temple, who liked one of my texts so much she agreed to memorize and perform it.

She's a big-boned, handsome dyke. Her menstrual lingerie consists of a velvet burgundy teddy under a see-through yellow tunic and sky-blue suede hotpants. I hand her the microphone.

"There's a German actor named Udo Kier," she begins. "He's a specialist in playing villains. I read an interview with him where he just about jacked himself off bragging and swaggering about his own idiotic nihilism. 'Evil has no limit,' he sneered, as if he were the first genius in the history of the world to arrive at that piercing insight. 'Good has a limit,' he blustered. 'It's not as interesting.' Here's what I have to say about that: *What a hackneyed, pompous ass!* Though it's true most of the journalists in the world seem to agree with him. And I'm obviously in a minority in my belief that evil is a fucking bore. But how dare Udo Kier or anyone else proclaim that 'good has a limit' when there are so few smart artists and thinkers who are brave and resourceful enough to explore the frontiers of goodness?

"Which is where I come in," Monika raves on, wrapping up her rant. "The way I'm killing the apocalypse is by studying really hard, working every day, to synthesize compassion and lust, irony and sincerity, bright enthusiasm and righteous rage. I've pledged not to automatically assume negative feelings are more profound and interesting and real than positive ones, or that pessimistic opinions are smarter than the optimistic kind. Amen and hallelujah, forever and ever. So mote it be."

As scattered cheers ripple from the crowd, a volunteer comes forward and clambers onto the float. He looks Native American. Dressed in a denim jacket, he wears his long black hair in two braids.

"There are two kinds of vision," he says carefully. "*Hard eyes* and *soft eyes.* The first is when you have such fixed concepts about a person or thing that you don't truly see it as it stands before you; you only see your own ideas about it. The second is when you strip away all prejudgments and view the person or thing freshly, as if God created it just a moment ago. When you use *soft eyes,* you're constantly amazed at how different the world is from what everyone says it is. When you use *soft eyes,* your capacity for killing the apocalypse becomes prodigious."

As quickly as he came up, he disappears. His rap is perhaps too subtle for the crowd to get worked up about. There's no big burst of hoots and applause. Myself, I loved it.

I sneak a peek at Jumbler. Her face is a mess of mixed emotions. Knowing how her mind works, I'm positive she loved the guy's testimony. But I'm also aware of how ambivalent she feels about men right now. It's not a rational thing—she'd be the first to admit. It's a gut reaction to the prospect of her boon companion breaking the alchemical seal to consort with a strange lover.

Among her feelings, I happen to know, is the certainty that the man I have chosen to be my first temporary husband is not good enough for me. He's too loud, too crude, too … manly. I've actually had the same inklings myself. I'm nobility, for Goddess' sake, and he's a peon. A talented peon, perhaps, but a peon nonetheless. Now and then, in harmony with the thoughts Jumbler carries more fixedly, I feel like I'll demean myself by letting him think he's important enough to touch my body with his own.

I first saw him last December. Though I rarely go out to hear live music, Monika had been bugging me to see the Sacred Sluts of the YaYa GaGa, a five-woman group that plays goth-tinged funk. I accompanied my friend to the Catalyst, where the Sluts were opening the show for another band.

I liked them, though they were too unsubtle for my tastes, with giant phallus-shaped candles burning atop their amplifiers and numerous songs with S & M themes, though I did laugh profusely when they played "Bend Over Boyfriend."

But it was the headlining band, World Entertainment War, that cracked open my doors of perception. The two women in the ensemble were smart and sexy, with far more soul, I thought, than the Sluts. And the male lead singer, who I found out later has appropriated the (presumably) ironic nickname of "Rockstar," was absolutely, inscrutably worthy of great study. On the one hand he was doing an excellent rendition of the orgiastic god Dionysus. I mean, he truly seemed to be in a *matriarchal* version of ecstatic trance, dancing and singing not with the typical rockstar's macho-bully squall, but with a graceful abandon that led him through an irresistible quick-change panorama of receptive and inviting moods.

At the same time, Rockstar was making fun of all the ways he seemed to be taking himself so seriously. For instance, during a song called "Thunder in the Earth," he periodically burst out of a yoga-like series of erotic movements to perform goofy flails and stumbles that sort of wrecked the sexy mood, but you didn't mind because it invoked a playful innocence that took the edge off the potentially overwrought mojo.

For another for instance, about halfway through the show, he disappeared from the stage while the band began a song on which the two women sang wordless vocals. Halfway through the piece, Rockstar emerged wearing only a red jockstrap stuffed with ten-dollar bills, then jumped into the crowd and pressed the money against audience members' foreheads. If dancing had made their skin sufficiently sweaty to keep the bills glued on, they got to keep them. Otherwise, he snatched them back. Finally, he leapt back on the stage and proceeded to dance provocatively as he donned, item by item, the uniform of a corporate CEO, down to the red power tie. "I performed the Reverse Strip-Tease Potlatch," he proclaimed after it was over, "in honor of the unsung suffering of the filthy rich."

I liked the way this dude piled up his metaphors in great big heaps. The scent of the Drivetime wafted from him.

Then there were the lyrics. I found almost all of them fascinating—highly unusual for me, being the picky, judgmental critic I am. "Pray to You" was one of my favorites. To the accompaniment of a sinuous rhythm and a Middle Eastern scale, Rockstar and the main female singer (they shared the spotlight equally) sensually intoned these lyrics:

> Those were the days when everybody prayed
> to the god with the biggest penis
> Those were the times when only one word rhymed
> with Isis or with Venus
>
> It's a mystery
> why history turned out to be a cover-up
> We're so sorry
> Allow us to offer up a remedy
>
> Pray to Her, Jesus
> Pray to Her, Buddha Allah
> Pray to her Zeus Jehovah Shiva Horus

The Sacred Sluts, who opened the night, were sacred in name only. They exploited the term without, apparently, knowing much about its meaning. I'm an expert on the subject, so I know.

The members of World Entertainment War, on the other hand,

created certifiably sacred space. They were also, for anyone who had the eyes to see, playing with real occult themes that I've never seen any professional entertainer refer to—let alone in a beer-stained rock and roll nightclub. "As above, so below," one of the core mantras of Western mysticism, was a chorus refrain in one song. Another piece, "Snake Dance," spoke openly about the alchemical and yogic principle of building an immortal "light body" by raising the sex force out of the genitals and up to the crown chakra.

About a third of the way into the "show," Rockstar even pulled off a somewhat disguised, comically mutated, but unmistakable version of a ceremonial magick rite, including all the elements you'd find in any self-respecting hermetic or pagan order. At this point I lost all doubt that he had been trained in a mystery school himself.

I left the Catalyst feeling nonplussed, not the least reason being that I felt a glimmer of attraction to Rockstar. For the first half of my adolescence I'd fantasized about having boyfriends, and I'd had an active relationship with my disembodied soul brother Rumbler, but since I met Jumbler the male gender had become an amorphous mass in which no individual face drew my attention. As I developed the details of my work in the world, I made plans to heal and correct the ravages of men's sickness, in part by taking on the role of "High Priestess of the Global Jiggy Snake." But I never felt any magnetic attraction to an actual guy.

Of course, I questioned my fascination with Rockstar. Wasn't I intrigued, simply, by his art and its implications for my own work? There was no need to imagine seeking a personal connection with him, especially since it was likely that his public persona was nothing like his private self.

When I bought all the recordings he and his various bands had made over the years, and when I began attending every one of his live shows, I told myself I was merely researching the career of an artist who might be able to teach me something. I used the same rationale when I showed up at the library to pore over old publications that might have reviews of his shows and records, or that might contain the little articles he writes. But as I uncovered more and more evidence of how artfully he had integrated his occult ideas into pop culture formats, it became more difficult to resist trying to arrange to meet him.

The front of the funeral parade has just left Pacific Avenue, turning right on Water Street and preparing to make a quick left on River Street. I'm glad to see the crowd has not thinned out. As the afternoon wears on (and maybe because intoxicating substances are taking effect), we're having no trouble getting volunteers to climb up on the float and testify about how they're killing the apocalypse.

"I invented the eleventh commandment," exults a thin woman with a slinky red satin dress on, "and I obey it always: Thou Shalt Not Bore the Goddess!"

"I've taught myself to think with my heart and feel with my head!" says a young man with delicate features and hair down to the middle of his back.

"I'm visualizing and praying that sometime soon we will see a headline on the front page of *USA Today* that says 'Why Do 95% of the World's Women Never Get Their Orgasm Experience?'" This testimony comes from a rowdy-looking redneck woman in her forties.

A school marm with an introverted-looking face but whose blouse is unbuttoned to her solar plexus says with pride, "I'm teaching eight-year-olds to honor and work with their dreams. Every morning, when their visits to the other side are still fresh, I ask them, 'Where did you go last night? What adventures did you have while you were sleeping? I bet they were better than any movie or TV show you've ever seen.' Together the kids and I remember the *other* world we live in. We honor the shades which have become so vengeful, so apocalyptic, because of the patriarchs' neglect."

Some rants are just silly, but I'm grateful for them. "I plunged butcher knives into accordions," says a grizzled poetry chick. "I hijacked a UFO and abducted some aliens, sold celebrity sperm on the home shopping channel, strolled around the mall with my sweetie wearing matching nipple rings peeking through our matching see-through plastic S & M blouses, jumped rope while wearing high heels, and spanked the devil with a ping pong paddle. But most of all I avoided thinking about winning the lottery while making love."

One of the most unexpected statements comes from a well-dressed older woman. "I'm celebrating the successes of patriarchy. Because I believe the only way to get rid of it is to love it to death. I'm praising the masculine. Hooray for suspension bridges. How'd they ever figure out how to make those things, anyway? Hooray for chemotherapy; I'd be nothing without it. Actually I'd be lying under six feet of dirt right now. Hooray for all the dead white men who wrote such great books. Kept me from getting bored. That's all I have to say."

Interspersed between the testimonials of people from the crowd are little speeches from some of the menstrual lingerie models here on the lead float.

Cecily, one of my moms (delivering a text I helped her write): "I work to repudiate the myth that men are more objective than women. In my opinion, a man's opinions are as rooted in his emotional fixations as a woman's are in hers. But men try to hide their irrationality behind a well-rationalized front of 'logical objectivity.' Just because they're so skilled at suppressing their emotions—or should I say just because they're so unskilled at knowing what they feel?—doesn't mean their ideas and opinions are any less driven by their emotions."

Artemisia, also one of my moms, delivers the wackiest spiel. "Well, I got sick and tired of all those mass hallucinations," she begins, "excuse me, I mean 'visions' of the Virgin Mary. In the clouds over Lisbon. In the plate glass window of the office building in San Antonio. In the tree-tops at Medjugorge. Et cetera ad nauseum. It was getting so you couldn't open a copy of the *National Enquirer* without seeing the so-called Holy Mother's ghostly ghastly smiling face. Which I wouldn't have minded except for the fact that the bitch is extremely fond of issuing death threats. In other words, she's a phallocratic stooge! Behind her mommysweet expression is one hell of a bad-ass Jehovah-like temper.

"'If you do not pray to me more often,' she scolds, 'I will incinerate your cities with fire from the sky! If you do not stop having so much sex, I will murder half the population with AIDS! If you do not stop having abortions, I will send an asteroid plunging into New York City!' Et cetera ad nauseum. Cranky jerk is just another secret weapon in the bad daddies' conspiracy to perpetrate the self-fulfilling prophecy of armageddon.

"So anyway, I took matters into my own hands. Me and my focus group. Started flexing our hex power. Meditated and visualized and shamanically-traveled like crazy. Yea for the Drivetime! 'O Great and Ever-Cackling Goddess Persephone,' we prayed, 'Burn that nasty Virgin Mary's goddamned "heaven" to the ground. Give us more interesting heavens, for anti-Christ's sake.'

"And guess what? It's working. In spades. Visions of Persephone are popping up everywhere! We call it Yo Mama's World Tour. Her ratings are starting to rival the Virgin Bitch's. Our Cackling Lady's been way up in the middle of a cloud in Buenos Aires. Smack in the heart of a billboard pizza in Cincinnati. Shimmering in an oil stain on the floor of a car repair shop's bathroom in Fresno. Everywhere She needs to be to help slaughter the end of the world."

Having made the turn down Coral Street, the parade finally arrives at Evergreen Cemetery. By rough estimate, gazing down the snaky line of floats, I'd say maybe four hundred non-Menstrual Temple people have followed us this far.

"Beauty and truth fans," I cry after waiting for more of the crowd to gather at the front float, "the apocalypse has been our totem. It has been the ultimately powerful and sacred taboo, the most terrible and the most valuable thing, the superhuman profanity on which all life depended and against which all values were tested. Shadowing every one of our personal actions, the apocalypse has been the fascinating blasphemy that wouldn't shut up unless we were all very, very good.

"We've fallen down before it, believing in it more fiercely than any other secret. We've agreed to be possessed by it, to be haunted by its image above all other images. Nothing else has had more deadly life.

"We've loved the apocalypse because it has been the most supernatural nightmare in the world, the only nightmare that has ever threatened to change all life on Earth instantly and forever. It's the dark and precious god, the promise of a revelation that would redefine the meaning of all history.

"And yet how few of us have ever stood next to the magic body of a nuclear bomb or a vial of anthrax, breathed in its smell, touched it, communed with its actual life? How few of us have actually seen any of the hundreds of species that are going extinct at a rate unmatched since the demise of the dinosaurs sixty-five million years ago? How few of us have actually measured the shrinking ozone layer or seen the rapidly melting ice of Antarctica as greenhouse gases warm the Earth? The presence of these things is rumor and mystery to most of us, like Christ and flying saucers. We hear stories.

. "At night our dreams have turned the apocalypse into the philosopher's stone, the ark of the covenant, the alchemical gold, the magic body of the messiah, the potent drug from the beginning of the world, the ecstatic and shocking moment of religious conversion. In our deepest darkest juices we have been alive to its divinity, as we are alive to any god that offers the brilliant and blinding flash of irreversible illumination. We have believed in the apocalypse because it has seemed to reveal what it is to melt back into the dangerous light that's as pure as the sun.

"Let's call the apocalypse a love that has been too big for us to understand until now. Let's say it has been the raging creative life of a cleansing disease that has wanted to cure us so it didn't have to kill us. Let's say it has been the last judgment that promises not to come true if we can figure out what it means. And we *have* figured out what it means.

"It's our apocalypse. We're the ones who made it, all of us. We've loved this apocalypse so much we imagined it could happen. We created this apocalypse so hard that it came alive and possessed us. We turned the apocalypse into our bodies; we gave messages to chemicals in our brains to make dangerous images of the apocalypse, messages to nurture and worship and flash those images through our nerves.

"The apocalypse has been the most beloved thing to us, because as we've all together imagined it our brains have been burned with the true hallucination that we are all one body. When we've fantasized the apocalypse returning us all to the primal ooze, we've remembered that you and I are made of the same stuff. The apocalypse has freed us to imagine that we all live and die together.

"Until now, we have needed the apocalypse.

"Until now, we have needed the apocalypse because only the tease of the biggest, most original sin could heal us. The apocalypse has been a blind, a fake, a trick memory we're sending ourselves from the future that has shocked us better than all the anti-Christs and AIDS and UFOs.

"So bless the fear, beauty and truth fans. Praise the danger. Let the great ugly power fascinate us all one last time, fix our terror so precisely that we become one potently concentrated ferocious imagination, a single guerrilla meditator casting an irreversible spell to bind the great satan apocalypse.

"There will be no apocalypse."

Monika leads seven Menstrual Temple pallbearers as they hoist the golden casket from the lead float and carry it into the cemetery. I wonder if anyone knows I lifted parts of my elegy from an old piece of writing by Rockstar?

I'll confess to him in person when I see him later. Tonight, this feast of Beltane will be the occasion of the first menarche for a member of the male gender in more than six thousand years. It will also herald a sacred boink between the Divine Avatar of the Cackling Vulture Goddess Persephone and a mildly amusing small-time rock star who may or may not be up to the task of embodying the sixty-six-million-year-old snake god.

As you commune with the Televisionary Oracle
Visualize the Silk Furrow and the Jade Stalk
Root for the Fluttering Phoenix and the Golden Bough
Pray to the Pearly Grove and the Justice Root
Exult in the Blooming Ha-Ha and the Starry Plough
Champion the Ambrosial Thicket and the Righteous Supplicant
Be curious about the Rumble Chamber and the Swooping Dabbler
Balance the Bombastic Lotus and the Tender Thunderbolt
Bear witness to the Chthonic Riddler and the Frisky Risker
Create sanctuary for the Rosy Manger and the Raunchy Weaver
Act crazy for the Honeyed Gateway and the Grateful Harvester
Look everywhere
for Quetzalcoatl's Gangplank and the Worshipful Pouncer

As far as the Goddess is concerned, beauty and truth fans, there's no such thing as heterosexuality. No such thing as homosexuality or bisexuality, for that matter. Even bestiality does not go far enough. Nor does the flower-boinking of the early Gnostics, or the sky copulations of the Essenes, or the fist-fucking of the holy ocean by the ancient Sapphic cults.

As far as the Goddess is concerned, there is only Pantheosexuality. Also known as Polymorphous Perverse Omnidirectional Goddess-Caressing. All else is a lie, an obscene limitation. You can only be in mad loving lust with ALL of Goddess, not some of Her. To be in love with some and not all of Her is to be in love with none of Her.

Therefore, we will now begin the ritual of the World Kiss. We will apply our tender loving lips and tongues to every quivering portion of the Goddess' outrageous joybody in this place. And we promise to keep uppermost in our emotions, with every smooch, a mood of demonic compassion, primordial sweetness, ironic sincerity, and blasphemous reverence. We will be always mindful that it's not enough simply to perform the outer gesture; we will aim to have heart-ons in all seven of our chakras.

Smacking our lips with a rat-a-tat of cartoon kisses, we glide over to the altar, which is built atop a giant old faux wood television. Here we do hereby kiss thee, candles and pomegranates and chrysanthemums. We press our warm lips against thee too, whooping crane feather and Venus of Willendorf figurine and silver bowl filled with good rich earth from the garden. Black knife, gold coin, and toy rubber unicorn, come hither: We wish to anoint thee with our love. Necklace of tiny dove skulls, chalice filled with dragon blood, sacred wand fashioned from the rod inside the toilet: As we bestow on thee our moist butterfly jiggles, we channel the pulse of our heart-ons into every luscious atom of the Goddess' sexy creaturehood.

But our Pantheosexual yearning does not end here. Onward! Towards new frontiers of kissability! Who or what offers itself up next to our osculatory worship? Djembe drum, thou strikes us as a pure embodiment of the Goddess' love of functional beauty. We pay homage to thee with flickering licks. Black flag, we smother thee with our blazing snuggles. Maypole with thy blue, red, yellow, and green ribbons, feel the fluttering graze of our undying devotion.

Though we've had erotic epiphanies while watching ruby-throated hummingbirds feeding from plum flowers, we've never enjoyed the shivering palpitations we feel now as we contemplate communion with the black carpet below us. As we swaddle thee with our yearning arms, dear carpet, we impregnate our shamanic intention deep into thy weave, deep into the lambs that sacrificed their wool for thee to live, deep into the hands that assembled thee.

At the foot of the altar, we slither our maws against *The Woman's Encyclopedia of Myths and Secrets*. We picture our righteous, tantrically sublimated kundalini, tinctured with heart medicine, spraying out the tops of our heads in a violet velvet cloud of blessing on every thought that was packed into thee, on the tree that died so that thy paper might live, on every ounce of ink shaped into thy magical words.

To the doorknob and the wall sockets and the light switch and the dead fly on the window sill, we pledge our undying adoration; and though we may later become separated in space, we will always remain joined in this exquisite embrace in eternity.

To the air itself, we send this message with our kisses: Since our particles and thy particles were ripped asunder at the Big Bang, we have fantasized obsessively of the rapturous reunion in which we now exult.

WE ARE THEE AND THEE ARE WE!

As a public service,
the Televisionary Oracle
reminds you of what Jesus said
in the gnostic Gospel of Thomas:

*If you give birth to the genius within you,*
*it will free you.*
*If you do not give birth to the genius within you,*
*it will destroy you.*

42

I am not easily thrown off-kilter. My own outrageousness has made me poised in the face of outrageous events. Did I lose my cool when the 7.1 Loma Prieta earthquake erupted moments after Demetria threw her legs around my waist and buried my jade stalk in her Greek crucible? I did not. I sensibly cruised us both, still joined, over to the nearest doorframe, best place to be in a quake, and continued our rock and roll while the walls of the house shimmied and groaned.

Did I, furthermore, reel with debilitating embarrassment at the age of nineteen when my astrologer pointed out she'd calculated my horoscope wrong, and that I had therefore spent three days and nights camping alone in the White Mountains of New Hampshire meditating on aspects of my destiny which did not exist? I did not reel. Rather, I hee-hawed and forgave myself on the spot.

Now, however, here in the kitchen of India Joze at 2:35 A.M. on a warm spring night, as I ply my new trade as janitor, my near-perfect record of unshockability comes to an end.

I've just fixed myself a big plate of gado-gado with lots of peanut sauce, plus a dessert of strawberry cheesecake. It's time for my break. I've been scouring and mopping and scrubbing for over two hours.

As I begin my stroll from the main refrigerator towards the dining area to sit down, I hear scuffling from the door at the rear of the kitchen. I curse myself. Shouldn't have left it open. Dave, the guy whose job I took over, said he'd never been bothered by bums strolling in looking for handouts in the middle of the night, but it seems I won't be so lucky.

I set my feast down on a counter, grab a butcher knife, and skulk back to investigate.

But it is not a grizzled homeless dude hovering in the doorway. It is a vision of bizarre loveliness. As I gaze upon it, my knees become the consistency of squid, and I half-crumple to the floor. An exotic blend of adrenaline and lust fountains out of my heart with such a sudden gush that I wonder whether I'm having a heart attack.

It's Rapunzel. In extremity. A grinning crazy pretty witch doctor from the pages of *Vogue*. A New Guinea supermodel on LSD.

She has woven giant silver seedpods into her disheveled auburn hair, which is half-piled Louis XIV-style on top of her head and half-streaming down. Somehow, a white and gold Pope's mitre decorated with a picture of a vulture balances tentatively on top. Her long hula skirt is composed in part of mummified snakes and animal tails. Her belt is a chain of shrunken heads with a suspicious resemblance to recognizable characters like Joseph Stalin, Ronald Reagan, Dan Rather, Carl Sagan, and Mick Jagger.

On top she wears a pinstriped baseball jersey which is a more colorful version of the one she gave me in the Catalyst bathroom. The first couple of buttons are unbuttoned, revealing a black lace bra beneath. On the left side of the shirt is an embroidered logo. The title, however, is not "Menstrual Temple," as I might expect, but "The Eater of Cruelty." Accompanying it is a depiction of a winged angel digging in a garbage can.

On the other side of the shirt is a large pocket with a brooch bearing a photo of one of my heroes, Antonin Artaud, the French playwright. Below the photo is a caption that reads "Use your nightmares to become rich and famous."

Lustful fantasies are immediately going full bore. I'm lying on top of Rapunzel, swimming madly as I pour my soul into her green eyes. But I'm also surging with a less familiar emotion: loving tenderness. My longing to bless her and give her presents is so strong it's scary. Am I really capable of feeling so sweet and soft and open-hearted? I just barely hold back my tongue from saying the words that are forming in the back of my throat.

*I'm amazed at how affectionate I feel towards you, how excited I am by your funny power. I love the way you change me. I love the way you crack me up.*

My dream woman has brought props. In one hand is a black bag similar to the kind carried by doctors who used to make house calls. In the other hand is a broom made of the trunk of a young tree with the branches lopped off. This tool hangs over her shoulder, and a gold bucket dangles from the end of it.

"Hi," she bubbles, "I'm Pope Artaud, Chief Tantric Janitor of The Eater of Cruelty."

I monitor the sparkling twists and turns of the wild mind behind her eyes.

"Do you need any help in scouring away your karma tonight, Osiris? You don't mind if I call you Osiris, do you? Seems like a more fitting name than 'Rockstar,' especially now that you've given up music for the janitorial life."

She has come close enough to swish the broom back and forth over my boots.

"Or would you prefer to alchemize your psychic crud indirectly, by cleaning the hell out of this grungy kitchen?" She waves her arm with a flourish, like an assistant on a game show showing off the new car that could be won.

*Teach me to understand what captivates your imagination. Don't hide anything from me. Let me listen to you talk for hours. I want to help you name your genius, coax it out, build it up. I want to be your muse.*

"Correct me if I'm wrong," I sputter, "but I thought you were the Supreme Arbiter of the Menstrual Temple of the Funky Grail."

"That's my other gig. Tonight I'm Pope Artaud, Spiritual Head of all Tantric Janitors."

"Pope? But why not Popesse? Doesn't Pope mean father? Better yet, why not call yourself High Priestess?"

"You should know by now that I can change into any gender I need to be. Those strict definitions of man and woman are the patriarchy's specialty, not mine. My archetypes are mutating."

"I know what the Theater of Cruelty is," I say. "I've been an Artaud fan since I was practically a toddler. But what exactly is The Eater of Cruelty?"

I'm going to pump her with questions, keep her talking. I want to bask in the majesty of her presence for as long as possible.

"Let's say it's the janitorial wing of the Menstrual Temple; the group that gathers the raw materials for the Menstrual Temple's eucharistic rituals."

"You must know," I say, "that Artaud himself would have considered the real Pope a mutilator of the heart. It was Nietzsche who called Christianity a religion for slaves, but I'm sure Artaud would have agreed. Aren't you blaspheming Artaud by associating his name with the enemy?"

*Take all you want from me. Show me your secrets so I can help them bloom and thrive. I want to be an expert at responding to your longing. Let me be the one who gives you yourself.*

"We're as opposite to Artaud as Artaud was to the Pope," she harrumphs as she sweeps the floor, heaping up a pile of food scraps I've missed. "Only we're also opposite to the Pope. That's the great thing about being a tantric janitor—you're opposite to everyone, even yourself. You get to blaspheme all of creation, especially the things you love best.

"And we especially love Artaud. That's why we take what we need from him, throw the rest away, and become the Anti-Artaud. We've transmuted his dark religion into a joyful game he'd never have approved of. Although, to be perfectly frank, we've been around for many eons before Artaud ever came along."

"And how exactly are you the anti-Artaud?"

Rapunzel reaches down into the midst of the pile of garbage she has accumulated with her broom. She plucks out some unidentifiable shred of black scum and holds it up to her lips as if to take a bite. At the last moment, just as I'm about to come to the rescue and snatch it out of her hand, she gives it a big smacking kiss and hurls it back over her shoulder.

"To Artaud," she says, "the world was God's abandoned rot. We think he didn't see deeply enough. The rot's there, all right, but the splendor's hidden inside it. We Eaters of Cruelty like to go rummaging around looking for all that good stuff. The treasure in the trash. The gold in the lead. The manna in the junk food."

Rapunzel heads into the bowels of the kitchen, carrying her black bag, broom, and bucket. I paddle after her.

*My bliss is to follow your bliss. I want to feel your nerve endings in my body. I want to sense your endorphins billowing in my brain.*

433

"I have a feeling," I say to her as I lean against a table, "that this has something to do with you telling me to get a job as a janitor."

"*Tantric* janitor, to be exact. But I didn't want you to get distracted by the sexy tantric part until you mastered the janitor stuff. And by the way, I didn't *tell* you to get a job as a janitor. I made you an offer contingent on you becoming a janitor."

From her black bag, Rapunzel removes a pair of red silk boxer shorts.

"Go ahead and change into these," she says. "They're more fitting for an aspiring tantric janitor like you. Don't worry, I won't peek. Go over there behind the cutting table."

I get up to obey her instructions, not sure I want to be so exposed around her but determined not to resist the will of the high priestess.

"The English word *janitor* is from the Latin word *janitor*," she says loudly, "which meant 'doorkeeper.'"

I'm receiving a lesson in etymology as I get nearly naked with a woman I passionately desire?

"*Janitor* is derived from the Latin word *janus*, which in its generic use meant doorway or threshold. Janus was also the Roman god of doorways, of beginnings, and of the rising and setting of the sun. He was portrayed as having one head with two faces back to back looking in opposite directions.

"In this sense of the word, every shamanatrix in the Menstrual Temple of the Funky Grail is also a janitor in The Eater of Cruelty. We hang out in the thresholds and root around for the beauty buried in the gunk that collects there. Where the coming meets the going. Where the contradictions are greatest."

"Because menstruators are threshold-dwellers? In what way?"

"Menstruators are right there on the edge where death and life meet, with their unfertilized egg dying and the next egg beginning to ripen at the same time."

"I can see how menstruation would actually be a good metaphor for all thresholds."

"Yup. Though the Drivetime is probably the ultimate metaphor."

"And Drivetime is what? The 4 to 6 P.M. rush hour?"

"The Drivetime is our term for the wormhole that connects the Dreamtime and the Waketime. It's the tunnel you inhabit—the hypnogogic state—as you flow back and forth between the two realms. The Great Inbetween. The mobius strip-like seam at the heart of the tantric yabyum."

"I love that place."

"I know you do, which is why you've got so much potential as a menstruator."

"So tell me more about this Drivetime of yours."

"It's the condition you embody whenever you master the art of simultaneously inhabiting both of *any* two polarities. It's the joyous celebration of contradictions. The attitude which is always loyal to both sides of every opposition. The power spot where you agree with everything you disagree with and disagree with everything you agree with—and vice versa."

I've finished removing my janitorial duds and slipping into the shorts. I leave my old clothes folded in a pile on the butcher block. As I return to where she's sitting, Rapunzel pulls out a vial of dark red liquid and holds it up so I can see what's written on it: "Dragon's Blood." She screws off the top and applies some of the viscous stuff to her finger. Then she pulls down my waistband a bit and daubs a red triangle about three finger-widths below my navel. My hormones are in danger of electrifying.

"Rowdy ruby glissando," she chants, closing her eyes. "Rowdy ruby glissando. Rowdy ruby glissando. Rowdy ruby glissando."

She reaches into her bag again and pulls out a tampon. Well, no, it's not exactly a tampon. It's a tampon and tampon applicator that have been modified into a toy flute, the kind you play by sliding a smaller cylinder in and out of a bigger one. Rapunzel demonstrates the technique, playing a loopy version of "Pray to Her," a World Entertainment War song.

"Another threshold metaphor," she says, handing me the thing, "is the archetype of the Great Mother Goddess, known by the ancient Greeks as Demeter. It's through her womb that we are all born into the physical realm."

"I had a past life reading once where the psychic saw me curled up in the fetal position inside the belly of a woman as big as the planet Earth."

"Yes, well, that was real, wasn't it?"

"As real as a red wheelbarrow, in my book. More real, actually."

"Red wheelbarrow?" she says, lifting a lovely eyebrow. "As in the poem by William Carlos Williams?"

"'So much depends/upon//a red wheel/barrow//glazed with rain/water//beside the white/chickens.'"

"The beauty of ordinary things."

"Yes," I declare, feeling my own power returning. It is getting a little old, isn't it, for me to exude such relentless deference towards Rapunzel. And I can't imagine that she could find it attractive.

"But also," I press on, "it's a poem about the sensory world as the ultimate reality. The red wheelbarrow is Williams' symbol for the modern dogma that what you see is all there is, baby. Ain't no such thing as spirit or soul. And don't you go muddling up your brain trying to believe in such nonsense."

"I catch your drift," Rapunzel says. "And yes. The twenty-five-thousand-mile-circumference womb of Demeter is definitely more real than the red wheelbarrow."

"So you and I do live on the same planet after all." This is a daring flirtation.

"And then there's Demeter's daughter Persephone," she says, "the Underworld Queen. Also more real than a red wheelbarrow. She leads us over to the other side of the veil, either through dream or trance or death."

Uh-oh. She's fiddling around inside her bag again.

"Though to be honest," she says, "Demeter and Persephone are two faces of the same Goddess. One is the doorway in and one is the doorway out. As if the two together made up Janus the cosmic janitor."

"Sounds like the Hindu goddess Kali, too."

"Exactly. Kali is another Drivetime tutelary. Both womb and tomb, nurturer and destroyer."

"Though Kali's reputation is more as a destroyer, right? I read a hymn to her once that was titled, 'My Delight Is on Your Cremation Grounds.'"

"Propaganda, my dear. Vicious propaganda. Would you base your understanding of African-American folks on the rants of a white supremacist? The Drivetime-deprived phallocrats who're in charge of writing history have just never been able to get the hang of a divine intelligence who goes both ways. It's true that Kali burns heaven to the ground every day; it's true that she cracks your heart open and steals everything you own. But only so that you'll be empty enough to have room for her subtly stupendous gifts—which, by the way, include immortality and the ability to make love forever."

Rapunzel has laid down seven objects on the table. Like the flute, they began life as tampons, but their destiny is taking a different route. Rapunzel begins weaving them into my hair, turning them into curlers.

"Got to fix your hair for your date later on," she chirps as she works.

"What date is that?" I ask.

"Don't want to spoil the surprise, but here's a clue: She's got a twenty-five-thousand-mile-circumference womb."

"OK. Will you chaperone us, please?"

"If you're good."

She grabs a cannister of spray-on oil from one of the cook's stations and looks as if she's about to apply it to the areas she's bundling around the curlers.

"I must deny access to my hair with that noxious beauty aid," I laugh, playfully wresting the cannister out of her hand.

"I understand your concerns," she says evenly and goes back to putting in the tampon curlers. Am I fantasizing, or was that a test to see if I would stand up for myself? Maybe my ballsier attitude has caught her attention.

"So, Rapunzel. What's a practical example of living in the Drivetime?"

"Well. Do you know the books of Michael Harner? He's the pop anthropologist. A low-budget Mircea Eliade with more gnosis and less academic bullshit. Harner tells of conversing with a Jivaro shaman in Brazil who makes no distinction between his experiences in Dreamtime and waking life. One moment the shaman is describing how he used his magical powers to fly to a remote mountaintop cave and bathe in the medicine of a liquid rainbow; next moment he's talking about the delicious rabbits he caught while hunting yesterday, or the exceptional talent his wife's sister has for farting during solemn ceremonial occasions. This is one example of a person who knows how to live in the Drivetime."

"What's the difference," I interject, "between that and, say, the high school kids in Pennsylvania who got killed while imitating what they saw in a Disney movie? I guess they didn't make much of a distinction between fantasy and reality either. Just like the actors they saw, they played chicken by lying out in the middle of a highway at night and waiting till the last minute before dodging oncoming cars. Difference was the actors didn't actually die."

I hold up a shiny pan to catch a glimpse of my reflection. Don't exactly look my best. The growing bunches of rolled-up hair give my head an extraterrestrial shape.

"I'm sure you've also heard," I press on, "about how every time an actor portraying a doctor performs a particular kind of surgery on a popular soap opera, real doctors begin performing that same surgery at a dramatically higher rate in real American hospitals. All the poor jerks that thereby get unnecessary gall bladder surgery have a certain resemblance to the Jivaro shamans too."

"Well, that's very astute, Osiris—considering you don't really know what the hell you're talking about." Rapunzel cackles brightly, without a trace of hostility. "Certainly there is a superficial resemblance between the Jivaro shamans and the Pennsylvania high school fools. For both, there's a conflation of dimensions, an overlapping of worlds. The difference is that the Dreamtime visited by the Jivaro shamans is a real place. It's an objectively existing realm."

"I wonder if the Jivaro dudes could tell the difference between a Dreamtime red wheelbarrow and a Waketime one?"

"On the other hand," she says, ignoring my quip, "the kids in Pennsylvania were suffering from what you yourself call 'the genocide of the imagination.' They probably lost the ability to visit the real Dreamtime long about the three-thousandth televised murder they saw back in kindergarten. No, what overlapped their waking reality was, you might say, *Faux* Dreamtime. Once the entertainment criminals genocided their poor imaginations, they became eager receptacles for the withered hallucinations of Faux Dreamtime—deposited in them by those same entertainment criminals."

My infatuated fantasies have officially leapt to the next higher octave. Rapunzel is incorporating some of my own ideas into her rap, ideas I've proclaimed loud and strong from my bully pulpit as lead singer of World Entertainment War. "Genocide of the imagination" and "entertainment criminals" are virtually my trademarks. She also used them a few days ago when she invaded my home, true, but at that time they were merely fodder for her derisive attacks on me. Now she's weaving them lovingly into her analysis. I take this to be a sign that even if she does harbor serious criticisms of my work, she also regards it as interesting enough to steal from.

The implications of this make me giddy with greed. It means her potential is not just as a lyrical lover, not just as a challenging consort, but also as a rowdy partner in crime—a true equal with whom I can whip up twice the creative trouble I already do. I picture us sneaking out together at dawn to steal the garbage of a Bay Area celebrity, maybe Robin Williams or Adrienne Rich, and auctioning it off at an impromptu "Garbage Sale" during one of my shows. I visualize us collaborating on a rock opera about the Menstrual Temple and performing it at weekend-long salons which also include workshops on the Drivetime and rituals designed to foment holy mischief. I can even imagine us writing a book together. It could be called *How To Make Smart Love with Your Best Friend*.

"Drivetime is a hard-earned luxury," Rapunzel says as she steps back to admire her hairstyling efforts, "available only to those who've cultivated a vigorous relationship with the True Dreamtime while at the same time maintaining a practical grip on the very different rules of the Waketime. But oh is it a luxury."

"What the hell are those noises?" I say suddenly in response to sounds like voices and banging chairs out in the dining area. I'd heard them before but rationalized they were merely my overwrought imagination. Now they're getting too loud to ignore. "I'd better go check."

Rapunzel grabs both my arms and forces me to stay. "Don't worry about it," she says. "I invited a couple of friends in with me. They're out there straightening up."

"But how did they get in without me seeing them? The front door's locked."

"Never mind. It's time to get ready for the next part of your menarche." She reaches into her black doctor's bag. "Here's the rest of your menstrual lingerie."

The costume she hands me consists of emerald-green velvet knee pads, a satin plum-colored vest featuring an embroidered image of a vulture, and black satin slippers.

As I put on the rest of my outfit, Rapunzel leaves the kitchen and goes out to the dining area. A moment later I hear an explosion of many female voices doing that funny amazon ululation-cum-war whoop. My imagination gets goose-bumps.

Rapunzel returns and takes my hand.

"The Menstrual Temple's welcoming committee awaits you," she says invitingly. She walks me out of the dingy kitchen. Where the dining area begins there is a long, narrow red carpet, newly placed.

The room has been transformed by the addition of eighteen to twenty women, who're sitting at the tables. As I arrive, they applaud and blow me kisses. Though they're all ages, they have in common a slaphappy sartorial sense. I see a rainbow beret sprouting pheasant feathers and a khaki military shirt paired with yellow velvet overalls. There's a gold brocade frock coat and bulbous red clown nose and green silk pajamas and black chiffon skirt that looks like it has a bustle underneath.

The restaurant has mutated in other ways. Stretched across the back of the main room of the dining area is a banner that reads "The Eater of Cruelty Cafe." Below it is a neatly hand-drawn poster listing "Tonight's Specials":

> Breakfast of Amazons Cereal with Virgin's Milk
> Rosicrucian Coca-Cola
> Black Market Pudding from Below the Abyss
> Vinegar Tears of Lame Angels
> Loamy Ouroboric Christ Resin
> Tender Adrenaline Ice Cream with Ancient Spider Webs
> Sphinx's Bath Water with Chthonic Plum Ganglion
> Licorice Ash of Incinerated Testosterone
> Rowdy Ruby Glissando of the Silk Lotus

Near the menu, on two tables pushed together against the far wall, is what looks like a pagan altar. It's crammed with red candles and snapdragons and small animal skulls and a small cauldron and a hundred other things. The centerpiece is an odd television which resembles the one I saw in the gallery installation on the evening before World Entertainment War's last show at the Catalyst. It's either made of stone and mud or else is an ordinary TV with those materials glued on. In several places, vines sprout out of cracks in the mud.

The images on the screen are like those of intense dreams. At the moment, Abraham Lincoln is giving Mother Teresa a big wet hickey on her bare shoulder as they lie outside a Disneyland-like fortress called "Drug City" while an African grandmother dressed in a turban and a tuxedo holds up a sign on a stick that reads "This Bud's for you, Uberwoman."

When I arrived earlier tonight, the tables were covered with white linen. That has been replaced by red satin. Each table now sports a fanned-out deck of large Tarot cards, as well as an oversized silver goblet—about the height and heft, I fantasize, of the goblet used by the giant in the story of Jack and the Beanstalk.

"Here at The Eater of Cruelty Cafe we refer to that particular story as *Jill* and the Beanstalk, Osiris," Rapunzel says to me, although I haven't said what I was thinking.

"How could you have possibly known I was thinking about Jack and the Beanstalk?" I wonder.

"I have a telepathic homing device that turns on whenever I'm in the presence of a person who's ripe to have her archetypes mutated," she replies. "And I hope you'll forgive me if I use the feminine form as the all-purpose pronoun. Of course I mean to imply that my homing device also turns on in the presence of a person who's ripe to have *his* archetypes mutated. But you can't imagine how important it is to use 'she' and 'her' to refer to generic humanity. It could literally be a factor in whether or not all human life disappears from this planet in the next thirty years."

"I'll buy that," I say. "I've always wanted to save the world."

"Good, good," she approves. "I'm always looking for more soldiers to help me kill the apocalypse."

Rapunzel ushers me to a table in the middle of the room where there's a woman I recognize. It's impossible, but I do. She's Jumbler, the Norse leprechaun androgyne from my superdream. There's the same thick, flaxen helmet of hair, the pale skin and turquoise eyes.

A Napoleon-style hat made out of aluminum foil wobbles on top of her head. She's also wearing pointy green velvet shoes and a red leather pouch with a silver buckle cast in the shape of a bull skull. This all contrasts with her sheer black mesh catsuit, which is garlanded by organza ruffles decorated with intricate paintings of red and black vultures.

"Hi, Jumbler," Rapunzel coos to her, confirming that this person has the same name that she did in my superdream, "you look like you're in the mood to kick the apocalypse's butt tonight."

Jumbler places her two thumbs and two index fingers together, palms held up and spread out, and greets me with a perverse toast: "May Persephone annihilate the rotting patriarchal imprints within you—without killing you. Somewhere over the rainbow, may She inspire you to resurrect the splendorous beauty of poisoned masculinity."

She reaches into her pouch and produces an egg. I'm too startled to stop her as she reaches over, pulls forward the waistband of my shorts, and breaks the egg against my belly. The oozing slime only enhances the erotic fever I have been nursing steadily since Rapunzel's arrival.

"And may Persephone dissuade him," Rapunzel adds with a giggle, "from being just another boring example of the patriarchy's crowning achievement: the hate-everything-that-doesn't-adore-me and fuck-everything-that-adores-me hero."

Jumbler's greeting is scary. I don't like her broken egg and I don't like her violent references—"without killing you" in particular. Better not complain, though. Don't want to alienate Rapunzel's buddy on our first meeting.

As soon as we've eased into our chairs, a visitor from a nearby table glides over. A handsome, weathered woman with shoulder-length brown hair and a cracked smile, she looks about forty. She's holding a guitar and wearing a decal-bedecked black leather motorcycle jacket over a hunter-green satin mini-dress. One of the decals says "Menstrual Minstrel," which she proceeds to illustrate as she sings us a short ditty that consists entirely of variations on the phrase "The penis is just a clitoris suffering from delusions of grandeur." Rapunzel plucks out the tampon applicator flute that I'd stored in my vest pocket and plays along.

"What'll it be, televisionaries?" she asks us when she's done singing, pulling out a pen and notebook. "Breakfast of Amazons cereal? Rosicrucian Coca-Cola? Tender Adrenaline Ice Cream with Ancient Spider Webs?"

"Just the cereal for me, Artemisia," Jumbler says.

"Do you have the Unicorn Ovaries with Dragon Mucus and Sacred Cow Memories tonight?" Rapunzel says straightfacedly, whereupon Artemisia nods. "Good. And why don't you bring me a quart of Moon Flower Brine, too, OK?"

An aroma I'd been subliminally aware of before has now crept into my full awareness. How to describe it? Sweet almond blended with musky goat and wet feathers and vinegar mingled with rose. It's not coming from any particular direction. It's just in the air.

Jumbler chooses this moment to pinch me hard on the arm as she makes a throaty aside close to my ear. "Everyone in this place happens to be menstruating at the moment. Except you and me, of course. I'm a hermaphrodite. Don't know what your excuse is." She cackles at this comment.

"You know how it is," she adds. "Women who spend a lot of time together get their periods synchronized."

"What should I bring for the sperm pod?" Artemisia asks Rapunzel sardonically, ignoring me. "Is he in the mood to eat?"

"Let's not call him any bad names tonight, sweety," Rapunzel says, sticking up for me. "He needs our love and support. Besides, he deserves a little credit. He did read *The White Goddess* long before it was hip. He has Marija Gimbutas' photo in his wallet, and I dreamed that he once had a sexual fantasy about Gertrude Stein. I even heard he's got 'Listen to Women for a Change' tattooed in a very private place. This one's special. He's ripe. Maybe even a true Lesbian Man."

"Woooooooo! You gonna give him the full treatment?" Artemisia whistles. "Persephone-style immersion? The Honest-to-Goddess eucharist?"

"Could very well be," Rapunzel replies. "I'm proceeding with the Rowdy Ruby Glissando of the Silk Lotus spell."

"Yow! He must be a hardy one if that's his starter plan. Guess you don't want me to bring him any appetizers that might spoil his appetite, then."

"Yup."

I assume this exchange has been scripted ahead of time. It's flattering to contemplate the possibility that all these women have plotted and rehearsed tonight's festivities solely for my benefit. Though I'm also daunted by the responsibility of having to live up to such an immense gift.

As Rapunzel and Jumbler have a whispered exchange that is not meant for my ears, I examine the Tarot deck on our table. It's a bizarre hybrid. One side of each card has a mutated replica of an old baseball card with categories of statistics unlike what usually appears: "Ecstatic Prayers" instead of "At Bats"; "Sacred Pranks" instead of "Runs Batted In." My childhood hero, Al Kaline of the Detroit Tigers, appears in one image, except that here he's wearing a helmet with the horns of a bull protruding and a necklace of vulture figurines. Looks like he has amassed a good number of Ecstatic Prayers, but has been less prolific in the Sacred Pranks department.

On the other side of each Tarot card is a surrealistic photo collage of a female deity garbed in lingerie, below which is a written text. Al Kaline, for instance, is paired with Medusa. Though she has her usual writhing green snakes for hair, she's portrayed as a smiling, pregnant fashion model striding down a runway. The title at the top of the card is "Medusa the Sexy Mama," and an accompanying text, credited to Joseph Campbell, reads, "She is Black Time, both the life and death of all beings, the womb and tomb of the world; the primal, one and only, ultimate reality of nature, of whom the gods themselves are but functioning agents."

I've become aware of a twinge in my lower belly. It comes and goes, throbbing in a slow rhythm. I can't imagine the cause. No food has gone down my gullet for hours.

"So," Jumbler says to me, "would you like a Tarot reading?"

"Sure. Why not?"

Jumbler shuffles the deck several times, then has me draw a card. It's the old shortstop for the Washington Senators, Rocky Bridges. He's dressed in a loincloth and is depicted leaping over a bull in the manner of the athletic maidens of ancient Minoan culture.

"Ah yes," she sighs knowingly. "You are now on a rocky bridge between your old life and the new. You are perhaps leaving behind your role as rockstar and crossing over to the other side of the abyss. I say perhaps. There seems to be some doubt. The going may be rocky.

444

Here, draw another card."

This time I get Early Wynn, a pitcher in the 1950s.

"Yes. I see the problem. You are unfortunately seeking an 'early win,' a premature victory. Something about cheating. Fraudulence. You're trying to skip some steps. Cross the bridge without really crossing it."

I freeze. Could Jumbler have sensed that I'm being less than honest and complete in carrying out the program Rapunzel designed for me when she invaded my house? That though I've suspended the band's operations in order to take on the job as janitor, I'm not really planning to make it permanent?

"Take two more cards," she demands.

I draw Hall-of-Famer Nap Lajoie and an obscure old-time player I never heard of named Kid Maddox.

"Ah. I see. Kid and Nap are telling me that you are not performing your kidnap with a pure heart. I think you know what I am talking about—the self-abduction the avatar suggested you undertake. Do you see? Your kidnap must be done with 'la joie'—for joy alone. Not with covert agendas. Not with an acquisitive eye. And it must be done as 'mad docs' would do it—crazy doctors. The cards are advising you to trust the inscrutable wisdom of the wacky healer. Do not imagine that you know better than she who was born to administer the sacred prank medicine."

I look at Rapunzel, the most interesting beautiful woman I've ever known. Along with her pregnant silence, her amused but intense gaze tells me that she ratifies her friend's oracle. Guilt descends upon me, and worse, fear that I've irrevocably messed up. If she really knows that I've only been pretending to execute my self-abduction, will she cancel delivery of what she called, back in my bedroom a few days ago, "the majestic gift beyond my ability to conceive"?

How could she not be peeved to the point of ending it all right here? Look at the lengths to which she has gone to stage this evening's performance art event for my entertainment. There can be no question that she takes my "menarche" very seriously.

I am filled with the desire to atone.

I promise myself that if she forgives me for my deception, I will do what I should have done right from the start. I will completely, not halfheartedly, die to my old life. I will unconditionally quit the music business. I will renounce my quixotic but ultimately futile efforts to maintain my purity in an institution that makes it impossible. If nothing else, this will ensure that I'm in line to have more of the superdreams Rapunzel somehow delivered to me a few nights ago.

"Now pick one last card," Jumbler adjures. "This will be a picture of your soul's purpose. Of the glory you might possibly attain should you make it to the other side of the rocky bridge."

I draw Chick King, outfielder for the Chicago Cubs.

"Chick King," she intones tentatively. "King Chick. Chick King. King Chick."

She closes her eyes and pouts in concentration. Her eyelids quiver.

"I've got it," she beams finally. "It seems your new career as a tantric janitor is ultimately destined to be in the service of King Chick. Notice it's not *Queen* Chick, but *King* Chick. King Chick means, I think, that you are destined to help chicks overthrow this overly manly world. Ever hear that expression, 'Behind every great man is a woman?' You're going to be a man behind a great woman."

"So, like, I'm going to marry a woman who becomes President of the United States?" I ask.

"More like you'll be a muse for a woman who becomes President of the United Snakes. Now why don't you read the texts on the backs of your cards. They will provide additional oracular insight."

On the reverse of the Rocky Bridges card is a picture of a goddess who resembles the Hindu Shakti. She's dancing on top of an altar whose central feature is a large silver bowl. The title of the card is "Shakti Mutates the Blood Archetype," and the text, credited to Vicki Noble, reads: "In the *real* old-time religion, the sacrificial altar was graced with an offering of menstrual blood, gift of the priestess. It was understood to have special power to propitiate divine contact. Later patriarchal religions preserved the idea that blood is charged with sacred potency, but replaced the menstrual offering with the shed blood of a murdered animal or human."

Artemisia arrives and pours red wine from a carafe into the goblet on our table. She also leaves a bowl of cereal and pitcher of milk for Jumbler, and a big mess of purplish green blobs and reddish brown gravy for Rapunzel. There's nothing for me. Despite my desire to improvise within the framework Rapunzel and company are providing, I consider speaking up and placing an order. Hunger is beginning to assail me. I wonder if the aches I feel in my belly are hunger pangs?

"So King Chick, tell me true," Rapunzel says, interrupting my meditations. She picks up my right hand and places two popsicle sticks in it. Half of each stick is stained blue. "What exactly are you doing to kill the apocalypse?"

I don't know what to say.

"Huh? Huh?" she probes playfully when nothing flies from my lips. "Have you got any bright ideas about how to liquidate armageddon? Try rubbing those popsicle sticks together. They're my special magic wands. They could help." She shows me the proper motion.

Not too long ago, in the days before I met Rapunzel, my answer to her question might have been something like "I'm making subversive music that undercuts the ability of the entertainment criminals to genocide our imaginations." But in the wake of my apparent resolve to renounce the music business for good, I'm stumped.

"Would you like some clues?" Rapunzel teases.

"Just get me started," I plead, rubbing the sticks diligently.

"How about if you said, 'I'm resurrecting the splendorous beauty of poisoned masculinity'?"

"I'm resurrecting the splendorous beauty of poisoned masculinity," I repeat, injecting mock histrionics.

"And how specifically are you doing that?" Rapunzel quizzes.

I decide to risk a daring move. I'm going to be vulnerable and humble, but with a feisty edge. What I mean is that I'll really try to inhabit a state of humble vulnerability, not merely perform it as I have so often done in the past. My earliest insight about the seduction game was that women are attracted to men who confess weakness, but all these years I've used that as a crafty technique without actually doing it with complete sincerity. Back in the women's bathroom at the Catalyst, when I first met Rapunzel, was a perfect example. I pretended to be a self-effacing sensitive man even as I secretly billowed with pride.

In my defense, I should note that there has been a good reason for me to keep an ironic distance from the "sensitive man" act. The only version of it I've ever seen in other men is the one motivated by a frowning, judgmental radical feminist in their superegos. It's a whiny form of humble vulnerability, in other words, enforced by shame and guilt. But in the breakthrough I'm having here with Rapunzel, I can envision a spunky, truly masculine kind of humble vulnerability. It would emerge from my lust for life, not my fear of being a bad boy in the eyes of my inner matriarch.

Fascinating to contemplate the possibility that only by being more of a real man can I incorporate a healthy form of feminine behavior.

"One way I'll resurrect the splendorous beauty of poisoned masculinity," I respond finally, "is by admitting how terrified I am of receiving big beautiful gifts from amazing women like you. Not just terrified. Embarrassed. Deathly worried I don't deserve them. Am not worthy of them.

"Then there's the part about how weak and needy the big beautiful gifts make me feel. Not my usual self-sufficient self. And maybe the worst burden of all is the responsibility of having to give in return. I'm always convinced I can't possibly match the blessing."

"You fantasize that you're inferior to me," Rapunzel says understandingly. "You're afraid I'll think you're a stingy narcissist. In your eyes, I seem to have almost too much to give, much more than you, and you subconsciously resent it." She says this with sympathy, as if she's sorry, not angry.

"And yet to your credit," she continues, "you refuse to imitate the billions of men whose masculinity has been poisoned. You don't blame me for your fear and resentment. You don't withdraw into numb aloofness and try to punish me with mysterious silence. Instead, you struggle to change your feelings, to be a real magician. The problem isn't with me, after all, and you recognize that. You don't want to bully me into giving less."

"Yes, exactly." I feel like she's reading my mind again.

"And I can't think of anything that is a more potent weapon in our war against the apocalypse," she concludes.

"Thank you. I'm honored by your recognition."

I'm not sure I've ever used the word "honor" non-ironically before now. It stings a little to be so sincere. Besides which, as if to prove my confession, I've been pinched with the discomfort of receiving the enormous gift of Rapunzel's approval.

Momentarily unable to deal with my feelings, I turn my gaze to the rest of the dining room. Two women at one of the tables are peering intently at me, while the others seem occupied in playing cards with the Tarot decks. I'm surprised to see that a large but rather lovely shamanatrix in her twenties, a lesbian if I know my physiognomy, has doffed most of her costume. All she has on is a "skirt" that's nothing more than shreds of newspaper hanging from a belt, and a makeshift bra composed of two sewn-together floral shower caps. No undies! Two other women, including a fiftyish pixie with very pale skin as well as an exotic-looking mix of maybe Eskimo and African, have also lost their shirts. One reveals another strange "bra" made of two small gargoyle masks connected with a rubber band and the other a "teddy" that seems to be made of round slabs of baloney sewn together.

"I can think of another way I am resurrecting the splendorous beauty of poisoned masculinity," I bubble.

"She's taking notes," Rapunzel smiles, pointing to Jumbler, who pulled out a notebook a while back and is scribbling intently.

"I'm a good listener, but with an edge," I begin.

"You mean you get people to open up so you can use your sharp intellect to probe them, to push them to think deeper thoughts about their secret feelings?"

"Well, I suppose that's one way to describe it, yes."

"Sorry. I guess I wasn't being a very good listener, was I? Go ahead and say what you mean in your own words."

Wow. Rapunzel's being contrite.

"I'm forceful in the way I shut up and get my own opinions out of the way," I say. "I make an aggressive effort to be warmly receptive to what the other person is saying. I fight to ensure that I don't fall into acting like a know-it-all."

"I see. Using your masculine will to serve a feminine agenda."

"Yes. And the other quality in my listening is ferocious curiosity. I ask really good questions. Not just because I want to do people a favor, either. I mean I do want to do them a favor, but I also get a personal thrill from it. It's hard to explain why exactly."

"It's your way of making love to everyone. You send your feelers into their psyches and stir up their juices. You imagine you're impregnating them with your influence."

I've never thought of it this way, but again I feel like Rapunzel has understood me perfectly. I'm aglow and abashed with the notion that she might actually be attracted to me.

Riding my success, I flash on another thing I've always hated about average, boring, "sensitive man"-style vulnerability: Neurosis is its crowning testament. To be vulnerable in this way not only requires nonstop pretentious solemnity; it also seems to lead mostly to expressions of negative emotions.

Why, Lord, why? Why is that if a man lets down his guard and disavows the macho, in-control attitude that is the curse of his gender, he seems inevitably driven to confess his failures, his grief, and his weaknesses? I have nothing against doing this *some* of the time. But right now I can imagine a more celebratory style of vulnerability in which I might gravitate towards delight, too; in which I would feel an eager and innocent desire to be overwhelmed by beauty. What if becoming vulnerable could fill me with wild reverence?

"I've thought of another way I can resurrect the splendorous beauty of poisoned masculinity," I say bravely.

"By perfecting the art of being a staunch feminist with a raging hard-on, right?" Rapunzel laughs.

"Sorry," she adds quickly as she sees my eyebrows rise. "My telepathic powers are out of control tonight. I just couldn't help myself."

I wouldn't have used the words she did, but she has indeed zeroed in on my unspoken thoughts.

"I would prefer to describe it," I begin, summoning my eloquence, "as blending unbridled virility and sweet sensitivity. To be, ahem, compassionately horny.

"Be a big red hot man," she puffs, raising her shoulders and making a macho face, "all rebellious and restless and ambitious. And be a soft, warm, nurturing woman"—here she softens her features and goes all willowy—"dispensing thoughtful blessings with loving kindness."

"It would be interesting to see if I could actually be both at the same time," I muse.

"Are you familiar with the concept of the epicene?"

"Isn't that like being androgynous?"

"No, the *difference* between androgynous and epicene is exactly my point. Androgyny is a melting down of the gender distinctions into a single fuzzy neutral blah. But the epicene person—the model citizen for the Drivetime, by the way—is one who's both fervently masculine and vividly feminine. Not the grey, odorless pall that comes from eliminating the contradictions, but the magenta menthol spermatic emerald clitoral saffron that comes from weaving the contradictions together with their full pungent glory intact."

"You're so smart, Rapunzel. Thank you. I can't ever recall a feminist woman telling me to trust my lust."

"That's one of the ways *I* am killing the apocalypse. By helping a few select lesbian men realize how important it is for them not to shame their testosterone."

On the one hand I'm flattered by this last statement. On the other hand I'm deflated. There are other men she's courting like this?

"I'm still afraid I take it too far, though," I blurt. "I guess I don't even have to say this aloud since you seem to know what I'm thinking. But ever since I can remember, I've been addicted to fantasizing about mass orgies. With me as the only man in a sea of women."

I'm amazed to hear myself confess such an embarrassing secret. I can only imagine that I really must be undergoing some kind of initiation—not at all like the ceremonial initiations I've undergone during my work with my occult school, but like them in the way that it's stripping away my usual defenses.

"Yes. Interesting quirk," Rapunzel says.

"I never thought of it as a quirk," I protest. "I assume it's what most men idealize. I mean, isn't it every guy's dream to make love to an endless variety of perfect women? Something about the DNA commanding him to spread his seed to as many young, fresh, beautiful hosts as possible."

"But that's not exactly what your fantasy is. Your orgies are not the exclusive domain of young, fresh, beautiful hosts. There are a few very plain women in there. I've even seen a crone or two."

"Now how could you possibly know that? Just from studying my Wailing Wall? Or have you been spying on my meditations?"

"You'd be surprised what I can do with the help of our sixty-six-million-year-old technology. A portable sample of which is right over there. We call it the Televisionary Oracle."

Rapunzel is pointing towards the mud and stone television.

"So with the help of your magic box you sneaked into my psyche and found out I sometimes stoke my orgy fantasies with a handful of women who aren't supermodels?"

"Sort of, yes. Which is why I can say with confidence that you definitely don't trust your lust enough. Because if you did, if you exorcised the shame you've allowed to infect your orgy fantasies, you'd really jack up your ability to resurrect the splendorous beauty of poisoned masculinity. You'd shoot out to the frontier of an even more sublime taboo."

"What taboo could there possibly be beyond that? Beyond the desire to be a lone Dionysus with a gang of horny women?"

"The desire to be a lone Dionysus with a gang of horny women of all shapes and sizes and ages. A lone Dionysus who does not choose only the prettiest, youngest, most supple horny women to run away with into the woods. Who longs for and is available to *all* women."

Uh-oh. Red alert. So gradually I haven't realized it, most of the shamanatrixes in the room have removed major parts of their elaborate costumes. Were they playing strip poker with those Tarot cards? Vistas of flesh are exposed, along with a wealth of often comical lingerie. These are not stylish items from a Victoria's Secret catalogue, but bikinis made of brightly colored band-aids and yarn, camisoles with attached moss and Christmas tree icicles, and lacy nursing bras with rubber shark puppet mouths where the flap opens.

Furthermore, many of the women are now peering at me with some mix of sweet, sultry, and sympathetic expressions.

I will myself to deepen my breathing as I scramble to assess my feelings. My rational mind knows that if this were any other situation, I'd rate two of the women here as full-on sexy to me and maybe six mildly attractive, while most of the rest I'd feel neutral about except for two that arouse my repulsion. But I'm so far gone from my normal state that my old evaluation system does not hold. To my amazement, I feel a preposterous lust for every single woman here.

Or have I merely had my esthetic exploded by the prodigious titillation and by Rapunzel's quasi-hypnotic suggestions? Have all my habitual responses been rendered irrelevant?

"This potential of yours, to be an all-purpose Dionysian muse, is one of the qualities that makes you so deserving of your own personalized menarche," Rapunzel explains soothingly. "It's also a valuable asset for storming the precincts of the Drivetime."

"To long for and be available to *all* women?" I stammer.

"You want to live in the Drivetime full-time? Where nothing needs to be true and everything is sacred and Goddess is a tenderly lascivious prankster at your service? Then tap into your hidden talent for being as lusty towards everyone and everything as you are towards me. Meditate on how to rev up your testosterone until it's in love with great grandmas listening to talk radio in nursing homes and chubby Guatemalan peasant women pounding laundry down by the river."

"But if I'm equally carnal for everything," I protest weakly, "if there's no difference between my desire for you and my desire for the grandma in the nursing home, doesn't that make me a ball of mush?"

"Exact opposite of that. You can never be a ball of mush if you're stoked with gargantuan levels of passion."

Rapunzel has undone the rest of the buttons on her baseball jersey. All the other women in the room have abandoned their chairs and are doing yoga asanas or tai-chi moves. My eyes are in crisis mode, frantically reaching out to engorge the epiphanies of breasts and butts jiggling as bodies stretch. I flash on the myth of Semele, who was burned to ash upon beholding Zeus in his dangerous glory. Except that the roles are reversed here. I'm Semele.

The most limber of the teasers, a pretty young Asian woman wearing only loose white silk shorts, is doing an absurdly salacious yoga pose that might go well on a "Girls of *Penthouse* Workout Video." Balanced on her shoulders and neck, she thrusts one leg out sideways and one out straight, both parallel to the floor. She rotates slowly, like a graceful breakdancer.

In my altered state of exploded lust, though, she evokes no more shivering blithers than any of the other women in the room. I'm equally turned on by the woman with a thick scar on her cheek and a big crooked witch nose, and the forty-something matron with cellulite and sagging breasts that have obviously nursed several children. I seem to be in bloom with the state of omni-horniness that Rapunzel said was helpful for living full-time in the Drivetime.

Rapunzel motions for me to get out of my chair and come hither. I obey. She grasps me around the waist and pulls me down to sit on her lap. Peering down, I have a perfect view of her breasts surging in her black lace bra.

"So what do you say," she murmurs as her bouquet of fruity, musky aromas spills over me, "that we take an inventory of how well you're doing on the project of achieving gargantuan passion?"

*I'm hungry for the real goo,* I think to myself, *for the sauce and the splash and the balm. I seek the true lust unguent that binds and burns, that cures and incites.*

"Tell me now. Be frank. How, in your heart of hearts, do you feel about *hag marks* on your luscious females? Look around here at the holy host of menstrual geniuses for reference. Do you honestly, no bullshit, have a divinely inspired affinity for thick black hairs sprouting from nipples and navels and maybe even chins? How about pimples on the butt? Stretch marks on pendulous breasts and big noble witchy noses and week-old stubble on shaved legs? Did you really, truly mean what you wrote in your personal ad at the Catalyst, 'All my patriarchal imprints incinerated'?"

*Keep me close always to your real maw, rolling in the rose dark behind your lids and lips, under the thigh and over the fear and into the sweat and the fur, between the breasts and spirit straight to the taste of your shivering moist soul.*

"What I'm driving at, my dear, is this: Do you truly and without any reservations pledge to place yourself under the influence of the mysterious chemicals of *real* women? Or will you continue to harbor, under cover of your feminist rhetoric, hypocritical urges to love only a narrow simulation of the Goddess' panoramic beauty? I think it's time you took a stand one way or the other. Not just with your fine words. But with your actual body. Know what I mean?"

*I want to be awake to the actual low rumbling of your rant and shadow, stretching to hear the strong old medicines of your tongue, pulsing limbless in waves of your lunatic hair—staring, face loose, into your molten pores and through to the generous dreams of your glands.*

"In other words, beautiful, what kind of man do you want to be when you grow up?"

*The thrill of the menstrual dark will be my secret salvation; the uterine quiver will be the best hysteria of my obsession.*

"I vow to love the hag marks as much as the beauty marks," I speak aloud to the gathering, feeling as if I'm channeling the spirit of an Irish bard, who a psychic once told me I was in a previous incarnation.

"I will swoon for the bumps and the dangles and the wobbly foibles just as much as I will for the smooth, sleek swivels and the taut, trim treasures. Therefore I now and forevermore renounce my worship of the slutty madonna fetishes passed into law by every shit-hoarding religion, and the man-made surrogates called bitches on pedestals, and all the leached, face-lifted, fanny-tucked, depillatoried, silicon-enhanced Olympian cyborgs who pride themselves on having the freshest feminine smell in the history of capitalism. I renounce them all. Forever and ever, amen. Awomen."

Wow. Where did that come from?

Rapunzel smothers me in a big hug and then maneuvers me into a position where she can kiss me on the belly. "May you find the treasure in the trash, the gold in the lead, and the manna in the junk food!" she exclaims. The room explodes in a chorus of ululating Amazon yelps.

"May you use your nightmares to become rich and famous," Jumbler adds amidst the cacophony, her arms stretched upwards in a V like a baseball player who has just smacked a game-winning home run.

"Because you can have anything you want," an older woman pitches in, "if you'll only ask for it in an unselfish tone of voice."

As the hubbub rages on, with others calling out odd slogans, all but Rapunzel work to push the tables to the periphery of the room and form a circle of chairs around me. Eventually, everyone sits down. I am now astride Rapunzel's lap, surrounded by mostly naked shamanatrixes whose gazes are directed at me.

Jumbler, who is still fully clothed, fetches a curious object from the altar against the back wall. It's a crown made out of willow branches, woven grass, lilies, copper and silver crayons, and a Tarot card which shows the goddess Athena in a "Menstrual Temple" baseball uniform. Jumbler ceremoniously places the contraption on my head.

"Congratulations, initiate," she says, "and welcome to the Menstrual Temple of the Funky Grail! I am very pleased to inform you that you have won a free value-pack of prizes worth three million years of vacation time in the Drivetime, plus the psychoanalysis of your diamond wand, a fabulously useful new organ of perception where your pineal gland now sits, and a reserved monthly space in the menstrual hut of your choice!

"And that's not all. As an added special bonus, you have been selected to be a contestant in the Fuck Your Friends Dating Game. One of three lucky shamanatrixes is going to win the privilege of escorting you through the rest of your menarche. Are you ready to play?"

"Can I take my curlers out?" I say with exultant meekness. "Rapunzel said I only had to keep them in until it was time for my date."

"Of course," Jumbler smiles, and begins removing the tampons from my hair. "By the way, Osiris, I want you to know that the Fuck Your Friends Dating Game is reserved exclusively for Love Geniuses who have demonstrated a potential for juggling rugged individualism and radical intimacy. Think you can handle that?"

Radical intimacy? Don't know what that is, but with Rapunzel as muse I'd be highly motivated to master it.

"I have always wanted to be a Love Genius," I say.

The Asian woman of the sexy yoga pose fame produces a brush, and she and Jumbler tease my hair into a fright wig. Meanwhile, Rapunzel leads the other women in a spritely version of the World Entertainment War song, "Dance Your Monster." Artemisia plays guitar.

"Do you realize," Jumbler notes after they finish, "that the last time an actual male was called on to be in the Fuck Your Friends Dating Game, the ancient Sumerian city of Ur had not yet been built?"

"Considering how big an occasion this is, then," I say, "I think I should clean up that egg you anointed my belly with. I'm sure my date would appreciate it."

"Certainly," Jumbler says boisterously. "Let me get you a sanitary napkin." She hands me two maxipads from out of her red pouch. They're delicately decorated around the peripheries with lozenges, double-headed axes, snakes, and butterflies.

As I pull back the waistband of my shorts to begin the mop-up, I'm taken aback. There is a trickle of blood emerging from the exact spot where Rapunzel daubed the "Dragon's Blood" back in the kitchen. It's blending with the slime of the half-dried egg white. This must be related to the mild cramps I've been feeling off and on.

I wipe the red streak away with one of the maxipads and watch the area for a few moments. The dribble returns, but very slowly. I guess I'm in no immediate danger of bleeding to death. But how did it happen?

Jumbler and Rapunzel are seeing the ooze that I am.

"Are you having any cramps?" Rapunzel asks eagerly.

"A little," I report.

"Rowdy ruby glissando!" Rapunzel announces loudly, and again a cheer goes up from the assembly. "Just in time for the Dating Game!"

"Without further ado," Jumbler proclaims when the hubbub dies down, looking at me with glee, "let's introduce you now to the three friendly Fuckfriends who'll vie for your favor. One of them will be *your* date!"

"First up we have a thirty-five-year-old genius with Ph.D.s in both music and physics. A major Pythagoras fan, she just happens to be the one and only quantum physicist on the planet who has mastered the art of lucid dreaming. Her Fuckfriend code name is Wealthy Anarchist. She regularly plays violin in accompaniment with the music of the spheres, and she claims her guardian angel looks a lot like Malcolm X. Here she is!"

A Jewish woman with blonde hair teased out into an explosion that must exceed the afro I'm now sporting, Wealthy Anarchist is wearing nothing else but the largest pair of white cotton underpants I have ever seen. They're far too big for her actual butt, so they're always on the verge of slipping off as she wriggles around in her chair. She lifts the waistband up and plays peekaboo behind them briefly. Then she picks up a knife from one of the tables and pokes through the cotton. She rips apart a hole wide enough to fit her face through, and delivers her spiel.

"I'm a disgruntled postal employee looking for a zombie love slave or lonely bank teller to share erotic fantasies about IRS audits and root canals."

Everyone in the room shakes with laughter, especially Wealthy Anarchist herself. When she recovers her composure, she continues.

"Just kidding. Actually, I'm an angel-wrestlin', magic carpet-ridin', sky-kissin' lover of architects who moonlight as exotic dancers and vegetarians who sneak pork chops. So please don't confuse me by being simple."

Again, guffaws whoosh through the room. I'm beginning to like this woman.

"No, really," she begins again. "In absolute actual fact, I am an inveterate xeroxer of my own butt who's seeking a like-minded cynical optimist for clowny adventures like trading clothes and rollerblading out to the nearest bridge for a no-holds-barred spitting-into-the-wind contest. Wouldn't mind if you were also into pursuing a career in killing the apocalypse, cultivating weird companions, collecting the relics of female saints, and exchanging frequent piggyback rides."

I glance over at the stone and mud television—excuse me, the Televisionary Oracle—as Wealthy Anarchist talks. The screen now shows the top half of a naked woman sitting behind a news desk and holding a sheaf of papers, as if she were a newscaster. With voluminous auburn hair and bushy eyebrows, she looks like she could be Rapunzel's twin sister—except for a few other details. She has blue skin, for instance. And eight arms, like some swarming Hindu goddess. Her body seems to be on fire in places, though she shows no signs of alarm. And every now and then she thrusts her impossibly long tongue down and out to the bottom of her chin.

This is not a cartoon or computer animation. The blue goddess appears absolutely real, as does her towering gold crown, which is surmounted by what looks like a sentient eye.

"Thank you, Wealthy Anarchist," Jumbler is saying. "Our next Fuckfriend is a forty-two-year-old painter who claims to be a direct descendant of William Blake's housekeeper and a junk dealer who once punched Charles Darwin in the nose. She regularly dreams she's a tree with its roots brushing the sky and its branches nuzzling the moles and worms. Believe it or not, she also claims to be a close personal acquaintance of the magic bunny rabbit eyes that watch you around the clock in the mirror attached to the ladder to the underworld you built inside your dreams when you were five years old! Codenamed Personal Growth Addict, she was recently elected to serve as Keeper of the Mysteries of the Difference Between Wise Pain and Dumb Pain."

It's Artemisia, the menstrual minstrel. She has clamped red rubber clown noses over her nipples, and her thick brown pubic hair is manicured in the shape of a bull skull.

"I've eaten food without imagining the hands of the people who grew it and picked it," she begins with mock mournfulness, her eyes downcast and her posture slumped. "I've loved my own pain more than everyone else's pain. I have sought out the most unoriginal sins and cultivated the most boring problems. Do you love me yet?"

As she asks that question she turns her eyes up and gazes at me with demure fervor, pouting her lips and winking. Many of her compatriots around the room are giggling.

"I've gotten free cable by hooking into the main line illegally," she continues, averting her eyes again and drumming her fingers against her belly. "I've bragged that a priest said I would burn in hell when he didn't. I've failed to ridicule humorless authorities whose dogmas I agreed with. I've underlined all the important passages in *TV Guide* and secretly fantasized that life after the apocalypse would be more interesting. Do you love me yet? DO YOU LOVE ME YET? DO YOU LOVE ME YET?!!!!"

As Personal Growth Addict giggles out her final refrain, she leaps out of her chair and skips over. Before I can respond, she straddles me where I sit on Rapunzel's lap, jamming her breasts against my face.

Jumbler is quick to intervene. "Not allowed to unduly influence the contestant with heated displays of physical affection," she says sharply as she fights to peel Artemisia off me. "Against the rules."

Meanwhile, however, Rapunzel is swaying back and forth as she tries to tickle me in the ribs. When Jumbler yanks Artemisia off my lap, all four of us barely avoid toppling over.

Once Fuckfriend number two is led back to her chair, Rapunzel gestures to Jumbler to fetch the mud and stone TV against the wall. She does, setting it on the table where I'm sitting. It apparently does not rely on electricity to function.

The screen still shows the blue goddess with eight arms sitting behind a news desk. I say "screen," but it is much more than that. It's as if another dimension or two has been crammed into the usual three, and somehow depicted on a two-dimensional surface. The screen doesn't even look solid. More like a small vat of liquid crystalline mercury. The images roil and swarm as if bubbling up from a cauldron. I start to reach out to touch it, but Rapunzel grabs my hand and places it on her thigh.

"For our final Fuckfriend," Jumbler announces, "we have a special treat. Code-named Philosopher Queen of the Underworld of Fun and Games, she is celebrating her sixty-sixth million, two hundred fifty-fifth thousand, one hundred thirty-seventh birthday today! I don't think there'll be any argument when I describe her as the planet Earth's most primordial tantric janitor! Not to mention that she's by far the most experienced virgin in this or any other dimension, and when I say virgin I of course don't mean sexually naive but rather complete unto herself. Needs no other Fuckfriend to be happy, really, but enjoys liaisons now and then nonetheless.

"And now, riding the fallopian holograms direct from a permanent yet secret orgasm just north of all our medulla oblongatas, I'm proud to present for your approval the Philosopher Queen of the Underworld of Fun and Games!"

Rapunzel twists a knob shaped like a five-pointed star at the bottom of the Televisionary Oracle. The sounds of music and speech emerge, as does—am I hallucinating?—a wave of aromas.

"This is a perfect moment," the blue goddess murmurs in a voice that is soothing and thrilling at the same time, reassuring yet full of insinuation. The music playing in the background is a weave of women's voices. It's like a Gregorian chant sung with the lush and dissonant harmonies of Bulgarian choral music.

The smells emanating from the blue goddess have a rich and piercing effect as well. How to describe them? The English language is stingy in providing words to capture odors. Citronella is one strain in the mix. Cognac. The inside of a new car. Vanilla. The liquid acne medication I used as a teenager. A new box of crayons.

This cacophony of fragrance penetrates my head through my nose but does not stop there. It snakes down and out in all directions, as if my entire body were filling up with a sweet, earthy, liquid smoke. The feeling is unmistakably erotic, yet not in any way I recognize.

"This is a perfect moment," the blue goddess singsongs, "because I'm stoking up my most healing pathologies for you. I'm getting ready to unhex all the black magic you've practiced on yourself—if that's what you want."

A fresh wave of aromas invades me, circulating in figure eights from the spot behind my nose down to my thighs and back: warm maple syrup blended with menthol and sandalwood and freshly cut grass and piles of linen.

"I'm practicing," the blue goddess continues, "so I can get better at being your invisible playmate and your anarchistic anima and the anonymous celebrity who lives under your bed—if that's what you want.

"I'm doing everything I can to turn myself into the menstruating coyote angel helper who wants everything that you want—if that's what you want.

"So. What *do* you want, anyway?"

Pervaded by the exotic aromas, agitated in a most soothing way by her voice, thrilled by her beautiful face and the flames flitting harmlessly on her voluptuous blue breasts, I am in a state of grace and emergency. My entire body is doing a perfectly extrapolated imitation of what it feels like for the male sexual organ to go from tumescent to erect. I do not just have a hard-on. I *am* a hard-on.

"Be specific," the blue goddess encourages. "Tell me everything. What exactly would you like more than anything?"

I surprise myself with how simple my response is. It's a formulation that makes me feel once again as if I'm channeling the Irish bard: "I want to be the man behind the woman who overthrows the world."

"The choice has been made!" Jumbler spouts, jumping over to shake my hand.

What's she talking about? I appreciate the way the blue goddess has enhanced my already altered state, but I'm not quite ready yet to select her over the other two contenders. In fact, I might prefer an actual woman to a disembodied image.

"My fellow shamanatrixes," Jumbler rants excitedly, "in an unexpectedly snap decision, Osiris has chosen Fuckfriend number three to be his dream date! The Philosopher Queen of the Underworld of Fun and Games! Thank you so much, Wealthy Anarchist and Personal Growth Addict, for lending your exuberant grace to our proceedings." She twists a dial on the Televisionary Oracle, pumping up the volume of the Bulgarian Gregorian chant music.

"I protest!" Artemisia shouts out suddenly. "I appeal! The Philosopher Queen hypnotized him with her smellovisionary beams! She cheated!"

Artemisia hurls herself across the floor and yanks me free of Rapunzel. In seconds she has pushed me to the floor and locked me in a wrestling hold. I'm on my back. Her chest is pressed down on mine while her left arm coils around my neck and her right arm is looped through my crotch.

"You're my love bitch!" she yowls. "Say it! Say it! Say 'I'm your love bitch.'" She has her hand close to a very sensitive part of my anatomy, and I'm in no position to resist.

"I am your love bitch," I shout. "I swear I am your love bitch."

"He is not! He is not your love bitch!" Wealthy Anarchist leaps into the fray, tugging hard on my arm in an effort to drag me away from Artemisia. "He's my candy sucker."

The two women are using me to play tug-of-war. Artemisia is yanking on my right leg and Wealthy Anarchist on my left arm.

"What the Hades are you talking about?" Artemisa screams with gruff laughter. "What's a candy sucker?"

"A psychic told me he and I have a special destiny," Wealthy Anarchist shrieks back. "Together we will set the world's record for longest time a cherry Life Saver is kept intact while passed between two people's mouths. Fifty-seven hours! We'll be famous!"

I catch a glimpse of Jumbler and Rapunzel standing side by side a few feet away. With goofy grins on their faces, they're clapping rhythmically.

"Love bitch, candy sucker," they chant. "Love bitch, candy sucker, love bitch, candy sucker."

From behind them, drowning them out, comes a series of high-pitched cackling caws. It's the Asian woman, who follows her crow calls with a shouted announcement: "No one even asked me if I wanted to be a Fuckfriend!" She maneuvers towards me, pinwheeling her arms and unleashing shoulder-high karate kicks that barely avoid hitting some of the other women. Finally, she throws herself down to the ground near me, landing softly in a position from which she could do push-ups if she so desired.

"As the duly-elected Rabid Nibbler of The Eater of Cruelty," she bellows, "I hereby claim the right to bite the lesbian man's gluteus maximus!" She clamps her teeth on my butt, not hard enough to break the skin but strong enough to send half-pleasurable, half-painful ripples through me.

Meanwhile, Artemisia and Wealthy Anarchist continue to struggle for supremacy, dragging me this way and that. The Asian martial artist follows along, sometimes letting go and chomping down at a fresh location on my hindquarters.

The woman with the scar on her cheek and the big witch nose comes forward to stake a claim. Kneeling at my head, she grabs me by the hair and peers down into my face.

"How do you identify a bull dyke?" she demands to know.

"What?" I laugh.

"How do you identify a bull dyke?" she repeats more loudly and slowly.

"I don't know what you mean," I sputter above the noise and confusion.

"She kick-starts her vibrator and rolls her own tampons," she reveals, pulling my hair back and forth a few times in punishment for my ignorance.

"When you order a Bloody Mary, how can you tell if the waitress is mad at you?" she asks, giving me a chance to redeem myself.

"I give up."

"She leaves the string in."

"Of course, I should have known."

"How can you tell a Polish woman is having her period?"

"Don't know."

"She's only wearing one sock, of course."

She bends her head down and begins kissing my face tenderly. "As clever as you are, honey, I'm afraid you need an intelligence upgrade," she whispers between smooches. "I'm going to have to smother you with IQ-boosting joy bombs."

A short, thin Arab woman with wire-rimmed glasses joins the crowd. Her first act is to sip the trickle of blood leaking from the spot below my navel. Then she takes a deep breath, presses her mouth against my skin, and blows a big, sloppy, trumpet-like sound. Again and again she performs this music. Liberal amounts of her spit accumulate on my skin.

Another shamanatrix, the Eskimo-African woman, shoves her face right up against Witch Nose's face. Only she's not kissing, she's talking.

"You've got to promise me that you will always be unpredictable but trustworthy, OK?" she prods. "Mysterious but loyal. OK? Ever-fresh and a little tricky but kind and thoughtful, too. Do you know what I'm talking about?"

I nod.

"I want you to communicate clearly," she says, "but always keep me guessing what your next move is going to be. Promise me. Resurrect the beauty. Resurrect the masculine beauty. Promise me."

Witch Nose covers my mouth with hers as I try to say, "I promise." This prompts Eskimo-African to scold, "Say 'I promise' into *my* mouth, too."

She gently shoves Witch Nose out of the way, then covers my lips with hers and mumbles, "Promise me." Which I do. Witch Nose moves on to kissing my neck and shoulder.

The large young lesbian arrives at the pile-up for a piece of the action. She grabs my free hand and places my thumb firmly in her mouth.

"My thumbsuckomancy reveals," she prophesies after taking my digit back out, "that in the future this new menstruator will be famous with the Goddess for his ability to awaken masculine mojo in the female psyche. He will not be threatened in the least when women are strong, but will in fact be totally turned on by it."

She thrusts the thumb back in for another divination. "Ah, best of all. He will master the impossible art of achieving rapture without losing his desire. Of surrendering to climax and still wanting more."

This announcement rouses the excitement in the room to a new pitch. Whoops and cheers break out.

"So does this mean," gushes the fiftyish pixie, "that once he's done seducing me he won't lose interest? Does this mean he understands it's his holy duty to propitiate the edge where satiation and longing co-exist?"

"Orgasm without ejaculation," the lesbian says jubilantly. "He'll learn how different they are. I predict he'll learn that his bliss can go on forever when he doesn't give in to the urge to splurge."

"Won't just roll over and go to sleep!" someone cries.

"Epicene bliss!" exults another.

"Stroke like a man, come like a woman!"

A few feet away, Rapunzel is now utterly bereft of clothes. She begins speaking to me with her gorgeous body, never once taking her kind and seductive eyes away from mine. At first it's the Russian cossack dance. With her arms folded across her chest, she squats down and kicks out her legs like an athletic madwoman. Next she does a willowy, slow-motion series of devotional poses, as if she were a Hindu temple priestess addressing her god. Then she adds a clowny animal dance, rubbing her belly and licking her chops as she bares her teeth and growls affectionately.

As she finishes, she glides over to me and places her forehead against mine. Rubbing back and forth, she soaks my skin with her sweat.

"I want us to write a book together," she sings into my ear, the warm flow of her breath thrusting me past every inhibition. "I want us to trick the masses into enjoying sacred entertainment."

Maybe half the women in the room are touching me: kissing my neck, fondling my hair, biting my butt, massaging my foot, sucking my thumb, trumpeting into my stomach, lightly stroking my arm. All the others are holding hands as they slowly circle around us, murmuring a song in a language I don't recognize. I can't quite see what the blue goddess is up to—there are bodies between me and the Televisionary Oracle—but I can hear her singing along with the rest of the women, and I can feel new waves of fragrance all the time.

At last something like an orgasm arrives. I don't recognize it at first. It's a whirlpool, not a spurt. Like an implosion, it gathers but does not discharge force. Billowing, throbbing, coiling, its center is not even my genitals, but rather my heart. Soft volcanic waves erupt there and split into two streams, one spiraling up and one down my spine. Both then circle back to plunge silkenly into my heart again, where the cycle begins anew.

It's as if my heart were being inseminated. An image percolates up into my mind's eye: a spermatozoa piercing the membrane of an ovum.

I feel a relaxation so profound that I realize I've never really relaxed before in my life. As the love medicine begins to take effect, an age-old narcissistic ache—*pay attention to me, see me as special*—begins to ease dramatically. With this realignment comes a wave of self-forgiveness. I feel a raucous but merciful laugh rise up and threaten to dissolve my ancient habit of taking everything so damn seriously. Yes, I have a fine sense of humor; yes, I can mock myself with the best of them. And yet I'm embarrassed to admit that I've always remained fiercely attached to how meaningful all my idiosyncratic opinions are. Like the patriarchy itself, I've been fixated on the early, infantile stages of individuation: What's helpful or attractive to me I've regarded as good; what's useless or boring or repulsive to me has been bad.

But I sense that this pathological crime against the ever-fresh creation—hallelujah!—is ready to die.

As my heart orgasm swirls on, I conceive of a kind of freedom that has been invisible to me before. It would require me to stop careening back and forth from moment to moment between "I like this" and "I don't like that." Instead I would be equally open and equally skeptical towards all things, whether I have an emotional affinity for them or not, whether they reinforce my world view or not. I'd be objective but also tender. I'd be liberated from believing my biases are ultimate truths, but without taking on the psychotically detached way of knowing that is the hallmark of poisoned masculinity.

What if I can learn to feel deeply enough to love my enemy? I mean *really* love my enemy, not just give lip service to tolerating him because my moral code tells me it's the right thing to do. What if I can truly summon a warm sympathy—motivated by a lust for life rather than a shaming superego—for anyone or anything that has no power to increase my personal pleasure?

And it will all have to be done without giving up my discrimination. I want to have the critical thinking of an authentically objective scientist (I'm thinking of Max Planck or Richard Feynman) blended with the vigorously nurturing, emotionally smart compassion of a skilled psychotherapist.

I'm crying. I've been crying for some time. The women who were ministering so aggressively to my pleasure have taken a break, and I'm lying on the floor surrounded by them. Now and then one of them leans over to kiss my tears.

Someone has turned the lights down low in the dining room. The only illumination consists of a few candles and the glow of the Televisionary Oracle.

Rapunzel lifts the magic box and sets it down on the floor near my head. The blue goddess seems to be gazing at me with loving calm.

"Place yourself in a comfortable position," she tells me. "Breathe deeply and let confusion and remorse drain out of you. Let yourself unwind and surrender with a wild abandon you have not experienced since you were a child.

"As you inhale, become aware that your heart's beating is fueled by thermonuclear chain reactions that originate on the sun. As you exhale, imagine that every instant of joy you've ever experienced is resurrecting itself as an image of a snapdragon opening at dawn.

"Can you surrender this profoundly? You know you can. Allow yourself to feel more at home in the world than you have ever felt before. It's as if your soul were sending secret transmissions to you from the end of time. As if you were able to be both dead and alive at the same time.

"Now begin your prayer to the avatar. Not with the gesture of clasping your hands together, as if you were shackled. Not with a bleat of submission or whine of greed. Do it with uproarious reverence. Bestow upon her the dazzling grace of your disciplined exuberance."

And so I find myself kneeling before her at last, my inscrutable queen. My hands rest just above her knees as she sits on the throne of heaven, which to the naked eye appears to be a wooden chair in a restaurant. She jiggles her legs up and down waggishly, inviting me to play.

"Oh wacky priestess," I pray, "you who dare me to think of you as an irresistible siren even though I have seen you kiss a rotting shred of eggplant dredged from the kitchen floor: I have been sent by the god of lesbian men to assist you in burning heaven to the ground. Accept my raunchy yet righteous supplication!"

I butterfly my lips on her feet as I murmur, swelling not with pride but with giddy appreciation for the privilege. As I slither my hair and face on her legs, I become aware of the hint of stubble, suggesting she has not shaved in a while. My bottomless excitement deepens in response, and I surge with confidence to know that my adoration does not require her to be a perfect idol.

"Oh scary genius," I pray, "you who are so mysterious I sometimes can't tell the difference between your talents and your deficiencies: I will call you the queen of *wabi,* after the Japanese word referring to a beautiful flaw in a work of art that endows it with far more value than if it were merely perfect."

She impishly squeezes her knees against my ears and rains a flurry of swats down on my head. I visualize the slowly whirling spiral of violet and red gas that was the primeval solar nebula—our solar system before it was the solar system—and I muse on how every moment in the evolution of that masterpiece has conspired to bring me here now for the purpose of making the avatar laugh as I worship her with my love.

"Oh luscious maestro," I say, "I would help you sell the rights to your life story to a major Hollywood studio if it were within my power. I would lobby to put you on the cover of *Time* and *Newsweek*. I would wangle you a contract to do endorsements for Nike. I would pull strings for a city street to be named after you, and a mountain, and a thousand-year-old storm on Saturn."

I reach my hands underneath her hips and gently slide her towards the front of the chair. Lifting up her legs, I drape them over my shoulders. Her silk lotus, previously half-buried in the throne, is now billowing towards me with the blazing radiance of a thousand suns and the cool moisture of a thousand moons. I inhale the life-breath of this cosmos. It's tinctured with the aroma of amber and pomegranate juice and smoldering sage and carved pumpkins and the wood of a violin and the leathery sweetness of the Dead Sea Scrolls, whose fragments I once sniffed in a museum.

"What did the rubies say standing before the juice of the pomegranate?" I whisper, quoting the poet Neruda, as I lift my head to gaze up into her green eyes. I'm ecstatic to find no self-consciousness there, and this releases me into the gift of losing my own self-absorption.

I muse on the memories of other tantric rituals I've enjoyed. All too often, my ego has been on full alert, lusting to impress my partner at the expense of our souls' more mysterious agendas. In those other times and places I've wielded the jade stalk with impeccably wild precision, suavely jiggling the pomegranate juice free from the grotto of the tiger lily, lodging my tongue of blue fire against the starry veil, blah blah blah—all the while spraying my mind's eye full of pseudo-immortal pictures of what a vivid Sex King I am.

Not this time, though. All my greedy grasping is gone as I bring my supplicant's lips and tongue to the rosy fluting. My breathing is regal, saturated with humble confidence that I am worthy of this blessing.

With slow-motion wave upon wave of mercurial spirals, I honor and enjoy Rapunzel's silken furrows. There is no hurry. I have all the time in the world. Only after I satisfy my craving to taste the entire bouquet do I hold the satiny pearl gently between my pursed lips.

"Namaste," I hum, "I greet the Goddess within you." Sometimes I keep my tongue softly erect as I swirl it around the heart source. Other times I sup and nuzzle, swirl and flick, shimmer and trill. Throughout the celebration, I invoke all my powers of love, visualizing a cornucopia spilling out a thousand gifts for her: green velvet gloves, a canoe made out of jewels, a sad donkey clown piñata full of crickets, toasters made of pure gold falling through the sky at the end of magenta parachutes, a going-steady ring from a vending machine at the drug store, a protective gargoyle from the Chartres Cathedral, an antique hammer and sickle, a strawberry chocolate cake baked in the shape of a question mark, fistfuls of sparklers, a bottle of holy water from the River Jordan, photos of lightning on a giant poster, ruby slippers, a map of human DNA drawn up by the Human Genome Project, a refrigerator magnet cast in the likeness of the Dalai Lama, and a mask of her face fashioned from purple day-glo Play-Doh.

43

You're tuned to the Televisionary Oracle

But how?

Meditation?
Drugs?
Shamanic quest?
The Jungian technique of inducing a waking dream
or the mystical method of astral projection?

Maybe you're lying in bed enjoying a lucid dream.

Or are you one of those exceptional fuckers
who can see the unseeable
through the sheer power of your love-making?

Hope you're not among the minority of tormented souls
that does it the hard way:
getting yourself "kidnapped" by "aliens."

And Goddess forbid that you're one of those poor creatures
who's got to half-fall asleep on your couch
and hallucinate the Televisionary Oracle
surging out of a television or computer or radio
in subliminal blips.

Although on the other hand
we'll take you any way we can get you.


Here it comes, beauty and truth fans! Twenty-Two Days of World Orgasm! Guaranteed to be more thrilling and infinitely less alarming than a planet-wide near-death experience!

Take New Year's Eve and Christmas Day and Ramadan and Passover. Add national election day and Halloween and your birthday and the Superbowl and the start of the new fall TV season. Even then, you still don't have a holiday as stupendous as Twenty-Two Weeks of World Orgasm!

Imagine our most brilliant scientists pulling off a daring nuclear attack on a comet, diverting it from a sure collision with our beloved planet.

Visualize a mass landing of flying saucers on the White House lawn, as a peaceful diplomatic corps of angelic extraterrestrials delivers the gift of a technology that will provide free energy for all humans and turn the Earth into a garden paradise, creating a planet of six billion billionaires with six billion unique religions.

Picture the discovery of indisputable archaeological evidence proving that everything we ever thought about the history of our race is much stranger and more amazing than we could ever imagine.

Only then will you begin to fathom the spectacular catharsis that awaits us when Twenty-Two Months of World Orgasm finally arrives!

Are you ready to answer the call, beauty and truth fans? Have you learned to cultivate the sacredly uproarious oozeglimmer of your mysterious kundalini? Can you swirl and billow the slippery throbwiggle on command, uncoil it long and slow and sweet?

If so, congratulations and hallelujah!

But if you're still a little short of mastery, the Televisionary Oracle is here to help. Whether you're a tantric adept-in-the-making or a struggling neophyte just beginning to understand how important it is to involve your body in your spiritual quest, we're happy to welcome you now to the Kundalini Pledge Drive.

The Kundalini Pledge Drive is nothing less than the Dress Rehearsal for the Big Event ... the Warm-Up for the Ultimate Celebration ...

the Ritual Foreplay for the End of History! Guaranteed to whip your erotic riches into a reverent frenzy in plenty of time for the coming of Twenty-Two Years of World Orgasm!

I'm your co-host with the Holy Ghost grin, Rapunzel Blavatsky, and I'm proud to announce that this is a perfect moment. It's a perfect moment because even though none of us knows the exact arrival time of Twenty-Two Decades of World Orgasm, and even though we have not yet fully guessed all of its shockingly intimate secrets, the seductive signs of readiness are mounting.

Have you seen them, beauty and truth fans? The omens and hints? Have you sniffed the pheromones of the Cackling Goddess as she invades us with her full-scale, pull-out-the-roots anamnesis, Her Reverse Armageddon of Pure Joy? Have you caught a glimpse of the coming Covenant of the Global Jiggy Snake? Do you know the sweet, moist fire of the Fuckissimus?

Let us know. We want to hear. Report the healing emergencies you're witnessing ... the spiral lightning juice you're feeling on the inside of your endorphins ... the rowdy ruby glissando you're invoking as you die to the old way of dying.

Tell us every secret, beauty and truth fans. Amaze us. Reveal how many hours you're making love without losing your concentration, how deeply you're looking into your lover's eyes until you see the birth of solar systems erupting therein, how fiercely and craftily you're working to make your compassion and lust flow from the same primal reflex, how sincerely you're doing everything in your power to love every creature, every plant, every rock in the world with the same primrose hurricane juju you bestow upon the slippery sacred soul who excites you most.

Use your imagination! Surprise us. Unveil the idiosyncratic trick you use to stoke the old spiritus frumenti, the amethyst dragon gumbo, the fiery doppelganger blubber. Our Grails are standing by, ready to register the signature of your diamond moonflower chrism and pearly chthonic thunder.

Reveal your own personal strategies: What magic do you invoke to lust globally and fuck locally?

Now I'm going to turn it over to the chronicler of the Televisionary Oracle, my colleague Osiris Rockstar. Osiris would like to present his own special perspective on killing the apocalypse.

I'm pleased to call attention to the fact, by the way, that his ideas both dovetail with and contradict my own. And that's exactly the way we like it here at the Televisionary Oracle!

Osiris?

Thanks, Rapunzel, and hello everybody.

Excuse me a minute, please, while I shout.

WAR! FAMINE! PESTILENCE! EARTHQUAKES! CRIME! SCANDAL!

Those storytellers known as "journalists" love and thrive on the nihilistic vision of the world captured in screaming headlines like that. But they're not the only fabulists to do so. A majority of the prophets down through the ages have been allergic to the possibility that the future might hold something besides endless tragedy.

The sixteenth century's creepy horror-meister Nostradamus wasn't the first, but he has been one of the most enduring. "In the year 1999 and seven months," he bellowed back in 1555, "a king of terror will come from the sky." Nope. Didn't happen. Yet his mystique still infects the imaginations of millions.

Ghoulish modern soothsayers continue in the scare-the-crap-out-of-'em tradition. At last count, three hundred twenty-two notorious latter-day oracles foresee cataclysmic "earth changes" that will create beach-front property in Nebraska. There are innumerable other augurs who, though they agree that most of humanity will be wiped out any minute now, see the death blow coming via other means: lethal solar flares, nuclear war, incurable new diseases, global warming that leads to the melting of Antarctica and the inundation of coastal areas on every continent, or an evil artificial intelligence that achieves sentience on the Internet.

We shouldn't neglect to mention the sentimental old favorite, the plagues of the seven angels as promised by the Bible's Book of Revelations. Though conjured millennia ago, the vision is as fresh as a morning kiss for hundreds of thousands of fear-worshiping fundamentalists, who fantasize that it predicts the Lord will scour the Earth clean of everyone but them.

So why are only the most terrifying omen-slingers so popular and prominent, even though their track record is so dismal?

First of all, the few optimistic prophets that have arisen are usually so boring that no one wants to bother listening to them. In the last five hundred years, Jules Verne is one of the rare exceptions.

Secondly, zoom-and-boom seers typically offer up far more hard-to-believe scenarios than their doom-and-gloom counterparts. Millions of angels will swarm into view of our naked eyes, they promise, for instance. The restrictions of gravity will be abolished. Time will no longer move in just one direction. And it will all happen in a twinkling.

The third reason the terror-mongers sell the most newspapers and captivate the most imaginations—and it hurts me to say this—is that our culture treats cynicism as a sign of intellectual vigor. It's smart to look for the worst in everything!

What's my view? I confess that I suffer from that peculiar variation on chauvinism which leads me to fantasize that the historical era I live in is more glamorously important than all the others. Secretly, and to my embarrassment, I harbor the hope that we are indeed approaching a radical turning point in the history of humanity. What fun, what glorious delirious dangerous fun, it will be if Twenty-Two Days of World Orgasm really does occur, unleashing a series of planet-mutating events that will rapidly expedite the end of history and the beginning of a shatteringly different future.

And yet, there is a part of me, a part of me that feels older and wiser, who suspects that even if we ARE in the midst of the Logos Calling Us Home or the Collective Upgrade to the Fourth Dimension, it just won't be as simple and obvious as all that. The change will not be some overnight world-wide presto-chango like an asteroid plunging into the Earth or everyone instantaneously developing telepathic powers.

Happily, the jingoistic part of me that yearns to be alive when Everything Changes can find a common ground with the cool eternal part of me that regards the all-or-nothing mindset as the peculiar signature of patriarchy's death throes. Together these two aspects of my psyche conclude: We are living through the apocalypse and the resurrection right now. The corruption and redemption are happening and will continue to happen side by side. The collapse and the renewal. The grievous losses and the unpredictable awakenings. There will be no clean break.

But more than that. We are each living through the apocalypse and the resurrection in our own little personal way. The radical turning point, the death of the old order and bloom of the new, is framed in the storylines of our most intimate dramas. You are being pushed up to and over the brink that is most challenging and meaningful to you personally, and I to mine.

A Cosmic Crucifixion may indeed come—maybe even Twenty-Two Weeks of World Orgasm, who knows?—bringing a global brouhaha that whips up media hysteria to psychotic levels. But what's more likely is that you will be invited and divinely assisted to mercy-kill your life's most oppressive structures—thus clearing out an empty space for an as-yet unimaginable new groove in the shockingly beautiful future.

So will your own experience of the apocalypse and resurrection be excruciating or liberating—or both? It's up to you, beauty and truth fans. I truly believe that the Goddess (or whatever passes for the Goddess in your world view) will conspire to corrode, dismantle, or blow up anything that's getting in the way of you expressing your soul's code—the blueprint you came to Earth to embody. Will you cooperate or not?

My own personal soul's code, by the way, compels me to ask whether our expectations actually help create the future. What if there is even a grain of truth in the notion that what we *think* will happen tends to come to pass? No need to get fanatic and literal about the idea; just imagine it has *some* credibility.

By this hypothesis, it is both insane and stupid to revel in visions of doom to the exclusion of other scenarios. And it is just as dumb and crazy to be entertained by bad news and to yawn in the face of good news.

One of my favorite games here at the Televisionary Oracle is to pose and then answer the question, "How can we kill the apocalypse?" In other words, what leaps of the imagination and ingenious actions can we take to crush rampant pop-nihilism? What entertaining tricks can we employ to create an environment in which it is more fun and interesting to play with prophecies of boom and zoom instead of prophecies of doom and gloom? How can we reinvent ourselves so as to interpret the Goddess' daily little deaths as a gift to outwit the huge, irrevocable annihilations?

Here is one of my answers to the question: Cultivate a tradition of *pronoiac* prophecies. *Pronoia,* for those of you unfamiliar with the term, is the sneaking suspicion that the whole world is conspiring to shower you with blessings.

I would like to get started on those prophecies immediately. Here's my first batch for you, beauty and truth fans.

- A rowdy new class of genetic engineers will arise. They'll have little interest in creating oil spill-eating bacteria, frost-resistant strawberries, or other useful hybrids. Considering themselves to be a cross between computer hackers and performance artists, they'll create fun monstrosities that appeal to their sense of play and perversity, like winged horses and trees that grow leaves resembling one-hundred-dollar bills.

- The rise of the pantheosexual movement will present a new threat to sexual law and order. Describing heterosexuals, gays, and bisexuals as narrowminded, pantheosexuals will claim to have erotic feelings for everything from tornadoes to garden hoses to rose bushes to all twenty-two genders of human beings.

- A new breed of well-read, charismatic homeless people will arise. They'll spread understanding and laughter through their communities and will be routinely feasted in the homes of grateful Americans.

- Nintendo will shock its target audience with the release of its "Codependent Bodhisattva" video game, the first-ever model with socially redeeming value. In it, kids must negotiate all eight levels of Buddhist enlightenment with a grinning, bespectacled, red-robed character who resembles the Dalai Lama.

- Cities strapped for funds will create a 900-number option for the 911 emergency line. Wealthy users will pay one thousand dollars per minute for the privilege of having their calls answered first and fastest. Poorer users may get slower response, but at least the service will remain operational—thanks to the 900-number subsidies.

• Supernatural apparitions of the Cackling Vulture Goddess will outnumber those of the bitchy Virgin Mary four to one. Furthermore, unlike the Virgin Mary's, the Cackling Goddess' chimeras will appear to people of all socio-economic classes, appearing on the hoods of lobbyists' BMWs and the wine glasses of legitimate scientists, as well as on pizza billboards or oil slicks in parking lots.

• Citing the growing threat from "entertainment criminals" who relentlessly create soul-shriveling films, TV shows, music, and magazines, Amnesty International will launch a campaign against a previously unacknowledged form of terrorism: the genocide of the imagination.

• The national murder rate will plummet after a cable TV network begins to broadcast live childbirths twenty-four hours a day.

• The average length of an act of heterosexual intercourse in America—which is currently only four minutes—will jump to eighteen minutes by the end of this year.

• An organization calling itself Morality Is Trendy will launch a successful boycott of all products that advertise on TV shows that refuse to depict in a favorable light the following: talking hummingbirds, green eggs and ham, senior citizens playing water polo, and healthy people with multiple personalities.

• Stunning new trends will include gay children, holistic crack, and computers that can talk to the Goddess. Also look for digitally remastered CDs of the Big Bang, prestigious vacations in refugee camps, and an aphrodisiac that stimulates compassion even more than sexual passion.

• A mass ecstatic frenzy will infect more than twenty thousand housewives in Iowa next summer. Much like the maenads of ancient Greece, they'll renounce their volunteer slavery and take to the woods and hills for an orgy of singing, dancing, and dramatic readings of *Women Who Love Too Much*.

- Shamanic scientists at Drivetime University will reveal the process by which the pineal gland in the human brain can be turned into the "Televisionary Oracle." They'll describe the Televisionary Oracle as a kind of naturally occurring "television" that serves as a switching station for one's "Holy Guardian Angel."

- The recovered memories movement will take a bizarre turn when many adults begin to recall under hypnosis long-suppressed memories of joy and peace experienced when they were children.

- Biologists at the Menstrual Temple of the Funky Grail will furnish conclusive evidence that men have "periods" analogous to a woman's menstrual cycle. They seem to correspond to changes in the relationship between Earth and the planet Mars, the biologists will claim. At the peak of the male "marstral cycle," which can last up to ten days every month, the adrenal glands release a hormone that makes men more likely to be irritable, more skilled at disguising their irrational impulses with logical explanations, out of touch with their feelings, and prone to violence and poor judgment. There's also a vulnerable phase preceding the period, which the biologists will dub PMS, or Pathological Macho Stress. Fortunately, revolutionary new meditation techniques also developed by the Menstrual Temple of the Funky Grail will offer hope in the struggle to reduce the social costs caused by this under-recognized natural problem.

That is it for "Pronoiac Prophecies," beauty and truth fans. Hope you enjoyed them. I would now like to turn things back over to the Head Shamanatrix herself, Rapunzel Blavatsky.

Rapunzel?

Thanks, Osiris, and hi again, beauty and truth fans. I'm very pleased to let you know that this is an incredibly perfect moment. It's a perfect moment for many reasons, but especially because I have been inspired to say a gigantic prayer for all of you. I've been roused by your gorgeous vibes to unleash a divinely greedy, apocalyptically healing prayer for each and every creature who can hear me—even those of you who don't believe in the power of prayer.

And so I am starting to pray right now to the God of Gods ... the God beyond all Gods ... the Girlfriend of God ... the Teacher of God ... the Goddess who invented God. ...

O Dear Goddess, Who Never Kills But Only Changes:
I pray that my exuberant, suave, and accidental words will move you to shower ferocious blessings down on all the beauty and truth fans who hear this prayer.

I pray that you will give them what they don't even know they want. Not just the boons they think they need, but everything they've always been afraid to even imagine or ask for.

Dear Goddess, You Wealthy Anarchist Burning Heaven to the Ground:
Many of the divine chameleons out there don't even know that their souls will live forever. Please use your blinding magic to help them see that they are all wildly creative geniuses too big for their own bodies.

Guide them to realize that they are all completely different from what they think they are and more exciting than they can possibly imagine.

Make it illegal, immoral, irrelevant, unpatriotic, and totally taste-less for them to be in love with anyone or anything that's no good for them.

Oh dear Goddess, Who Gives Us So Much Love and Pain Mixed Together That Our Morality Is Always on the Verge of Collapsing:
I beg you to cast a boisterous love spell that will nullify all the black magic that has ever been cast on all the wise and sexy geniuses out there.

Remove, banish, annihilate, and laugh into oblivion any jinx that has clung to them, no matter how long they've suffered from it, and even if they've become accustomed or addicted to its ugly compan-ionship.

Conjure an aura of protection around them so that they will receive an early warning if they are ever about to act in such a way as to bring another hex or plague or voodoo into their lives.

Dear Goddess, You Sly Universal Virus with No Fucking Opinion:

I pray that you will help all the personal growth addicts within the sound of my voice to become disciplined enough to go crazy in the name of creation not destruction.

I pray that you will teach them the difference between oppressive self-control and liberating self-control.

Awaken in them the power to do the half-right thing when it is impossible to do the totally right thing. Arouse the Wild Woman within them—even if they're men.

And please, dear Goddess, give them bigger, better, more original sins and wilder, wetter, more interesting problems.

Oh Goddess, You Pregnant Slut Who Scorns All Mediocre Longing:

I pray that you will inspire all the compassionate fuckers out there to love their enemies just in case their friends turn out to be jerks.

Provoke them to throw away or give away all the things they own that encourage them to believe they are better or more special than anyone else.

Show them how much fun it is to brag about what they cannot do and do not have.

Most of all, Goddess, brainwash them with your freedom so that they never love their own pain more than anyone else's pain.

Dear Goddess, You Psychedelic Mushroom Cloud at the Center of All Our Brains:

These curiously divine human beings I am communing with deserve everything they are yearning for and much much more.

Please arrange for a statue to be built in their honor, or a memento of their genius to be launched into orbit around the Earth, or a flurry of gossip to be spun out by smart people who adore them.

Help them win the battle against time, and learn to talk the language of the most scientific angels, and master the zen of temper tantrums, and get a fabulous mommy and daddy in their next incarnation.

Teach them to push their own buttons and unbreak their own hearts and right their own wrongs and sing their own songs and be their own wives and save their own lives.

And please give them lots of gifts, dear Goddess. More gifts than they think they deserve. Bless them with lucid dreams while they are wide awake and solar-energy-operated sex toys that work even in the dark and vacuum cleaners for their magic carpets and a knack for avoiding other people's hells and a secret admirer that is not a psychotic stalker and a thousand different masks that all fit their face perfectly and their very own 900 number so that everyone has to pay to talk to them.

Oh Goddess, You Fiercely Tender, Hauntingly Reassuring, Orgiastically Sacred Feeling That Is Even Now Running Through All Our Soft Warm Animal Bodies:

I pray that you provide all the compassionate fuckers out there with a license to bend and even break all rules, laws, and traditions that keep them apart from the things they love.

Show them how to purge the wishy-washy wishes that distract them from their daring, dramatic, divine desires.

And teach them that they can have anything they want if they'll only ask for it in an unselfish tone of voice.

And now dear God of God, God beyond all Gods, Girlfriend of God, Teacher of God, Goddess who invented God,

I bring this prayer to a close, trusting that You have begun to change everyone in the exact way they've needed to change.

And if I've forgotten anything that will help their cause, please flash it into my imagination in the coming days and months and decades, and motivate me to perform any tricks or carry out any project that will encourage an abundant flow of sweaty creativity to flow through them, inspiring them to become more wildly disciplined, compassionately horny, aggressively sensitive, ironically sincere, lyrically logical, insanely poised, and macho feminist.

Amen. Awomen. And glory halle-fucking-lujah.

There you have it, beauty and truth fans. A personalized prayer just for you. A prayer that'll probably come true simply because you didn't even ask for it.

You may now kiss yourself on your own lips.

Calling all wise fuckers

Calling all love bombs
skilled in the art
of lusty compassion

Calling all sexlaughers
whose every burst of love
recreates the divine joke
that birthed the cosmos

Prepare your gorgeous self
for
Twenty-Two Months of World Orgasm

If we've got to annihilate the boundaries,
let's do it with eros, not thanatos

LUST GLOBALLY, FUCK LOCALLY

*Author's Acknowledgements*

Delirious waves of gratitude are pouring out from me towards Jennifer Welwood, Suzanne Sterling, Zoe Brezsny, Gretchen Giles, Joseph Matheny, Paul Foster Case, and Ann Davies. Their help and inspiration were crucial.

Sincere yowls of thanks go to Shoshana Alexander, Richard Grossinger, and Chuck Stein for extremely useful feedback on the ripening text, as well as to Kathy Glass for stupendous copyediting.

Booming thunderclaps of lusty reverence spiral out to the best deity in the universe—the funniest, smartest, and most lovable deity—the Great Goddess Herself.

*About the Author*

Rob Brezsny is the author of "Real Astrology," a weekly column that reaches an audience of over nine million readers in 118 publications and his website, www.realastrology.com.

As much a storyteller as astrologer, Brezsny brings a literate, myth-savvy perspective to his work. When *Utne Reader* named him a "Culture Hero" in its Fall, 1997 issue, it summed up his role this way: "With a blend of spontaneous poetry, feisty politics, and fanciful put-on, Brezsny breathes new life into the tabloid mummy of zodiac advice columns."

While not plying his trade as a writer, Brezsny has also been a janitor, performance artist, poet, songwriter, and singer. During the course of a twenty-year career, he has been managed by one of rock's top impresarios, the late Bill Graham, and has released four albums, including a major-label CD that was nominated for a "Bammie," California's version of the Grammies.